Magic

With a sprinkling of *f*...   ...*agical*
things can happen—*bu*...   ...*ver of*
love.

Sea S'pell

Tess Farraday

(June 1998)

*As a child, Beth fell into the churning sea, only to be lifted gently
out—by a dark-haired youth with a knowing, otherworldly smile—
who then vanished into the mist. Somehow the young girl knew her
elusive rescuer was a powerful, legendary selkie, who could become
the love of her dreams . . .*

Once Upon A Kiss

Claire Cross

(July 1998)

*For over a thousand years—so legend has it—the brambles have
grown wild over the ruins of Dunhelm Castle. Many believed that
the thorns were a sign that the castle was cursed, so no one dared
to trespass—until an American hotelier decided to clear away the
brambles himself, and found a mysterious slumbering beauty . . .*

"A wonderful tale . . . exhilarating . . . enchanting. If this is an
example of the publisher's new Magic line, it's obvious they
will have a smash series to their credit."

—*Painted Rock*

A Faerie Tale

Ginny Reyes

(August 1998)

*According to legend, a faerie must perform a loving deed to earn
her magic wand. So, too, must the leprechaun accomplish a special
task before receiving his pot of gold. But the most mystical, magical
challenge of all is . . . helping two mortals fall in love.*

Once Upon A Kiss

CLAIRE CROSS

JOVE BOOKS, NEW YORK

MAGICAL LOVE is a trademark of Berkley Publishing Corporation.

ONCE UPON A KISS

A Jove Book / published by arrangement with
the author

PRINTING HISTORY
Jove edition / July 1998

All rights reserved.
Copyright © 1998 by Claire Delacroix Inc.
This book may not be reproduced in whole
or in part, by mimeograph or any other means,
without permission. For information address:
The Berkley Publishing Group, a member of Penguin Putnam Inc.,
200 Madison Avenue, New York, New York 10016.

The Penguin Putnam Inc. World Wide Web site address is
http://www.penguinputnam.com

ISBN: 0-515-12300-5

A JOVE BOOK®
Jove Books are published by The Berkley Publishing Group,
a member of Penguin Putnam Inc.,
200 Madison Avenue, New York, New York 10016.
JOVE and the "J" design are trademarks
belonging to Jove Publications, Inc.

PRINTED IN THE UNITED STATES OF AMERICA

10 9 8 7 6 5 4 3 2 1

For Ingrid and Kate . . .
Two strong and compassionate women
I'm proud to call my friends.
Thanks.

Once Upon Upon
A Kiss

Prologue

"Ships!" The sentry's hoarse cry carried over the heavy walls and made every inhabitant look up with alarm. "Ships on the horizon!"

Aurelia crouched lower as her father darted up a ladder with the agility of a man much younger than his own fifty summers. Hekod's long golden hair, now threaded with silver, lifted in the stiff sea breeze as he reached the summit, his feet braced against the stone.

Aurelia pulled her hood further over her face. The last thing she needed was for her father to guess of her disobedience after they had argued so long over her role. She watched her father's expression avidly from below, her mouth so dry that she could barely swallow.

Was it Bard, son of Erc, who came to take his avowed revenge?

Or had her father's Viking relations arrived with aid?

Hekod's expression turned grim as he scanned the seas. He swore with rare eloquence and Aurelia's heart sank, the truth clear before he even spoke.

Hekod's eyes blazed like sapphires as he pivoted to address his men. "That can be no Viking sail!" he roared. "Bard, son of Erc, dares to attack Dunhelm! To arms! *To arms!*"

With those words, chaos erupted.

The ladders leaning against the defensive wall creaked with the warriors' haste to climb to the summit. Swords caught the sunlight as they were unsheathed, the freshly honed blades of battle-axes gleamed dangerously. Prayers were muttered and amulets kissed. Helmets were donned and leather jerkins laced among the Viking warriors, while the Picts boldly bared their tattooed flesh.

"The murderous swine dares to tempt a father's wrath!" Hekod raged above the confusion, waving his own sword high in the air. The men stamped their feet in support. "Let him taste the bite of my blade!" the warriors bellowed. "Like father, like son, say I. Let Bard meet the Nairns by my hand as did his sire before him!"

The fighting men shouted their approval of this sentiment. The war horns were blown in a cacophony of sound and all attention turned to the sea.

Aurelia took advantage of the moment to dive out of her hiding place and hastily retrieve her bow. Her heart was pounding with the threat of discovery as she discarded the cloak that had hidden her garb this morning. The tunic beneath was purposefully short, the leggings and boots practical garb that Aurelia had worn little since her sire determined her to be of marriageable age.

Evidently, in her father's mind, even marriageable Viking women did not wear short tunics or shoot crossbows. But Aurelia knew the defense of her home was more important than mere modesty and protocol, whatever Hekod's views to the contrary.

She tossed her long fair braid over her shoulder as she turned, standing as tall as a woman of tiny stature could. Aurelia was ready to face condemnation, yet found none aware of what she had done.

Perfect. There was no time to waste on such nonsense, at any rate.

Aurelia simply could not sit by when all she held dear hung in the balance. Even her sire could not dispute that she was the best archer in Dunhelm—and Aurelia's duty could be nowhere else but in the defense of her home.

Hekod was not the only one who thirsted for vengeance, after all. It was no small thing for Aurelia to carry the proud legacy of Viking blood and, to her mind, Hekod—the Viking responsible for that mingled blood—should have understood.

Aurelia scrambled up the ladder and posted herself a goodly distance away from her perceptive sire. The men on either side of her did not even consider her arrival worth a questioning glance. Aurelia lifted her face to the sea, triumphant at her success thus far, but her heart trembled at what she saw.

A trio of ships crested the brilliant blue of the seas, their prows cutting through the waves with a purpose that could not be denied. Not one but *three* ships came to battle!

These certainly were not the graceful Viking ships that all had hoped would arrive at Dunhelm first. These vessels were all of diverse and humble origins, their sails patched, their paint chipped, and their hulls devoid of ornamentation.

Such sorry craft befitted a thieving vagrant like Bard son of Erc. A dark hatred filled Aurelia's heart and a tear blurred her vision as she recalled how this loathsome man had deceived her sole brother.

If Aurelia had anything to say about the matter, Bard, son of Erc, would not survive this day. She looked to her sire and saw the same grim determination harden his weathered visage.

The waves pounded on the wooden hulls of the ships as they drew near, the wind snapped the sails. Two men leaped from the lead ship and hauled it in toward shore, the waves coming above their waists. The individual men aboard the ships became distinguishable as the crafts were drawn closer.

Aurelia was dismayed to see how numerous they truly were. The deck of each ship fairly bristled with weaponry.

There was a strange interval of silence on the walls in this moment, as though all looked into their hearts in the face of such odds and understood that this day would change their very lives. Many would not survive this battle, Aurelia knew, for Bard brought greater forces than anticipated. And without the Vikings to swell their ranks, Hekod's forces would be hard-pressed to hold Dunhelm.

Aurelia knew she was not the only one to wonder at their chances.

"Bard, son of Erc, is mine alone," Hekod declared coldly. The silence was such that his voice carried along the entire wall, the dark menace of his tone sending a shiver down every spine.

Aurelia had the sudden thought that the first strike could be telling. A quick gain for Hekod's side could lift the spirits of Dunhelm's troops. Aurelia knew enough of war to understand that that alone could send them surging to victory.

Without questioning her impulse, Aurelia loaded an arrow into her crossbow, silently beseeched the Goddess for favor, aimed, and fired.

The arrow whistled through the air and was quickly lost in the sun. It buried itself with a barely audible thump as Aurelia strained to discern its landing point.

A heartbeat later, one of the men hauling the lead ship faltered, then fell into the blue of the sea.

He did not stand again. The end of the rope he had held trailed away into the waves; his alarmed partner missed a step before boldly surging forward again.

The men on the walls of Dunhelm cheered boisterously. Bard's forces launched a volley of arrows that fell far short of the stone walls. Aurelia felt a surge of victory before her sire's voice boomed across the ramparts.

"Aurelia!"

Too late Aurelia realized that the accuracy of the shot betrayed her hand.

All eyes turned to Aurelia when Hekod spotted her and glared dangerously. Aurelia stubbornly held her ground. Hekod muttered a curse, then pushed aside warrior and mercenary as he carved a path along the wall to his errant daughter.

And Aurelia knew she would not have another chance to fire a shot. She had to make this fleeting moment count! The men around her murmured in dismay, but Aurelia quickly fitted another arrow and lifted her crossbow to aim once more.

She squinted and adjusted her sight on the second man in the sea. He had taken an uneven gait, presumably to foil her efforts. Precious moments passed before Aurelia was satisfied with her aim.

Just as she was about to let the shot fly, heavy hands landed on her shoulders. Aurelia jumped and lost her aim, her fingers fumbling with the arrow.

Pain burned in her left thumb. The sensation was hot enough to bring tears to her eyes.

"Aurelia!" Hekod cried out in dismay.

In that instant, a curious glow swirled around Aurelia. Everything around her seemed enveloped in shimmering silver, distant and otherworldly. Aurelia herself felt buoyed by nothingness in a most unnatural way. It was as though she had been surrounded by a glittering fog.

Gods and goddesses! What was happening to her?

Aurelia glanced to her father, only to find him as ethereal as all else around her. His anger was gone, dissipated as quickly as it burned bright, and now his features were lined with concern.

"The prophecy!" he murmured hoarsely, and his grip tightened on her shoulders. "It was true, after all!"

Aurelia tried to laugh at such foolishness but failed. The swirling gossamer haze had eclipsed the pain so thoroughly that Aurelia felt as insubstantial as a morning mist. In fact, she tingled lightly all over. Aurelia had the odd sense that if her father let go of her shoulders, she would be swept away to forever in the blink of an eye.

"It is only the loss of the blood that ails me," she managed to say. Aurelia frowned, feeling as though the cloud had numbed her reason as well. Had she felt so odd when wounded before?

Hekod lifted his daughter's wounded hand, his great paw gently cradling Aurelia's much smaller fingers. "But Aurelia, there is no blood."

No blood? There must be!

But when Aurelia looked at her hand, she saw that Hekod was right. The arrow had fallen away, leaving behind no more than a gaping hole in Aurelia's left thumb.

Right in the middle of the whorl, just as the prophecy made so long ago had clearly declared. And her very fingers sparkled against her father's lined palm, as though she was wrought of something other than flesh and blood.

Aurelia blinked, unable to accept the evidence before her own eyes. The prophecy was a lie, after all!

But before Aurelia could argue, the whirling iridescent cocoon surrounded her and caressed her, lifted her so high that she could not even feel the weight of her father's hands, let alone see the anguished blue of his eyes.

She could not leave him! She *would* not leave him!

But Aurelia was to have no choice. She faintly heard the clash of steel on steel. She struggled to join the fight to defend Dunhelm, but felt herself swept away. She could see nothing but thousands of shimmering lights dancing all around her.

And then Aurelia knew no more.

One

DUNHELM CASTLE
MARCH—PRESENT DAY

The thorny brambles had no chance.

The hedge clippers Baird had borrowed from the grounds-keeper were fiercely sharp and he wielded them with characteristic determination. The brambles, though, refused to surrender without a fight. Baird had never seen brambles grow so big, so tangled, or so robust.

They must be ancient, like everything else at Dunhelm Castle.

Another massive thorn bit at him and Baird cursed under his breath. No wonder the groundskeeper had refused to clear this corner! Talorc could blame local superstition but the truth was that he was just avoiding a miserable job.

It was raining this morning, as it had rained every day since his arrival at his new holding, but the light drizzle didn't bother Baird. He was getting used to Scotland's wide variety of rains, as well as the national refusal to let poor weather change plans for the day. After all, the skies could change in the blink of an eye.

What wasn't changing was the way Baird felt at Dunhelm,

and he wasn't having an easy time getting used to that. He felt as though nothing else mattered in the world except Dunhelm and his being here.

Baird felt at home in the old ruins.

For a man who had never had a home, who had been certain he never wanted one, and who had always made a point of not settling anywhere for any length of time, this was more than unusual.

It was downright weird.

Baird meant to put a stop to Dunhelm's strange effect on him, and he was going to do it today.

Dunhelm Castle—or what remained of it—occupied a jagged point of an island dropped into the misty gray of the North Sea. Although the grass was as level as a bowling lawn where Baird worked, rocky cliffs fell unevenly to the crashing sea beyond the encircling stone walls. There was a beach on the east side of the peninsula, though the wind was cold enough to flay the skin of anyone foolish enough to swim there.

All around Baird were the walls, the crumbled ruins that once had been towers and halls and kitchens. The wind from the west whistled through the ruins, and at dusk, the castle seemed alive with whispers of forgotten times. Baird did not consider himself an imaginative man, but Dunhelm seemed to pulse with the heartbeats of all the people who had lived here over the millennia.

He wondered whether it was the age of the place that entranced him. Certainly he had never owned anything a thousand years old. And he couldn't think of any other reason why one sight of Dunhelm had been enough for him to make his decision. It was almost as though he recognized the castle from some long-forgotten dream.

But that would have been irrational, and Baird Beauforte was a supremely logical man.

All the same, from that very first glance, Baird had *known* that this was the property for Beauforte Resorts to establish its toehold in the European market. He told himself that this was finely honed instinct at work, an understanding of the market based on years of experience. A logical recognition of opportunity.

But even to Baird's own ears, that claim was beginning to ring hollow.

One thing was for sure—Baird had never felt such satisfaction in signing his name to a contract for a property before.

It was good that he was so committed to this place, for Dunhelm was the largest renovation Beauforte Resorts had ever undertaken.

And by far the most expensive.

But all the costs of restoration would be worth it. Dunhelm would be spectacular, the crown jewel of the Beauforte chain. Already the main circular tower rose restored behind Baird and the restaurant at the top with its panoramic view was being roughed in.

The massive wrought-iron double gates Baird had commissioned had been installed just the day before. They were the perfect accent to the long stone wall that marked the perimeter of the property and cut off the peninsula from the rest of the world. The Beauforte Resorts's logo was forged into the gates and dramatically silhouetted against the sky before the approaching visitor.

The work was a bit behind schedule, but Baird's vision of Dunhelm was taking shape. There was no reason why he shouldn't leave this job in the capable hands of his staff, as usual.

Except that he couldn't bring himself to leave Dunhelm.

Even worse, he wasn't sure why.

This tangled mound of briars had aroused Baird's curiosity from his first tour of the property. His interest was only strengthened by Talorc's, and every other local workman's, refusal to go near the briars.

Not one to back away from a challenge, especially with no reason other than superstition to do so, Baird had taken on the task of cutting back the thorns himself.

He was sure that revealing Dunhelm's every hidden corner to the pale sunlight would loosen the place's hold over him. After all, this was the last part of the estate still hidden away. And he had always liked to solve puzzles.

That must be at the root of his fascination with this place. Once he cleared the thorns, Baird was sure that all mysteries would be solved. Then Dunhelm's grip over him would vanish.

Every fallen branch fed his conviction. Baird had to conquer these thorns, and he had to do it today.

Baird had worked up a good sweat when the briars reluctantly parted to reveal a flat stone on the ground before him.

It was just a stone, but he had a strange certainty that it was a step. Baird hacked with renewed vigor, smiling to himself with satisfaction when a second step was revealed.

He was right! There *was* a secret in this corner and he was about to uncover it.

Although the briars seemed to be suddenly more resistant to his efforts, nothing could have stopped Baird now. The rain fell like a protective mist all around him, a light fog hiding the other workers from view. The mist even seemed to muffle the sounds of construction.

It was as though he were alone in the world. No stranger to that feeling, Baird shoved up his sleeves and methodically sliced back the stubborn growth.

The steps appeared before him, one after the other, descending into the earth. Baird, hot on the heels of solving a mystery, worked his way down them, his anticipation rising with every minute.

What could be down here? Who had made the steps? And why?

On the eighth smoothly fitted flagstone step, the brambles became thinner. It was chilly down here, the shadows of the walls on either side embracing him coldly.

Just a little farther and he would know.

"Baird? You down there?"

Baird jumped at the sound of the familiar voice. He wiped a hand across his brow and felt the exhaustion in his muscles for the first time. How long had he been at this? Baird turned back and spied Julian's silhouette against the gray sky.

"Down here, Julian."

"Down *there*?" Baird could imagine the grimace his words earned and almost laughed. Julian and his damned shoes. "Won't you come back up?"

"Nope. Got to finish." Baird bent back to his task, Julian's muttered curse not low enough to be inaudible.

He was probably meant to hear it.

"I don't know why you had to have this place," Julian muttered as he trudged down the stairs. "It needs more work than any other property we looked at, and it's miles from London. No one will come all this way, especially since all it does is *rain*!"

"They'll come." Baird's voice was low with conviction. "They always come to Beauforte properties."

" 'Every guest is royalty to us' and all that," Julian echoed the firm's motto. "But all the same, this is a *miserable* place."

Baird caught a glimpse of Julian's Italian leather loafers, their patina looking somewhat the worse for wear. Typically, the lawyer was dressed to the nines. Julian would never abandon his suit and tie, even in the most inclement weather.

But Julian was too much of a Californian to ever completely succumb to the conservativeness of business dress. Though he wore a suit and tie, the boldly cut Armani suit was of a grayed eggplant shade, the tie a brilliant yellow.

Julian had only recently allowed his signature blond ponytail to be lopped off—after a young, attractive woman had joked that he was compensating for the increasing baldness on the top of his head by growing what hair he had overly long.

The ponytail had not survived the hour.

Thirty-five could strike a man hard, even one so trim, well-groomed, and successful as Julian.

Baird, on the other hand, had taken to jeans and Gore-Tex within hours of arrival here. It was true it had rained in some way or another every single day, but he loved all the myriad shades of blue and green mirrored in the shifting sea, not to mention the clouds drifting above it.

Baird's newfound attraction to the sea was odd, really, given that he had been raised in the Southwest, far from a sea of any kind.

"I think it's beautiful," Baird said mildly, earning a scathing glance from Beauforte's legal counsel.

Julian snorted. "Beautiful? Far from it."

"Just look at the sea. It's quite a soothing place."

"Ha! I don't have to look any further than my own stomach. This is no place for a vegetarian. No country that willfully murders innocent vegetables could be beautiful!"

Baird had to grin despite himself. An ardent vegetarian, Julian should have become accustomed by now to having culinary adventures whenever he ventured far from a city's bright lights. "It's not that bad."

"Oh, yeah? Last night in that horrible dark pub in town—you know the one—the only vegetables they could give me was this heap of something called clapshot." Julian flung out his hands in exasperation. "Clapshot! Even the name is horrible! What the hell is *clapshot*?"

"You should know." Baird returned to his clipping with a philosophical shrug, more than used to Julian's monologues on the subject of food. "You're the one who ate it."

"I did *not*!" Julian grimaced. "It was orange and lumpy, like it had been put through a blender or something. Baby food."

Baird grunted as he conquered a particularly thick vine and cast it aside, only to find another right behind it. A more whimsical man might have thought the briars were deliberately blocking his way. "Could be neeps and tatties together in one."

"Neeps and what? I can *guess* that tatties must be potatoes in some overcooked form, but what the hell's a neep?"

"Turnip. Or rutabagas. Those orange things, whichever they are. Mashed."

Julian shuddered with mock horror. "Just like Mother used to make. Ugh! I'm *glad* I didn't eat it."

Baird's mouth quirked. "Maybe we should bill this as a weight-loss resort for vegetarians."

"Very funny." Julian folded his arms across his chest and tapped his toe. "I'm not asking for much, you know. Why not a few roasted red peppers? A little rosemary? Maybe they could let some daylight in the place, instead of all that brooding dark wood. Ferns. Brass. Here's a thought—*attractive* waitresses."

Baird spared his friend a glance that spoke volumes before

turning back to his clipping. He cleared another step. "Just like some chichi bistro in North Hollywood?"

"Well, yeah. I mean, why not?"

Baird shook his head. "Because it's not California. Wouldn't the world be boring if everyplace was the same?"

"Hardly." Julian snorted. "We'd eat better, at least."

Baird decided to offer Julian a choice morsel of news. "If it makes you feel any better, Sebastien's coming to manage the restaurant here."

"Sebastien? *Here*?" Julian looked incredulous. "You've convinced Sebastien to leave Manhattan? To come *here*?" The lawyer glanced about himself in amazement, as though he had been magically transported somewhere other than the Orkney Islands, then scrutinized his employer. "How did you manage that?"

"He thinks it's 'elemental.' " Baird watched Julian struggle to come to terms with the concept.

It was obviously an uphill battle.

"Well, maybe it *could* be, with Sebastien cooking," he conceded reluctantly, then closed his eyes in rapturous remembrance. "The things that man can do with portobello mushrooms!"

Julian sighed, then fixed Baird with a bright glance. "When is he coming?"

Baird shrugged. "A couple of weeks."

Julian groaned. "It's like an endurance test," he muttered, then snapped his fingers in recollection. "Oh, hey, Darlene called. That's why I came looking for you."

"Again?" Baird was glad he had missed another worried call from his secretary.

"She wanted to know when you'd be back in the head office."

"Soon," Baird said, emphasizing the word with a decisive snip of the clippers. "*Very* soon."

"Great." Julian's tone implied that the news was far from that.

"I thought you hated it here."

"I do! But now we'll be gone by the time Sebastien gets here." Julian scuffed his toe. "It's just not fair."

Julian pulled a determined branch away from his face and frowned at it. "These thorns are unbelievable. Look at this thing!" Baird obediently looked at the thorn offered for his perusal, a thorn not unlike the hundreds of others that had already made a grab at him today. "It must be three inches long!"

"And probably too tough to sauté in unsalted butter."

"Very funny." Julian let the branch go with a snap and peered into the shadows below for the first time. "Where does this staircase go?"

"That's what I'm trying to find out." They had to be a dozen feet below the surface of the ground, the skyward view tangled with healthy briars. Baird grunted as he cut back a final tough curtain of branches.

The two men froze and stared at the heavy stone portal that was revealed.

The doorway was made of three massive rough-cut stones, two standing on end to support the weight of the third. The darkness within was complete, though cold air wafted toward them. It smelled like wet stone.

"Where does it go?" Julian whispered.

"Let's find out." Baird stepped through the doorway. Julian glanced about himself, then tentatively followed suit.

The sound of dripping water echoed loudly in the small space they entered. It was bone-chillingly cold here, the smell of the dampness and the silence emanating from the stone making Baird feel as though he had entered a strange, maybe enchanted, world far from the one he knew.

Julian shook the rainwater off his Burberry trench coat and looked around the dim, roughly rectangular room. His words revealed that his mind had not taken the same fanciful turn as Baird's.

"Doesn't look like much. Are you going to put the sauna down here, or something? It could be expensive for heating. And you'd have to run some sort of covered walkway for guests who didn't want to go out in the rain. . . ."

Baird switched on the flashlight he had brought.

Hotelier and lawyer gasped aloud simultaneously. A slab of stone, as tall as Baird and covered with fantastic carving, filled the wall directly before them. They gawked silently at the treasure that just a moment before had been hidden in secretive shadows.

The slab was made of the same local gray stone as the rest of the castle ruins. At the top was a massive crescent carved in relief, almost like the curve of a sundial, points down, its interior writhing with Celtic knots.

On closer inspection, the knots were made of fantastic animals, all twined around each other. The imagery reminded Baird of the illuminations in the Book of Kells.

A bent arrow made a V across the crescent, its crook at the lower center of the crescent, its head pointing to the top right corner, its fleche to the top left.

Below this was a backward Z, about a foot high, which seemed to have flames erupting from both ends. On either side of this character were two disks, again filled with knots made of entwined creatures. A snake writhed around the perimeter of these elements, its body an intricate braid, the end of its tail in its own mouth.

The lower half of the stone was graced with the image of a woman in repose. Though her features were not clearly etched, it was obvious that she was a beauty. She looked to be sleeping, her hands folded across her chest and garments pooling about her slender form.

"Whoa!" Julian breathed. "It would be good to move that somewhere more visible in the resort."

Baird bent and ran his fingertips over the row of cross-hatched lines that ran up the right side. "It must be an inscription," he mused, recognizing runic letters and wondering what they said.

Julian showed no interest in such mysteries. He shivered and shrugged, throwing Baird a smile as he shoved his hands into his raincoat pockets. "Definitely worth a visit. Now, let's get a brandy."

"Not until we see what's behind it." Baird pushed on the slab, but it did not give in the least.

"Behind it? It's just a frieze, Baird."

"No, it's a door."

"A door? Come on, where could it go? It's just a wall mural or something, maybe some kind of pagan altar." He shuddered elaborately and looked around himself as though expecting hostile pagans to spring from the shadows. "Do you think they *slaughtered* things here?" he demanded in a horrified whisper.

"It's a door," Baird repeated. He was oddly convinced of his conclusion, though he refused to think further about that. "Now, are you going to help?"

Julian winced. "It doesn't even *look* like a door to me. I mean, where's the knob? How do you open it?"

"It's a door. Trust me. We're just going to have to figure out how it opens." Baird set his lips grimly, resolving that he would not leave before seeing what was behind this door. "Then you can have your brandy."

Baird turned back to the carved stone, scanning its width and breadth. There had to be a lever or a hinge somewhere, probably concealed if something precious was hidden behind the door.

And Baird knew in his heart that there was.

Julian cleared his throat, an annoying habit that usually indicated he was going to be particularly lawyerlike. "If it *is* a door—and I'm not in the least bit sure that it is, mind you— there is some question as to whether there might be historic artifacts within. As your legal counsel, I would strongly suggest we summon authorities of antiquities to be present—"

"Forget it, Julian," Baird interrupted crisply. "We crossed every t and dotted every i acquiring this place. I've had it up to the eyeballs with paperwork."

Julian inhaled sharply, but Baird tossed his friend a wry grin. "Come on, what can it hurt to look? You know me better than to worry about the fate of anything we find here."

"You are painfully scrupulous, much to my ongoing disappointment," Julian acknowledged with a rueful smile.

"So, how can we open this? Any ideas?"

But Julian was not prepared to abandon his argument so easily. "Baird, we could get someone down from PR, you know, and manage this opening as an event—"

"No!" Baird was surprised by his own vehemence. "Forget PR!"

"We never forget PR."

"This time we will." Unable to explain his need to do this alone, Baird turned back to survey the door. "Look, the sooner we get this open, the sooner you can have your brandy."

It was troubling to feel so strongly about something he knew nothing about, especially when he made it his business to feel as little as possible in the course of life. Feelings got a man into trouble. They were unpredictable, unreliable.

They made a man hope for things that could never be.

But still Baird couldn't even consider walking away from this door before it was opened. This was the root of his fascination with Dunhelm. Baird knew it. He couldn't turn away and leave the job half done.

He had to solve this puzzle now.

When Baird said nothing more, Julian did not hesitate to warm to his theme. "Baird, this is about more than brandy! You can't simply barge in and do whatever you want here. We're in a foreign country, after all, and it won't pay to step on any toes."

"It won't hurt to look, if we can even get the door open," Baird corrected with growing impatience. "And if there isn't anything there, summoning someone would have been wasting their time, as well as our own."

"We shouldn't do it."

Baird's lips set in a tight line. "Look, Julian, I don't have to tell you that we're way behind on this restoration, mostly thanks to bureaucrats. And I am not going to spend another six months in government offices getting the right to open a door on an estate when the title to that estate is in my pocket and the bill for the property taxes lands on my desk, especially when there's probably nothing in it!"

"Well!" Julian's nostrils flared. "I don't know what you pay me for, if you aren't going to listen to what I have to say!" The lawyer smacked the wall to punctuate his frustration.

Julian yelped and swore, Baird turned to argue, then a low rumble stole away anything either man might have said. They pivoted to find the carved stone sliding slowly to the left, revealing a dark space.

Baird glanced back to find Julian nursing the back of his hand, his eyes round. "What did you do?"

"I hit that thing." Julian pointed to a gargoyle grimacing on the wall beside him. It was the only decorative detail in the small space at the foot of the stairs and Baird only now noticed the oddity of that.

Baird shone the flashlight on the gargoyle. He touched its outstretched tongue and discovered that it was actually a lever. When he carefully depressed it, the door slid closed with a grating of stone on stone. Baird repeated the move and the door opened once more.

"Well, we have to look now," Baird said with a smile that he hoped hid his burgeoning anticipation.

Julian took a tentative step forward, as though fighting his own legal instincts, and peered over Baird's shoulder into the shadows. "I can't believe that you were right," he breathed. "It *is* a door."

"I told you to trust me." Baird ducked through the portal and flicked his flashlight around the revealed chamber.

A woman, garbed precisely like the one on the door itself, was sleeping on a slab on the opposite side of the room.

Baird stopped so fast that Julian bumped right into his back. The glow from the flashlight bounced off the walls and seemed to illuminate the entire chamber.

But Baird had eyes only for the woman.

Her long golden hair spilled over her shoulders and the stone, a garment that had once been richly embroidered, clung tenuously to her curves. Baird's mouth went dry and he nearly dropped the light.

"How in the hell did she get in here?" Julian muttered, but Baird wasn't interested in anything his friend had to say.

Because the jolt of recognition Baird had felt upon seeing Dunhelm was nothing compared to this.

He found himself halting beside the stone slab without any recollection of deciding to cross the chamber. Baird stared down at the woman, astonished at the turmoil of emotion let loose within him.

How did he know her?

Her heart-shaped face was delightfully feminine, her ruby

lips sweet and full. She was small and delicately built, her hands slender and gracious.

And Baird wanted to kiss her more than anything in the world.

Which had to be the weirdest damn thought he'd had in quite a while, perhaps ever.

Baird couldn't explain his conviction, illogical as it was. It came out of nowhere, but seemed incontestable. Baird found himself bending closer to her as though a will greater than his own drove him on.

He couldn't stop.

"Baird!" Julian exclaimed in horror behind him. "What are you doing? Have you lost your mind?"

But Baird was deaf to his friend's protests. A sweet perfume rose from the woman's skin, a beguiling mix of flowers mingled with her own scent that swept every objection from his mind.

He had to taste her. Baird knew when his lips were a finger's breadth from hers that he should stop, that he should step away, that this was crazy.

But he couldn't. It was as though there was nothing else he could do in this place at this moment. The woman seemed to sense his intent, for her head turned slightly toward Baird and her lips parted in mute invitation.

His gut clenched at the sight. And Baird bent to brush his lips chastely across hers. The welcoming heat of her lips burned against his mouth, their breath mingled, and time stood still for a tantalizing moment.

Then the woman's eyes flew open, their blue-gray shade echoing the colors of the sea just beyond the walls. She caught her breath in alarm and sat up hastily as Baird took a guilty step back. Her hands clutched the shreds of her dress to her breasts, but not before Baird glimpsed their creamy perfection.

Then she glared at him with undisguised hostility.

And Baird didn't need Julian to tell him that he had just made a big mistake.

Two

What was this?

Two strangers bursting into her chambers. And her robe in tatters about her! Aurelia would have words for the seamstress about this garment, that was for certain!

The tall one who led the way was oddly dressed, his heavy blue chausses showing the lean strength of his legs to shocking advantage. He was dark of hair and broad of shoulder, square of jaw and proud of profile. He was a handsome man, a warrior by his stance, his stern expression, and the determined line of his lips.

But the bright gleam of his eyes unsettled Aurelia so much that she had to look away. Something lurking in those green depths gave her the sense that this man could read one's very thoughts.

Had he had the audacity to *kiss* her? Aurelia hated that she could not be certain. Her mind was filled with stardust and she could not manage to collect her thoughts.

But he had been dangerously close when she awakened. And her lips were warm in a most odd way.

The second man was dressed strangely, too, a bright length of silk knotted around his neck and the finest leather shoes Aurelia had ever seen upon his feet. His cloak was fabulously detailed, though the familiarity of the plaid lining was oddly reassuring. The top of his head was bald, his fair hair left in a thick ring from temple to temple.

Had she not heard that the priests from Rome shaved their pates in such an unusual fashion?

Aurelia tried to sit up straight and hold the shreds of cloth over her nakedness with a measure of decorum. She would need all the grace drilled into her to meet the measured gaze of the tall one once more.

But what were foreigners doing in her father's home, so free with their ways that they could burst into her chambers? Her mind felt as fogged as the bay on an autumn morning, but Aurelia fought to collect her wits.

And this place smelled like a cellar! With a start, she realized that she was not in her chambers at all.

"Who are you?" she demanded regally. "What gives you the right to invade my privacy unannounced? And where is my father?"

The men exchanged a glance, though their features did not show any sign of comprehension. Where had they come from that they did not understand the Pictish tongue?

Aurelia repeated her questions in the Gaelic of the Scots and that of the Irish, then in the Briton of the south, finally in the Norse tongue of her father. All to no avail. Even the Latin of the cursed priests earned no response.

"What the hell is she saying?" the man with the bald pate asked.

The tall man shrugged, his perceptive gaze not wavering from Aurelia's own. "I have no idea. Maybe she's cold."

A twinkle danced within Aurelia's mind and she felt the power of the first gift granted at her naming surge to life. For years, she had trained and honed this ability, and now the dividends were her own. She silently thanked the great priestess who had paid her homage with this gift.

For Aurelia had been granted, as a babe, the gift of tongues.

It was fitting for the daughter of a great sorceress to be endowed with such a magical gift, and useful, as well. Aurelia habitually translated messages from afar at her father's court, for she had only to hear a language to have not only an understanding of it but to be able to converse in it.

That did not mean she understood all of the words within that language, particularly when parallel words did not exist within her own mother tongue. The second man's next speech made that tellingly clear.

He scratched his forehead. "She must be a vagrant—just look at her clothes!—who somehow has gotten into this place to sleep. We can't afford to have this kind of PR liability connected with the resort before we even open." He rolled his eyes and shuddered. "I can't believe you *touched* her without having any idea where she's been! What were you thinking?"

The tall man's expression turned grim, but he did not respond. Even Aurelia could see that he did not intend to defend his actions.

He was obviously the leader, this priest his advisor. Her father had often said not to trust a man who put too much faith in the soothsaying of priests of any faith and she admired that this one questioned his counsel.

But precisely *how* had he touched her? Aurelia licked her lips nervously and found a taste upon them that was not her own.

What manner of man kissed a sleeping stranger?

The priest sighed. "Look, let's take her into town and . . ."

"And what?" the tall man demanded impatiently. "Toss her out in the street? How is *that* good PR?"

He waved off whatever the priest would have said, his green gaze fixing on Aurelia once more. "Can you understand me?" When she nodded, he went on. "Have we met?" he asked in a far more gentle tone than he had used with his priest.

"No."

Something flickered in the depths of those eyes, as though he did not quite believe her. "Are you lost? Do you live near here?"

"I live *here*!" Aurelia almost laughed at the foolishness of his question, but a shadow crossed the warrior's eyes.

Why was he troubled by that claim? It was perfectly true. Aurelia frowned, sensing there was something critical she should remember, but the memory shimmered elusively just beyond her grasp.

The priest sighed again, a sure sign that his course of action was getting short shrift to his mind. "Look, Baird, I don't know what's going on here, but sentimentality has no place . . ."

Bard! Aurelia straightened with a shock she could not hide. This was *Bard*, son of Erc!

Aurelia had never met the cursed dog, but certainly had not imagined he would be so handsome. There was an air about him that tempted one to trust him, a characteristic all the more foul given what Aurelia knew of his deceitfulness.

Memories tumbled into her mind like a river unleashed from a dam. Bard's ships had arrived at Dunhelm this very morning! And Aurelia had killed the first of Bard's own men.

And now Bard, son of Erc, stood boldly before her, his progress unobstructed. Her father would never have allowed this.

If Hekod had had a choice.

A trickle of dread slithered down Aurelia's spine. She thought frantically, but she could not remember anything beyond pricking her thumb.

And being surrounded by a dizzying shimmer. Clearly she had fainted from the shock of her wound and the battle had raged on without her.

Suddenly Aurelia recognized the room. They were in the bowels of the old ritual well, though that made little sense. How did she get from the ramparts to the well while the battle for her home raged?

She must have been taken prisoner.

Aurelia's mouth went dry. Bard had singled her out, no doubt to pay for her early assault upon his forces.

Bard suddenly cast aside his unusual green cloak. He shrugged out of his heavy cream-colored knit tunic and Aurelia inched backward in sudden understanding of the price she would pay.

He would rape her!

"You must be cold," he said smoothly. Ha! Aurelia would never give him the chance to warm her flesh with his own!

Bard stepped closer, his emerald gaze fixed upon her as though he would lull her into complacency. Aurelia stared back at him with feigned innocence and secretly felt for the blade she always carried.

The sheath hanging from her belt was empty. The treacherous dog had seen her disarmed, while she lay in a stupor!

But Aurelia was not without defenses. Bard took another step and Aurelia coiled herself tightly, waiting for the moment he came near enough for her kick to be disabling.

But Bard halted two steps away. He held out his garment at arm's length and Aurelia's breath caught in her throat.

Had he guessed her intent?

"Take it." Bard gave his garment a little shake when Aurelia did not move. "You'll catch cold otherwise."

Aurelia did not want to take any garb that had graced Bard's sorry hide. All the same, she did not want to sit virtually nude before that perceptive gaze.

It left her at a disadvantage, to say the least.

Certain that there must be a trick, Aurelia snatched hastily at the tunic. She moved quickly, but not quickly enough to avoid the heat of Bard's fingers brushing against her own. The contact sent a shiver running along her flesh, and shock made her stare into his eyes for a dangerously long moment.

He arched an ebony brow, as though surprised by her reticence to touch him. Aurelia's heart stopped before it lurched forward again.

Oh, he had a charm, that much was certain, but Aurelia knew the darkness that filled his heart! She hauled the knit tunic hastily over her head and closed her eyes against the seductively masculine scent that rose from the garment.

She felt suddenly much, much warmer, though she fought hard against her instinctive attraction to this man. Aurelia had no doubt Bard cultivated this calm manner, perhaps practicing the bone-meltingly low pitch of his voice, as it would serve his ends well. All the better to disarm those he would destroy.

Had her own brother not been seduced by Bard's deceitful talk?

"I thank you," Aurelia managed to say with some decorum. The tunic covered her hips and would probably fall halfway to her knees when she stood.

Her suspicion must have shown, but Bard's gaze did not waver. Aurelia folded her arms across her chest and glared at her captor, determined to know the truth. "What have you done with my father?"

The men seemed surprised by this question and exchanged a glance before Bard's dark brows drew together in a frown.

"Who?"

"My *father*, King Hekod the Fifth, King of Dunhelm and Lord of Fyordskar across the sea."

Bard's lips curled in an unwilling smile that transformed his features. A unexpected twinkle gleamed in his eyes, like sunlight dancing on the sea. Bard was no longer the stern warrior, but an indulgent lover.

Lover? What had summoned such a foolish thought? Clearly he smiled because he was pleased to have her parentage confirmed.

"King Hekod?"

"The Fifth," Aurelia corrected haughtily. "I would see him now, if you please, and ensure his welfare."

Bard's smile faded. "I don't know your father," he said gently. "Much less know where he is. In fact, there was no one here when we came to Dunhelm."

That Bard should lie to her so baldly stunned Aurelia to silence. No one here? What of the warriors she had joined on the walls this very morning?

Her heart clenched in fear. What had Bard done to her father?

Aurelia pushed to her feet and determinedly folded her arms across her chest. "He *must* be here!" she insisted.

Bard's lips quirked as though he wanted to reassure her. "Well, there can't be that many Hekods in the vicinity. And he can't be far. Maybe we could find him together."

Aurelia was astonished by the suggestion. Either Hekod had already died a gruesome death, or he was imprisoned and awaiting a sorry demise. How could Bard pretend Hekod did not even exist?

He had sworn vengeance upon Hekod, after all.

"Do you have any other family?" Bard asked with a concern Aurelia knew was feigned.

Clearly Bard meant to exterminate *all* of her family to see his claim to Dunhelm uncontested. Well, Aurelia was not go-

ing to supply the names of her Viking kindred to make that
task any easier!

"No, none, I am afraid," Aurelia lied.

Bard had the audacity to look sympathetic.

The cur! How could he imagine that she would forget that
he had killed her sole brother in his drive to possess Dunhelm?
Bard must think Aurelia a fool.

Though Aurelia longed to set him straight on that score, she
suddenly realized that it might be useful to encourage this
view.

Aurelia's mind flew like quicksilver. She was Bard's prisoner, that much was clear. If she were believed harmless and
given free rein within Dunhelm's walls, she would be better
situated to aid her father's Viking cousins when they arrived.

And it was so easy to trust a half-wit.

"Well, if you have no other family, we'll have to make sure
we find your father," Bard asserted.

Determined to play the idiot, Aurelia clasped her hands and
let her voice rise slightly, as though she were but a trusting
child. "You would have time for such an endeavor?" she
asked with feigned delight.

"Of course." Bard smiled warmly at her, then a shadow
flickered over his expression. "Losing a father must very difficult." The glimmer of pain in his eyes was gone so quickly
that Aurelia wondered whether she had imagined its presence.

"Baird! What are you doing?" The priest was agitated, obviously at having lost control of events. "Are you feeling all
right?"

Bard interrupted his priest in a tone that brooked no argument. "I see no reason why she can't stay here until this is
resolved." He smiled for Aurelia and her heart thumped.

"I can see a thousand!"

Bard propped his hands on his hips and pivoted to glare at
the priest. "What about your old favorite—liability?"

What was liability? Something that enraged the priest,
clearly, but beyond that Aurelia had no idea. Perhaps it was a
fancy word for her not being Christian.

The other man hissed through his teeth. "There is no Ki—"
he began, but Bard did not let him finish.

"We don't know that," he interrupted crisply, command obviously coming easily to him. "And there's no reason not to be cautious."

"Except that you never have been before," the priest muttered with dissatisfaction.

Bard grinned outright, his teeth flashing in the darkness of the chamber. Aurelia could guess that women came out of the woods when he smiled like that—and melted when he turned that smile upon them. "So, your tirades haven't fallen on deaf ears all these years, after all."

The priest opened his mouth and shut it promptly.

Bard turned crisply, ignoring the way the priest's nostrils flared with disapproval. He offered Aurelia his hand gallantly. "May I offer you accommodations?"

Accommodations in the home he had stolen from her family.

Aurelia bit her lip before she said too much and fought to appear simple. "You *have* claimed Dunhelm, then?" she asked with wide eyes.

"Yes," Bard declared in a tone that brooked no argument. "Dunhelm is all mine." He was once again a grim warrior and Aurelia had no doubt that Bard would be a formidable adversary.

And he was the new king. Dunhelm had been lost, her father's fate was unknown. Aurelia refused to be daunted by the prospect of her being able to change any of that.

She was the only hope her father had.

Aurelia stood tall and slipped her hand into the broad strength of the warrior's palm. His skin was warm, his grip over her own small hand both strong and gentle.

But Aurelia would not be fooled. She summoned every vestige of regal training she had and turned a polite, if vacant, smile on her companion. "I thank you for your hospitality, King Bard."

The priest snorted. "King? More like your knight in shining armor! He's awakening you with a kiss, just like some goddamned fairy tale, and now you want us to believe your father's a king." The priest folded his arms across his chest and glowered at Bard. "Just let me know when reality can intrude again."

The words made Aurelia's cheeks burn. Did Bard know the ridiculous prophecy of her birth? Had he arranged this awakening to trick her into believing that *he* was her destined lover?

That *would* explain his kiss. He was using an old bit of whimsy to his advantage. Aurelia's heart went still.

And then her anger erupted. Oh, his ploy was lower than low. Any fool could see that the curse placed upon Aurelia was meaningless! Whoever heard of someone sleeping for eons, let alone until their one true love awakened them? It was beyond reason!

These two must think her stupid indeed!

But, all the same, this was a perfect opportunity to bolster their expectation of her intellect. She could play the witless woman as well as anyone, if it meant saving her sire and her home.

Without another thought, Aurelia spun and clutched at Bard's hand. "Truly?" she demanded with a cloying sweetness alien to her. "You have come for me, just as it was foretold?"

Bard opened his mouth, but Aurelia was not going to give him any chance to make his lies yet worse.

Instead, she flung herself into his arms. "I was so hoping you would come soon, warrior of mine!" she cooed.

And Aurelia stretched up to kiss the deceitful murderer full on the lips.

Three

Her soft lips were on his and the breasts he had glimpsed were pressed against his chest before Baird guessed what the woman was going to do.

And then nothing else mattered but her kiss.

Baird's fingers of their own accord fitted to the neat indent of her waist. She was so tiny that his hands nearly encircled her completely, her curves fitted against him as though they were made for each other.

And Baird, a man not given to impulse, only cradled her closer and deepened his kiss. She trembled, as though she was also surprised by the heat of their kiss and just as powerless to end it as Baird. A protective tide swept through him and he lifted her to her toes, slanting his mouth across hers.

There was a *rightness* about kissing her, a sense of home-coming, a rush of victory that made absolutely no sense. In this moment, Baird didn't care about what made sense. Her lips were as soft and warm as summer rain, her kiss as sweet as honey.

Baird knew with sudden clarity that he had come to Dunhelm precisely and purely to find this woman. It was no co-incidence she was here, he was oddly certain of it. This woman was the lure that had drawn him not only to Dunhelm but to this chamber.

He had been looking for *her*.

What? How could he look for someone he didn't even

know? That kind of thinking had no place in Baird Beauforte's supremely rational mind!

Baird tore his lips away from hers, but his odd certainty didn't fade. He stared at the woman as he backed warily away, and his hand rose to wipe away the nectar of her kiss. She was possibly the most beautiful woman he had ever seen, as perfectly made as a china doll, but she must be a few bricks short of a full load. She had just kissed him as though she couldn't get enough of him, and for no reason at all!

And Baird had—very uncharacteristically—kissed her back.

In fact, he had kissed her *first*.

The whole situation was enough to make Baird deeply uneasy. He had a very definite sense that this woman knew more about him than he did about her.

Baird was no stranger to manipulation by the fair sex, but he had decided a long time ago that he wasn't going to be tricked again.

Okay. This woman had lost her father—in one way or another—and was obviously upset, maybe upset enough to be confused. And she was on Beauforte Resort property, which must be the reason Baird felt so responsible for her. He had offered to help her find her father and he would keep his word.

But that was *it*.

Baird swiftly turned his back on the woman before she could mess with his thinking any more than she already had. "Julian, find her a room in the renovation until we get this resolved," he commanded crisply. The weight of her gaze bored into his shoulders, but Baird refused to turn and look at her. "It doesn't matter where."

Julian's brow furrowed with concern. "But—"

"Just do it!" Baird snapped in a rare show of frustration. "Just do it and do it now!" He stalked toward the stairs, fighting the urge to take one last survey of the woman.

Baird forced himself to think of the appointment with the interior designer. They would talk prices and availability of materials, they would plan, they would be reasoned and unemotional.

He could hardly wait, Baird told himself grimly.

"King Bard," the woman called softly from behind him.

Baird froze with one foot on the first step and hesitated for just a moment, bracing himself for another view of her feminine vulnerability.

But the sight still made his gut clench.

It seemed impossible that she could appear softer than she had after their kiss, but she did. It was easy to imagine long sunny mornings spent in bed. . . .

Baird pulled himself up short. Julian was right—the woman must be a crazy vagrant. Wherever she had come from, obviously she had been out in the elements too long.

But Baird's lips burned. As much as he knew he should just march right out of there and put the woman out of his mind, he just couldn't do it.

And she seemed to know it. She tucked a strand of blond hair behind one ear, the move accentuating the soft sweep of her jawline. She stepped closer, her fair hair swaying behind her like a satiny curtain, and her blue, blue gaze locked with his.

Baird could feel that uncanny allure working its magic on him again. He forced himself to look away, to look anywhere other than her eyes, and his gaze had the misfortune to fall on her feet.

Baird had always had a weakness for the feminine foot. So different from his own, women's feet spoke of delicacy and grace, of suppleness and strength. These, unfortunately for his determination to leave and ignore the woman, were among the finest pair he had ever seen.

Baird swallowed and stared.

Just to make matters worse, those tiny feet were bare against the accumulated moss on the stone floor, the contrast highlighting their dainty femininity. Baird gritted his teeth and struggled not to wonder how soft the pearly skin on her instep would be.

He failed utterly.

"I thought we were going to look for my father." There was a thread of steel in her tone that had not been there before, but Baird overlooked it to seize on her words.

Could her father, whoever he was, really have some claim

on Dunhelm? Could Baird lose Dunhelm, after all he had been through to acquire it?

No way! An irrational panic swept through him and Baird knew he couldn't let that happen at any cost. He shoved one hand through his hair. "I'll get to it after my meeting with the designer."

"Oh, yes, we can't keep our precious Morticia waiting," Julian muttered.

Baird glared at his friend, his patience with dissenting opinions completely gone. "Our designer's very good at what she does, whether you like her or not."

Julian grimaced. "I wouldn't know how *good* she is. What I do know is that she's very—how should I put it?—*ambitious.*"

Baird stifled a growl, wishing for the umpteenth time that Julian and Marissa could put their differences aside. There were days when he felt more like a mediator than an employer.

And that was the last thing he needed today.

"Just leave it, Julian." Baird turned back to the stairs, his gaze unwillingly drawn one last time to those enticing feet. It was too easy to picture one cradled in his hand, cleaning the dirt away, sliding his palm over that graceful ankle. . . .

He *was* losing it!

"Take care of her," Baird commanded, then swung around and started up the stairs. "After the meeting, I'll start looking for Hekod."

"King Bard?"

What now? Baird reluctantly glanced back to find the woman standing ramrod straight, her chin high, his sweater hanging nearly to her knees. Her blue eyes shone with a clarity that made Baird wonder whether she was really as dumb as she seemed to want him to believe.

He refused to look below the hem of his sweater.

"I am the Princess Aurelia, a Pictish priestess and daughter of the king," she said with the same pride with which she had declared her father's title. "If I am to be your *guest*, I can only ask that you address me properly."

Princess? Baird blinked but her gaze did not waver.

"No one calls me '*her*' in my own presence," she clarified, obviously mistaking the reason for his silence. "I do not take offense, for a barbarian such as yourself cannot be expected to know better, but in future, you could *try* to be decently mannered."

Baird gritted his teeth and bit back a defense of America with an effort. Aurelia certainly wasn't the first he had met in Britain who thought everyone from beyond their own borders was an illiterate colonial redneck.

Especially Americans.

But considering herself royalty was another thing entirely. He wondered briefly if she would think it a royal insult if he decided to correct the slight mispronunciation she gave his name.

"*Princess* Aurelia?" he echoed skeptically.

Aurelia's smile was dazzlingly bright. "Of course, I'm a princess!" She giggled like a teenager that he would question something she found self-evident. "King Hekod the Fifth is my sire, as you well know."

Baird didn't know any such thing.

What he did know now was that Aurelia was crazy. There was no doubt about it. She thought she was a princess, that her father was a king, and that this was her home.

Such as it was.

Aurelia's smile slowly faded when Baird said nothing. A wariness dawned in her expression again, as though the silliness was a mask that had slipped away.

Baird found himself intrigued by the hint that there was more to her than met the eye. Which was the real Aurelia?

Baird told himself that he shouldn't care.

He certainly shouldn't be replaying Aurelia's luscious kiss over and over again in his mind.

"Well, I'm late, *princess*." Baird bowed ever so slightly in her direction, and caught a wayward glimpse of her pale toes. The sight did hard and thick things to him that had no place in this situation. "Julian will find you a room."

"Don't worry, I'll take care of everything." Julian waved him off and Baird didn't need any more encouragement to take the stairs two at a time.

• • •

Baird's heart was still pounding when he reached the graciously wide entry to the hotel. Though he told himself that it was because of the run across the lot, Baird wasn't as sure of that as he would have liked to have been.

It certainly wasn't because he was anxious to pore over marble samples with Marissa Witlowe.

In fact, he couldn't remember exactly why he had agreed to let Marissa come early to Dunhelm. Keeping her and Julian from each other's throats was not going to be a treat.

Marissa pivoted at the sound of Baird's arrival, her slender curves perfectly accentuated by her slim black suit. A pretty woman, she was impeccably groomed, as always, and right on time. Morticia was not such an unlikely moniker for her, with her preference for black clothes, her fair skin, ebony hair, and love of dark lipstick.

Marissa raised one hand to pat the elegant coil of her hair and smiled at the sight of him. "Baird!" She waved with her fingertips, her high heels clicking as she crossed the new granite floor. Baird wondered whether he imagined the accentuated sway of her hips.

Marissa Witlowe had been hired by a human resources expert who hadn't lasted long at Beauforte Resorts. All the same, Marissa had remained, and shown rare determination in working her way to the top. She was a competent designer, though not brilliant, but even Baird was quick to admit that hotels seldom require decorating brilliance.

Marissa not only understood the Beauforte look, but she was good at digging out new suppliers and good prices for the materials that the resorts needed. Baird gave her credit for that—and no more.

There certainly was nothing else between herself and Baird—never had been—they simply weren't each other's types. Marissa was simply Too Much Trouble. She took hours to get ready for the smallest occasion, and invariably broke nails or lost eyelashes or found minute snags in her stockings that required long sojourns in the women's room to repair. Marissa was allergic to a change of plans and was almost as fussy an eater as Julian.

And apparently, somewhere and sometime, Marissa had

adopted a flowery, extravagant way of expressing herself—not to mention a glaringly phony British accent—that she obviously thought suited a creative personality like her own.

Having Marissa on the Beauforte team for even the most mundane business function was such a huge pain that it cured Baird of any desire for female company for a good month afterward.

The sight of her, here in Dunhelm but dressed as though she were popping out for a goat-cheese-and-endive salad at one of Julian's chichi bistros, was a tangible reminder of the real world that should have been more welcome than it was.

But Baird had to force his smile. He found himself half wishing that the real world had stayed safely ensconced in the head office, where it belonged.

"How was the flight from London?"

"Uneventful." Marissa waved the question off dismissively, then leaned closer. The move granted Baird a view of her cleavage and a waft of her musky perfume.

Before Baird could do more than wonder whether the view was deliberately offered, much less why, Marissa's gaze dropped to his jeans. Baird hoped she hadn't noticed what he thought she had noticed.

He *knew* he should have gone for relaxed-fit jeans.

Silently he blamed Aurelia for getting under his skin in a way that no woman ever had done. And more quickly than Baird would have thought possible.

Aurelia was going to be trouble with a capital T. Why had Baird listened to impulse and invited her to stay? He was *never* impulsive!

Worse, he couldn't stop thinking about her. He couldn't even concentrate on Marissa's chatter, his mind replaying that hot kiss over and over again.

And Marissa evidently had noticed the result.

"The gates look simply *divine*! And this place is absolutely *fabulous*!" Marissa smiled with something more than professional respect gleaming in her dark eyes. Baird felt the back of his neck heat in embarrassment, but Marissa continued merrily along, kissing her fingertips dramatically. "Of course, you always have the most *impeccable* taste, darling, you truly do."

"The logo on the gate was your idea," Baird reminded her, his tone coolly professional. "I'm just glad it worked out so well. Did you get pricing on the travertine marble?"

Marissa's lips thinned ever so slightly before she ducked her head and dug into her briefcase. "Why, of course, darling! Why else would I be here other than to work, work, work?"

Aurelia certainly had not expected Bard, son of Erc, to find her kiss repulsive! Her feathers ruffled with feminine pride and she glared at the priest to whose company she had been abandoned.

The insult was even worse given the tingle of awareness that kissing Bard had awakened within her.

After all, Aurelia knew she was not plain! Men came from far and wide to court her, but Aurelia turned them all aside. She wanted a partner who cared for *her*, not merely her face. Beauty, after all, would fade and it was the person within who endured.

Aurelia had learned much of the power of that kind of partnership from her parents' example and she wanted no less for herself.

All the same, Bard's rejection irked her. Why, she had even been called a *beauty*!

But the new King of Dunhelm could not bear to have her touch him. That just proved he was an unmannered barbarian!

The priest urged Aurelia impatiently toward the stairs. "Come on, let's get out of here. I don't know about you, but I could use a brandy. Let's find you a guest room pronto."

Guest? Ha! No doubt this priest would toss her into some dank and dour prison, crawling with rats.

Aurelia tightened her lips and stalked toward the stairs. They would drag her out periodically to interrogate her—perhaps even torture her!—then cast her back into misery.

Oh, she knew well enough the kind of brutality of which Bard was capable! But she, *she* would not bend readily to his will. Somehow she would find her sire, and somehow she would prevail against this villain.

Or Aurelia would die trying.

Decision made, Aurelia stormed to the summit of the stairs, then froze on the spot. She stared dumbstruck at the changed scene before her.

What had happened to the holding she knew as well as the palm of her own hand?

Walls had been ruined, the rubble moved so that the structures Aurelia knew were virtually obliterated. Her father's great wooden hall was gone so completely that it might never have existed. And she had raised a chalice of mead within those carved walls this very morning, before the battle.

At least, it *seemed* as though it had been this very morning.

Aurelia frowned and eyed stones heavy with moss where there had not even been stones. She chewed her lip with uncertainty and she had the odd sense that her mind taunted her to reach for a truth hung just out of reach.

She must have been drugged. There were plants Aurelia knew well, which were more than potent enough for such a task.

"Come on," the priest urged impatiently. "Let's get out of this miserable rain already. God, I hate this place. Beats me why people *choose* to live here."

Aurelia stepped forward at his demand, all the while fighting to hide her response to Bard's wanton destruction. If she had not recognized the ritual well, Aurelia might have doubted that she was home.

Aurelia looked to the sea, knowing that it would tell her no lies. She eyed the sweep of the coastline, the reassuring shade of hazy blue with which the sea always met the sky.

That was familiar, at least. She recognized the crags and beaches, the great stones and the waves that stretched to the horizon, and felt her fears settle as surely as the waves pounding on the shore.

Back across the island and in the other direction, Aurelia could barely discern the silhouetted towers that had been falling apart as long as anyone could remember. The dimple of an old chambered tomb, left by people long forgotten, could be seen if she squinted into the morning sun.

Were the crumbling towers shorter than before? And what had happened to all the trees surrounding her father's hall?

Bard's men must have raided the towers for material to build his great stone hall, just ahead. And the trees could have been burned with alarming speed.

This *was* her home, regardless of how quickly Bard had managed to make his mark upon it.

Aurelia took a deep breath and looked once more at the construction they approached. Workers crawled over the site like bees in a hive, their clothing different but no less strange than that of Bard and his priest. The great stone hall rose high behind them, higher than any hall Aurelia had ever seen.

Surely everyone she knew could not have been slaughtered? It looked as though Bard had need of every strong man for the ambitious construction he made here.

Encouraged by the thought, Aurelia focused her attention on the men themselves, hopefully seeking a familiar face. She scanned the first workman that she and the priest passed by, but did not know him. Nor the second, nor the third. Aurelia returned more than one questioning glance, and hoped desperately that the priest did not notice her curiosity.

But there were no faces she knew in the yard.

Aurelia refused to despair. Maybe the women, at least, had been allowed to survive as household slaves and whores. They would be hidden away at this hour, working in kitchens and storerooms and fields. With so many men filling the courtyard, Aurelia knew there must be women kept to service their needs.

It was the fate of conquered women everywhere to roll to their backs, willingly or not. Somewhere on this holding, Aurelia would find someone she knew.

The priest led her through a wide portal set beside a soaring tower that had not existed before. The portal was thrice as high as Aurelia stood, its wooden doors heavy with iron studs and folded back against the inside. As they passed beneath its shadow, Aurelia looked up and saw the spikes of a wicked iron gate that could be dropped across the passage.

She had never seen such fine ironwork in all her days and shot a glance at the priest. Aurelia knew well enough that blacksmiths possessed a secret power and taught their songs only to specially chosen apprentices. Had this priest been responsible for increasing the power of the smiths' songs?

The high walls were wrought so carefully of stone that they seemed perfectly smooth. Aurelia touched one as she passed through the passageway behind the portal and marveled at the thin line sealing each stone to the next.

The craft of the stonemason had also been taken to new heights by Bard's men.

The truth could not be denied. There was powerful witchery at work in this place.

Aurelia gazed sidelong at the impassive priest, much impressed by his influence. Perhaps her father had underestimated the powers of the men from Rome.

Another pair of doors—these wooden ones ornamented with swirls of gold or brass—opened at the priest's touch to reveal a hall of such sumptuous design that Aurelia halted and gaped.

The floor was like a gaming board, alternating dark and light squares, but wrought of some infinitely smooth stone that was cut with incredible precision. The ceiling arched high overhead and Aurelia could not imagine what magic possessed the slender columns that they could hold up a roof made of stone. The interior was in the midst of being painted most artfully with writhing Celtic dragons and knots.

On the far side of the hall, a pair of staircases wound skyward like two embracing arms, their curves smooth beyond belief. Rails gleamed gold on either side of each staircase and red tapestries were being laid against the stone stairs.

Despite her determination to despise everything associated with Bard, son of Erc, Aurelia was impressed.

A long table of dark wood was being assembled between the ends of the staircases, its front rich with ornamentation. The wood gleamed with a reddish hue alien to this corner of the world. Where the staircases met high above, Aurelia could just spot a wide double doorway.

The hall was filled with the sounds of hammering and men muttering. She assumed they chanted the spells that made such wizardry possible. And such power!

Aurelia feared suddenly that her abilities might be as nothing compared to the sorcery of Bard and his priest.

But it would not do to let this priest see her doubts.

The priest shook his head impatiently. "I know it isn't done, we're *weeks* behind schedule, but it doesn't look so bad that you have to stare! Surely you can see that the reception area will be stunning when it's finally finished?''

The reception area?

This was not even the king's hall?

Aurelia swallowed with an effort. She had never seen such wealth and could not imagine that anything could be more ostentatious than this. For the son of a reviled and deposed king, Bard was unexpectedly affluent. How had he amassed such awesome wealth?

Through no honest means, Aurelia was certain of that.

Four

"*Hellooooooo*, Julian! Darling, how *are* you?"

The priest and Aurelia swiveled as one to find a woman waving her fingertips from the other side of the hall. Aurelia's heart lurched at the sight of King Bard looming behind the slender woman, and she cursed her own feminine weakness. His arms were folded across his chest and he looked doubly grim.

The woman's black garb fit her every curve and did not even fall long enough to cover her knees. Her features were beautiful, her skin pale, her lips full and reddened, her eyes thickly lashed. She tripped across the floor, somehow keeping her balance in ridiculously restraining shoes.

None of the other men in the hall seemed to take notice of the woman's bold display of her assets, though the priest's lips thinned tellingly.

Aurelia understood immediately. This woman was competition for the king's attention, for she was obviously Bard's whore. What priestly advisor would not resent such influence? A whore had more than the king's ear in her keeping!

And clearly, by his expression, Bard did not want his whore showering her attention on anyone but himself. He stalked behind her across the floor, as though he abandoned their private conversation only because he had little choice. His brow was as dark as thunder.

No, he was not pleased. Aurelia concluded that the whore

must be expensive to indulge, and that Bard, reasonably enough, considered that his indulgence should earn him her exclusive attention.

The whore evidently had other ideas. She laid a hand on the priest's arm in a most friendly manner, and even had the audacity to give him a peck of greeting on one cheek, then the other, then the first again.

The priest stiffened and did not return her salute.

The whore, though, was too preoccupied to notice. Her cold gaze swept over Aurelia, and a glint flashed in her eyes, revealing that she recognized the garment as the king's own. The tightening of those reddened lips showed what she thought of that.

Aurelia knew enough of whores to understand that the woman considered her a competitive threat. As laughable as that was, Aurelia instinctively braced herself for a fight.

"How *are* you, Julian, darling? It's been so terribly long!"

"Really?" The priest's tone was cold, undoubtedly for the benefit of the king now closing the space between them with long strides. "Perhaps not long enough."

The woman laughed. "Oh, Julian." She rapped a fingertip on his arm playfully. "Darling! You're such a kidder." She leaned against him, her breast pushing against his arm, and eyed Aurelia with open assessment. "Isn't he just the most *hysterically* funny man?"

She batted her lashes at Aurelia, then gave Julian a playful pinch. "Come along now, Julian, my darling man. Don't be shy! Tell me now, is this your new flame? Don't be naughty, darling—introduce us, do! She looks like such a *precious* little waif."

The priest coughed in agitation, and though Aurelia didn't understand what fire had to do with anything, she caught the woman's meaning.

Then Bard loomed beside her, his deep voice interjecting before the priest could sputter an answer. "Princess Aurelia is a guest of the estate." His tone was resolute.

Aurelia was perversely pleased that he used her title and acknowledged her rank, then chided herself for being so easily charmed.

Again.

"Really?" the woman purred, her dark gaze gobbling up a thousand details. "*Princess*, is it, darling?" she asked, her smirk condescending. "I suppose you must be on terribly close terms with Queen Elizabeth, then? I would so love to have tea with her, you know, and talk woman to woman. I could straighten out those children of hers, I'm just sure they only need a good talking-to. . . ."

Aurelia blinked in surprise. "I know no Queen Elizabeth."

"Europe, then, darling? Prince Rainier is said to be the nicest person, once you get to know him on a more *personal* level, you know, darling. I suppose you do?" The whore's wide gaze implied that she supposed no such thing.

Fortunately Aurelia had been raised with impeccable manners, even if these barbarians had not. She drew herself up tall and did not miss the fleeting smile that curved Bard's lips.

"I am afraid I do not know this prince of your acquaintance," Aurelia admitted with a smile far more gracious than the whore deserved. Two could play this old game of one-upmanship. "Perhaps you might introduce us, at your own convenience, of course."

The whore caught her breath, but before she could speak, the priest interjected. "Oh, yes, why don't you have them both over for tea one day?" There was an edge underlying his tone and the whore fired a hostile glance in his direction. "When are you planning to see dear *Rainier* next?"

The whore gritted her teeth and looked daggers at the priest. Apparently any hostile feelings were mutual. "I have yet to make his acquaintance, darling," she admitted in a low growl.

"Really?" The priest's surprise was obviously feigned. "And here I had thought you were the *best* of friends. How could I have gotten such an idea?"

"Back to your corners," Bard interjected. "We don't want Aurelia to imagine that you two don't like each other." He quirked a brow at Aurelia with such a conspiratorial air that she knew the truth was exactly thus.

Her foolish heart fluttered at his attention, and she fought to hide any sign of her response from that perceptive gaze.

"Oh, no, never that," the priest muttered.

Aurelia ignored him and summoned her most regal manner—disregarding for the moment that she was wearing no more than a tunic—to address the whore with a winning smile. "We have not been introduced, of course, but you must be Morticia."

The priest choked and the whore gasped in outrage.

Aurelia looked between the two of them in confusion, then to Bard, unable to guess what she had said wrong. His eyes flashed and she knew that somehow she had put her foot right into it.

Not that that was a new experience for Aurelia.

She quickly decided to take refuge in her guise of stupidity. Aurelia opened her eyes wide and blinked owlishly at the king. "But you said you had an appointment—" she began in a childishly high voice.

"With *Marissa*," he interrupted tersely before Aurelia could finish. "This is Marissa Witlowe, our interior design consultant."

The introduction meant nothing to Aurelia, beyond the woman's name, which made it easier to smile like an insipid fool.

Marissa did not smile. "I do *all* the interiors, darling," she echoed in a low voice, a warning light in her dark eyes. She looped one hand through Bard's elbow and looked up at him with a proprietary smile. "Baird and I work *very* closely together, darling, especially on a project of the magnitude of Dunhelm, so don't be terribly surprised if he can't manage to find a *speck* of time for you."

She turned that cold smile on Aurelia and her eyes were dark with what was clearly a threat. "Even if you are royalty." Marissa's tone implied that she suspected precisely the opposite.

The priest chose that moment to intercede. "Well, it's time we found Aurelia a room," he said with false cheer. He continued in a cutting tone. "As delightful as it has been to see you again, Marissa, unfortunately duty calls."

Marissa's cold gaze scanned Aurelia from head to toe, then locked with Aurelia's own once more. "You know, darling, I do understand that spring is coming, but it might be a teensy bit premature to dress so"—she waved a hand vaguely—"understatedly."

"Good point, Marissa." Bard's tone was even, as though he had either not noticed his whore's antagonism or had chosen to ignore it. "Perhaps you could help Aurelia with that. She's without anything to wear right now and Tex said you flew in enough luggage for a family of five."

Marissa's finely arched eyebrows shot skyward, but Bard did not give her an opportunity to protest.

"Surely you could lend Aurelia something to wear at dinner?"

Marissa's lip curled in a disgust Aurelia was sharing, but the smile she turned on Bard was demure. She even raised one hand to her throat as though something had stuck there.

"*She's* going to eat dinner with us, darling? But she's just a guest! And I had thought that we would have a *private* dinner to discuss the decor."

The whore fluttered her lashes so provocatively that Aurelia knew "decor" had something to do with matters of intimacy.

At dinner. Shameless slut.

"Of course she's going to eat with us." Bard turned a smile on his whore that was obviously designed to dissolve feminine resistance. "There are so few of us here, it would be ridiculous to split up for dinner."

When the whore said nothing, Bard took her elbow with an ease born of familiarity, and lowered his voice to a confidential tone. "I'm sure you can find something, Marissa. I might need my sweater, after all," he said with a wink that could melt knees.

The whore's defiance faded into a compliant smile. "Whatever you like, darling," she murmured, staring up at Bard, and Aurelia knew it was time they parted ways.

She had no desire to watch this seduction unfold.

Fortunately the priest seemed to feel the same way. "Good, that's settled." He tapped Aurelia's elbow crisply. "Why don't we head upstairs and find you a room, hmm?"

Aurelia needed no encouragement to follow his lead, though she did not imagine the other pair even noticed them leaving. That irked her, but Aurelia told herself that it was just the breach of good manners that burned.

It could be nothing else.

• • •

"Just what we need—things going from bad to worse," the priest muttered under his breath as he trudged up the stairs.

It was obvious he referred to the whore and equally clear that he was not ashamed of expressing the sentiment.

"I mean, I *knew* she had to show up sometime but was hoping for *later* rather than sooner, if you know what I mean."

Aurelia watched him from the corner of her eye, uncertain what to make of this confession. For once, she held her tongue.

He sighed. "She's so high maintenance—God! She just drives me crazy. At dinner, we'll be hearing about all the burdens she has to bear, you can be sure of it." The priest's voice rose to a falsetto mimicking Marissa's accent. " 'My blow dryer isn't wired in yet, Baird, *darling*, can't you just come along to my room tonight and fix it for me, darling?' "

The priest shrugged as though he would dismiss his irritation and forced a smile for Aurelia. "Sorry. This has nothing to do with you. I shouldn't be venting."

"I understand how you feel," Aurelia said carefully. "An influential whore can be a great trial in a household."

The priest sputtered, then turned an incredulous look on her. "You're serious!" He gasped.

Aurelia was confused by his surprise. "You do not agree?"

The priest's lips twisted, then he abruptly laughed out loud. "Well, yes, I do, actually, but people seldom state the truth so bluntly." He chuckled to himself for a moment, then shook his head.

Aurelia was unable to see the difficulty in calling someone by their station in the household, let alone what was amusing about it. "If that is her place, then there's no point in garnishing the truth."

The priest shrugged. "Well, I suppose not, though calling Marissa a whore might be a bit harsh."

Aurelia blinked. "Is that not what she is?"

The priest fired a sidelong glance in Aurelia's direction. He coughed behind his hand. "Technically, *I* wouldn't know precisely what happens in Baird's bed," he said archly. "She *does* do the interiors of every Beauforte Resort, though I have to say that I don't think she's overly talented." He sniffed with obvious disdain. "I suppose anyone could draw their own conclusions from that."

" 'Does the interiors?' " Aurelia echoed.

The priest waved to the hall below as they reached the landing. "She buys stuff, picks colors, chooses furnishings, wallpaper, lamps, flooring tiles. You know, she *does* interior design."

It seemed ridiculous to make up a new name for a practice as old as time. Obviously the pleasures Marissa gave Bard in bed loosened his purse strings, and her position as his mistress granted her a household position similar to a wife.

Aurelia leveled a knowing glance at the priest as they mounted the stairs. "She spends his coin."

The man's lips quirked at her terse summary. "Yes. In a way, yes, that's what she does." The priest gestured to the lavish room behind them. "She bought all that. And all this." He threw open the carved wooden doors at the summit.

The doors swung inward silently despite their obvious weight and a long hallway hung with glistening crystals was revealed. Countless doors marched on either side of the corridor, following one after the other as far as Aurelia could see.

The tapestry cast on the floor here was crimson, crisscrossed with a rope pattern worked in shades of gold. It gleamed with the luster of silk, was as thick as a cushion, and stretched on seemingly forever. Aurelia could not even imagine how long it would have taken to weave, let alone how many women would have to lend their hands to the task.

It was shocking to think of walking on such a work, but the priest strode across it without a second thought. He paused before the fourth door on the left side of the corridor.

"And this." The priest slid a thin square into a slot above the door handle. Aurelia saw something red flash, then he pulled back the square into his hand, as though he would conceal it from her. He opened the door.

It was a ritual, obviously, a protective spell.

But now the priest had disappeared inside and left her behind. Aurelia took the two longest steps she could manage, on her tiptoes, across the magnificent tapestry to reach the narrow strip of wood flooring revealed on the far side. She sidled along the wood, careful not to step on the tapestry again, and peeked through the door that the priest held open.

And was amazed by the magnificence of the furnishings. The room was ornamented in a deep and pleasing sapphire hue, the bed hung with heavy tapestries, the floor thick with rugs.

"King Bard's chambers," Aurelia whispered, certain that this luxury could be for no one else.

It was shockingly intimate to look upon his private chambers. Aurelia was certain the king would have words for the priest, had he guessed that she was here.

Perhaps it was the fact that this was a stolen view that made a heat unfurl in Aurelia's stomach as she eyed the great bed. It was so easy to imagine Bard sleeping there.

Nude.

On his back, as all warriors slept, one hand flung out across the pallet. His broad chest would be tanned golden, the dark hair that adorned it slightly curly. Aurelia's toes curled at the vivid image she had of him. He would smile that provocative half smile when he awakened and his eyes would glitter that dangerous sea green.

And his strong fingers would rest on the hip of his whore, who curled by his side in a most proprietary manner.

Aurelia inhaled sharply and glared at the priest, uncertain why the thought of Bard's whore troubled her so much. The pair deserved each other!

The priest shook his head. "No. Baird's room is the first one." He nodded to the left. "This one might as well be yours."

Aurelia blinked, but he was not teasing her. Though she was a noblewoman, Aurelia had expected accommodation markedly more austere.

Like a dank, stone cell.

"It's no big deal," the priest said with a shrug, evidently noticing Aurelia's surprise. "It's just one of the guest rooms."

Such a room for guests.

For *any* guest who stumbled into the hall.

Aurelia wandered into the room in disbelief. She touched

the silken softness of the thick bed curtains and felt the carved solidity of the bedpost beneath.

Suddenly she thought of all the doors facing this corridor and swiveled to face the priest. "And the other doors?" she demanded, half expecting his answer but not daring to believe such whimsy possible.

The priest shoved his hands into pockets hidden in his chausses. "They'll all be guest rooms, once they're finished."

All of them! Aurelia's mind darted ahead. There had to be fifty rooms in this hall alone. And Marissa had made each one finer than the last—simply to entertain guests!

Oh, she was an expensive indulgence, to be sure.

"How can you imagine that she is not his whore?" Aurelia demanded, before realizing she had given voice to the thought.

The priest hooted with laughter and Aurelia felt her cheeks stain pink. But his twinkling glance was without condemnation and oddly enough, his merriment put her in mind of her lost brother Thord.

The memory saddened Aurelia.

The priest sobered when she did not share his laughter. "Whatever she does now, Marissa hasn't made any secret of her ambition to marry Baird, at least to everyone other than Baird himself." He frowned. "I wish he'd open his eyes for a change."

Aurelia's mind flew. Marissa as wife would be even more influential than she was as whore. It made perfect sense that she would seek such a position.

And just as much that the priest would be adverse to having such a powerful adversary lodged at Bard's side over the long term. Evidently it pleased him that Aurelia and the whore had not taken to each other.

But why?

The pieces fit together with horrifying precision. The priest *had* mentioned the prophecy of Aurelia's birth in the well. Further, the priest had not made a murmur of protest when Aurelia had seized the excuse for looking like a fool and kissed the king.

Finally and perhaps most tellingly, the priest had chosen this fine prison for Aurelia.

Could the priest be planning for *her* to marry Bard, son of Erc, instead of that man's whore? Aurelia's mouth went dry. There were too many things lining up to be counted to be accidental.

She had to know the truth.

When Aurelia spoke, she was careful to keep her tone frivolous. "But what does King Bard think of such plans? Surely he has picked a bride for himself?"

"Right. He can't see for looking when it comes to women." The priest was skeptical. "And he'd do better to marry someone with connections anyhow."

Aurelia toyed with the bed curtains. "Connections?"

"Sure! A woman from a prestigious family, you know, one with property that Baird could develop, or with an influential father. That's the kind of wife he needs, not the daughter of some bank teller in Des Moines who only wants to spend his money as quickly as he can make it."

"Des Moines?"

The priest grimaced. "It's infinitely forgettable. I'm not surprised that you haven't heard of it." He wagged a warning finger at Aurelia. "But I'll tell you one thing, they don't talk like *that* in Des Moines."

Aurelia kept her mouth shut, because she could not understand what he was talking about.

"She's as fake as a three-dollar bill. Watch the accent," the priest whispered. "When she gets ticked off"—he snapped his fingers—"it's midwest twang all over."

The priest shook his head and shoved his hands into his pockets, the very image of a discouraged man. "I can't figure out why he can't see that she's not his type at all." He sighed. "It's Jessica all over again."

And who *was* Bard's type, to the priest's mind?

A woman with a prestigious family. A woman with a powerful father. A woman with a property Bard wanted.

A woman just like Aurelia.

Knowing it had been done a thousand times before did not make the reality any easier to face. Aurelia's heart trembled at the prospect of being wed to a deceitful murderer, a conqueror with an iron will and an enchanting kiss.

Against her volition.

And apparently against Bard's. But this priest was powerful, that much Aurelia knew already. Bard *had* staged her reawakening to comply with the prophecy of her birth, evidently at the priest's bidding—or at least, he had not fought the priest on this.

Was he already bowing to the priest's scheme?

Bard wanted Dunhelm and at any cost, Aurelia knew that. And with her father missing, Bard could secure his ascendancy over Dunhelm by marrying the former king's daughter.

Aurelia swallowed and let the drape slide through her fingers. Her imagination supplied the image of Bard nude in this bed once more.

Except this time, his hand was on her own bare hip. Aurelia felt the strong imprint of his lips moving against hers, felt again the weight of his hands locked around her waist.

It was Bard's fault that her thoughts were muddled, Aurelia concluded savagely. His kiss had confused her.

No. *Liking* his kiss had confused her.

Aurelia crushed the rich fabric in her hand. She hated that she had already been so readily manipulated. Would she be able to resist Bard's charm if it was turned fully upon her? Or would her feminine weakness betray both her and her family?

She suddenly became aware that the silence between herself and the priest had stretched overly long, and rushed to fill it with the first thought that came to mind.

"My mother oft said that men do not marry their whores." Aurelia heard a sharpness in her voice that she had not intended. "Even if they indulge them."

The priest chuckled and watched her with twinkling eyes. "Why would a man buy the cow when he can have the milk for free, right?"

It was an apt parallel. Aurelia met the priest's dancing gaze and was reminded again of her lost brother. Even knowing his intentions for her, Aurelia could not help but smile tentatively back.

He grinned and stuck out his hand. "Julian Preston. Call me Julian."

Aurelia stared at his hand, then took it, as that seemed to

be his expectation. Julian squeezed her fingers, pumped her hand up and down twice, then released it.

A strange gesture indeed. Aurelia wondered what it meant.

"And you may call me Aurelia."

"Instead of Princess?" Julian seemed to be struggling not to laugh. The similarity to Thord was most telling when his eyes danced, and Aurelia, despite her determination not to like the priest, felt some sisterly affection dawn within her.

"Only in private, of course," she advised him, much as she would have advised her brother with his short memory for such details. "In the hall, you will still have to use my title." Aurelia frowned, unable to understand why this was so amusing to the priest.

Did they not have decent manners in Rome either?

"Well, make yourself at home." Julian waved cheerfully and tossed his blessing square toward Aurelia.

She no sooner caught it than he was gone, leaving Aurelia alone in the chamber decorated by Bard's whore. The door closed with a solid click that made her realize this chamber, regardless of its richness, was a prison, after all. And, as his prisoner, Aurelia was subject to the whim of Bard, son of Erc.

Whatever that might be.

Five

Aurelia waited a few moments, then surreptitiously checked the door. She fully expected it to be secured from the outside.

But it was unlocked.

To Aurelia's further amazement, the corridor outside was empty. The distant sounds of hammering carried to her ears, but no guard was posted watchfully outside.

Ha! They must think her witless, after all! She propped open the door with her toe and slid Julian's magic square into the slot, exactly as he had done.

Nothing happened.

But there had been a light when Julian did it. Perhaps she did not know the proper incantation. Who knew what Julian might have muttered under his breath, or whispered in his mind? She stepped out into the corridor, trying to examine the slot in better light.

The door closed with a resolute click.

Aurelia turned the handle, but the door was locked against her! She was trapped in the corridor, of all foolishness! What kind of malicious magic was this?

In desperation, Aurelia shoved Julian's card into the slot once more, but this time, a red dot glowed thrice.

It was a sign. Three was a powerful number, that much was certain, and red a color of protection for ages past.

It must be safe to enter the chamber once more.

Aurelia cautiously tried the handle again, and magically the door was now unlocked. She darted inside, fingering the card, and marveled at Julian's power. Aurelia fought to make sense of Julian giving her the ability to lock herself *outside* of the room and could not.

Perhaps his spell had twisted itself backward. Such things happened when magic was wrought in haste.

Or perhaps Julian was less powerful than Aurelia had feared. Now, that was an encouraging thought! Aurelia grinned with satisfaction and her mind worked furiously. What should she do? At any moment, Julian could repair his spell and trap her inside the chamber.

This might be her only opportunity to find her sire without observation.

Clearly her father was either dead or imprisoned. And if Aurelia were in Bard's place, intending to let Hekod be forgotten, where would she have imprisoned the deposed king? The answer was simple beyond all.

In the sea caves.

Aurelia clutched Julian's magical talisman, scanned the corridor once more, then abandoned her room. She darted down the corridor in the opposite direction of the great reception hall. When Aurelia opened the last door at the end of the corridor, she found a flight of stairs markedly less ornate than those she and the priest had climbed.

No one was behind her. Aurelia lunged down the stairs. There was only one door at the bottom, red letters above it declaring FIRE EXIT.

On the door itself, a sign read: For Emergency Exit Only. If Door Is Opened, Alarm Will Sound.

Aurelia hesitated, then frowned. Who would sound this alarm, if no one saw her open the door? She looked over her shoulder, but she was definitely alone.

Ha! More lies! Aurelia was developing a very low opinion of Bard's household security. She shoved open the door and a shrill ringing suddenly filled her ears.

Oh, no! Julian had laid a spell on the door!

Aurelia muttered something unladylike under her breath. Her heart thundering in her ears, she fled Bard's hall as fast as she could. Hopefully there was no witchery left to discern her path.

Baird's head snapped up from the travertine marble samples when the fire alarm went off. "Is this another test? I thought they were done yesterday."

"They were," the job foreman confirmed, then looked worried. "It might be a real fire, sir."

The intensity of Baird's response surprised him. He wouldn't let Dunhelm burn under any circumstances. He scanned the hall anxiously but, to his relief, saw no flames.

"Well, better safe than sorry." Baird's tone was calmly authoritative despite his fears. People immediately turned to do his bidding. "Everybody outside—get all your team out— we'll meet on the lawn in front of the main entrance and have a head count."

"Yes, sir."

Marissa looped her hand through Baird's arm and her voice dropped to a throaty purr. "You're so very decisive, darling! I just *love* a man who takes charge of things—"

"Marissa, there may really be a fire," Baird interrupted tersely. "Why don't you go outside with the others?"

"But it's raining!" Marissa raised a meticulously manicured hand to her cheek. "My hair will be ruined, darling!" She chuckled huskily and wrinkled her nose as she leaned closer. "Why don't we just stay inside together, darling, and look for that pesky fire ourselves?" She walked her fingers up his arm. "We might start in *my* room."

Fortunately Julian darted down the stairs and across the room, his arrival saving Baird from making a reply. "Is there really a fire?" Julian eyed the departing workmen with concern.

"There might be. Where's the princess?"

Julian shrugged. "In her room, I guess." He glanced over his shoulder and coughed. "You know, fires can move through a building this size with remarkable speed, making our liability quite considerable. The greater weight of our insurance coverage, as you know, does not begin in earnest until the grand opening of the resort. We should think about getting everyone out as quickly as possible and minimizing our risk in this.''

"Oooh, Julian, darling, you don't say?'' Marissa batted her lashes at Baird. "We could be in *dire* peril at this very moment!''

Baird shook himself free, his mind on other concerns. The hall was emptying quickly, but Aurelia had made no appearance at the top of the stairs, despite the insistence of the alarm. What if she had fallen asleep? Or hadn't heard the alarm?

Or didn't know what it meant?

"I have to go check on Aurelia.''

"Fourth room on the left,'' Julian supplied.

"But Baird, *darling*!'' Marissa wailed. "You can't abandon me here in the midst of this chaos!''

Baird looked pointedly around the nearly deserted foyer. It was far from a disorganized scene. He looked at Julian, who winced as though he guessed what Baird would say.

"Julian, could you make sure Marissa gets outside with the others? I'll be right there. I just want to check that our princess isn't left in her room.''

Marissa inhaled dangerously, but Baird was already striding away. He scrutinized the hall as he went, fearful that his renovation would be lost to flames even before it was done.

But he couldn't catch even a hint of smoke in the air. There was no evidence of fire at all in the hall upstairs.

Baird knocked on the fourth door, but no one answered.

He knocked again, more insistently, but there was still no response. Baird leaned closer and listened.

There wasn't a sound from inside. Baird knocked again, more forcefully this time.

Where *was* she?

When his fourth heavy knock brought no answer, Baird hauled his passkey from his pocket and opened the door.

Not only was there no sign of fire, there was no sign of the Princess Aurelia.

In fact, it was as though she had never even been in the room. A primal panic swept over Baird and a single thought echoed in his mind with startling clarity.

He had lost her again.

An odd sense of loss swept over him, one greater than anything Baird had ever felt before. He was bereft, as though a part of himself had been torn away.

And he knew without a doubt that he had felt this way many times before.

Great. Baird shook his head savagely. Now she was making *him* nuts.

But Baird couldn't completely dismiss his fear, even knowing it was irrational. What if something had happened to Aurelia?

Baird ran for the stairs, fighting for his usual calm as the alarm rang insistently. He met Julian halfway down the stairs.

"The *fourth* room?" Baird demanded.

"Yeah. But one of the guys saw a woman leaving from the back fire exit." Julian's sober gaze locked with Baird's. "Blond hair, wearing only a sweater. Looks like your princess set off the alarm when she ran away from here."

Baird exhaled in a relieved rush and shoved one hand through his hair. "Where did she go?"

Julian shrugged. "He said she ran toward the sea."

Baird caught his breath. One false step could send anyone plunging to their death. And it would be all too easy to slip in this weather.

Aurelia wasn't safe after all.

"I tell you, Baird, this woman is a lot of trouble and I really think you should reconsider the wisdom of your offer." Julian coughed into his hand. "If anything happens to her, we could be found liable since you invited her to stay. Having her here as an unpaying guest clouds the assignment of responsibility. . . ."

Baird pushed past Julian and bolted down the stairs.

Aurelia raced along the uneven rocks, the path she had known now obscured. Her certainty that Bard had deliberately hidden this way grew with every moment—it could not have changed so drastically otherwise!

The wind whipped her hair around and the cold rain splashed on her face. Bard's tunic was little protection against the bite of the cold, and her feet were freezing, but she thought only of her sire.

Her heart twisted as she imagined him trapped in the wretched prison of a sea cell. Though Hekod was strong, he was no longer a young man—he could already have caught a deathly chill.

Aurelia paused on the lip of the cliff and scanned the rocks below. This was the spot. Aurelia could fairly taste the despair.

It was a desolate and lonely place, isolated on the northernmost crag of Dunhelm. In broad sunlight, it gave a person gooseflesh, no doubt because the torment of countless prisoners had left its mark.

From the crest of the cliff, the slope of rock looked as though it continued unbroken to the edge of the cliff, where it dropped straight down to the sea far below.

But Aurelia knew better. Halfway down the ragged descent of the cliff, there was a black and jagged opening in the rock. That hole was the only entry to the dreaded sea cells. Aurelia glanced back and thought she discerned figures erupting from the castle.

She did not have much time. She scrambled down the steep rock face, scratching her bare feet in the process but continuing undaunted. She tasted the salt of the sea spray and her mouth went dry at the proximity of the crashing waves.

The wet rocks gleamed like jet and were slick with moss. One false step and she could slide to the edge of the cliff, then straight down into the sea. There would be no easy landing on the rough rocks below. Aurelia concentrated on finding a secure footing on each rock, telling herself to ignore the hypnotic pounding of the sea.

The opening to the sea cells was closer to the cliff edge than she recalled. Aurelia gripped the rocks and leaned over the hole, closing her eyes at the dizzy drop to the cell's wet floor.

There was no escape from these dismal cells. It was here that the worst criminals had always been abandoned to die. Aurelia was certain that the repetitive crash of the sea would drive them to madness first. Or the crush of bones beneath one's feet, a tangible reminder of the fate of previous occupants, and a fate ultimately to be their own.

Aurelia could see no movement in the fathomless shadows

below. She peered into the darkness and shivered when she thought she saw the glimmer of a pale bone.

"Father?" she called, but there was no response.

Her voice echoed slightly in the cavern below and made a lonely sound. She raised her voice and called again.

The sea rushed and withdrew, the wind whistled over the rocks. Gulls cried far overhead, but Aurelia strained to see some sign of life below.

"*Father*! Father, answer me! Father, are you here?"

"There is no one here, Gemdelovely Gemdelee, no one but you and now there's me."

Aurelia jumped at the gently spoken words. She spun to find an ancient crone behind her.

The woman leaned heavily on a cane to survey Aurelia with twinkling eyes. Her face was wreathed in wrinkles, her hands gnarled, but she exuded a good-humored charm and a strength unexpected.

Her bright pink dress flapped around her knees and danced with large blossoms. Her silver-gray hair was pulled back and pinned, but seemed to have a wavy defiance. Quite a lot of it blew freely around her face.

She must have been a beauty when she was young.

There was something familiar about the woman, but Aurelia knew they had never met before. She would have remembered those eyes, she was certain of it. All the same, she found herself returning the woman's smile and felt oddly comforted by her presence.

"Who are you?" Aurelia asked. "I did not hear you come near."

The woman's smile broadened. "Oh, I know well enough who I am and who you might be, Gemdelovely Gemdelee. The question is only—what do you seek, pretty you, pretty me?" The woman's voice was delightfully musical in cadence.

"My father. King Hekod the Fifth."

"Ah!" The woman's eyes lit up, as though she laughed at a secret joke, then she turned to walk away. Her cane tapped on the wet rocks, but she climbed the slope with the assurance of one who knew her way well.

Aurelia guessed from that expression that the woman knew

something she was not prepared to tell. She rose to her feet and anxiously gave chase. "Do you know where he is? Have you seen him?"

The woman sent a glance Aurelia's way. "I have seen many come and many go, Gemdelovely Gemdelee. Some call themselves kings, some merely believe themselves to be."

Hope rose within Aurelia. Could this woman have aided her sire? "But have you seen my father? Was he imprisoned here? Did you help him escape?"

The woman climbed, apparently untroubled by either Aurelia's questions or her concern. "No one can escape their fate, Gemdelovely Gemdelee. Any task left unfinished must be done, any debt settled and balance paid." She turned and glanced piercingly at Aurelia. "There was a time when you understood such things."

Aurelia had a sudden recollection of her dame giving her just such a look when she had forgotten a vital lesson. She gaped at the old woman, and realized belatedly that the woman's eyes were the same silver-gray as her mother's had been.

And they twinkled with the same vigor.

As Aurelia fought to make sense of this, the woman smiled and turned back to her climbing. "You are not afraid of me, Gemdelovely Gemdelee. Can you tell me why that might be?"

Aurelia exhaled slowly. "You remind me of someone." A lump rose in Aurelia's throat. "Someone I loved very much."

"Do I that, and can that be, Gemdelovely Gemdelee?" The woman seemed to find this amusing, though Aurelia could not guess why.

Aurelia climbed behind the woman, hoping neither of them would stumble and fall. "I think you may have me confused with another. My name is not Gemdelovely Gemdelee."

The woman gained a rise near the summit and turned, her brief flash of a smile almost mischievous. "And I think I know what it is that I do see, Gemdelovely Gemdelee." Her lips twitched as though she would laugh out loud were she alone, and Aurelia was again reminded of a trait of her mother's.

Aurelia's mother had often stifled her laughter in Hekod's presence precisely thus, especially when it was something

Hekod had done that she found amusing. The remembered bellow of her sire when he thought himself mocked echoed through Aurelia's ears, followed by her mother's lilting laughter.

They typically had retired to their chambers after such exchanges. Much laughter had carried from those rooms throughout the night, as well as various mysterious thumps and bumps.

Of course, all that had changed when Gemma died.

Tears blurred Aurelia's vision and she suddenly felt very much alone. She folded her arms around herself, unable to deny the chilly fingers of the wind any longer.

"Do not cry, Gemdelovely Gemdelee," the old crone advised with a gentle tap on Aurelia's arm. "What you seek is closer than you might see."

She knew something, that much Aurelia could read in the eyes so disconcertingly like her mother's. "Will you not tell me whether you have seen my father? Was he brought to the caves? Did he escape the new king's vengeful hand?"

The woman shook her head slowly, then turned away to finish her ascent. "Do you not already know the answer, Gemdelovely Gemdelee? It lies before you, as clearly as can be."

Ha! Aurelia's heart skipped a beat. The woman *had* helped Hekod escape! It was only natural that she was circumspect, for the new king would not be amused by this development.

"Then he has not died!" Aurelia whispered with delight. "He escaped! Do you know where I might find him?"

The woman reached the summit and turned to watch Aurelia scramble impatiently in her wake. The wind lifted a strand of her silver hair free and the lock waved over her head like an unruly ribbon. She took the pose of a warrior, her ancient hands braced on the cane like a man's on the hilt of a blade, her shoulders square and her stare unflinching.

She arched a silver brow. "Oh, you will find him, Gemdelovely Gemdelee, of that I am certain as can be. Though you will find nothing as you believe it should be—'tis always thus for the seeker and for thee."

"Then where shall I find him?"

The crone smiled. She looked toward Bard's castle and

lifted her cane to point in that direction. "The seeker comes for you, Gemdelovely Gemdelee. Mind he sees what you want him to see."

Aurelia pivoted just as Bard's outraged cry rang out across Dunhelm.

"Princess! What in the hell are you doing out here?"

Aurelia glanced back but the crone was already a goodly distance away, the sound of her tapping cane swallowed by the bellow of the sea. The woman's words echoed in her mind.

Bard must not realize that her father had escaped!

Well, Aurelia was no witless fool who would betray her own sire's plans to regain his holding! She had to intercept Bard before he drew near the sea cells and guessed where she had been.

Aurelia recalled suddenly how Bard had turned in revulsion when she had kissed him in the well. And he had beaten a retreat out of that place without looking back.

Aurelia squared her shoulders and strode toward the self-proclaimed king, knowing exactly what she had to do.

"Are you out of your mind?" Baird stalked across the wet green turf, stunned to find Aurelia on the edge of the cliff. She wore no more than his sweater and was obviously soaked to the skin, but her expression was mild as she walked toward him.

They might have been meeting for tea on the lawn, on a sunny Sunday afternoon, not braving the elements on the edge of a damn cliff! Baird was more angry than he could ever remember being, though he was sure that was because Julian's dreaded liability had been narrowly averted.

Of course, he had never felt so relieved at avoiding liability before.

"Are you nuts or what?" Baird planted his feet against the mud when they were only a few steps apart. "No, don't answer that." He flung out his hands, more than ready to vent his frustration. But Aurelia walked toward him silently, the mud sliding between her bare toes. Baird caught his breath at the sight.

"You could catch your death of cold out here in that

sweater!'' he raged. "Why couldn't you just stay warm and dry in your room?''

His arguments fell silent when Aurelia came to a halt directly before him. The rain beat down on him with new intensity, the sea churned, and he thought he could see the ruddy pink of her nipples through the lattice stitches of his sodden sweater.

Her eyes were so very blue that a man could drown in their depths. As Baird stared at her, his heart clenched.

Aurelia reached up and cupped his face in the delicacy of her hands. Her fingers were light against his jaw, her room key pressed wetly against one cheek, and Baird was powerless to step away from her. One pale toe landed on Baird's boot, and he tried to swallow the lump that rose in his throat.

If she kissed him again, Baird wouldn't be able to stop so easily this time.

"Did you desire me after all, King Bard?'' she whispered, then stretched against him without waiting for his response.

Baird closed his eyes as her breasts pressed against his chest for the second time in short order. An achingly long moment later, the soft sweetness of her lips landed on his.

And desire took the reins, kicking anger out in the cold.

She tasted so good. Baird tried to resist her siren's call and failed so quickly that he knew resistance was futile. He made a sound in the back of his throat that was halfway between a groan and a growl, then pressed his lips possessively over Aurelia's. She arched against him, as though helpless against an answering tide of passion, and Baird hauled her even closer.

Vaguely he heard her room key clatter to the ground.

The sea spray mingled with the sweetness of her own taste, the combination intoxicating. Baird wanted more, he wanted all she could give. He wanted to meld their bodies together, right here and now.

It felt so right and for once, Baird Beauforte didn't question his instincts. He cupped Aurelia's tight buttocks in his hands and lifted her closer as he slid his tongue between her teeth.

Aurelia sighed and arched her back bewitchingly, the sound of her pleasure firing Baird's need as nothing else could have done. Her tongue dancing boldly with his, her fingers latched into his hair to pull him closer. They kissed hungrily, greedily, as though they had both awakened from a long slumber to find the world brighter and better than imagined. The fever between them was all consuming, as though they had found a treasure long lost.

The cold rain sluiced over them and Baird's hand slid beneath Aurelia's sweater. His fingers cupped the ripe perfection of her breast and he marveled at the softness of her skin.

Her nipple instantly became a hard bead beneath his caressing thumb. Baird ducked his head and nudged the neck of the sweater aside, running a row of kisses across her flesh and capturing the nipple between his teeth.

Aurelia moaned. She slid her foot up his leg and Baird's blood sizzled. He suckled her until the nipple was taut, then Aurelia rolled her hips against his raging erection in a silent demand. Baird captured her lips beneath his own once more, sampling her deeply and leisurely, trying to tell her with his kiss what he could not explain in words.

This was not lust. This was something more, some connection on a deeper level, some recognition of a passion that had been between them before. A legendary passion, a desire for which he sensed he had paid a heavy price not once but many times.

A passion that Baird could not remember.

When Baird lifted his head, Aurelia's azure eyes were drowsy with desire and her lips were softened. Baird cupped her head in his heads as he caught his breath, knowing he had come within a hair of making love to this stranger in the rain.

He was still thinking about it.

But she couldn't *really* be a stranger. It would be crazy to feel such a strong attraction to someone he had never met. They must have been together before, even though Baird couldn't remember it.

But he never forgot anything or anyone. Baird's photographic memory was legendary.

It made no sense. How could Aurelia turn him inside out, remind him that they had been together, yet slip out of his memory as elusively as a ghost? Baird stared down into Aurelia's fathomless eyes as though he could will the truth out of her.

"Who are you?" His voice was unexpectedly hoarse, even to his own ears. "Who are you *really*?"

Six

Aurelia raised a hand to her burning lips, shocked by her own response to the kiss she had initiated. Oh, the man had a dangerous allure!

And contrary to expectation, this time he had more than responded to her kiss. What had changed? A dangerous heat flared deep within Aurelia and she was unaccountably grateful that *he* had stopped their embrace.

She was honest enough to admit that she could never have done so.

Had her wits abandoned her? This man had killed her only brother! And even though Hekod had escaped the sea cells, it had been no kindly gesture to abandon him there.

Aurelia forced herself to step away from the villain and proudly lifted her chin. "I have told you that I am the Princess Aurelia."

"There are no princesses anymore," he growled.

Aurelia inhaled sharply at his obvious dismissal of her parentage. She was right—he intended to have everyone forget about her sire!

Well, Aurelia was not prepared to comply.

"Then I shall be only Aurelia," she retorted, and headed back to his hall. She hoped desperately that he would not be able to discern the effect his kiss had on her own ability to walk. Her knees were quivering and she had a hard time marking a straight path. This was not a good time to realize that her will was more feeble than she knew.

Bard swore under his breath behind her but Aurelia did not look back. She heard his footfalls, but determinedly headed for the palace. "Don't forget your key, Princess."

Aurelia glanced back to find him offering her the magical square, though now it was dark with mud. They certainly took such powerful witchery for granted in his domain! Aurelia snatched it back and wiped it pointedly on the front of his sweater.

Bard did not seem to notice. He gripped her elbow and fairly lifted Aurelia to her toes. "Let's hurry it up, then. Julian will have my head if you catch pneumonia out here."

Aurelia was more than happy to quicken her pace. The heat he had awakened beneath her skin was sliding away, leaving her feeling chilled in its wake. "It is you who insisted on lingering in the rain for no good reason," she retorted.

Bard rolled his eyes. "And you had nothing to do with that?"

Aurelia shrugged deliberately. "What can I do when a warrior so much larger than myself forces his attentions on me?"

"*Forces!*" The word exploded from Bard's lips. "You were the one who started it!"

Aurelia tossed her hair. "And you were the one to prolong it."

Bard shook his head and rubbed his brow with his free hand. "I'm sure I'd remember a woman as troublesome as you. Where have we met before?"

Aurelia glared at him, not liking his choice of words in the least. "We have never met."

His green gaze locked assessingly with hers, the heat in his eyes sending an answering shiver over her flesh. Aurelia again had the uncanny sense that he could read her thoughts.

Oh, no! She had forgotten to pretend to be simple!

Aurelia summoned an elaborate shiver and rubbed her arms. She batted her eyelashes and contrived to look stupid beyond all. "Why, look at the foul weather! Hasten yourself! Do you not have the sense to come out of the rain?"

Bard eyed her skeptically. "I went out in the rain to get you," he observed.

Aurelia giggled and danced a few steps ahead of a newly wary Bard. "And now we are all *wet*!" She spun and wagged a playful finger at him. "I shall want a bath now, a very hot one, if you please!"

Bard shook his head and looked puzzled. "Then have one." He seemed to notice his own wet clothes for the first time. "It doesn't sound like a bad idea, actually."

"But I am your guest, so I must have mine first!" He leveled a glance at Aurelia that she chose to ignore. "I will have mine *now*!"

They were near the hall now, and before Bard could say anything more, Aurelia turned and darted into the building. She was up the stairs in the blink of an eye, fumbling with Julian's token as she raced down the corridor.

To her relief, the light glowed red thrice as soon as she shoved the square into the narrow slot.

And she was safely inside. Aurelia closed her eyes and leaned her back against the door, her heart pounding in her ears. She had nearly ruined any chance of being underestimated by this wily conqueror. Bard had nearly guessed that she was clever, and even now she had left him wondering.

Curse her unruly tongue! Aurelia shoved a hand through her wet hair and shivered, hoping her bath would come very soon.

But time passed and no bath came.

The heady scent of masculinity teased her nostrils and Aurelia realized suddenly that she still wore Bard's tunic. She hauled the garment over her head in disgust and cast it across the room, not wanting anything that had graced his treacherous hide against her flesh longer than necessary.

But his scent clung to her own skin in a most troubling way. Aurelia scrubbed at her upper arms, but Bard's musk rose even stronger, as though it would taunt her with her unhealthy attraction to him.

Aurelia would not think about his kiss. She would not think about how her skin tingled beneath his touch. She would not relive the slow caress of his thumb across her breast.

Her renegade nipple, though, tightened in defiant recollection.

And Aurelia would not, under any circumstance, think about Bard's tongue, let alone its beguiling dance. She could have melted before his amorous assault without so much as a whimper of protest.

Curse Bard for not responding as she had expected him to! He was *supposed* to be revolted by her.

Aurelia conceded that he seemed to have recovered from that at a most inconvenient time.

Was the priest's counsel gaining appeal in his mind?

Aurelia's heart skipped a beat and she refused to even consider the prospect of wedding the cur. No, her time would be better spent in studying her luxurious prison. There might well be another means of escape, one that Julian had not bewitched with ringing bells.

Aurelia let her gaze dart over the room's finery and noticed a small room immediately to the left of the bed. Aurelia held the magic card tightly, for a protective talisman was no small thing in this palace of marvels, and stepped cautiously into the chamber's darkness.

The floor was shockingly cold beneath her feet. Aurelia jumped back against the wall and something dug into her shoulder.

Light flashed overhead and she cringed in terror at whatever she had done. She wildly waved Julian's card skyward in supplication, but the light stayed on.

Aurelia slowly opened her eyes, her heart still pounding in her throat. A row of bright orbs on the far side of the room glowed with fierce intensity. She scanned the room suspiciously, but could find no explanation for the change she had witnessed.

Darkness had changed magically to light when she came into the room. Aurelia stepped back over the threshold, but the lights remained bright. She jumped on the floor tiles, with no effect. She waved Julian's talisman in and out of the chamber, but the lights burned on.

Inexplicable. Aurelia looked to see what had dug into her

back and found a little lever. She peered at it, then touched it again.

It moved.

The light went off.

Aurelia jumped in alarm at the sudden darkness, then looked to the lever once more. While the room was wreathed in shadows, the lever glowed with an eerie orange light.

A sign of its magic, most certainly. And orange could only mean the element of fire, the source of light and heat. Respectfully, for its size belied its power, Aurelia moved the fire lever with gentle fingers again.

The chamber was once more flooded with light.

This delighted Aurelia no end. There were no spells or incantations to recite, no candles or herbs to be burned. This magic was simple enough for a babe. She even put down the magic card and the fire lever *still* worked.

Finally Aurelia tired of the fire lever and explored the chamber itself.

Everything was smooth and shiny within it. There was a table wrought of stone set right into the wall, and with a hard basin inserted into its midst. Strange golden shapes arched over the basin, but Aurelia was fascinated by the mirror that lined the entire wall behind the table.

She had never seen a mirror wrought so fine. Aurelia had a mirror of her own, to be sure—she was a noblewoman, after all!—one that had been her mother's, though it was made of polished bronze. And small. Round with a handle, she could hold it in one hand.

Never had that mirror returned an image so faithfully as this one did. Aurelia could see the scar on the back of her shoulder clearly for the first time. A symbol of her love of her crossbow, it had been earned on her first, illicit, lesson from the archer.

Aurelia touched the scar and remembered. Her mother had long forbidden such lessons, a demand that was not surprising given that Gemma had believed in the curse laid upon Aurelia at her naming. Aurelia, despite her skepticism of such portents, had not had the heart to defy her.

But when Gemma died, Aurelia could resist the crossbow's

allure no longer. This wound had been no one's fault but her own, although the flow of his sole daughter's blood had made her father bellow like a cornered bear.

After that, her lessons had been furtive no longer.

Aurelia smiled in recollection. The wound had been mended quickly, as had her sire's blustery temper once he realized the damage was slight.

Concern for Hekod's present predicament stole away Aurelia's smile. Somehow she must find that old woman again and learn whatever she knew.

On the back of the door of the little room, Aurelia found a veritable treasure. A robe of deepest blue hung there, its fabric thick beyond all. She liked the gold embroidery on its front—it was stitched with great skill and precision with the words *We Treat You ROYALLY* stitched around the crest.

Obviously the robe was meant for her. Aurelia immediately wrapped herself in its welcoming softness, rolling up the ample sleeves and knotting the belt about her waist. It was fine, far finer than a prisoner of war like herself could expect.

Gratitude warred with her distrust of Bard's intentions. The robe was lovely, but she would not be so readily swayed by gifts.

There was a little basket reposing before her and Aurelia emptied its contents to push such thoughts from her mind.

Toothpaste, she read on the side of a crimped little tube. She opened it and found green gel inside. It smelled of wild mint. Aurelia checked her teeth but found them well secured, as usual. Obviously she did not need this frippery, though she wondered why Bard's household felt compelled to glue their teeth in place.

Bath Oil, declared the next bottle, much to Aurelia's delight. Nothing like the oil from herbs in the bath! She sniffed the turquoise liquid within and identified both elder flowers and meadowsweet. Aurelia set the little bottle aside with approval, drummed her fingers, and glanced around the chamber.

The very sight of the tub made Aurelia's skin itch. Surely, in a hall of this size, water could have been heated by now? There could be no dearth of servants in this place.

Where *was* her bath?

Aurelia stalked back into the main chamber. Was this some kind of torture, tormenting her with the possibility of a bath while withholding the water? Did Bard mean to let her languish in her fine prison, ignored and unattended, despite his pretty words?

Aurelia prowled the perimeter of the room restlessly, examining each stick of furniture that the whore had bought. She must be making good progress in emptying the king's treasury.

The tapestry on the far wall hid a massive window that overlooked the sea. Aurelia shoved the fabric aside and tentatively touched the clear barrier against the wind and rain.

No stretched pig's gut this. It was clear as rock crystal and hard as stone. The rain spattered against it on the far side, not a drop leaking through to this rich chamber though the water coursed down its other side.

Aurelia shook her head, suddenly feeling very tired. She could marvel no more, so overwhelmed was she by what she had already seen this day.

The rolling waves made Aurelia think of her father's cousins. She scanned the horizon, unable to spy a single great sail drawing near. How could this massive place have been built before her relatives completed the two-day journey from Norway?

Could the priest from Rome have cast a spell across the seas? Or had he managed to have this stone hall spring skyward in but a single day? Either prospect was daunting to imagine, but there could be no other explanation.

It could be that she had been drugged for weeks, but if that were the case, where were the Vikings? Her family would not abandon Hekod when he needed their aid, Aurelia knew it, or have lingered in answering his call. They must be en route, even now, even if Julian's sorcery had delayed their progress.

The Vikings would come. And by the time they did, Aurelia would find her father, so he would be prepared to assume his kingship once more. Aurelia would have to do so without Bard guessing she had managed the deed.

It was her only hope.

•   •   •

The old groundskeeper approached Baird and Marissa as they considered the site where the main restaurant was being built. The rain had stopped, but the wind was still high. Fortunately there was a bit of a lee on this side of the building.

All the same, Marissa had thoroughly communicated her disapproval of the situation and suggested twice that they retire to her room. Baird wondered what had possessed him to let her come here.

Marissa was much easier to deal with by facsimile.

"Mr. Beauforte, sir, I'm not meaning to be bothering you, but have you finished with those hedge clippers?" Talorc turned his battered felt hat in his hands and periodically shot a very blue glance from beneath his bushy silver brows at Marissa.

Baird found the older man's response amusing. Certainly Marissa was from a different world in comparison to the groundskeeper. Talorc looked to have stepped out of an age gone by, dressed in worn brown dungarees, held up with antique suspenders that might have been his grandfather's. The groundskeeper worked with slow effectiveness, each twig on the estate apparently having a story to whisper to his attentive ears.

But if Talorc seemed ancient, his mother was even more so. The two had evidently lived in a little cottage on the property for as long as anyone could remember. It had quickly become clear to Baird that acquiring Dunhelm had meant also acquiring its self-appointed groundskeeper.

Fortunately, Baird liked Talorc. The old man certainly knew a lot about plants, not to mention the castle itself, and he worked diligently at any task he undertook.

Even if Talorc had refused to have anything to do with clipping back the thorns.

Marissa sighed theatrically when Baird excused himself. "Do hurry, darling, it's beastly cold out here."

Baird retrieved the clippers from the corner where he had left them and smiled as he handed them back to the older man. He shoved his hands into his pockets, more than glad to take a break from Marissa. "They may need to be sharpened, Talorc. Those thorns were pretty tough."

"Were they, now? Well, sir, they've been growing on that site for more than a thousand years as the story goes. I'd expect they'd have grown tough roots in that time." Talorc grimaced and turned the clippers in his calloused hands, as though checking the state of a precious charge.

Baird's curiosity was piqued. "There's a story about the thorns?"

Talorc shrugged. "If you're wanting the truth of it, you'll be needing to ask my mother." He flicked a look at Baird and his tone was gruffer than usual. "She's the one as recalls every little bit of every tale she ever heard, and tells it as though 'twere her very own." He smiled wryly. "I'm only the one as can listen, if you know what I mean."

Baird considered the offer for only a moment. This story might reveal something about Aurelia and where she had come from. "Maybe I will."

"Well, my mother is always pleased to have company, Mr. Beauforte, and you know where to find her, that much is for certain."

The groundskeeper might have turned away, but Baird suddenly realized he was the perfect one to ask about Aurelia's father. "Talorc, do you know anyone around here named Hekod?"

"Hekod?" Talorc's eyes brightened and he almost grinned. "Oh, you'll be sounding like a history lesson soon, sir! My mother will be taking to you like a duck to water."

"I don't understand." Baird frowned. "Is Hekod a common name?"

"No, far from it, far from it, indeed. It would be a Norse name, as with the Vikings, you know, and very few now take those names to their own. There's one Hekod I know, and he would be famous around these parts, maybe even part of the reason the name fell out of favor as it's told."

A local scandal, Baird concluded, realizing that some kind of family troubles could be at the root of Aurelia's predicament.

Talorc shook his head and his heavy brows drew together. "But as I said, I'm no good with a story."

Baird could easily imagine the kind of gossip that would

run rife in such a small community. He wondered what this Hekod had done to earn himself such a reputation.

"You'll be wanting a wee book I have at home," Talorc continued with a frown. "I'll drop it by for you, if you be interested."

Talorc didn't seem to be the kind of man who would endorse gossip. Probably he thought Baird should get the story from Hekod's own lips, which seemed reasonable enough.

It must be a phone book he was offering.

"Thanks, Talorc. That'd be great."

"Ah!" The old man pursed his lips and nodded solemnly. "I knew 'twas only time before you showed an interest in what you've got here. These old stones have tales to tell, Mr. Beauforte, more tales than you can imagine."

With that enigmatic conclusion, Talorc shuffled off, whistling through his teeth with characteristic tunelessness.

What could Dunhelm have to do with this Hekod?

Baird shook off the question, knowing it wasn't the first time he hadn't exactly understood Talorc. The good news was that if there weren't many Hekods around, then this one Talorc knew could be Aurelia's father.

Once Baird found her father, well, maybe he'd be able to figure out where he had met Aurelia before.

He watched the old man go, barely aware that a grim-faced Marissa had come to his side. "Are you finally done with the help, darling?" she demanded tightly when he didn't acknowledge her. She shuddered theatrically.

"Yes. Let's go back inside," Baird suggested easily. "I want to have a look at that reception counter again."

The rain slowed and stopped, the sun crawled across the sky, its glow evident behind the thinning clouds. Aurelia's stomach grumbled, she felt the dirt press on her skin and smelled Bard's masculinity. She licked her lips and the taste of his kiss made the secret part of her tingle.

How she longed to scour herself from head to toe!

Suddenly Aurelia realized why no maid was being sent. Had she not guessed that her women had been taken prisoner? And if the women of Dunhelm had been enslaved, then Aurelia might recognize one sent to service her.

And she might learn where her sire had fled.

Oh, it was an old trick to keep a prisoner isolated and secured from news! And part of a captor's devious means to earn their victim's trust and manipulate their thinking. Well, Bard would not succeed in doing any such thing to Aurelia!

Aurelia almost charged out of the room to confront him before she recalled herself.

She was trying to play the fool! She could not challenge Bard openly with such accusations and risk arousing his suspicions about her intellect.

Aurelia paced the length of the room and back as she worried about her course. What would a witless woman do? Assume she was being denied a bath—perhaps because men of war were not known to trouble themselves with matters of hygiene.

Yes! Aurelia smiled to herself. A fool would think no further than her own comfort!

She looked down at the robe and tugged at its hem with impatience. The garment was too short for her taste, but the only other option was Bard's own tunic.

And Aurelia would not don that again, under any circumstance.

But clearly she had to demand her bath. Aurelia nibbled on her lip and worried over the issue for only a moment before her decision was made.

As the better of two poor options, the robe would have to do. Aurelia lifted her chin proudly and sailed toward the door. Despite her qualms, Aurelia found herself looking forward to matching wits with Bard.

Not that that was of any import at all.

Seven

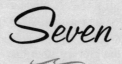

Marissa's arrival, a false fire alarm, the complication of Aurelia, and now the arrival of the exercise equipment before the spa area was finished.

So much for the uneventful day Baird had expected to have.

Marissa and the foreman were exchanging insults over who was to blame about the poor coordination of events, Julian was flipping through contracts, the electrician was venting about the premature use of his alarm system, and Baird was trying to find a solution as to where the exercise equipment could be stored until the spa was done.

Anything had to be better than paying to ship it back to Sussex, then back here in a few weeks time.

"Mr. Beauforte?" The head plumber was closing fast and Baird groaned silently, certain he didn't need another thing to juggle right now. "I'm needing you to have a look at what Joe has found. We're going to be having a wee problem with installing the fourth septic tank as planned—Joseph, Mary, and all the saints above!"

At the unexpected curse, Baird's head snapped up.

And his heart sank. He should have guessed.

All eyes were fixed on Aurelia as she bounced down the stairs to the reception area. Her hair was still loose and damp, but his sweater had been abandoned in favor of a resort bathrobe.

It covered even less of her thighs than his sweater had.

Her skin was unexpectedly pale. Hadn't she had a hot shower yet? Baird muttered an oath under his breath, uncertain why he felt protective of a woman he barely knew, let alone one whose mind seemed to have a precarious grip on reality. He scanned the hall to find work stopped completely as every man in the place gaped.

Not that Aurelia would have noticed. Her gaze was fixed determinedly on Baird, her full lips pouted like a child denied a chocolate bar in the grocery store line. Despite her expression, Baird felt a prickle of awareness, as though they were the only ones in the massive hall.

"Well!" Marissa sniffled in disdain. "Well, darling, I can't imagine where you scraped up this sorry little bit of baggage, but she truly has no concept of what is *appropriate* to wear—"

Baird impatiently waved the designer into silence. "I'll handle this."

"But darling, surely you could send along some minion to talk sense into the woman. . . ."

It was easy to ignore Marissa's plaintive voice though Baird wished, again, that she had not managed to persuade him to let her come to Dunhelm. Oddly enough, Marissa was not spoiling him for *all* female company this time.

He wouldn't think about that.

Baird determinedly crossed the floor, but Aurelia was not backing down. She didn't slow her own course until they stood toe to toe and, despite himself, Baird admired her boldness.

There was something on Aurelia's mind and Baird knew she was about to set him straight on whatever the issue was. When was the last time he had met a woman who was so direct?

And why couldn't he recall this one?

Baird scanned her features with frustration. He wondered suddenly whether there was some reason that she didn't *want* him to remember. Aurelia flushed when Baird looked into her eyes and her gaze flicked away. Was she trying to hide something from him?

"Where are the maids?" Aurelia asked in the high voice that she only used some of the time. She sounded childish and dumb when she talked this way, and Baird preferred her lower tones.

Baird frowned, both at her tone and her question. "There are no maids here yet. If you need more towels or anything, there's a supply room at the end of the hall. Your key will work—"

"Me?" Aurelia chuckled as though he were joking, although Baird didn't know what he had said that was funny. "There *have* to be maids here somewhere! There were *dozens* of maids this very morning." She smiled up at Baird and batted her eyelashes. "Surely, you did not send them *all* away?"

This morning? Baird's heart sank. Aurelia was confused, that was for sure. She and her father must have been very close for his loss to affect her so deeply.

Baird felt a pang of compassion and knew he had to help Aurelia. Baird was used to solving problems—one more wouldn't add much to his burden. Aurelia had no one else to count on, after all.

At least not until he found Hekod.

Baird heard his tone soften as he placed one hand gently on Aurelia's shoulder. He leaned closer and was surprised to see something flash in her eyes.

"There are no maids, Aurelia," he explained quietly, "and there were none this morning, either."

Aurelia stared back at him for a long moment. Baird had the sense that her mind was going a mile a minute and wished heartily that he could have known what she was thinking.

"I'm sorry, princess, but there won't be any maids here until the building is done."

She stiffened beneath the weight of his hand and her fair brow arched. "You do not mean to bathe before the building is done?"

Baird stifled a grin, not wanting her to think he was laughing at her. "It's not *that* serious. The plumbing works already."

But Aurelia didn't seem to understand. She folded her arms across her chest and took a trio of deep breaths. She appeared to be choosing her words carefully.

"If there will be no maids until that time," she said tightly, "then, of course, I am obligated to wait."

Now *Baird* was confused.

Aurelia fixed a very blue glance on Baird and he knew in that instant, from that one look, that Aurelia was not as dumb as she wanted him to believe.

Then she met his gaze so blankly that Baird wondered whether he had seen anything at all. The sense that she was playing games with him irritated Baird immeasurably.

The last thing he needed was another Jessica in his life!

"What's the problem?" Baird propped his hands on his hips with sudden impatience. "Just draw the bath yourself."

"Myself?" Aurelia's disgust with that idea was tellingly clear.

Which could only mean that she wanted someone else, some paid help, to draw her bath for her! Baird had never heard anything so lazy in all his life! The embroidered motto on Aurelia's bathrobe taunted him, but Baird knew the resort had never been asked to do such a menial task, even for a paying guest.

"There's a tub in your room," he reminded her, biting off each word with precision.

"That tub has a hole in its bottom," Aurelia retorted with a flighty toss of her hair. "And there is nary a drop of hot water to be seen!"

This was ridiculous!

"You are not going to have a maid or anyone else prepare your bath," Baird asserted in a far more reasonable tone than circumstance demanded. "You are simply going to have to do it yourself, as everyone else does, whether you think you're a princess or not."

"Think I'm a princess!" Aurelia's cheeks burned bright and her voice dropped. Her eyes snapped with intelligence as she wagged a determined finger beneath Baird's nose. "I *am* a princess and you know it as well as I do. And I am *not* going to haul water up those stairs like some common serf captured on a raid in the East!"

She folded her arms across her chest and glared at him as

though daring Baird to insist otherwise. Aurelia certainly wasn't afraid to speak her mind.

All the same, Baird didn't understand her. He frowned in confusion. "Up *what* stairs? What are you talking about?"

"Do not play games with me!" Aurelia glared outright at him. "I will not be mocked by the likes of you! Perhaps *you* do not see fit to bathe, or perhaps you find it amusing to torment me like this—gods and goddesses only know what passes for cleanliness among barbarians!—but understand that neither I nor my father will readily forget such rudeness. . . ."

Barbarians? There was another reference to his being American! Did these Brits never get over themselves?

"Rudeness?" Baird retorted. "I'm putting you up for free in a luxury resort!"

"Your terms are hardly gratuitous!" Aurelia snapped. "My birthright entitles—"

"That's enough!" Baird roared, and everyone who wasn't already watching this exchange turned to have a good look. "We'll see this settled, once and for all!"

Before Aurelia could launch into another lecture about his poor manners, Baird gripped her elbow and propelled her toward the stairs. She had to take three steps to match every two of his because she was so much shorter, but Baird didn't care.

She wanted someone to draw her bath and, by God, Baird would do it—though not likely in the way *Princess* Aurelia had planned.

He had had enough insults about his nationality to last one day.

"Baird! What about these samples, darling?" Marissa called.

"And Mr. Beauforte, the plumbing—"

"Where shall we put the step machines?"

"I'll be back shortly." Baird nodded to the plumber and delivery team. "And Marissa, the tiles will have to wait until the morning, there's too much on my plate right now." Baird threw a telling glance over his shoulder that Marissa would have been wise to heed.

She ignored it.

The designer pouted, her gaze darting to Aurelia and back

to Baird. "But Baird, it's absolutely *no* trouble at all. You'll be back in—what? Five minutes, darling? I can wait right here."

Baird glanced grimly down at Aurelia and caught a glimpse straight down the front of the bathrobe that made his gut clench. Down there, just to the right of the creamy flesh he could see, was the nipple that had responded so pertly to his touch. Heat coursed through him at the memory of that soft curve beneath his hand.

Aurelia looked up in that moment and proudly held his gaze, not even trying to hide the sharp gleam in those blue eyes. Baird's heart leaped. Maybe she wasn't crazy, after all, but just pretending to be.

Which left the intriguing question of *why*.

One thing was for certain, Baird Beauforte was going to get to the bottom of this puzzle. And he was going to do it now.

"This may take a while," Baird said, and forced a polite smile for Marissa. "And we've done more today than I expected. Why don't you take the chance to relax after your flight?"

Marissa exhaled in a hiss of dissatisfaction, but Baird didn't care what she thought. He was much more interested in the fact that his words seemed to trouble his tiny companion. It was almost as though Aurelia guessed Baird's intention and didn't want her mysteries solved.

She caught her breath, then tried to shake off Baird's grip on her arm. "You are *not* coming to my chambers! I do not need your accompaniment!"

"You obviously do if you want that bath."

She glared at him and twisted her arm some more. Just on general principles, Baird held on.

Firmly but gently.

This, after all, was the woman who had landed two soul-searing kisses on him, without any preamble. This was the woman who had turned his day upside down, forced an evacuation of the hotel, and denied having met him before even though Baird recognized her. He didn't know who she was, he didn't know what she wanted, but letting Baird guide her by the elbow was peanuts in exchange.

And besides, Baird liked having the supple strength of Aurelia's arm in his grip. He told himself it was because that was the only way he would know exactly where she was. Princess Aurelia was already showing a marked ability to find trouble when she wasn't watched.

It certainly had nothing to do with the tingle of awareness Baird felt in her proximity.

"Bullying me is not going to solve anything," Aurelia declared with bravado.

"I'm not bullying you, princess. I'm just escorting you to your room in the most expedient fashion."

What Baird had meant as a gruff assurance only seemed to agitate Aurelia more. She twisted and wriggled, trying to pull her elbow free from his fingers.

"You'll bruise me!"

"I will not, unless you keep fidgeting," Baird retorted.

She inhaled sharply. "If you mean to torture me, I have to tell you right now that I will *never* betray my father."

"Torture you?" Baird arched a brow and marched her up the stairs. "We gave that up in the States long before you people did."

"Ha! A likely story." Aurelia glared up at Baird and he was surprised by the intensity of her obvious distrust. Then her eyes widened and she changed to the high voice that grated on Baird's nerves. "You already *are* bullying me, and I have to tell you that this is not the way I expect to be treated—"

"Don't you think you're overreacting?" Baird dryly interrupted her tirade. "We're just going to go up to your room and—"

"Ha!"

Baird's calm words seemed to infuriate his guest so much that she couldn't keep her voice high any longer.

"And I can guess what will happen after that! Will rape be part of your torture? Even if you cannot bear to touch me yourself, I am sure you'll find some underling to do the deed! Either way, I will not make it easy for you!"

Before Baird could make sense of that bizarre volley, Aurelia kicked him in the shin.

Hard. Baird's eyes widened in shock, then Aurelia bent and

bit at his fingers where they still grasped her elbow.

Baird bellowed in pain. He muttered a curse as his hand flew open.

"What in the hell is that all about?" he roared, but Aurelia was gone.

She had turned and fled like a doe, straight back down the stairs. A hoot of laughter rose from the workmen, but Baird was concerned for his tiny charge. She was running wildly, without care for her own safety, taking the steps three at a time.

And in outright fear of *him*.

That was not a good feeling. Baird had never sent a woman fleeing before, but this seemed to be a day of firsts. He was determined to set Aurelia straight.

But first, he had to catch her. Baird bounded after his resort's first guest. Aurelia glanced over her shoulder and ran faster.

She'd kill herself!

Aurelia leaped down the last four steps like a bird taking flight. She just brushed the floor with one bare toe before Baird snatched her up from behind. She was light, but fought like a tigress.

Baird tossed her over his shoulder, hoping it looked effortless, and turned in one smooth move to begin up the stairs again. The workmen cheered, but Aurelia seemed less than impressed.

"No! I will not permit you to do this!" Aurelia struggled and squirmed. She pounded her fists against his back and kicked him as hard as she could, but Baird marched impassively toward her room.

"Quit your fighting! You wanted a bath," he growled as they gained the summit. "And by God, you'll get one."

Aurelia froze, then struggled with renewed vigor. Baird clamped his arm over her knees and held on tight. It was high time that he and Aurelia got a few things sorted out between them.

And there was no time like the present.

•   •   •

The way Aurelia wriggled against him was not helping Baird collect his jumbled thoughts in the least. Even through her robe, he could tell that the buttock bumping against his jaw was round and firm, that the breasts that brushed periodically against his back were temptingly full.

And those feet. As Aurelia struggled, her delicate feet danced before Baird, challenging every scrap of his self-control. He half wished he *was* the uncivilized barbarian these Brits expected Americans to be.

Instead Baird used his passkey, then shoved open the door to her room. He stalked into the bathroom, flicked on the light, and dumped the lady on her feet.

Before she could start to make wild accusations, Baird sat on the side of the tub, locked the drain, and turned on the water. Steam rose from the cascade of water spilling into the tub, and only then did Baird look at the woman who had fought him tooth and nail.

She was backed against the far wall. Her eyes were narrowed with suspicion and she held her room card out between them as though it would ward him off.

So much for hoping she wasn't nuts.

Baird shoved one hand through his hair and let a smile quirk his lips as he watched Aurelia, hoping he could reassure her. "See? Bath right on cue."

"You stay away from me," was all she said.

Trust him to have a chivalrous impulse to help the first lunatic who came along. This would have been a lot easier if there weren't something about Aurelia that reached right into the core of Baird.

And twisted hard.

Baird kept his tone low and even to reassure her. "Don't worry. I'll stay right here."

But Aurelia did not step forward. "Save your lies! You brought me here to torture me!"

"I brought you here to show you how the bath works," Baird corrected matter-of-factly. "You wanted a bath, didn't you?"

Aurelia's gaze flicked to the running water as though she couldn't control her curiosity any longer. Baird watched

amazement cross her expression, then her wary gaze flashed
back to him. "How did you do that?"

And suddenly her argument made sense.

Aurelia just didn't know about indoor plumbing. She must
have thought that someone would have to haul buckets of water from a well, then heat it on the stove for her bath. And
haul it up the stairs from the foyer.

No wonder she had been so annoyed when he told her to
do it herself!

There were people at home who had never seen indoor
plumbing—why should he be surprised that someone who had
lived on these remote islands might be similarly amazed?

The irritation slid out of Baird like magic and he pushed
one hand through his hair. He found himself oddly relieved
that Aurelia's thinking was really very logical now that he
knew her assumptions.

Maybe she wasn't crazy after all. Baird found that possibility more encouraging than he thought he should have.

"You just turn the knob." He demonstrated with one hand
and beckoned to her with the other.

Aurelia recoiled. "I will fight your foul intent with every
fiber of my being!" She waved the room key at him wildly.
"Do not imagine that I will easily surrender to the likes of
you!"

Right. Torture and rape were on the agenda, though not
necessarily in that order. How could Baird have forgotten such
pertinent details?

It must only be his injured pride that insisted he make sure
Aurelia recognized his sterling character.

Baird deliberately kept his tone even. "I'm just here to
show you how the bath works." Aurelia eyed Baird and
clearly did not believe him. "The knob was a bit tight, probably because it's new, but you should be able to manage it
now. Come here and see."

"I will not make your rape easier!"

"I'm not going to rape you."

Aurelia arched a dubious brow. "Torture, then!"

Baird shook his head. "Nope. No torture either. Wouldn't
know where to start."

She chewed her lip and lowered the room key a little. Her voice was low and her eyes narrowed. "You *swear* that you have no intent to rape or torture me?"

This was far from the most flattering exchange Baird had ever had. "I swear it. Not now or ever."

She still didn't look convinced. "Your word of honor?"

Well, she didn't give up easily, did she? Annoyance swept through Baird. Had there ever been a woman who found him more offensive than a three-inch cockroach?

Baird gritted his teeth. "I give you my most solemn word of honor."

To his relief, that seemed to satisfy her.

Aurelia kept the room key steadfastly between them as she came closer, though Baird couldn't imagine why. Those little feet with their delectable toes halted uneasily just an arm's length away from Baird's boots.

There was still a vestige of mud in between the toes.

Baird's pulse accelerated as his imagination supplied the possibility of his thoroughly cleaning each toe in succession. They were so tiny and soft, so perfectly shaped. Her foot would fit snugly in his hand, he just knew it. Baird's pleated cords got a little tighter and he forced himself to examine the wall tiles.

He really could pick them, that was for sure.

"I do not understand," Aurelia confessed, her fair brows drawing together in a frown.

"Hot, cold." Baird seized on practical matters. He gestured to the brass knobs in question, then turned the hot one. "On, off. Same as everywhere else."

But Aurelia's expression revealed that she had never seen anything like it. Baird slid toward the base of the tub and gestured to the taps in his most nonthreatening manner.

"Try it," he encouraged.

Aurelia fired a glance at Baird. "I will not interfere with your magic," she insisted.

"Then the water will overflow." Baird's tone was matter-of-fact. Her gaze darted between him and the rising water as though she weren't sure whether to believe him.

But then, people were always suspicious of new technology—or old technology that was new to them.

"Come on. It won't bite. Adjust the temperature." Baird stood and put even more distance between them. He shoved his hands into his pockets.

Aurelia crept toward the tub, one wary eye on Baird's precise location as she sidled past him. Aurelia flashed a glance to him—just checking!—and her eyes were so wide that he could see the silver-gray perimeter around the intensely blue iris of her eyes.

There certainly had never been a woman who was outright terrified of him.

That must be what was bothering him. Baird must just want to see the record set straight. He knew he had never done anything to inspire a woman's fear, especially this one's.

Or had he? Could he have met Aurelia, hurt her feelings in some way contrary to how he always treated women, and then forgotten her? That was too much to believe.

But how could he have recognized her if they hadn't met? The hair on the back of Baird's neck stood at attention and he had a very uneasy feeling that he wouldn't like the truth.

Aurelia tentatively turned the hot knob as he had done, her tiny fingers barely making their way around the knob. The strength of the water coursing from the tap changed and she gasped.

But before Baird could show her, Aurelia reached forward again. She certainly wasn't shy once she had the hang of things. Baird smiled to himself, liking the way this woman seemed to grab life with both hands. Aurelia adjusted the temperature with dawning confidence and grinned like a child with a new toy.

Baird put the lid down on the toilet and sat there, bracing his elbows on his knees as he watched her play.

"So, you see, you *can* draw your bath alone."

Aurelia turned a bright gaze on Baird and an enchanting flush rose over her cheeks. "I am sorry," she admitted. "I did not know such marvels existed."

Her heartfelt apology made a part of Baird melt like butter in the sun. He cleared his throat, unaccustomed to such a feeling, and arched a brow that he hoped looked skeptical. "Perhaps the next time, you might give me the benefit of the doubt."

She said nothing, but again Baird had the impression that she was thinking furiously. What was in her mind? And why was she so determined to distrust him? He wasn't that bad of a guy!

Hoping to encourage Aurelia's trust, Baird dared to smile at her.

She flushed scarlet and dropped her gaze in obvious discomfort.

So much for his charm. Baird cleared his throat. "Could you tell me where we've met before?"

Aurelia frowned. "We have never met before."

"But we must have! I feel as though I know you, as though I recognize you. . . ." Baird's voice faded before her steady gaze.

She looked as though she thought *he* was crazy.

Now there was irony.

"Never," she repeated with quiet determination.

Then how had Baird recognized her? It made no sense!

But Aurelia stared steadily back at him, her wide blue eyes all innocence. The rushing water made the bathroom humid and unexpectedly intimate.

Baird's errant mind supplied the feel of Aurelia's breast in his hand at this most inopportune time.

Powerless to stop himself, Baird glanced to Aurelia's perfect feet. She was wriggling her toes against the bath mat. His mouth went dry as desire roared to life once more.

A hot flush passed over him, heating his flesh from head to toe. Baird wanted to kiss Aurelia again, taste her, caress her, savor the weight of that breast in his hand. He wanted to peel off his clothes, tear off that bathrobe with his teeth.

Baird wanted to climb into the tub with Aurelia—or better yet, the shower—massage her, lather her with soap, tease her until she moaned with pleasure. He wanted to bury himself to the hilt in her softness and never come back. His need for her was primal and so overwhelming in its intensity that he felt dizzy.

It was the steam from the bath. Baird was too hot, in more ways than one.

He had to get out of here.

"Well! That's settled, then." Baird pushed to his feet, not believing that for a minute. "So, now you know how the bath works. I guess I'll see you at dinner, say about six?"

Aurelia frowned in childish confusion. "Six?"

"Six o'clock, in the west hall where the restaurant will be." Baird cocked a finger at the rising bathwater and ducked toward the door. "You'd better get that before it runs over."

"Oh. *Oh*!" Aurelia pivoted and dove for the tap. The steaming water had nearly crested the overflow valve, and she scrabbled at the knobs in her haste to turn off the water.

The pose showed her legs to distinct advantage, making Baird suddenly very glad that he had ordered the short bathrobes for the resort.

Even if it meant special torment for him in this moment.

"Enjoy your bath, princess." Baird ducked for the door and problems multiplying faster than even he could solve them.

It wasn't any help that one particular issue on that list had claimed his attention wholesale. That just meant, Baird resolved grimly, that it had to be solved first.

He had to find Hekod and he had to find him soon.

Eight

Aurelia sank up to her chin in the scented bathwater and considered her predicament. Bard, son of Erc, was a man full of enough surprises to keep any woman on her toes. Never would Aurelia have imagined that he would make a pledge to her—though what his word was worth remained to be seen.

The gesture alone was astonishing and hinted at a man of vastly different character than she had expected.

But perhaps he only toyed with her. Aurelia chewed her lip and hated that she could not be certain of his intent. Clearly Bard's priest believed that Bard should wed Aurelia, though his whore, not unexpectedly, did not share that view.

But what did *Bard* think?

He had been uncommonly gracious in showing her this water marvel that they all took for granted. And he had not pressed any advantage he might have seen by being alone with Aurelia in the chambers she had been given for her own.

That made *twice* he had not raped her.

It was most unlike a savage barbarian—which she knew Bard to be—to show such restraint.

Oh, he was handsome, that was for certain, and his charm was undiminished with further acquaintance. That little smile that tugged at his firm lips, the warm gleam in his eyes when he looked upon her, the way he arched a dark brow as though they two shared a jest. Aurelia's breath caught at the mere recollection.

And the way he kissed.

Aurelia sat up hastily and felt around for the soap, determined not to let her mind dwell on such inappropriate thoughts. She took a soapy cloth and scrubbed the taste of his kisses from her lips with a vengeance. Her breast earned an extra, savage cleansing.

Here was a man who knew his assets and played it masterfully. And, just to make matters worse, Aurelia could not keep herself from responding to his touch.

She had to find her father, before it was too late.

And what of the others? There had been hundreds on the walls this morning to counter Bard's attack, yet Aurelia had not seen one familiar face.

Had Bard slaughtered them all?

There were the dungeons. Perhaps they survived there.

One way or the other, the truth of Bard's deeds would be discernible. No one could hide the fate of hundreds. At first opportunity, Aurelia would check the dungeons. Just one warrior left alive might have news of her sire.

Marissa was not amused to have a tempting package like Aurelia materialize out of the blue. And just to add insult to injury, she had to outfit the invader or risk looking petty in Baird's eyes.

As if looks like that needed any help at all. Every man in the place was watching Aurelia like a dog in heat, and her skin—well!—you didn't get skin like that living out in the wilds of Scotland. Marissa knew the work of a good spa when she saw it.

Which meant that Aurelia was far from the wacko innocent Julian thought she was.

More like an opportunist on the hunt. Marissa easily recognized her own kind and didn't appreciate the competition. The entire point of Marissa being in this godforsaken place was to have Baird to herself.

Period.

This was supposed to have been *her* moment in the sun, her chance to persuade Baird once and for all that they two were made for each other.

Not that Marissa really believed any such romantic nonsense. The math alone said that Baird Beauforte was the man
for her, and said it loud and clear.

But Baird just didn't seem to get it. Oh, Marissa had tried
to get him to notice her feminine charms, but Baird seemed
so oblivious that she wondered whether he was made of stone.

Marissa dug savagely through one of her Louis Vuitton
trunks. Baird had *never* come to meet her with a rise in his
Levis before. For a breathtaking moment, Marissa had dared
to hope that she was making real progress.

At least until the blonde appeared and the rise became the
size of Florida. Marissa didn't need to be a rocket scientist to
notice the way Baird's gaze followed Aurelia and know what
it meant.

And when they had gone upstairs? Well. Baird hadn't come
back to look at her travertine marble samples, that was for
sure! Imagine, luring Baird upstairs with some nonsense about
not being able to work the bath! And Baird hadn't seen
through the ploy—almost as if he *wanted* some excuse to go
to Aurelia's room.

Marissa ground her teeth in frustration. Having to lend
clothes to a woman who had already claimed Baird's attention
made her want to spit.

Her only hope was to come up with something hideous.

It was no help at all that Marissa's trunks were carefully
packed with clothes that showed her figure to particular advantage—sensuous silks and delicate lingerie that would contrast wonderfully with rugged outdoor wear. It was clothing
she had planned to wear herself to capture Baird's attention
and she didn't want to part with the advantage of a single
item.

Marissa came up with her favorite silk dress and nearly
shoved it aside before she froze midgesture. She stared at the
soft shimmer of the silk pouring over her hand for a long
moment. Its creamy hue highlighted her dark coloring spec-
tacularly well.

But blond Aurelia would look like dirty dishwater in such
a pale shade.

Marissa fanned out the dress's fullness across the top of the open trunk and a hint of a smile curved her lips. The dress brushed her own ankles with dramatic flair—but she was a good six inches taller than the blonde.

All these yards of silk would dwarf the little unfortunate. With luck, despite the luster of the fabric, she'd look like a lost child dressing up to be a woman.

Wouldn't that be sad.

And Marissa, by lending a silk dress Baird knew she favored, would appear to be sweet and generous.

Perfect. Marissa tossed the dress over her arm and smiled. This could work to her advantage in the end.

Marissa rapped on the door of the room Julian said he had given to Aurelia. The door swung open immediately.

"Oh! Hello." Aurelia was obviously both surprised to see Marissa and fresh from the bath. Her hair hung damp and gleaming past her hips, the towel she had wrapped about herself covered her only from underarm to midthigh.

And there was not a dot of cellulite on what Marissa could see of those slender but muscular thighs. Aurelia was the very image of dewy innocence. Thank God Baird wasn't here to witness this!

Anger surged through Marissa at the thought. She gritted her teeth and managed a smile that she hoped appeared friendly. "Didn't you look through the peephole before you opened the door, darling?" she asked sweetly. "You never know who could be knocking at your door otherwise and you certainly wouldn't want to just let them in!"

Aurelia blinked, obviously not understanding.

"The peephole, darling."

Aurelia's blank expression didn't change.

"In the door. The peephole in the *door*. Surely you've noticed it?" Marissa tapped impatiently on the brass insert in question, amazed that the ditzy blonde didn't seem to know what it was. "You look through it, darling, to see who is outside *before* you open the door."

Aurelia frowned. "There is no hole in this door," she said carefully, looking at Marissa as though *she* were the dense one.

Marissa barely controlled her exasperation. "You know, you can't just open the door, especially dressed like that! What if there had been a workman here?"

Or Baird. He'd likely blow a seam in his jeans!

Marissa refused to think any further along such lines. "Go inside and look through the peephole, darling," she instructed, incredulous that she had to explain something so simple. "You'll see exactly what I mean."

Was it true that blondes were as dumb as bricks?

Aurelia shut the door obediently. Marissa waited a second, then waved and smiled. There was an audible gasp from inside the room and Aurelia tore open the door, her eyes narrowed with suspicion.

"How did you get in there?" she demanded.

Marissa barely refrained from rolling her eyes. Dumber than dumb. But then, hadn't Aurelia insisted that she was a *princess*? Obviously reality was a distant concept for this one.

"I'm not in there, darling, I'm out here," Marissa explained patiently. "You looked through the peephole in the door and saw me out here in the hall. That's how it works, very *simple*, really."

Aurelia appeared unconvinced. She glanced at the peephole, then back to Marissa, her doubts clearly unabated.

Did she think Marissa was *lying* about something so painfully pedestrian?

"You were only this big," Aurelia insisted, holding her finger and thumb an inch apart. "How did you make yourself so small?"

Marissa blinked, but Aurelia held her gaze stubbornly. Incredibly, the woman was not putting her on. She might be drop-dead gorgeous, but Baird's attraction wouldn't last long if he had to explain every little thing.

Maybe she really *had* been incapable of drawing her own bath.

Maybe there was hope after all. Marissa's spirits soared and she felt uncharacteristically generous.

"It wasn't me, darling. There's a lens or something in there, a special kind of glass that makes things look smaller when you look through it. It lets you see whatever—or whoever—

is out here before you open the door. It's perfectly marvelous, of course.''

Aurelia went back and looked through the peephole again, swinging the door and staying right behind it to stare through the peephole as the door moved.

Pathetic. When Aurelia reluctantly abandoned the game, she looked impressed. Marissa's bored tolerance must have shown.

''You are used to this magic,'' Aurelia commented.

''Oh, yes, I wouldn't have a door without it.'' Marissa shrugged. ''You never know who is going to come knocking these days, darling, do you, and one can only be prepared for *every* eventuality.''

Aurelia nodded understanding, her gaze trailing back to the marvel in the door once more. Marissa, though, had no intention of wasting any more time watching Aurelia gawk.

''Look, darling, I've brought you some clothes, nothing too terribly swish but something to get you by. Here's a dress for dinner and some undies—don't worry, of course they're clean!—some pantyhose. I'm not sure whether any of my shoes would fit you, darling, but here's a pair just in case they do.''

Marissa handed over the lot. Aurelia fingered the silk and Marissa smiled with the certainty that she would take the bait and wear the dress.

That made her almost laugh out loud. ''Oh, and here's a bit of makeup that just might be *perfect* for you, darling.'' Marissa handed over a vibrant pink lipstick and a glaringly blue eyeliner that she hadn't gotten around to pitching. ''I thought the colors would suit you.''

In one way or another.

Aurelia stared at the cosmetics as though she had no idea what they were. Maybe they packaged them differently here. God knew almost everything else was backward in one way or another. People even drove on the wrong side of the road!

''At any rate, it will get you by until you can get some things in town.''

Then Aurelia glanced up and something flashed in her eyes that made Marissa wonder whether she had underestimated the woman's intelligence.

The expression was gone so quickly that Marissa immediately doubted what she had seen.

"Thank you very much for your generosity." Aurelia smiled. "I hope that you have not done yourself a disservice."

"Oh, no, darling, don't fret!" Marissa, her optimism restored, gave her trademark trill of laughter. "I'm sure I'll find *some* little rag to wear!"

"No doubt you will," Aurelia said sweetly. She firmly closed the door before Marissa could wonder what was being implied.

Marissa stood there for a moment, then shook her head. Diverting Baird's attention from Aurelia's charms would take virtually no effort at all. Marissa was certain that Aurelia could manage the job just fine, now that she had had a little bit of assistance.

Aurelia tossed the armload of clothes across the room, outraged that Baird's whore would try to cast her in the same role. The garb of a harlot was what she had shared, that much was clear, for no woman of honor could afford such fine fabric.

'Twas the mark of a whore to be indulged with silk. Aurelia supposed she should have expected no less.

But wait—*who* had chosen the garb? Certainly the whore was adverse to any competition for Bard's eye and would have shared millet sacks, given her choice.

Not garb wrought so fine as this.

Which could only mean that *Bard* must have dictated what would be bought.

But why? Aurelia thought furiously. Had the priest been successful in coaxing Bard closer to his own view?

Why else would his kiss have changed so seductively?

Aurelia examined the sheerness of the silken chemise once more. It was thin enough that any man would see the flesh beneath. Even a whore would have to be bold—or well claimed—to wear such attire into the evening revelry of the hall.

Especially in a holding so apparently devoid of womenfolk. Aurelia's mouth went dry at the import of this garb. Wearing this to the board would make Aurelia a temptress—and any results the fault of no one but herself.

Clearly Bard meant to add her to the ranks of his whores! Why else would he insist Marissa share *this* garb?

Why, he might even have planned to bend his considerable charm upon Aurelia this very night! Perhaps she would be fed tender morsels to fuel her desire, or plied with mead until she was too drunk to fend off Bard's advances.

And once her maidenhead was gone, Aurelia would be compelled to wed the cur or shame her family. It was reprehensible—yet curiously evocative of how Thord had been coaxed to his death.

Aurelia paced her chamber at breakneck speed as she worked through the repercussions of this deed. She would not drink a single sip of mead at the board this night. And she would not eat of any special dish prepared for her alone. She would eat and drink only whatever Bard ate or drank first. Her chastity was not to be begged or bartered at any man's command!

Especially the murderer of her only brother. Aurelia would rather starve than go to the hall and make such a spectacle of herself!

On the other hand, she was *very* hungry. She drummed her fingers and considered the problem of how she might foil Bard's plans, at least long enough to fill her belly.

Suddenly Aurelia glimpsed the linens adorning the bed. She hastily peeled back the coverlet and was astonished at the lush beauty of the smooth cloth revealed. Somehow a pattern had been made upon the fabric, though it was not woven there, its hues echoing the shades of the room.

Aurelia recalled the sewing needles in the little basket in the small chamber. There *was* another option! Oh, she would show Bard that she would not readily become his whore!

But she must hasten, lest she be too late to the board. Who knew when this "six o'clock" might be? The sky was already darkening outside the room and Aurelia was certainly hungry.

She might already be late!

• • •

The rain had stopped and the dark clouds had parted in the west to frame a magnificent orange sunset when Baird came downstairs. The dramatic light streamed through the tall Gothic windows along the west side of the old castle and painted the unfinished room in shades of gold.

Baird refused to look at the cut thorns marking the place he had met Aurelia.

Instead he stared at the sunset, certain he had never seen another so beautiful. Baird's senses seemed to have awakened after a long sleep when he had taken up residence here. Not only was every hue more intense, but the simplest food seemed more flavorful, and he felt as though he could hear a thousand voices in the wind.

Dunhelm had enchanted him.

Was that why Aurelia affected him so strongly?

Baird dismissed his whimsical thoughts and surveyed the construction critically. This was currently the tidiest public room in the renovation, though folding tables were the extent of the furnishings.

It was a far cry from his plans, though Baird could see hints of what the space would become. Although the main restaurant would be on the east side, stretching down the slope toward the beach and a stunning view, this would ultimately be a smaller restaurant. It would boast a comparatively small kitchen, and be a good place to have drinks or perhaps a casual lunch.

Right now, it was a less daunting unfinished space than the cavernous main restaurant.

The old stone walls of the thirteenth-century castle exuded a cozy intimacy here, as would the great stone fireplace, once it was refurbished. Yet the high ceiling would absorb the murmur of several dozen conversations easily.

And the view was magnificent, whatever the weather. The large windows granted a sweeping view of Dunhelm's natural site. The sea stretched out to the west, shimmering in the evening light like an endless blanket of jewels, and waves crashed on the ragged coastline.

Currently, though, the space in the east restaurant destined to be filled with gleaming stainless steel was still a gaping hole filled with wires and sawdust. Baird tapped his toe and wondered how long it would take for the food he had ordered to be delivered from the village.

Or how cold it would be when it got here.

Baird spotted a package wrapped in brown paper on one of the folding tables. He picked it up and noted that it was addressed to him in Talorc's spidery handwriting. Baird smiled with satisfaction.

The mystery of Hekod was close to being solved. He could call the man tonight, maybe head to his place with Aurelia after dinner and get the whole tangle sorted out.

Whatever story Aurelia had concocted or whatever family complications had brought her ultimately to Dunhelm, it would all be shortly laid to rest. Then Baird could focus on solving the question of how he recognized her, and from where.

Baird tore the paper away with purpose, but paused to frown at the package's contents. Instead of the telephone book he was expecting, he held a beaten-up copy of a book called *Sorensson's History of the Orkney Islands.*

A history book?

A slip of paper was tucked into the middle of the book and Baird opened the volume to that page. There was more of the shaky writing on the slip.

"Here you will find the only Hekod that I know, he would be the famous one I told you about this afternoon, to be sure."

The page marked was entitled "The Dark Ages in the Orkney Islands."

Obviously Talorc had mistaken Baird's meaning, but a little history about the area wouldn't be unwelcome. He had a few moments to wait for the others, anyway.

So Baird settled into a chair and read.

The Arrival of the Vikings

 The Vikings first landed on the shores of the Orkney Islands sometime shortly after their raid on Lindisfarne, the famed monastery on the east coast of England, which occurred in A.D. 793. Some scholars maintain that the attack on Lindisfarne was launched by a fledgling Norse colony in Orkney, but whatever the chronology, within a century, the Orkney, Shetland, and Faeroe Islands were all major Norse settlements. The Orkney Islands remained a holding of the Norwegian Crown until 1468.

One of the first established Viking kings in the Orkney Islands was Hekod the Fifth, King of Dunhelm and Lord of Fyordskar.

Hekod the Fifth, King of *Dunhelm*?

Nine

Baird slammed the book closed. The hairs on the back of his neck were standing on end. Aurelia had claimed her father, Hekod, was King of Dunhelm and lord of somewhere else. Surely her father couldn't be this eighth-century Viking conqueror?

No, no, that was nuts! She hadn't said Fyordskar. She *couldn't* have. How could her father be twelve hundred years old, give or take a few decades?

Baird was connecting dots that didn't deserve the link.

Obviously.

Okay, he'd never heard the name Hekod before, but it might be popular here, regardless of what Talorc said.

It was illogical for Aurelia's father to be twelve hundred years old, plain and simple. He must have been named after this Hekod, and when Aurelia lost him, however that had happened, she was so upset that she confused the past with the present.

Baird was no psych. major but that made sense. Aurelia could spend her whole life looking for this historic Hekod and never find him—just as she would never find her father if he had abandoned her.

It was a familiar enough story to Baird Beauforte. Baird had to admire the way the human mind rationalized things to save its own sanity. His compassion for Aurelia grew with the certainty that they had both been dealt the same lousy hand.

But unlike Baird, Aurelia remembered her father, she had known him and obviously cared for him. Baird's lips thinned. There was no way Hekod should be allowed to get away with that.

No one should have to go through what Baird had. He would make sure Hekod gave his daughter a straight answer, if nothing else.

Baird deliberately shook off any intuitive feelings that argued with his conclusion—intuition, after all, was illogical—and opened the book again.

> *Comparatively little is known of Hekod, other than the fact that he married a Pictish woman. There is some scholarship indicating that Hekod's queen was linked to the Pictish List of Kings, the only Pictish document that survives. This could imply that his marriage was a strategic move designed to assure his suzerainty in his new home. Appearances would support this, for unlike many conquerors whose reigns were short, Hekod sat upon his throne for at least twenty-five years.*

A Pictish woman? Aurelia had mentioned the same thing. But what was Pictish? Baird fanned back to the table of contents and discovered that a good third of the book concerned the Picts.

> *Little is known decisively about the Picts, and there is wide dissent in academic circles about even their origins. A prevailing opinion is that the Picts were a remnant of the Celtic society that once spread across all of Europe. When the Romans began to defeat the Celts, they moved to the margins of Europe, the Picts being those Celts ousted to the northern fringes of what is now Scotland. Other scholars maintain that the Picts were simply the descendants of Iron Age peoples in the area.*
>
> *At any rate, even the word Pict is not their own, it is derived from the Roman* Picti *or "Painted Ones." The Romans were continually harassed by the Picts, eventually resorting to the construction of Hadrian's Wall, and*

the Antonine Wall, further north, designed to keep these "barbarians" out of Roman Britain.

The moniker Painted Ones derives from the Picts' purported fascination with body tattoos as ornamentation. These they created by piercing the skin with needles in intricate patterns, then rubbing the juice of an herb—woad, used as a blue dye in the area until the importation of indigo much later—into the punctures to make a fairly permanent stain.

If, like other Celts, they waged war in the nude, the Pictish warrior would have been an imposing sight.

No doubt.

Baird ran a fingertip across the swirling tattoo designs illustrated in the margin and considered to be characteristically Pictish. Intrigued as much by the story as the fact that Aurelia had chosen to use it, he turned the page.

But Baird wasn't going to have the chance to read any more.

"Delivery from McNally's Fish and Chips Shop! Someone order pizzas?"

The shadow of a gangly boy could be spotted in the corridor that stretched back to the entryway. He juggled a trio of boxes and peered into the sun.

"In here!" Baird called, and jumped to his feet. He put the book aside reluctantly and rummaged for his wallet. "One's vegetarian?"

"This one, sir." The kid looked about himself with wide eyes and gave a low whistle. "This here is looking to be some kind of place, sir."

Baird smiled with proprietary pride. "It certainly will be."

"It has changed and then some, sir. We used to play hide-and-seek out here, sir, when I was a wee lad."

"Did you?" Baird peered at the unfamiliar banknotes, trying to make sense of them quickly. "Must have been a bit dangerous. There were a lot of holes where floors had fallen in."

"Don't I know it! Part of the game, sir." The boy's eyes glinted with mischief. "But don't you be telling my mam we done it, will you?"

Baird smiled. "Not me." He handed a couple of bills to the boy and waved away the offer of change. "It's a long drive from town. Keep that for yourself and your car."

The kid scanned the notes, then grinned from ear to ear. "Thank you, sir. Petrol's freaking expensive up this-away. That's right generous of you, sir." He bobbed his head, took one last gawk around his old haunt, and was gone.

Baird was sure all the former playmates would hear at the pub tonight what had been done to Dunhelm, at least so far.

Julian sauntered into the hall, his tie loosened in an apparent concession to casual dining, and took a disdainful sniff. "Fish pizza?"

"No. Regular pizza, but the fish and chips shop is the only place that makes any." Baird plopped the boxes on a folding table and opened one. The pizza inside proved to be heavily laden with sausage. "One's supposed to be vegetarian. I forget which."

Julian grimaced and poked open the second box with a fingertip. "Probably got *turnips* on it," he muttered, and sniffed suspiciously.

"Well, good evening, darlings," Marissa cooed from the doorway. "I certainly hope I'm not late."

Julian didn't even look up. "Just in time for something Baird optimistically calls pizza."

Undeterred, Marissa smiled sunnily and swept into the room, dressed in a flowing pantsuit of sage green. Probably silk, Baird guessed, because he knew more about Marissa's extravagant taste than anything about women's clothes. Her hair was loose, an uncharacteristic choice, and Baird was sure it was the first time he had seen her without dark lipstick.

Go figure. He'd never imagined Marissa dressed in anything other than black. Baird's glance slid to Julian, noting again the lawyer's loosened tie.

Dunhelm apparently worked its magic on everyone.

Marissa sniffed, then shivered indulgently. "Pizza for dinner? It smells positively divine!"

Julian cocked a brow at Marissa. "You're joking, right? Either that or you've been living on airline food too long. This pizza smells like *fish*."

"Julian, don't be silly, darling. I'm sure whatever Baird ordered will be simply marvelous." Marissa's voice dropped to a seductive murmur. "Aren't you just famished, Baird?"

Aurelia swept into the room in that moment, and anything Baird might have said to Marissa was completely forgotten.

She looked like a Dark Age goddess come to life. The light of the setting sun toyed with the gold of her hair and made the proud tilt of her chin look more regal than ever.

Her hair was plaited with an intricacy that rivaled the carving on the stone before her chamber, countless blond braids tucked and woven and looped into a headdress of fantastic design. She wore a tunic of a sapphire blue print that seemed vaguely familiar to Baird, though he couldn't place where he had seen it before.

It certainly didn't look like anything Marissa would wear, so it couldn't have been The Loan.

The tunic was pinned at Aurelia's shoulders, then fell open to reveal the creamy sleeves of the dress she wore underneath. Long silken sleeves nearly covered her hands, a sweep of ivory brushed the floor in her wake. The tunic was hemmed with a wide border that fell just below Aurelia's knees, its fullness pulled in by a glossy golden cord hung with lavish tassels.

If nothing else, she was playing any eighth-century fantasy to the hilt. That confusing protective urge roared to life once more and Baird promised himself that he would not only solve the mystery of Hekod's disappearance, but see Aurelia's confusion sorted out before he left Dunhelm.

It was the only decent thing to do.

Aurelia stepped forward, her azure gaze locked challengingly with his own and Baird realized, to his dismay, that her feet were bare.

His mouth went dry.

"The bitch!" Marissa whispered. She pushed past Baird so impatiently that she nearly sent him sprawling. "She's torn up one of my sheets!"

Baird looked again, recognized the print of Aurelia's tunic, and realized simultaneously that her belt was a curtain tie-back.

His lips quirked despite himself.

But Marissa was across the room like a shot, her hand shaking as she scooped up a fistful of the sheet Aurelia had fashioned into a dress.

"My sheets!" she murmured, turning the fabric over and over in her hands. "My *precious* sheets! Two-hundred-and-fifty-count Egyptian cotton percale. Special ordered, a design exclusive."

She glared lethally at Aurelia, who stood as straight and impassive as a queen. Marissa's fingers clenched in the fabric and she gave it a savage shake. "How could you destroy my bed linens?"

"Bed linens?" Aurelia blinked in obvious astonishment. "You mean only to *sleep* on such fine fabrics?"

"Of course!" Marissa raged. She flung out her hands, but Aurelia did not even flinch. "Why else would they have been on the bed? What kind of a backwoods upbringing have you had, that you don't even know a *sheet* when you see it?"

Aurelia's lips tightened and her blue gaze turned glacial. "I have always slept in a fur-lined cloak, wrought of samite carried by my sire from the markets of Micklegarth." She fixed a stern glance on Marissa. "Bed linens, as everyone knows, when used over and over again, do nothing but promote fleas."

Julian choked back his laughter.

"Fleas? Ugh!" Marissa grimaced, then she seemed to recall where she was. She flicked a look to Baird and summoned a falsely sweet smile. Her voice dropped to a friendly tone that Baird knew was contrived and her accent made a curtain call. "Wasn't my favorite silk dress *good* enough for you, darling?"

"Such a fine chemise is a wonder next to the skin, but hardly appropriate to wear alone to the board." Aurelia's tone was cutting, and Baird marveled at the intelligence shining in her eyes. This time he knew without a doubt that she wasn't as dumb as she would have him believe.

And that fired his blood even more than her bare feet did.

"Not appropriate?" Marissa's mouth worked silently for a moment. "Not *appropriate*? I'll have you know that *that* is a Donna Karan pure silk dress that cost a fortune at Bloomingdale's, darling! It has seen more fine restaurants in style than the likes of *you* could even begin to imagine!''

Baird decided it was time to intervene, before Marissa said something they would all regret.

''Well! Enough about clothes.'' His tone was deliberately cheerful. ''How about dinner?''

''These pizzas aren't going to be any better cold,'' Julian added. ''Can't you two have your catfight later?''

''Catfight?'' Marissa rounded on Julian with flashing eyes and must have caught a glimpse of Baird stepping closer in the process.

Her mouth twisted for a moment, then she turned back to Aurelia with a honeyed smile. ''You were supposed to wear the undies next to your skin, darling,'' she said through gritted teeth. ''Poor Aurelia, all this proper dress must be so very *complicated* to you after the simple rural life you've lived. Don't worry, darling, I'll be perfectly happy to explain *every* little detail to you.''

'' 'Undies?' '' Aurelia sniffed with disdain. ''What kind of a woman wears such little bits of nothing as that?''

Baird looked to Aurelia in amazement. Could it be that more than her feet were bare? It was too easy to remember the lean perfection of Aurelia's legs, legs that might right now be brushing against the creamy silk of Marissa's dress without interference.

''Could we just eat already?'' Julian demanded in exasperation.

''Marissa, leave it be,'' Baird interjected firmly, putting his own tempting thoughts aside with an effort. ''We have plenty of sheets, and tomorrow I'll take Aurelia to get more clothes. You'll have your favorite dress back.''

''I'm not even sure that I'd want it back from someone who knows so much about *fleas*!''

''I'll have it cleaned.'' Baird looked sternly at each woman in turn. ''And now, let's eat.''

''Hey, Mort, I need an expert opinion. Do you think this is a red pepper?'' Julian's attempt to redirect the conversation wasn't subtle but it worked.

Marissa took a deep breath and crossed the floor, her lips

still tight. "Maybe the pimento out of an olive, darling. Surely there's no *hope* for decent antipasto here."

Julian winced. "From a jar!" He shuddered dramatically. "I knew a fresh bell pepper was too much to hope for."

Baird glanced to Aurelia when she didn't move. "Do you want some pizza? It's getting cold."

Aurelia looked him up and down. "I know nothing of this pizza you offer."

"Well, don't judge all pizza by this particular example." She looked puzzled, but Baird shrugged. "The real chef is coming in a couple of weeks. Until then, we take what we can get."

Aurelia still didn't move, and Baird again felt that urge to make her smile.

Well, she thought she was a princess and seemed determined to play the role. It was harmless enough. Why not play along?

Baird bowed slightly. "My lady?" He offered Aurelia his hand in a gallant gesture that seemed to suit her manner. "May I escort you to dinner?"

Aurelia stared at his outstretched hand for a long moment, then carefully—as though she didn't trust him not to bite—laid her delicate fingers across his own.

And Baird felt a disconcerting sense of recognition again. Aurelia's gaze flicked to his, and an answering heat burned into his own. Aurelia certainly had a strong effect on him. Was it just the puzzle of trying to remember that was responsible for his powerful attraction?

Right now, Baird didn't care.

On impulse, he leaned over her hand and brushed his lips across its back. Aurelia shivered and her lips parted as she stared at him.

But she didn't pull away.

Baird couldn't think of anything other than the sweet press of those lips beneath his own. Everything else faded before his need to taste her again. He had to know whether it had just been surprise or something deeper that burned between them today.

Baird stepped closer and Aurelia didn't step away or protest.

Slowly he lifted her small hand toward his chest, watched her sapphire gaze dance over his face. . . .

"Come *on*, already!" Julian complained. "Don't make me eat this travesty of a pizza cold, too!"

Aurelia's head turned with a snap and she hauled her fingers out of Baird's grip. She scooped up her skirts and joined the others so hastily that she seemed to be taking refuge in their midst.

The tantalizing moment was gone.

And, against all reason, Baird found himself hoping it would return soon.

Aurelia's very flesh seemed heated after Bard's touch and she had a hard time thinking with any kind of sense.

He was bending his charm upon her without delay, and she was falling prey to his seduction so readily! Aurelia could not seem to help her instinctive response to his touch—though now, she hated the fact that she had *wanted* him to kiss her again.

Bard was following his plan to the letter, and Aurelia, even though she had guessed his intent, was powerless to stop her traitorous body from responding.

What had happened to her resolve?

But even as she wondered, Aurelia was reliving the fan of Bard's breath against her lips, the resolute grip of his hand upon her own, the heat of desire that glowed in his eyes.

The way he held her hand was so gallant, so different from the coarse behavior she expected of him, that Aurelia did not know what to think. She swallowed her unwelcome response with difficulty and focused on the oddly small board.

To her astonishment, there was no mead.

"Will you have some Chianti?" Bard asked.

Aurelia was so shocked that he intended to pour the beverage himself that she did not immediately comprehend his question. Were there no servants for the king himself? He truly did have a barbaric court!

"Aurelia?" he prompted. "Chianti? There's water, if you prefer."

What kind of fool drank water? Especially after a battle had been waged? Who knew what foulness had trickled into the well?

Aurelia examined the red liquid in the glass flagon. "I do not know this Chianti," she said carefully.

"It's cheap," Julian confided, his tone making his opinion more than clear. "I never drink the damn stuff—much prefer a good Châteauneuf-du-Pape, myself—but there isn't a lot of choice around here."

"Sebastien will take care of all of that, darling." Marissa seemed to have recovered, both her accent and manner securely back in place now that she was beside the king once more.

"You know he's coming?" Julian looked surprised, whoever this Sebastien might be.

Marissa chortled. "Oh, of course, darling! I helped to *convince* him!" Her expression hinted at powers of persuasion that Aurelia didn't even want to imagine.

Whores and their tricks were of no interest to a well-bred woman.

Julian grimaced. "I should have figured *you* would have had something to do with stealing him away from New York."

"Aurelia, would you like some wine, cheap as it is?" Bard's voice was tinged with impatience and Aurelia could not blame him. His minions were far from respectful of his position.

Unfortunately there was no one else to ask what was probably a silly question except Bard, for the other pair had begun to bicker about this Sebastien.

But perhaps that was best. It could do no harm to appear foolish to Bard, after her many slips on this day. Aurelia leaned closer and dropped her voice. "What is *wine*?"

Bard did not mock her. Nor, unfortunately, did he act as though she was slow of wit. "You do have things pretty simple up here, don't you?" he mused, just taking the question in stride. "It's made from grapes."

"Grapes?" That did not tell Aurelia anything and Bard evidently guessed as much.

"They wouldn't grow here, but I thought they might be shipped in." His glance was questioning, but Aurelia shrugged her incomprehension. Furs and slaves were shipped, to her knowledge, and settlers brought livestock and tools. Certainly one would not make a beverage of any of those things.

Bard swished the red liquid in the glass flagon. "Grapes are a fruit that grows in warm places, warmer places than here."

The juice of a fruit. There could be no harm in that. And it would certainly be safer than the water. Aurelia nodded. "I would like to sample some of this Chianti, if you please."

Bard poured her a finger's depth in the bottom of a glass and offered it to Aurelia. "Try it first. See if you like it."

The vessel he handed her was like a chalice, stemmed and shaped like an inverted bell, but wrought of very thin glass. Aurelia was amazed yet again at the craftsmanship they all took for granted.

Their fingers brushed in the transaction and Aurelia fought to hide any sign of the way her heart stopped. Those green eyes never wavered from her, though, and she deliberately turned her attention to the wine. Her very flesh tingled in awareness and, yet again, Aurelia felt that Bard could read her thoughts.

Why could he not have been born a wretchedly ugly man?

Aurelia sniffed the wine and found its aroma quite pleasing. Under Bard's watchful eye, she cautiously sipped. The juice tasted of richness and sunshine. Aurelia closed her eyes as she rolled this wine across her tongue and imagined herself in this warmer clime, a place so warm that she could bare her very flesh to the sun. In her mind's eye, a handsome warrior who was not entirely unfamiliar bent to brush his lips temptingly across her own.

Then she heard Bard chuckle. Aurelia's eyes flew open.

He *had* read her thoughts again!

And now he laughed. Oh, he must think her a fool to have fallen so readily for his scheme! Aurelia felt herself flush scarlet.

"You look completely entranced." Bard's voice was low with a thread of humor, his lips quirked at one corner. His eyes gleamed as though he were talking about more than the wine.

Had he guessed that she found him dangerously handsome?

Aurelia felt uncharacteristically flustered at the prospect. She was not used to people reading her thoughts so easily—usually *she* was the perceptive one!

And she certainly was not used to being so aware of a man. There had been warriors in her father's court anxious to win her attention, but Aurelia had easily ignored them.

Bard, however, was markedly difficult to ignore. He spoke to her as though he cared for more than her fine features, which proved to have a dangerous allure.

That he knew her weakness for him only rubbed salt into Aurelia's wounded pride.

"I like it very much," she said formally.

And she held out her goblet for more.

Ten

This pizza, however, did not rate so well in Aurelia's estimation. A kind of bread, it was slathered with a red sauce of considerable spice, the entire thing smelling of fish. She certainly had known better fare, but hoped no one noticed her circumspect examination of the food.

She had no such luck.

"Disgusting, isn't it?" Julian asked, and tossed his piece back on the board. He took a deep draught of his wine as though he would wash the taste from his mouth, then reached for the glass flagon to refill his goblet. "Aurelia? Could you use a bit more?"

Aurelia nodded. To her surprise, once Julian was done, he lifted his goblet in a toast. "To Aurelia's superb taste! May none of us ever have to eat pizza like this again!"

And he drained his goblet once more.

Aurelia, not wanting to antagonize the priest after having won a measure of his acceptance, followed suit.

"You don't have to eat it," Bard muttered darkly.

Julian filled his glass to the brim. "Good. More wine?" His question came too late for Aurelia to have stopped his refilling of her goblet. He winked. "It gets better by the fourth glass."

This made no sense to Aurelia but she said nothing, stoically continuing to eat her pizza.

"Really, Baird, darling, it's just too terribly fishy!" Marissa dropped her pizza back onto the board. "I don't even eat *fish* with this strong of a flavor!'' She sipped at her wine, her gaze locked on Bard.

''I thought you were ravenous,'' Bard commented.

Marissa rolled her eyes. ''Desperation, darling, is quite another thing. And I'm certain I couldn't possibly eat another bite.''

Bard eyed the whore's half-eaten slice of pizza dubiously, then his glance met Aurelia's. She saw a skepticism there that she certainly shared—why, Marissa had not eaten enough to sustain a mere rat!

''Well, it's all there is,'' Bard said tightly. He looked at Aurelia again, his eyes tellingly bright. ''Will you have another piece?''

Aurelia was not about to slight the hospitality of her host, however barbaric his court might be. A princess had to show some dignity, after all.

And she was very, very hungry.

She wiped her hands fastidiously on her oddly thin napkin and eyed one of the other pizzas. Aurelia was curious to know what all three tasted like but was mindful of her decision to eat only what Bard ate first.

''Shall we try the other one?'' she suggested, and Bard grinned.

''Absolutely.'' He sent an arch glance to his courtiers, both of whom grimaced with distaste and drew back.

''Looks like it's just you and me, Princess.'' Bard offered the pizza and Aurelia took a piece, sipping her wine until he had taken the first bite.

Then she practically inhaled her second piece. Gods and goddesses, had she ever been so hungry?

''Whoa!'' Julian whistled through his teeth. ''You look like you haven't eaten in a thousand years!''

Vulgar man! Aurelia glanced scornfully in his direction. ''I have always been blessed with a healthy appetite.''

Marissa snorted. ''I should say so! I could *never* have eaten more, even if it had been one of Sebastien's glorious pizzas!''

To Aurelia's surprise, it was Bard who came to her defense. ''There's nothing wrong with a woman being honest enough to eat like a human being.''

The whore straightened proudly. "What is *that* supposed to mean?"

"Only that most women pick at their food and eat about three bites a meal. It's not good for you to eat so little." Surprisingly, he granted Aurelia a smile. "The princess obviously has a good appetite and enjoys food. There's nothing wrong with that."

The glint in Bard's eyes made Aurelia's resistance to him melt a little more. She felt that the room had become much warmer, though maybe it was from finally having something in her belly. Aurelia cleared her throat, uncomfortable to be the sole point of his interest, and tried to laugh.

"One must always take advantage of an opportunity to eat," she said lightly. "My mother often said that one never knew when there would be a meal again."

"Let alone a good one," Julian interjected.

Bard ignored his priest. "Sound advice," he concurred.

Marissa snorted. "For vagrants, it makes wonderful sense."

"My third foster mother said the same thing and I always believed it," Bard retorted. "Despite an unsettled childhood, I've never actually been called a vagrant before."

Marissa's eyes went round and she immediately began making fulsome apologies.

Bard ignored his whore and offered the third pizza to Aurelia. "Should we try this one, princess? I don't think Julian's going to do this Vegetarian Special justice."

"Oh, yes!" Aurelia took a piece and Marissa inhaled sharply.

"Give me that!" she snapped, and snatched up a slice of pizza.

The priest chuckled to himself and drained his wine once more. "Is the prey really worth the price of the hunt, Marissa?" he murmured inexplicably.

Aurelia glanced between them all in confusion and caught the end of the wicked look the whore fired Julian's way. There was the evil eye in action, if ever she had seen it! Aurelia concentrated on her pizza for fear of attracting such malice to herself.

"You just go ahead and finish up that cheap wine, Julian,

darling." Marissa's voice was low with animosity. "You'll regret it in the morning, you can be sure."

"Oh, I don't think so." Julian leaned forward unexpectedly, the flagon in his hand. "What do you say we make a bet, Aurelia?"

She looked warily to the priest, wondering what his game might be. "A bet?"

"Sure. You may be able to eat more pizza than our Marissa, but can you drink more wine than me?"

Aurelia surveyed the priest who was her competition in more matters than this. "You mean to make a wager."

"Yeah, just a little friendly competition." Julian topped up her goblet with a flourish and waggled his eyebrows expressively. "There's nothing else to do around this damned place."

"Careful, princess," Bard warned with a smile. "This man likes his wine." He offered the first pizza again, much to Aurelia's relief. This fare was not terribly filling. Aurelia took another slice while she considered Julian's offer.

A challenge over fruit juice. The Viking pride Aurelia had inherited from her sire would not let her turn him down.

"And what do I win?" she demanded saucily.

"Satisfaction!" Julian said, and lifted his glass high.

Oh, there would be that, Aurelia was certain! If she could best Bard's priest in any matter, even one so minor as this, she would be more convinced of the power of her own abilities against his own.

And less convinced of the efficacy of his own. That would be no small thing.

Aurelia lifted her glass high. "To the end of the wine," she declared, and Julian laughed aloud.

"Or of us, whichever comes first!"

Two hours later, Aurelia and Julian had drunk the better part of four bottles of wine and Julian was wrestling with the cork of a fifth. Aurelia was feeling very, very relaxed.

And more than a little bit happy. She liked the Chianti well, and felt more carefree than she had in quite some time.

Perhaps it was because Bard had settled back in his chair,

his green gaze burning bright as he watched her. Aurelia supposed that they were all providing his entertainment, but for the moment, she did not care.

She felt very feminine beneath his regard and very much alive. A small smile toyed with his lips, and with each glass of juice the hum of desire deep within Aurelia buzzed a little harder.

Julian tugged savagely on the strange curly implement he had inserted into the cork, but to no avail. "Whoa! This is a tight one!" He turned it some more, grimaced, and pulled again.

The cork did not move, but Aurelia laughed at Julian's antics. Truly, Bard had no need of a fool with this priest in his household!

"Oh, you make too much of too little!" she scoffed, the curious heat in her veins making her playful.

"Oh, yeah?" Julian grinned. "You're drinking as much of it as me—*you* open this one."

"I do not know the spell!"

Julian managed to look innocent. "What spell?"

Aurelia chuckled. "You will not trick me that easily into matching my powers against yours!" She shook a finger at an apparently astonished Julian. "You do not fool me with your jest!"

"What jest?"

"Pretending that you cannot conjure that cork out of the bottle in the blink of an eye!" Aurelia scoffed. "A powerful priest such as you. For shame!"

Marissa trilled the same odd laugh she had given when explaining the magic of the peephole to Aurelia. No one joined her laughter, or even acknowledged it.

Julian blinked and sent a glance to Bard.

Bard leaned forward and braced his elbows on his knees. "Priest?" he echoed quietly.

"Oh, surely anyone with their wits about them could see that Julian is your advisor! Who else would have the king's ear but a priest? Julian is certainly not a warrior, with that strange garb!" Aurelia chuckled to herself that they should pretend the truth was anything other than what it obviously was.

Silence filled the restaurant, but Aurelia was oblivious to the stares of her three companions. She drained the last of her wine and held out her goblet for more with a winning smile.

For fruit juice, it was quite good. A bit of a tang—probably the grapes had been tainted slightly during the shipping Bard talked about—but it was a flavor one could grow to like.

"If I concede that the powers Rome grants to its priests are far greater than imagined, would you open that cursed bottle and share its contents?"

Julian sat down with a thump, his grip loosened on the flagon of wine. He held her gaze as steadily as an owl. "I'm not a priest, Aurelia. I'm a lawyer."

Lawyer? There was a word that had no meaning for Aurelia—it must be simply some distinction between grades of priesthood.

"Call yourself what you will!" Aurelia waved off this qualification. "Let us have the wine." Aurelia dropped her voice and leaned closer to Julian, taking a confidential tone. "You know, for mere fruit juice, this wine has an effect not unlike mead."

"Mead? Dear God, you have drunk *mead*?" Marissa looked to be smothering a laugh. "Darling, I thought only rural heathens drank that stuff. Probably because they could not afford anything better."

Aurelia gazed sternly at the other woman. Her garb this evening was no less revealing, for all its apparent modesty. Marissa's ankles were on full display and her chausses emphasized the roundness of her rump in a most forward manner.

"I suppose," Aurelia said with all the hauteur she could summon, "that mead is beneath the fine tastes of an overly indulged whore like yourself."

"*Whore?*" Marissa blanched and her mouth dropped open before she bounded to her feet. "*Whore*? How dare you call me a whore?"

"Oh, I dare," Aurelia said smoothly. She eyed the emptiness of her goblet pointedly, then glanced to Julian. He seemed to be struggling not to laugh and had apparently forgotten the wine completely. "Though it matters little. The truth is painfully obvious to anyone who even glances at this travesty of a court."

"Well, I never—!"

"I should think you have," Aurelia retorted. "And often." She met the other woman's gaze with a serene smile and shrugged. "Why else would the king indulge you so freely?"

Julian began to laugh, but a hard light glittered in Marissa's eyes. "The *king*, well!" The whore laughed awkwardly and looked at Bard. "Where did you find her, darling? Under a rock?"

"Close to it," Bard commented evenly without turning to Marissa. "Why don't you tell us who you really are, Aurelia?"

Aurelia tried to sweep to her feet regally at the implication that her word was not to be believed, but stumbled instead.

Gods and goddesses, but this juice had an unexpected power!

She lifted her chin proudly all the same. "I am Aurelia, daughter of Hekod the Fifth, King of Dunhelm and Lord of Fyordskar over the sea, princess of the Royal House and sole heiress to the throne of Dunhelm." She met the invader's considering gaze squarely and arched a brow. "Who else could I possibly be?"

Bard glanced at a bound volume by his foot and then back to Aurelia, his brows pulling together in a frown.

"Anyone you can imagine, obviously," Marissa said tartly.

"Marissa, that's enough." Bard's voice was stern.

"Hardly!" Marissa snorted, and fired a lethal glance at Aurelia when there was no response. "Well, it's obvious that no one has any interest in *my* perspective about all of this!" She stormed toward the door, clearly expecting someone to stop her.

But Aurelia was snared by the intense green of Bard's concerned gaze and could not look away. They stared at each other, the whore's displeasure a distant annoyance.

The power of Bard's effect upon Aurelia was astonishing. She was sorely tempted to trust Dunhelm's new king, even knowing all she did about him.

Aurelia was vaguely aware that Marissa sniffed with displeasure before stalking through the portal.

"Good riddance," Julian muttered. He conquered the cork and splashed wine into all three goblets, taking a hearty swallow himself.

Bard leaned closer and Aurelia's heart began to pound. "Princess, you can tell me the truth, you know," he said in a sympathetic voice. His gaze was mesmerizing, his softly spoken words hypnotic.

Aurelia was horrified to find her will bending to mesh with his own. "But you know the truth!" she retorted. "Why else did you imprison me in the well?"

Bard laced his fingers together and held her regard, his voice low and authoritative. "No one imprisoned you, Aurelia. We simply found you in that room, the well, as you say. How did you get in?"

Aurelia did not know what to say to that.

Bard's tone was so gentle that a less worldly woman than herself might have been fooled into believing he cared for her welfare. "Aurelia, your father is not the king. . . ."

"He was, before you came," she said tightly.

Bard's lips thinned, but his tone did not change. "Did your father abandon you here at Dunhelm?"

Aurelia was appalled that he would try to twist the truth to leave her honorable father looking responsible. "No!" she retorted hotly. "My sire loves me! He would *never* abandon me. We are each all the other has left in this world!"

Bard's expression turned grim. "Did your father *die*, Aurelia?"

How could Bard not know her sire's fate?

Aurelia's heart leaped. Her father *had* escaped Bard's vengeance, no doubt with the aid of the old woman on the rocks.

Then her heart fell like a stone. Because Bard *knew* Hekod had evaded him. She was the one who had been fool enough to lead Bard to the sea caves! Aurelia groaned inwardly, hating that she found herself in a predicament of her own making yet again.

Clearly Bard thought Aurelia knew her father's hiding

place. That was why he was treating her so kindly. Oh, she had made a mess and a half of this!

And what else had she revealed this evening? Aurelia knew all too well that she had talked overmuch, but her recollection was already fogged.

Aurelia looked to the goblet of wine and suddenly understood what had loosened her unruly tongue.

The drink had been enchanted!

Baird stared into Aurelia's magnificent eyes, once again certain that her mind was whirling. He could almost hear the wheels turning—and wished desperately that he knew what she was thinking.

Julian chose that moment to end his contest with Aurelia.

The lawyer hesitated uncharacteristically in the act of taking a sip of Chianti. When Baird glanced his way, Julian wavered for a moment, his eyes rolled back, then he slid bonelessly to the floor.

Aurelia waved her goblet over her head, a flush not purely from victory staining her cheeks. "I win!" she crowed, and danced to her feet. "He could not face his own brew!"

Her change of mood was breathtakingly quick and Baird considered her uncertainly. Aurelia changed from woman to child in the blink of an eye—and usually right after she got that look of terror in her eyes.

Her strong response to the idea of her father being dead made Baird think he had hit a nerve. That Aurelia, who faced life full-out, couldn't bring herself to confront the idea of her father's death was obviously important.

She was such a strong person that her vulnerability over even one issue tugged at his heartstrings. Baird resolved that he should be more gentle with Aurelia in his search for the truth. If her father was dead, that wouldn't be easy for her to face.

And Baird was oddly determined to protect his princess from hurt.

A less-than-festive Julian groaned from the floor and his glass slipped from his limp fingers. It rolled across the floor, spilling its ruby contents, but the lawyer did not move.

Baird suddenly saw disaster in the making.

"The new tiles!" He swore and ducked his head under the table to wipe up the wine, Aurelia following suit. They bumped heads and she sat back on her heels with a giggle. She clapped a hand over her mouth, fell back on her butt with a thump, and watched him with twinkling eyes.

She was just so damned cute. Baird had to admit that he liked how enthusiastically Aurelia had met Julian's challenge and liked even better that she had beaten the lawyer soundly.

Julian would never live this down.

At least, if Baird had his way.

And if Baird could do anything about it, he'd have Aurelia's eyes sparkling routinely. Baird had to help Aurelia face the truth, however painful it might be.

But right now, he had to ease away the shadows he had unwittingly put in her eyes.

"What do you seek beneath the board?" she asked.

"I was looking to see where you hid all that pizza and wine." Baird met her gaze solemnly. "Are you sure you don't have a hollow leg?"

"Not me!" Aurelia laughed heartily, a far cry from the contrived trill that Marissa periodically let herself utter. "You have seen my legs enough to know the truth!"

Oh, that he had. Baird snuck a glance at her dancing toes and told himself that the heat in his veins was because of the wine.

"What about a dog?" he demanded with mock skepticism. "Have you been slipping all your pizza to some hungry mutt?"

"No! There are no dogs in your hall."

"Hmm." Baird stood and propped his hands on his hips, making a great show of looking around the room. He fixed a stern eye on Aurelia. "But you're too small to eat more than me and drink more than Julian, let alone at the same time. Are you *sure* you don't have big pockets in that dress?"

Aurelia scrambled to her feet and lifted her chin proudly. "Do you doubt the word of a Pictish princess?"

"No, just her capacity." Baird closed the distance between them, fighting against a playful smile. "Maybe I should check,'' he suggested wickedly and snatched at her.

"Oho! You will not touch me!" Aurelia danced away evasively, holding up her left hand to ward Baird off.

It worked.

Three delicate, very blue whorls uncoiled on Aurelia's left palm, the trio radiating from an ornate spiraled core. Each curve was as graceful as a fern in the spring forest. It almost reminded Baird of drawings of galaxies before he realized exactly where he had seen this pattern before.

It was in Talorc's book.

The hair on the back of Baird's neck rose right on cue.

"What's that?" he asked, and his voice was unusually strained.

Aurelia looked at her hand as though it were no big deal. "It is the mark of the onset of my courses and the pledge of my vows. Surely you have seen one like it before."

Oh, he had, but how could she know that? Baird refused to even look toward the book. He took a step backward, his gaze locked on the tattoo. An eerie tingle danced over his flesh.

It couldn't be a Pictish tattoo!

Baird must have drunk more than he thought he had to even be considering such a possibility! Anyone could have a tattoo made in any city in the world. It wasn't hard to do, and if Aurelia had wanted to play the Pictish princess with conviction, she might have deliberately chosen this design.

If nothing else, Aurelia had done her homework.

But all the logical explanations in the world couldn't undermine Baird's intuitive certainty that this was the real thing.

Which was not the way Baird thought at all. He wasn't intuitive, he didn't have any use for instinct, he certainly put no value in emotion. Only logic served a man well.

Even if logic was coming up a bit short in this circumstance. Maybe it wasn't Dunhelm that had cast a spell over him, after all.

Maybe it had been Aurelia.

His blood ran cold at the thought. "It can't be real," Baird argued, but there was no conviction in his voice.

"It most certainly is real," Aurelia scoffed. "I still recall the pain."

"Then why do it?"

Aurelia lifted her chin proudly now as though insulted. "I am half Viking blood, by my sire, and unafraid of anything laid before me. A Viking neither backs away from a challenge nor forgets obligation, nor leaves the field in defeat."

She cast a scathing glance at Julian, now snoring on the floor. "Tell your Roman priest that the power of the old ones is yet strong."

There was that talk about Julian being a priest again. Baird shifted his weight uneasily and refused to look at Talorc's book.

Aurelia would have strolled from the room regally, no doubt, but she stumbled on the hem of her dress. She did an intricate little two-step toward the stairs and she caught her balance before Baird could even move to help her.

Then she took a deep breath and pivoted to look Baird right in the eye. "And tell him that the spell he laid on the fruit juice was weak indeed."

Spell?

Before Baird could ask, Aurelia turned away. She must have done so a little too quickly, for she wobbled on her feet, then gripped the doorframe for a long moment. She crossed the foyer without looking back, the faint sound of a hiccup carrying to his ears.

Baird stood and stared after her for a long moment. She didn't know what wine or pizza was, she drank mead, she didn't understand indoor plumbing. Aurelia couldn't really be from the eighth century.

She just couldn't.

Baird eyed his snoring lawyer and realized that although one contestant had made it to her room under her own steam, the other one would need a little assistance.

And he was the only one left to provide it.

Eleven

Aurelia peeled off her clothes and cast them impatiently on the floor when she reached her room. She knew it was not her imagination that the whore's chemise nearly burned her skin. The woman's malevolence was powerful enough to have a life of its own.

The moonlight was spilling through the window in her chambers and Aurelia pressed against the clear pane to look. The moon was waxing toward full.

It had been the last new moon before the Moon of Eostre when Bard had attacked Dunhelm, she remembered. And the plants showed that it was still early spring, she could tell by the growth around her.

Aurelia guessed that she had slept for at least seven nights. Which could only mean that the priest *had* drugged her.

And that his power to see great buildings rise from the ground was beyond anything Aurelia had ever seen before.

But she had bested him in a simple contest of will. Aurelia rubbed her temple in confusion. Clearly Julian had bewitched this wine to prove the strength of his power over hers.

But he had fallen prey to his own spell. It was a sign of incredible incompetence. Just like his spell on her room door.

Though both were odd contrasts with the other signs of his power.

And where had her sire gone?

The moonlight splayed across the tapestry on the chamber

floor, painting an inviting square of silver light. Aurelia tugged the draperies back and made the square into a large rectangle.

Aurelia's second gift was the ability to see her way most clearly when she beckoned prophetic dreams to her sleep. On this night, in Bard's dangerous den, she needed that gift's aid more than she ever had in all her days.

Aurelia stood in the rays of the glowing moon, her flesh bare to its cool light. She closed her eyes and began to chant the words her mother had taught her from the cradle.

The chant surrounded and embraced her, lifting her above the limitations of the earth. Deep in a hidden corner of her mind, Aurelia reached into a deep well of shadows and pulled to light the dreaming stone.

Aurelia felt its smoothness as though she held it within her hands, knew that it was magically wrought of the spittle of countless snakes. In her mind's eye, she stroked the veined red and gray of the stone, and urged its power into herself.

The stone began to glow. Aurelia felt its strength build within her, felt the tide rise in her favor, and smiled with certainty that this night's dream would be powerful in its insight.

In the peril confronting her, Aurelia needed no less. She tipped back her head, stretched her arms wide to embrace the moon's silver light, and boldly beckoned to the Dreaming.

Baird tossed restlessly in his sleep. He saw himself descending the stone stairs, cutting back the thorns as he had this very morning.

But Baird *never* dreamed.

Never had, never would. Dreams were for other people. Even in sleep, a part of his mind pointed out logical inconsistencies.

But the dream continued, all the same, apparently unaware that it was unwelcome on this foreign turf.

Baird noticed suddenly that the light was different than it had been that morning. He saw the flaming torch held high in his own hand, the golden firelight dancing off every surface and making intriguing shadows. The night pressed against him from all sides.

And despite himself, his attention was snared.

Baird caught a glimpse of a long, full ostrich feather bobbing in his peripheral vision, and knew it must adorn his hat. A long sword with an elaborate hand guard bumped against his leg. His feet, when he looked, were shod in high, cuffed leather boots.

He had stepped into a *Three Musketeers* movie.

The cold shadows of the stairwell rose higher and higher around him, the damp smell of the underground chamber filled his nostrils. He looked up, just before ducking beneath the portal as he had this morning, but was shocked to find the sky overhead a star-studded bowl.

It had been raining and gray this morning.

To Baird's further surprise, the stone portal before him was slightly ajar. This wasn't the same at all.

The dream Baird slipped through the doorway cautiously, blinking in the shadows and shivering in the chill sheltered within. He stepped forward, slowly at first, holding the torch this way and that. His hand was on the hilt of his sword.

Baird could see the silhouette of Aurelia's sleeping form. She breathed slowly and deeply, the sound a soft whisper in the dead silence of the well. The lady slumbered like a corpse, the flickering light giving the impression that her lips moved ever so slightly.

Baird drew nearer to Aurelia's side, feeling the same weird magnetic pull he had experienced this morning. His heart thundered in his ears with the audacity of what he meant to do.

Aurelia lay undisturbed as Baird reached her side. The musty smell of the chamber enveloped him, the sweetly familiar perfume of Aurelia's flesh rose to tease his nostrils. He held the torch high, seeing the way her delicate hands were folded across her chest, and felt the satisfaction of a man who had reached his goal.

What goal?

Gemdelovely Gemdelee. Should her true love kiss her, his bride she will be.

The strange phrase made Baird toss and turn in his sleep, as though he would tear free of his mind's games.

But the dream Baird was undeterred. His hand came to rest

on the stone beside her hip. Baird had the same sense of pow-
erlessness he had felt this morning. He was startled to see his
hand garbed in heavy green leather and lace spilling from his
sleeve. In his mind's eye, he bent over the sleeping woman,
his heart racing.

He was going to kiss her.

Baird's attention fixed on the shadowed silhouette of her
sculpted lips. His mouth was only a finger's breadth from hers
when a bellow erupted immediately behind him.

Baird straightened with alarm. He pivoted on his heel and
saw the flash of the knife just before he was struck. Baird
dropped the torch with a cry and hauled his own sword from
its scabbard, too late to make a difference.

A searing pain erupted in his chest. Baird looked down in
disbelief, the torch still burning fitfully from the stone floor.

A knife with an ornately chased grip was buried to its hilt
between Baird's ribs.

And his own blood ran in a dark, sleek current to puddle
on the stone floor. A clatter of footsteps betrayed his attackers'
flight, then there was no sound beyond the lady's faint breath
and his own labored breathing.

A strangled cry broke from Baird's lips, then he roared in
mingled pain and disappointment. He tried to run toward
moonlight and assistance, but his legs refused to support him.

Baird fell to his knees and fought to crawl out of the well,
but without success. His limp fingers touched the growing pool
of blood as though he could not believe it was his own. The
room began to fade to black from all sides.

He had failed.

Again.

No!

Baird sat bolt upright in his bed, shaking from head to toe.
The sweat was running down his back in a cold river. His
heart hammered, his breathing was labored, and his fingers
rose instinctively to touch the burning of his lethal wound.

But there was no ragged hole in his chest, much less an
ornate knife.

Baird swallowed his fear with difficulty. He ran his fingers across his unblemished flesh and breathed a shuddering sigh.

There was no knife. He had not been attacked.

He wasn't dying.

He wasn't even bleeding. Baird took a deep, steadying breath and heard it rush out of his lungs.

He was in his room, alone, safe in his new hotel.

And outside his windows, the moonlight toyed with the incessant waves of the sea.

Baird couldn't help rising from his bed. There was no way he would sleep now. He shoved a hand through his hair, drawn to the window by some force he could not explain. His gaze sought the shadows shrouding the steps he had cleared only this morning.

Nothing moved on the resort grounds. Baird could see the outlines of the briars and barely detect the shadow of the descending stairs.

Baird hadn't known Aurelia was there this morning—he *couldn't* have known she was there. He had just wanted to uncover Dunhelm's secrets because Dunhelm was old. And he had found a gorgeous if unbalanced woman that even now he felt compelled to protect.

Mr. Responsibility, that was Baird.

Baird had always loved the challenge of untangling a mystery, and Aurelia was an enigma and a half. His interest in her was perfectly logical, if he thought it through. She was beautiful and beguiling, a double whammy for a red-blooded man who loved mysteries. Baird almost believed his own explanation.

He looked back at the tangled sheets on the bed and swallowed awkwardly.

Almost.

Baird tasted again the agony of his failure and couldn't explain its source, much less his certainty that it was not the first time he had been here.

Oddly enough, Baird's gut demanded that he go to Aurelia right now and make sure that she was all right. It made no sense at all. She would be asleep!

As he should be.

Baird paced the length of the room and back. What *had*

Aurelia been doing in that well? How had she gotten in there without disturbing the briars? There must be another entrance. . . .

But Baird knew he had seen no other entry point to the stone chamber. He looked to the right, pressing his hot face against the cool glass, knowing her room was three doors down the hall. But he couldn't see Aurelia's room from this vantage point. Of course not! The wing was built perfectly straight.

Gemdelovely Gemdelee. Should her true love kiss her, his bride she will be.

Bride. Baird wasn't the marrying kind, he knew that without a doubt. Only one other woman had kept him awake nights with desire, one other woman with plans for marriage.

And that had been nothing compared to this. Maybe that was what had prompted his nightmare.

Maybe he shouldn't have had so much Chianti.

Aurelia sat up in her room and watched the moon climb higher as she puzzled over what she had witnessed.

Why had the dream come from another's perspective?

Whose perspective had it been? Who had come to her while she slept? Why did she feel he had come more than once? If only he had awakened her and she could have witnessed the truth!

And what did the name Gemdelovely Gemdelee have to do with anything at all?

Aurelia frowned. The Dreaming was supposed to provide clarity, not more questions. It was clear there was more at work here than she had guessed.

Her head ached with the aftermath of the wine's enchantment and Aurelia could think no more. What she needed was a good night's sleep, for morning would undoubtedly bring some answers her way.

Perhaps there would be something better to eat in Bard's hall than there had been on this night. Reassured at the prospect, Aurelia burrowed beneath the duvet and was asleep as soon as her head hit the pillow.

• • •

Baird was feeling far from his best the next morning.

Chianti had more of a bite than he remembered. That was the only possible explanation for his headache. It certainly couldn't have anything to do with his nightmare.

Or his restlessness afterward.

It was indicative of how he was feeling that Elizabeth's coffee didn't taste half bad. There is nothing more frightening to someone who relies on a good cup of java to start their engine than the thin instant coffee offered in Britain.

Baird sipped and struggled not to groan.

What he needed was a couple of aspirin.

"There you are, Mr. Beauforte!" Elizabeth erupted from the little nook that she had made her own with a perkiness that Baird could not have returned to save his life.

Elizabeth was a woman in her midfifties whose hips showed a lifelong love of simple hearty food and whose laugh lines indicated her merry good nature.

She was also as much of a morning person as Baird was not. Elizabeth reminded him of his fifth foster mother.

"Nothing like a good hot breakfast to get a man going in the morning!" she declared cheerfully, and bustled about, setting the table with alarming efficiency.

Even watching her made his headache worse.

Baird shoved his hand through his hair as Elizabeth fixed him with a bright gaze. "Will you be starting with oatmeal this morning, Mr. Beauforte?"

"No, not today, Elizabeth. Maybe just the coffee. . . ."

"Mr. Beauforte! Why, you can't be eating so poorly in my kitchen, even if it is only my kitchen for a wee while." Elizabeth waved off any potential objection before it could be uttered and trotted back to her lair. "You just sit right there and I'll have a fine Scottish breakfast ready for you in no time at all."

Baird sipped grimly, and true to her word, Elizabeth was back in record time. With a flourish, she slid a plate loaded to overflowing with eggs, bacon, and sausages onto the table in front of him. Baird eyed the three eggs and what looked like half a pound of meat with doubt.

Never mind the six slices of wafer-thin toast.

His stomach rolled in protest, but he knew that anything less than cleaning the plate would hurt Elizabeth's feelings. Even though she was paid, it was awfully good of Elizabeth to come all the way up here every morning, just to fix breakfast for himself and Julian.

"You're sure you're not wanting oatmeal this morning, Mr. Beauforte?" Elizabeth asked, her ruddy face wreathed with concern.

"No, really, Elizabeth, this is more than enough." Baird patted his abdomen and smiled. "I'm not usually a big breakfast eater."

She looked unconvinced. "First meal of the day, Mr. Beauforte, and the most important of the lot. You should see Talorc put the sausages away."

Ah, so there was more than himself and Julian benefiting from Elizabeth's culinary efforts.

"Really, Elizabeth, this is plenty. I don't even know that I'll be able to finish this."

She leaned closer and twisted her hands in her apron as her voice dropped. "Mr. Beauforte, are you feeling well? It's not right and proper for a man to be greeting the morning without an appetite. Talorc, now, he'll eat twice this and then some if I don't put a stop to it!"

It looked like Baird was going to need an excuse.

"Well, to tell the truth, I didn't sleep well last night," he confessed, and Elizabeth clucked her tongue.

"I've just the thing for you, Mr. Beauforte!" She bustled back to the nook where her hot plate and toaster were rigged up and emerged victorious with a small jar. "Some of my sister Mary's marmalade will have you set straight in no time."

The marmalade jar in question landed on the table with a thump.

"Now, Mr. Beauforte, if you don't mind me saying so, tonight when you go to bed, you take a bit of Mary's marmalade and you drop in a wee dram of whisky."

The thought made Baird's stomach roar an objection, but Elizabeth nodded sagely at his glance. "You try it, sir, and mark my word, in the morning, you'll be fit as a fiddle."

Baird couldn't help but wonder what Mary put in her marmalade.

"Fit as a fiddle?" Talorc echoed cheerfully from the doorway. "Elizabeth, are you advising folks to be destroying good Scottish whisky again? How many times have I been telling you that's *blasphemy*? Trust a woman to be spoiling the only decent pleasure left to a man!"

Elizabeth straightened and fired a scowl across the room that would have sent a lesser man running for cover. Talorc puffed up his chest and glared back at her, his blue eyes dancing merrily.

Not only were they both disgustingly cheerful morning people, but the pair of them obviously loved to spar.

"Talorc! If you're thinking that you can sniff around my skirts and get yourself another breakfast, then you've another think coming, sir! Off with you and see to Mr. Beauforte's hedgerows. Mr. Beauforte isn't paying you to eat every speck of food in his larder. Go on! Get on with you!"

When Talorc took a tentative step toward the kitchen nook, Elizabeth let loose a cry of protest. She snatched up her broom and chased Talorc back out into the foyer.

"Talorc Sinclair, you're no better than a stray hound, coming into my kitchen begging for scraps. . . ."

Baird shook his head and grimaced as he took another swig of coffee. The eggs weren't going anywhere without his help.

What he wouldn't give for a decent cup of coffee. Another fortifying sip and Baird picked up his fork.

Julian strolled into the room in full sartorial splendor, his olive double-breasted suit accented surprisingly well by his turmeric tie.

But despite his dapper dress, Julian looked the way Baird felt.

"Oh, my head," he groaned. "Have you got any aspirin?"

Baird touched his knife to the marmalade jar. "That's the only cure-all around."

"Jam. Refined sugar. That stuff will kill you." Julian dropped into a chair and eyed Baird's plate with a grimace. "Looks like you've got everything but the squeal."

"Careful, careful." Baird wagged his knife at his friend,

immeasurably pleased to find that he wasn't suffering alone. "If Elizabeth sees you, she'll be loading up the frying pan."

Julian shuddered. "Won't she just. Why can't the woman understand the simple fact that I'm a vegetarian?"

"It's unnatural, laddie." Baird tried his Scottish accent, but it was as bad as ever. They both winced, then Baird poked his fork at his legal counsel. "She's trying to convert you. Or save you."

"And not successfully either way. There's enough grease on that plate to lube a midsize car."

"It's not that bad." Two slices of something dark lurked beside the eggs. Baird couldn't guess what it was, resolved it was some kind of sausage, and cut a slice.

Definitely sausage.

And kind of good. Baird cut another slice.

"Ooooh, Mr. Preston! There you are, looking as splendid as ever, our gentleman from Savile Row!" Elizabeth beamed from the doorway, her hands rubbing together in anticipation of more cooking to be done. "Will you be having eggs and sausages? The butcher has brought us some lovely haggis this morning."

Baird froze midchew, suddenly certain of what he was eating.

His gaze flicked to Julian, who was not hiding his laughter very successfully. "And how *is* the haggis this morning, Mr. Beauforte?" he asked wickedly.

Twelve

Baird wasn't quite so badly impaired that he would miss such an opening.

"Very, *very* good," he said enthusiastically, then turned to their expectant cook. "You know, Elizabeth, I'm certain that Julian would just love this haggis. We might make a meat-eater of him yet!"

"Oh, truly!" Elizabeth smiled with delight at the prospect. "It'll just be a moment, Mr. Julian! You stay right there!"

"I only want coffee!" Julian wailed as she disappeared into her nook. He glared at Baird. "*You* get to eat the haggis."

"Mmm, are you sure?" Baird granted his friend a knowing look. "If I eat yours, she'll be convinced that you loved it."

"And if I don't touch it, she'll be insulted." Julian gritted his teeth. "Thank you very much."

"What are friends for?" Baird was feeling much livelier as he refilled his coffee cup.

Elizabeth trotted back to the table with a cup and saucer and a second steaming thermos of coffee. One thing she had learned about "her Americans" was their need for copious quantities of caffeine.

Regardless of its quality. Julian rolled his eyes and poured as Elizabeth trotted away.

"She's in her element," Baird whispered with a wink.

"Like I wasn't last night. Guess I lost that bet, hmmm?" Julian took a swig of coffee as Baird nodded.

"Oh, yeah."

"Well, the consolation prize will be seeing the state of your princess this morning," the lawyer said grimly. "If we even see her at all."

"I bet you will."

Julian glanced darkly at Baird. "No more bets, at least until I get rid of the hangover."

"Don't underestimate her. She wasn't very drunk when she went to bed."

"Mmm. All that vile pizza probably soaked up the booze. Or she's got a cast-iron gut." Julian shrugged and took a sip of his coffee. "Too bad you can't say as much for her sanity."

Baird frowned, unable to explain his desire to defend this woman who thought so little of his character. "She's had a shock, apparently from losing her father."

"She's wacko." Julian waved his cup for emphasis.

"I don't think so." Baird's frown deepened. "It's all very logical, if you start from her premise."

"Which would be?"

"That she's the daughter of Hekod the Fifth."

"That would be Hekod the Fifth, King of Dunhelm and Lord of Fyordskar." Julian grimaced. "Nobody I've ever heard of."

Baird indicated the book Talorc had loaned him with one finger. "Hekod was an eighth-century Viking who conquered Dunhelm and married a Pictish woman."

Julian glanced at the book, then back at Baird. "You don't see any *logical* problems with her thinking her father is over a thousand years old?"

Baird shrugged. "If you start from that premise, her behavior makes sense. The clothing, her not understanding the taps in her room, not knowing what wine or pizza is. It's all logical—an eighth-century person wouldn't understand these things."

Julian leaned forward and his eyes gleamed. "An eighth-century person would be really, really dead by now."

Baird grinned despite himself. "I know, I know, she's *not* an eighth-century person, obviously, but she *thinks* she is, and everything she does follows from that."

Julian looked skeptical. He coughed. "I hate to spoil this theory that Aurelia is perfectly sane except for one comparatively minor delusion"—he widened his eyes to show his judgment of that—"but only a *lunatic* would accept the premise that they were actually over a thousand years old."

Baird stabbed a sausage. "Yeah, well, there is a little glitch in the system there. She and her father must have been really close. I wish we could help her somehow."

"A little good PR for the grand opening?"

Baird scowled. "This has nothing to do with PR."

"Wow!" Julian shook his head. "I must be hungover. That sounded like the second time in less than a day that you've said 'Forget PR.' What's that, now, twice in your life?"

"Laugh if you want," Baird growled. "She needs someone."

"Doesn't have to be you."

Baird frowned, not liking the idea of anyone else helping Aurelia, though he couldn't explain why to his own satisfaction. "Dunhelm is my property, which makes this my responsibility."

"And never was there a nobler impulse." Julian drank his coffee thoughtfully. "She certainly is entertaining, I'll give you that. I'd pay good money to see her bait Marissa again."

Baird fired a glance at his legal counsel. "You two really have to get over that."

Julian's answering glare was just as sharp. "Well, I don't see that happening before you get married to someone else and put an end to Marissa's ambitions."

Baird felt his expression turn sour at another mention of marriage so soon after his nightmare. "Marriage is not an agenda item. You know that."

"Then neither is Marissa and me settling our differences."

Before Baird could comment, Elizabeth gasped from behind them. "Oh, and who might this little Gemdelovely be?"

Baird choked on his haggis. His fork clattered to the table as he spun in shock.

It was Aurelia, of course.

Baird's heart thumped. Aurelia was dressed the same way as the night before, although this time her hair hung in one long braid down her back. She looked disgustingly well rested.

"Bright-eyed and bushy tailed," Baird muttered.

"Fourth foster mother?"

"Fifth."

"Mmm. Mrs. Morning Sunshine, didn't you call her?" Julian drank deeply of his coffee.

Didn't it just figure that Aurelia showed no ill effects after the night before? Baird forced himself to turn back to his breakfast, retrieved his fork, and determinedly ignored Julian's obvious inquisitiveness about his response.

"Good morning. But my name is Aurelia, not Gemdelovely."

Elizabeth laughed. "Oh, lass, that's what we call all the pretty lasses up this way. On account of the story, as you know."

"The story?"

Baird's ears pricked with curiosity, but he wasn't going to turn around again. He ploughed through his eggs purposefully.

"Oh, you'll have to be having one of the old ones tell the tale, for they know it best." Elizabeth rubbed her hands together in anticipation. "*Aurelia*! Such a lovely name! Could I be getting you a wee breakfast, lass?"

"Yes, please! I am quite hungry."

Hungry? Baird met Julian's astonished gaze across the table, certain his own was just as surprised.

"She must have a tapeworm," Julian declared, and buried his nose in his coffee cup. Baird chuckled midsip at the unexpected conclusion and snorted some of his coffee.

"Serves you right," Julian muttered unsympathetically. *"Haggis."*

"Well, then, lass, you'll be wanting a good hot bowl of oatmeal before your eggs. With bacon or sausages or both? Would you like a bit of haggis?"

"Must I choose?"

"Of course not, lass, there's plenty to eat! There's coffee on the table, lass, and I'll be right along. Don't you fret, Mr. Preston, I've not forgotten you!"

Elizabeth scampered away, quite beside herself with excitement.

"How's your head?" Julian asked wryly as Aurelia came to the table.

She blinked in confusion at him and settled into a seat. "My head?"

"From the wine."

Aurelia looked at Baird, her eyes wide. "I do not understand."

"Oh, no." Baird winced at the childishly high pitch of her voice and waved his fork at her impatiently. "None of that today. You may be nuts, but we know you're not stupid."

He pushed the plate away, the better part of his breakfast untouched, and growled into his coffee cup. "Don't play that game with me today, princess."

Aurelia frowned and to Baird's relief, her voice lowered slightly. "But I still do not understand."

"The wine!" Julian confirmed expansively. "We drank a lot of it. We were *drunk*! Falling-down drunk. Doesn't your head hurt? Mine is killing me."

"You are a fragile sort for a priest," Aurelia said scathingly. "A sore head from *fruit* juice." She rolled her eyes, then examined Baird's abandoned plate with obvious interest. "Are you going to eat that?"

"No. Do you want it?"

Aurelia tucked in as soon as Baird pushed the plate her way. She used neither knife nor fork, to his surprise. She ate even the eggs with her fingers by sliding each one carefully onto a piece of toast. She was quite graceful about it and both men watched with fascination as she methodically cleaned the plate.

Baird had to hand it to her, she never missed a beat.

"What is the matter with you?" Aurelia asked, looking from one to the other. "Have neither of you learned to eat with any grace?"

Before Baird could summon an answer to that, Elizabeth appeared at his elbow, her hands buried in thick plaid potholders.

"Oh, lass! I've just brought your oatmeal and you'll be all filled up!" Elizabeth was obviously crestfallen, but Aurelia accepted the steaming bowl appreciatively.

"It smells wonderful!"

"And here's a cup for your coffee, lass. Mr. Preston, here's your oatmeal, as well." Elizabeth folded her hands together, her eyes hopeful. "Unless you'll be wanting tea? Talorc always has a hot cup of tea in the morning."

Aurelia passed a glance over the woman's expression, then smiled. "I would love to have this tea," she said graciously, and Elizabeth, transported with delight, raced back to her kettle.

Aurelia looked to the men and shrugged philosophically. "It was of such import to her," she murmured, then slid a spoon into Elizabeth's trademark oatmeal.

It was so thick that Baird was convinced they could use it for mortar on the brickwork. He had only faced it with success once and was not entirely sure that it was edible.

But Aurelia's oatmeal disappeared in record time. Julian was slower but when Aurelia cast a longing glance at his bowl, he possessively pulled it closer. "You can have my haggis," he muttered, and Aurelia's eyes lit up.

She considered Baird for a long moment. "Your charm is markedly lacking this morn," she commented finally, then tilted her head to watch him like a perky sparrow. "Are you irked with me?"

"He's just not a morning kind of guy," Julian confided. "His bark is definitely worse than his bite." He eyed his employer. "Though today, he's barking—and looking—a bit worse than usual."

"Thanks for the character reference."

"Least I could do." Julian smirked.

"I thought perhaps you might have slept poorly," Aurelia suggested quietly. She watched Baird steadily, her blue gaze seeming to see more than Baird would have liked.

He actually felt like fidgeting.

"Were you troubled by dreams last night, King Bard?" she asked softly, her eyes wide. "I had a most *unusual* one, myself."

Baird's heart lurched, but her fathomless eyes revealed nothing. How could she know?

She couldn't!

Baird jabbed a finger through the air at the woman he knew was the source of his troubles. "Let's get one thing straight, princess. I *don't* dream."

"But everyone dreams," she protested. "It is a natural part of sleep. . . ."

Baird impaled her with his sternest look, the one he had perfected in the boardroom and which sent most men running for cover.

Aurelia didn't even flinch.

"*I* don't dream," Baird insisted. "Never have. Never will. And that's final."

Aurelia frowned, but Elizabeth brought in the teapot at that moment. Although Aurelia looked unimpressed at first sip of the beverage, once she had dropped a third of the sugar bowl's contents into her cup, she seemed to like it more.

Baird told himself that he was irritable not only because it was morning, but that his head hurt and, just to add insult to injury, the one who had drunk the most showed the fewest ill effects.

Maybe it was just his headache making him more grumpy than usual. He sipped his coffee, well aware that he had affected the mood at the table.

Just the mention of that dream had Baird all jangled up inside once more. Dammit, this wasn't like him and he wasn't going to put up with it. He was going to find Hekod today, if only to end his obligation to that man's daughter.

But first, Aurelia had to get something to wear. There would be hell to pay if Marissa didn't get her Karan dress back. Baird would rather that happened sooner than later.

To Baird's amazement, Aurelia consumed the better part of all three breakfasts before sitting back with a sigh. She surveyed the men and patted her stomach with contentment, treating them both to a sunny smile.

Baird drained his cup and pushed impatiently to his feet. "Come on, princess. Let's get into town and find you some clothes."

The cab Baird had ordered was waiting in the circular driveway in front of the hotel. It was one of the boxy black cabs typically found in London, but looking more than a little the worse for wear. Garth, its driver and owner, leaned against the bumper, reading a tabloid and smoking his pipe.

There was a rumor that Garth, disenchanted with the London scene around 1970, had headed north with his cab, vowing not to stop until he found someplace simpatico. Whether he had chosen this island or simply run out of any more Britain to explore was unclear, but here he had remained.

It could be said that Garth matched his cab, for both were a conglomeration of the unexpected. The once all-black cab had gotten a brilliant yellow front quarter panel at some point in its life and the front bumper, which should have been chrome, had been removed to make space for an electric winch. The muffler and tailpipe hung low enough that they scraped the ground at regular intervals, and obviously nothing more than divine Providence kept them attached to the car.

Garth had confided once that the sheep were terrified at the sight of his cab.

Baird couldn't blame them.

Garth's clothes were as mismatched as his cab, but he was a genial sort beneath his crusty exterior. He had a penchant for wearing a blue plaid shirt with orange shorts that were an unwelcome reminder of the psychedelic sixties. The ensemble coordinated with a pair of green Wellington boots, none of it varying, regardless of the weather.

It was frightening to think that a man could have more than one pair of shorts like that. Baird didn't want to know.

Garth's carrot-orange hair always resembled a severely abused steel-wool pad and his eyebrows seemed to crawl across his brow with a life of their own. His nose was permanently red and it was no real surprise that the phone number for Garth's Cab Livery was exactly the same as that of the Boar and Thistle Pub.

Garth had taken it upon himself to give his conveyance the decoration he thought it deserved as the island's sole taxi for hire. The inside had originally been upholstered in crimson vinyl, but now that interior had seen better days. It was patched with mismatched strips and lavished with mementos of Prince Charles's wedding to Lady Diana Spencer.

A cross-stitched cushion illustrating the glorious event was sealed in plastic for all time and held a position of honor in the center of the backseat. Stickers and posters covered the interior walls of the cab.

Aurelia's eyes rounded like saucers when she climbed in, and Baird couldn't blame her. He'd had a good look himself when he'd first stepped into Garth's cab.

Garth started the vehicle and the pair of commemorative teaspoons hanging from the rearview mirror shuddered. The cab coughed, farted, wheezed, then settled into an approximation of a consistent hum.

"Where you off to today, guv?" Garth came complete with a diluted variant of a Cockney accent.

"Just into town." Baird leaned forward as the car slid into gear with a whine. He thought he heard Aurelia gasp, but then, he had been surprised that this dilapidated cab could actually move, as well. He braced his elbows against the back of the front seat. "Is there a women's clothing store there?"

Garth whistled through his teeth. "You'll be needing to see Marge, I'll wager. She's the only one as follows the trends."

Baird shrugged, hoping that Marge had something worth buying. "Then Marge's place it is."

Aurelia caught her breath when Garth cleared the resort's new gates and accelerated to a dazzling twenty-five miles an hour. The sheep ran in all directions, fleeing in terror before Garth and his trusty cab.

Aurelia looked as spooked as the sheep. She gripped the armrest as though she were seeing her life pass before her eyes.

"Don't be afraid," he said in a low voice that Garth wouldn't be able to hear over the grumbling engine. "He's not that bad a driver."

"I am afraid of nothing!" Aurelia retorted, though her death grip on the armrest said otherwise.

"Right. Half Viking. I remember."

Baird settled back in his seat and wondered whether Aurelia had only been used to horses and carts. He certainly hadn't seen a lot of cars out here and this might just be another unfamiliar experience for her.

At any rate, shopping would cheer her up.

It worked for women everywhere.

The strange chariot carried them away from Dunhelm and around the curve of the coastline. After Aurelia gave up looking for the horses that pulled the chariot, she was amazed at the smooth black surface of the road that had recently been a track in the dirt, riddled with ruts. The only thing familiar about the scene before her was the slope of the land and the hundreds of foolish sheep, bolting in every direction.

Aurelia attributed this to Julian's magic, because she could think of no other reasonable explanation.

The chariot lurched to a halt in the midst of a cluster of stone homes that Aurelia did not recognize. There had been no dwellings here, she knew very well, though these looked soundly rooted to the spot.

A stone cross rose high in the middle of the cobbled square, a reminder of the ascendency of Julian's faith. It was amazing that so much could have been constructed so quickly, let alone that it could look so aged.

Aurelia wondered again how much time could have passed while Julian's herbs kept her sleeping.

Could it have been an entire year? Her father could be far across the sea if that were so!

Aurelia watched with fascination as Bard doled out pieces of vellum to the driver. That remarkably garbed man grinned from ear to ear as he closed his hand over the notes.

"Thank you, guv! You'll know where to find me when you're set to go back!"

Bard nodded, flicking a wry glance Aurelia's way. The driver winked, left his chariot where it stood, and trotted toward a building wrought of dark wood with wattle and daub between.

The Boar and Thistle, read the sign, though Aurelia could make no sense of that.

Aurelia glanced in Bard's direction to find him looking thoughtful. "Why is he so glad to have vellum from you? Is it scarce in your kingdom?"

Bard glanced at her in what must have been surprise. "It's money. I was paying him for the ride."

Aurelia frowned. "With *used* vellum? What merit is it to him with its surface already covered?"

Bard studied her for a long moment. "It really is like stepping back into the Middle Ages around here, isn't it?" he murmured finally.

Aurelia did not understand the reference.

"It's money, paper money." Bard pulled out a couple of banknotes and she studied them with curiosity. "I guess you still barter for most things."

Aurelia looked up in surprise. "Barter?"

"You know, trade some of this for some of that. My oats for your hay. That kind of thing."

Aurelia shook her head. "We grow our own oats and hay. You must have found all the stores when you took Dunhelm."

Why would Bard pretend he knew nothing of this?

"What about your clothes?"

Gods and goddesses! Did the man understand nothing of domestic matters? What kind of upbringing had he had?

"We have sheep, as you well know," Aurelia explained patiently. "And my father employed many spinners and weavers to make cloth, dyers to color it and seamstresses to make garments of it. Were I not nobly born, I would know how to do it myself."

Bard snapped his fingers as though remembering something. "What about that cloak you told us about? The one made of the fabric your father brought from somewhere . . ."

"It was samite. From Micklegarth. We cannot make such fine cloth here and it was a treasure to be cherished." Aurelia's eyes narrowed suddenly as she realized that her cloak had disappeared.

Had the whore taken it for her own?

"Right. Wherever that is."

Aurelia was incredulous. "You do not know of Micklegarth?"

"No." Bard shrugged, looking untroubled by the stunning inadequacy of his education that admission revealed.

"How could anyone know so little of the world?" Aurelia

demanded. "Even I have had enough teaching to know Mick-legarth!"

Bard looked grim again. "Let's just say we've had enough of this colonial stuff, all right? I've had a perfectly good education, even with the remarkable omission of your Mickle-garth."

Aurelia folded her arms across her chest, unconvinced of that.

Bard shoved one hand through his hair. "My point is that *wherever* Micklegarth is, your father must have bought that samite stuff there."

"Bought?" Aurelia arched a brow skeptically. "No Viking exchanges hard-won coin for whatever he desires." She waggled the banknotes at him. "Nor even used vellum."

Bard's brow darkened. "You don't really expect me to believe that your father is a *Viking*, do you?"

"No longer," Aurelia conceded. "But he went a-viking when he was a young man, as does every man worth his salt." She glanced at Bard consideringly. "Did you not go a-viking in your youth?"

"I'm not that old."

Aurelia shrugged. "Old enough to be done with such things."

Bard's lips tightened. "I went to college." At Aurelia's blank look, he continued. "School."

"But your tutor did not teach you of Micklegarth!" He was lying and Aurelia did not care whether he knew that she knew it. "All men go a-viking."

Bard grimaced and shook his head. "No one does that anymore."

Aurelia was unconvinced. Any inadequacies in his upbringing did not reflect the world as she knew it.

"Perhaps not in *your* sorry kingdom!" she maintained archly. "*My* relations do precisely thus and with great success." She turned to sweep away, not at all certain where she was going, and could not resist a parting shot. "Of course, they are truly men, not mere barbarians."

And she turned to stalk away.

Aurelia did not get far before Bard caught at her elbow and

pulled her to a halt. His piercing gaze locked on hers and Aurelia braced herself against his ability to read her thoughts. "Wait a minute. Your relatives can't be Vikings!"

Aurelia tossed her hair, proud of her mixed descent. "Of course they are!"

"You mean they're from Scandinavia," Bard corrected. "They have Viking ancestry, but there aren't actually Vikings anymore."

His words recalled Aurelia to her senses. What was she thinking? She would destroy any chance her cousins had of surprising him with their attack!

"Of course, you are right," she said hastily. "I have no Viking relatives." She giggled foolishly. "Indeed, I have no relatives at all! They are all dead, except for my sire."

Aurelia pivoted and marched quickly down the street. Bard seemed to have rooted to the spot behind her and she hoped desperately that he was not seriously considering what she had said in error.

Had her fickle tongue betrayed her relations' plans?

Thirteen

~

Aurelia became aware as she walked that many eyes were on them. Behind lacy curtains and in shadowed doorways, people had paused to watch their arrival and discussion. Even now, heads were bending together and Aurelia heard the whispers begin.

She wondered whether they were calling her the king's new whore and felt her cheeks heat.

Stones crunched as Bard strode up behind Aurelia and he caught up her elbow with a proprietary gesture. "I thought we had that all straightened out," he growled. "No more playing dumb."

Aurelia lifted her chin proudly. She tried desperately to think of something to say and failed.

Bard, apparently undeterred by her silence, steered her into an adjacent building. Bells tinkled as he opened the door—obviously a crude copy of Julian's alarm—and she knew they would be caught as intruders.

"You cannot simply barge into people's homes!" she hissed, and tried to step back into the street.

Bard determinedly pushed her forward. A slender older woman inside the home watched the byplay with interest and Aurelia's cheeks burned even more hotly. Bard smiled for the woman with all his usual charm.

"It's a store," he muttered through his teeth. "Anyone can come in here."

"A store?"

"A shop. Where a merchant does business." His voice was gritty with impatience. "Where they sell their merchandise."

Understanding dawned. "Oh! There was once a merchant who brought his wares to Dunhelm on his back," Aurelia whispered, her gaze dancing over the goods displayed. "But my sire oft told of the merchant's stalls in Micklegarth."

Baird breathed a sigh of relief. "Right. Just like that."

"May I help you?" the woman asked.

Bard loosened his grip on Aurelia. "You must be Marge. I'm Baird Beauforte, from Dunhelm." Aurelia hated how the woman's manner became coy once she knew who had crossed her threshold.

The vain cur had to have every woman groveling at his feet!

Bard gestured easily to Aurelia. "This is Aurelia—perhaps you've met?"

"We have not met," Aurelia said stiffly, and the woman shook her head in turn.

Bard looked disappointed, though how he imagined Aurelia would know a merchant from his kingdom, Aurelia did not know.

"Well, Aurelia needs a few things."

"I see. Lost luggage?"

Aurelia did not know what that meant, but Bard quickly agreed. The woman erupted from behind the table with purpose in her step. She scanned Aurelia, then fixed Bard with bright eyes.

"Anything in particular we have in mind?"

"I'm sure that your advice will be invaluable to the lady," Baird said smoothly. He dropped into a chair by the door and scooped up a wad of colorful vellum. "You do take American Express, don't you?"

The woman smiled.

And Aurelia wondered what in the name of Odin had just been transacted.

It quickly became clear that the merchant woman had been hired by Bard to assist Aurelia in choosing more garb. Though she could have found the intimation that she did not know her own mind insulting, Aurelia was soon glad of the advice. The array of colors, the choice of fabrics, the variety of cut of the garb in even this one shop was completely overwhelming and Aurelia was grateful for the woman's patient guidance.

She argued briefly with Bard about his buying her garb, but he was adamant that she was his "responsibility," at least until her father was found. He was obviously trying to win her approval, but the prospect of shedding his whore's chemise was simply too tempting to be refused.

Aurelia settled on the familiar, or at least the closest thing to it that she could find. Their leggings were made of a wondrous stretchy matter and were wrought in the most delightful array of bright colors. These were no herbal dyes that Aurelia knew! And if the cloth was woven of wool, then even the spinners had been bewitched by Julian's spells. Aurelia had never felt cloth so smooth.

This merchant, too, insisted on the same "undies" that the whore had tried to foist on Aurelia. She finally conceded to the briefs, but would not have anything to do with the harness for her breasts.

They had tunics and shirts of gossamer fabrics, though none had the embroidered hems Aurelia so favored. She imagined another merchant sold lengths of embroidery, or perhaps one was expected to do that oneself. The merchant had a great creamy knit tunic, not unlike Bard's own, and Bard insisted on a burgundy cloak of the same strange fabric as his.

Aurelia liked the pockets and the strange manner of fastenings, though she was skeptical of the merchant's claim that it would repel the rain.

She found but one dress—and that at Bard's insistence— that she could bring herself to wear in public and its texture was well familiar. "Wool challis," the merchant called the fabric, though the design wrought upon it was as marvelous as that on Marissa's sheet.

The "paisley print" was all blues and greens with a touch of purple, the very colors of the sea and the sky around Dunhelm. Though it had no embroidery, the hem and cuffs were bordered in the same magical way as the overall pattern.

And no man could see through it. Its hem, though a far cry

from the floor, hung just below Aurelia's knees. The merchant matched the dress with a short jacket of boiled wool with the most wonderful silver buttons Aurelia had ever seen.

Bard's eyes glowed when she came out of the little chamber to which she had been dispatched to change. Aurelia felt a perverse tingle of pleasure that he found her pleasing.

She knew it was only because he had finally acknowledged her beauty, not because his approval in itself mattered in the least.

"Shoes," Bard said simply when she thought he might say more, his gaze traveling to her bare feet as though he could not help himself from staring at them.

Aurelia wiggled her toes playfully and marveled at the way he caught his breath.

Was it possible that she had some effect on him?

The merchant summoned another merchant who evidently made shoes, for he brought a variety of awesome footwear for Aurelia's perusal. She flatly refused the whore's shoes that they all encouraged her to try—obviously her role in Bard's life had been mistaken! They were of fine enough leather, but the spikes under the heels made it nearly impossible to walk.

She liked instead a marvelously wrought pair of purple leather shoes. They had virtually no heel but were delicate and feminine. And they matched the hue of her dress perfectly.

Bard had considerable opinion about the matter of sensible boots and she let him argue with the shoe merchant. He got down on his hands and knees, to Aurelia's amazement, to check the fit of what he called "hiking boots."

They were comfortable indeed, but Aurelia could not help but catch her own breath when Bard closed his hand around her ankle. He checked the solidity of her stance, then shot a glance through his lashes so hot that it nearly stopped her heart.

She stared back at him and her mouth went dry. A snippet of the dream trotted through her head and she wondered whether it had been Bard's dream she witnessed.

The prophecy nudged at Aurelia's memory but she would not heed its foolishness.

Nonsense! There was nothing that said it had been *his*

dream she shared! Why, it could have been the priest's—indeed, it would have been far more reasonable for the priest to be meddling with her dream power.

Or trying to steal it.

But there was a knowing in Bard's gaze that set a heat simmering deep within Aurelia. She broke free of his grip and fled to the "changing room."

Aurelia dressed hastily in the boots, the burgundy leggings, a teal shirt, and the tunic like Bard's. She returned to the shop to find her "Gore-Tex" on the counter, everything else folded and packed away in great bags. Bard was handing a gold card to the merchant, a card not unlike Julian's talisman.

To her relief, he did not so much as glance her way and she took the opportunity to gather her wits about her.

The woman toyed with the card, something beeped, then she smiled at Bard. "Thank you so much for your patronage, Mr. Beauforte."

Bard scrawled on the paper she gave him, then handed it back to her. The woman smiled again and handed back Bard's card. She beamed at Aurelia and handed over their packages. "Have a lovely day, dear."

They left the shop without any coin or fancy vellum changing hands.

Aurelia snorted under her breath, Bard's lie obviously exposed. "And you say you do not go a-viking."

"What do you mean?"

"You did not pay for those wares!"

"Of course I did!" Bard had the grace to look sheepish. "Or, at least, I will once the bill comes."

But Aurelia had not been born the day before. "That is the import of your note? That you will pay later?" Bard nodded, but Aurelia laughed. "That merchant was well fooled by your charm, but I know a-viking when I see it!"

She poked the new king solidly in the chest with her finger. "You are a rogue, sir, and people will learn soon enough the manner of your dealings. Even Vikings do not pillage in their own towns."

Bard's lips thinned. "Look, just because you don't have a credit card doesn't make one a bad thing. They're handy and as long as the debt doesn't get out of hand, are useful.''

That meant just about nothing to Aurelia.

"And now," Bard said firmly, "we'll ask about your father."

Aurelia, though, had more immediate concerns on her mind. They had been in the shop a good while and such decision making was always a tiring business. She scanned the square as her stomach grumbled loudly.

"Have you charmed anyone in this village with a good kitchen?"

Bard looked confused.

"I am hungry," Aurelia clarified. "Where can we eat?"

Hungry?

Baird couldn't believe it. After the breakfast she had put away?

But Aurelia was serious.

He sighed with resignation and steered her to the pub, where she consumed a fish-and-chips lunch in short order. Baird barely ate half a dozen bites of his, because his cell phone kept screaming for attention.

By the time Aurelia began making his lunch disappear as well, Baird knew reality couldn't be avoided any longer. The plumbers couldn't go any further without the placement of the fourth septic tank being solved and it wasn't going to happen without him being there.

Baird didn't want to even think about how much it was costing him to have all those plumbers sitting around doing nothing more productive than twiddling their thumbs.

Baird watched Aurelia eat and wondered how she would take to this change of plans. After all, he *had* promised to help her find her father today.

But Dunhelm was calling. And the huge financial obligation of this resort could not be ignored. Baird leaned forward and watched Aurelia carefully for her response, hoping this would be easier than he thought it might be.

If she panicked, he would just have to find another solution.

"Look, princess, I've got to get back to Dunhelm," he said gently. "There are all sorts of people who need decisions made. Do you mind if I don't help you look for your father today?"

"No." Aurelia shook her head readily, returning her attention to consuming the last of his chips with gusto.

Baird blinked. She agreed so easily that he was almost insulted. He eyed her carefully but her expression was blank.

Well, he certainly wasn't going to force his company on her!

"Fine. Do you want to stay in town or go back to Dunhelm?"

Aurelia barely considered the question. "Back to Dunhelm, please." Then her lips set with such purposefulness that Baird had the feeling his decision had perfectly dovetailed with Aurelia's plans.

Whatever they were.

Aurelia was delighted by this turn of events. The last thing she wanted was Bard hot on her heels while she looked for her father.

Bard kept looking at her on the way back to Dunhelm and once or twice started to ask her a question, but the small ringing box he carried kept interrupting. Aurelia was well pleased with its timing, though the way he talked into it confused her utterly.

Though that was not the only thing about Bard, son of Erc, that did not match expectation. Aurelia glanced at her companion as they passed through the gates of Dunhelm. His strong fingers drummed on his thigh, he frowned as he listened to the little box.

Dunhelm Castle rose in silhouette before them against the silver gray of the sea. Aurelia's heart skipped a beat at the sight of her home, changed yet still familiar, and resolve grew within her.

She had this one afternoon to search for the truth of what had transpired. What had happened to all the men who lined the walls and the women who waited anxiously below?

Aurelia meant to find out. Once she knew the fate of her father's faithful, she might learn more of her father.

And who knew when she might have such a golden opportunity again?

In the Hampstead offices of the National Heritage Preservation Society, Colin Russell was drumming his meaty fingers on his desk. He hated the feeling that he was waiting on a very junior member of his staff—it was against every hierarchical belief he held about the world—but that was precisely the situation.

How could he have let this ingrate win such power over him? It was unnatural. It was against the normal order of things. It was *wrong*.

But Colin hadn't had the nerve to call a stop to it all.

And he hated the recognition of his own weakness even more.

There was a rap on his door and his secretary, the wraithlike Miss Patterson, ushered Darian Mulvaney into the office.

"Mr. Russell? You wanted to see me?" Darian smiled guilelessly and Colin's hackles rose. He really did not like this young man, and he particularly did not like the means Darian had chosen to get ahead.

But he would be damned if he let his animosity show.

He was British, after all.

Darian Mulvaney had looked like a promising candidate for the society, an attractive young man with fixed goals and a doctorate from a prestigious American university fresh under his arm. Darian had impressed the entire society committee during the interview process with his fervor for the Picts, his dedication to his career, and his boyish enthusiasm.

Giddy with the prospect of recruiting from the "first crop" of graduates, instead of picking over everyone else's leavings, the meagerly funded society had acted with uncharacteristic haste.

And made a tragic mistake.

By the time Colin knew that the doctorate was faked, Darian Mulvaney already had his ace in the hole. Ousting the young man would bring scandal on the fledgling society in more ways than one, and havoc into Colin's personal life.

Because Darian had already begun blackmailing him, not only could Colin not risk angering his newest employee, but he also had to perpetuate the sham of Darian's credentials.

At least until he could think of an alternative.

"Yes, I did, Mr. Mulvaney," Colin agreed as sternly as he could manage. He smoothed the facsimile that had arrived that morning against the broad oak expanse of his desk. "We have word today of a discovery at Dunhelm Castle in the Orkney Islands, an ancient site that might have Pictish origins."

"Yes?" Darian's excitement was tangible and he looked almost innocent in his enthusiasm. But there was a hard glitter in his eyes that was evident to anyone who looked.

Or anyone who had *learned* to look.

But they had a bargain, as much as Colin would like to deny it. And Colin Russell was a man of his word.

"Yes," Colin admitted with a sharp glance at the newest member of the society's staff. "Just as you suspected it would be, oddly enough." He pursed his lips. "One might almost think you knew in advance that the site would be found."

Darian swallowed a coy smile. "That would be rather unlikely, wouldn't it, sir?"

"Quite." Colin shuffled the paperwork on his desk, sickened that he had to do this. There were half a dozen researchers on his staff more experienced and, frankly, more deserving of this plum. How could he ever have guessed that a quick tumble would put him in the predicament of betraying so many dreams?

"As you may have guessed," he said gruffly, "I need to send a staff member to Dunhelm to investigate the site so that an appropriate course can be decided."

"Of course," Darian said smoothly, anticipation gleaming in his eyes.

Colin cleared his throat. "Per our earlier discussion, I have chosen to send *you* to Dunhelm." Darian smiled a very cold smile of satisfaction and Colin latched his nervous fingers onto a heavy glass paperweight.

The worst must be said.

This had to be stopped right here and right now. Colin tried to toy with the paperweight as though unconcerned about what he intended to say, but suspected that he failed.

"I believe, Mr. Mulvaney, that this act will fulfill the

bounds of my obligation to you here at the society.'' Colin took a deep breath. ''Your credentials in coming here show an impressive level of work in researching the ancient Picts—however questionable they may be, it is evident that this area is of a profound interest to you. This opportunity—granted at the expense of many others, I might add—should give you the chance you desire to prove yourself.''

Darian said absolutely nothing, a fact that Colin found terribly unsettling. ''Needless to say, I consider our bargain to be a matter forgotten as of this moment.''

He threw his most quelling glance at his subordinate, but Darian's smile did not waver. When the young man spoke, his voice was dangerously low. ''Unfortunately, sir, we aren't in agreement.''

''What?''

''I don't consider our business to be completed.''

Colin dropped the paperweight and it rolled heavily across his desk. He ignored it and jabbed a thick finger into the solid wood. ''You cannot continue to milk a single comparatively minor incident to fuel your entire career! I will not have it! It is a disgrace to the society!''

Darian arched a fair brow. ''Would Mrs. Russell consider the widow on Rosehill Road to be a single comparatively minor incident?''

The men's gazes locked and held for a long moment. Colin sat back heavily and poked at the fax in dissatisfaction.

Mildred. The Russells's marriage was not a love match, by any means, but it was one firmly rooted in mutual respect. They passed each other periodically in the house Mildred had inherited, but by and large, lived separate lives.

Mildred had her horses, her friends at Ascot, her big straw hats and social teas. Colin had his tweeds and his archaeological digs.

And his society.

Established with a juicy grant from Mildred.

''You're right, of course, sir,'' Darian said cheerfully when Colin glared at his desk. ''I'm certain Mrs. Russell would see no harm in this at all.'' Darian reached for the phone. ''Why don't we just give her a call and set this matter behind us, as you wish?''

Darian picked up the receiver but Colin snatched it out of his hand and dropped it back into the cradle.

He glared at the audacious young man who had invaded his life.

Darian smiled with open malice. "Mrs. Russell is an *understanding* woman, isn't she?"

Mildred was *not* an understanding woman, never had been and never would be. If she found out about Colin's dalliance, there would be hell to pay for the rest of his life.

Colin drew himself taller and made a bluff of having some dignity left in this exchange.

"I'm warning you, Mr. Mulvaney, I will not permit this to continue," he declared. "It is a travesty of the code of the society and an affront to serious scholarship everywhere."

But Darian clearly knew as well as Colin did that the words were empty. The younger man laced his fingers together and looked steadily at his superior. "I only want one more thing, Mr. Russell."

Colin's mouth went dry. "What is that?"

Darian pushed to his feet. "I'll let you know when it's time for you to do something about it." He sauntered across the office, pausing with one hand on the door. "I'll call you from Dunhelm, *sir*."

And then he was gone.

Colin wadded up the fax and hurled it across the room. Insolent bugger! Maybe life would be easier with him at the other end of the country!

One more thing. Did Colin dare to hope that might be the truth?

He sighed, feeling suddenly very defeated by life's challenges, and retrieved the fax, smoothing it out on his desk. One last thing, he reminded himself, just one last thing and Darian Mulvaney would keep his mouth shut forever.

Colin could only hope it was something in his power to do.

Fourteen

~

Baird returned to poorly managed chaos. He listened and looked, pointed and prioritized, delegated and decided with an efficiency perfected long ago. Each felt they had their say, each respected his decisions, although new issues seemed to crop up faster than he could resolve the old ones.

Marissa cornered him after several unsuccessful attempts, though she would have been dismayed to know that Baird's mind was firmly locked on the problem of placing a septic tank. They had found a load-bearing wall where no one had expected one to be—and precisely where tank number four was supposed to be installed.

The backhoe was waiting for Baird to decide where to put the tank instead. He was up to his elbows in blueprints, had the architect on the cell phone, a building inspector hovered nearby, and the head plumber anxiously making suggestions.

"Baird, darling, whatever is going on in this place? The noise is so terrible that I can't even think straight!"

Baird glanced briefly at the designer and wasn't surprised. Her flowing skirt and pointed heels had no place in the mess of the construction site. "Then go to a hotel," he said tightly. "You can't be in here without steel-toed boots."

The architect barked in his ear, Baird located the spot he suggested, and looked to the plumber. He tapped the nearby wiring that they had penciled onto the plan the week before—

another unanticipated complication—and the plumber made a face. The inspector shook his head firmly.

"Where else?" he asked the architect.

"Baird, darling, I really must put my foot down. I know you've decided about the marble, darling, but we simply must go over the draperies and upholsteries for the Series B guestrooms. I've brought all the fabric swatches—"

"Fine. Later." Baird turned to the plumber. "What about here?"

The plumber considered the possibility and Baird was encouraged that he didn't immediately discard it. The plumber shoved his hands into his overalls and leaned closer. "Where's the restaurant relative to this?"

"Here," Baird said. "So we could make the access over here, maybe add a line of shrubbery, the driveway goes around the building there already."

"I like it." The plumber picked up the plan and frowned at it, obviously checking that he hadn't missed anything.

The inspector looked over his shoulder, nodding as his gaze darted over the plans. "Looks doable."

Baird was vaguely aware that Marissa was still chattering on to him. "It's not safe for you to be in here without proper boots," he reminded her tersely, then waited impatiently for the two men before him to decide.

Marissa leaned closer, but Baird wasn't listening. "Look, Baird, I have the most wonderful idea. Why don't we have a lovely intimate dinner tonight, and get all these issues settled? We could meet in my room, darling, don't worry, I'll arrange for the meal somehow. . . ."

The plumber nodded approval, the inspector concurred, and Baird picked up the cell phone, glad everything was resolved. "All right, we've got a deal," he informed the architect. "Let's do it."

Marissa trilled her odd laugh and attracted the attention of all three men. She kissed her fingertips and waved coyly to Baird, dancing out of the work area. "I'll take care of everything, darling! Sevenish would be good."

Baird looked at the inspector and plumber. He had an odd sense that he had inadvertently agreed to something, but didn't have any idea what it was. "What in the hell was that all about?"

Both men shrugged, the plumber tapping another section of the plan. "See? If we can fish the pipes through the cellar somehow *here* then we can hook up exactly as we would have if the tank had gone in the original location."

"That old wall is thick," the inspector observed.

"There has to be another way," Baird said, and the trio settled over the plans to work out their strategy.

Aurelia did not find the dungeons as easily as she had hoped. Once she could have walked there blindfolded, but now all had been changed around so thoroughly by Bard's workmen that she quickly became disoriented.

Her father's hall had been a simple wooden structure in the style of the Vikings, a long rectangular hall with a sloping roof and tables along its walls. It had been destroyed, as Aurelia had noted earlier, though not a single mark remained to hint at its precise location.

At least the ritual well was more or less as it had been. Aurelia started there.

The stone structure that Bard made his hall was new to Aurelia, though parts of it looked markedly aged. She suspected the stones had come from elsewhere, perhaps from the ancient crumbling towers on the horizon.

But roughly where Bard's hall stood, there had been an old settlement, long fallen into decay. A tumbling central tower had dominated a circle of cloverleaf-shaped homes, which Aurelia recalled had been waist deep in the turf. Certainly they had been too far gone to repair and she was not surprised that Bard had eliminated them.

Indeed, though she would never tell him as much, his hall vastly improved the appearance of Dunhelm. Aurelia would never have expected a barbarian to have such an aesthetic sense, but then there was much about Bard that surprised her.

She refused to think about that now.

Beneath the tower that no longer stood sentinel over the squarish peninsula of Dunhelm, there had been deep pits. A curved staircase followed the outer wall of the tower, descending to a small anteroom from which the pits could be reached. Once undoubtedly cellars, they had been converted to dungeons by Bard's own sire, Erc.

The only problem was that without the landmark of the tower, Aurelia was not certain precisely where they should be.

After a good amount of fruitless searching, she conceded defeat and resolved to circle the peninsula before the daylight was gone. She might well find the bodies of fallen warriors or some hint of what had transpired in the attack.

Maybe she would find a survivor willing to share a tale. Or see another angle of the land that would reveal the location of the dungeons.

Aurelia's spirits were high when she began, but quickly faded. The peninsula of Dunhelm was not a small one and she had a good bit of ground to cover. That, added to her determination to walk close to the edge of the cliffs—all the better to see the bodies cast below—made the walking difficult.

But she saw nothing other than myriad birds nesting on the rocks that fell to the sea. Aurelia was convinced every curve would reveal a horror to her eyes, but as the day passed and nothing suspicious came to light, she began to tire.

Aurelia walked until the sun was lowering toward the sea, her view filled with rocks, birds, and the occasional seal.

What had happened to everyone? The dungeons, even if she managed to find them, could never have accommodated hundreds of men. And how could Dunhelm have been captured without a resounding battle?

Even if the carnage had been cast into the sea, Aurelia knew full well that the sea returned such gifts in short order. But the beaches, far below, were barren.

Aurelia stared back at Bard's hall, distant calls of the workmen carrying to her ears. Could it be that Bard had let her father's men all go free?

It defied good sense! And she had seen well enough that he was a man with a logical mind.

Perhaps the warriors had been shipped off to some foreign estate, perhaps they toiled in whatever outpost the son of Erc had made his own, perhaps they had been shipped off to be sold as slaves in the markets of Micklegarth.

Such an expense. Aurelia winced, not certain it would be worth the trouble.

No, some must be here in the dungeons. Why else would those dungeons have been so artfully concealed? Aurelia stalked back toward the hall, determined to find those dank and dour cells.

She found them in a rather different way than she had expected.

Aurelia was marching resolutely across the lawn behind the hall when the ground suddenly gave way beneath her feet.

She screamed and scrambled for a grip as the earth fell away, taking her with it. Aurelia fought against falling into the gaping hole opened in the earth, even knowing it was hopeless.

She dropped a good thirty feet before she landed on her buttocks with a solid thump. Dirt showered around her and a chunk of turf landed heavily beside her foot.

The sounds of the world seemed distant and muffled in the eerie silence that surrounded Aurelia. Far above her, the hammering and shouting of the construction continued undisturbed.

No one had heard her scream.

Aurelia tried again, just to be sure, but there was no response. She winced and moved slightly, knowing that she would have an enormous bruise in short order.

Aurelia reached out and touched a damp stone wall. She called a greeting, but the words echoed through the stone and came forlornly back to her.

She had found the dungeons all right, but there was no contingent of warriors wasting away in these forgotten shadows.

She was alone. Aurelia bellowed again, but with no discernible effect. She was alone and evidently destined to stay that way.

Well, she was not going to sit back and wait to be rescued! Aurelia pushed to her feet, determined to explore her prison thoroughly.

She stared into the darkness surrounding her as she tried to remember exactly how the dungeons had been laid out. There were half a dozen cells, as she recalled. She might find some sign of her father's warriors, though her heart doubted they had ever been here.

The dungeons, after all, smelled dead and disused.

Aurelia folded her arms across her chest, already feeling the chill of the coming night, and set to exploring. What had happened after she pricked her thumb?

What if her father had seen his forces so outnumbered that he surrendered himself to Bard rather than see his men slaughtered?

What if Bard, having won what he saw as his due, had been persuaded to let her father's men leave Dunhelm freely?

There would be neither bodies nor prisoners, then.

But, of course, there would be a legion of men not particularly well disposed to the new upstart king.

Unless Julian's plan succeeded. Their marriage would ensure that all those formerly loyal to her sire would turn their loyalty to Bard. And when her escaped father returned to reclaim what he had lost, his own men would be pledged against him.

Despicable! Fortunately, Aurelia had deduced the truth. Bard would fool her no longer with his lingering glances and little smiles! She would teach Bard, son of Erc, that she was not a woman with whom he could trifle.

Although a more pressing issue in this moment was how Aurelia was going to get out of the old dungeons.

Baird was dead on his feet by eight o'clock that night. He ached from stooping and scrambling through the nether regions of the castle. He had bumped his head and scraped his knee, missed his dinner, and wished heartily that he hadn't let Aurelia eat his lunch.

But the fourth septic tank was secured in its new home and ready to accept donations.

Now all Baird wanted was to sleep. He made his way through the silent hotel, permitting himself a thrill of pride at how it was all slowly coming together, and climbed the stairs to his room.

What they needed was an elevator in this place.

•   •   •

Talorc's book taunted Baird from the end table when he
climbed into bed. Baird didn't remember bringing it upstairs,
but he found himself reaching for it without hesitation.

It fell open where he had been reading before.

> *The most obvious and enduring legacy of the Picts, of
> course, is the vast number of standing symbol stones left
> scattered all across Scotland. These stones are carved
> with heavy relief and mounted at great effort to stand on
> their ends. There is remarkable repetition in the range of
> symbols employed on these stones, though no script on
> the stones or Pictish documents survive elsewhere to ex-
> plain their import.*

> *There is considerable controversy as to whether these
> stones are territorial boundaries, memorials to the dead,
> announcements of treaties and alliances, or whether they
> mean something entirely different and as yet undeter-
> mined.*

Baird glanced at the photograph at the bottom of the page
and his heart jumped. The symbol stone was just like the door
to the well!

Well, not exactly. A closer look revealed that there were
common elements—the crescent, for example—but that this
stone was slightly different.

Still, it was weird how closely the two resembled each other
and how neatly this dovetailed with Aurelia's story. Baird
glanced at a map on the next page that marked every Pictish
stone in Scotland with a dot and was reassured. There were
hundreds of the damn things!

And it didn't mean that the slab in the well had been there
since the time of the Picts. One thing that struck Baird about
Europe was that people reused every little thing, artifact or
otherwise. If that stone was lying around here just when someone wanted to make a stone door, they would have thought
nothing of using it.

The carved slab in the well could have originally been anywhere within a couple of miles.

Although that wouldn't explain why the woman carved on it was dressed exactly as Aurelia had been. She certainly couldn't have moved it there herself, even if it had cohered perfectly with the story she had concocted.

Baird's gaze lifted of its own accord to the mysterious shadows lurking far beyond his window, shadows that marked the stairs descending into the well. Instead of solving a mystery when he laid those stairs bare to the sunlight, Baird had opened a nest of enigmas.

All centered around Aurelia.

Maybe that stone wasn't as much like her as he recalled. Suddenly Baird's exhaustion slipped away. He had to go and see the stone again, right now.

A walk, after all, would do him good.

Aurelia was cold and cramped, damp and irritable by the time she heard the faint crunch of footsteps overhead.

Someone to help her!

She screamed as loudly as she could and barely dared to breathe until she heard the steps hurry in her direction. The arc of a light cut through the night, and she blinked as it shone directly on her.

"What in the hell are you doing down there?" Bard demanded, and Aurelia's heart sank.

Trust him to be the one to find her!

"I fell," she admitted irritably.

"So I see." The light flicked away and Aurelia could see Bard crouched on the edge, his elbows braced on his knees. That wry smile was tugging at the corner of his lips and her defiance melted just a little.

Oh, the cursed man fairly oozed with charm!

"So, are you naturally this much trouble, princess, or do you have to work at it?"

Trust him to find it amusing that she was trapped here! Why, it probably suited Bard well to see her in such foul circumstance!

"You may find this humorous, but I do not!"

He considered the depth of the pit she had fallen into, then looked back to her with a heart-wrenching grin. "It's a good thing you're so cute, because you sure are a lot of trouble."

There was a charge that hit too close to home. Such belit-tling compliments had been the reason Aurelia learned to fire the crossbow. "I am not *cute*!" she cried. "I am a warrior!"

"A regular Amazon," Bard agreed easily, and she knew he was mocking her even though she did not understand the ref-erence. "My seventh foster mother would have said you were in a fine pickle, Princess. Seems your warrior skills aren't getting you out of it."

Bard might be in a teasing mood, but Aurelia's sense of humor had been chilled out of her hours before. "Seventh foster mother? No one has that many foster mothers!"

"Wrong, princess." His expression turned grim again. "I had fourteen. And foster fathers to match."

"What need had you of so many?"

Bard's lips thinned. "I didn't *need* any of them," he said tightly. "Just like they didn't need me." He pushed to his feet and cleared his throat. "Now, do you want some help?"

As much as it galled Aurelia to accept his assistance, there was no other means of escape. "Yes, please." She wrapped her arms around herself and felt a shudder ripple through her, despite her determination to appear strong.

"Then let's get you out of there." He straightened and was back with a rope in short order.

And when the warm grip of his hand finally closed over her own, Aurelia hated that she felt safe and secure once more. She could not help but shiver at the contrast between her cool flesh and his warmth.

It could be no more than that.

Bard's voice dropped and his gaze sharpened. "Your hands are freezing, princess! How long have you been down there?" The concern in his eyes nearly undid her resolve.

Oh, the man could feign caring for her so well that even knowing it was a ploy did not strengthen Aurelia's resistance!

"Since shortly after we came back from town," Aurelia admitted, feeling her cheeks heat at her own foolishness.

He swore under his breath and peeled off his own jacket, wrapping its welcome warmth around her and bundling her back into his hall. Aurelia let him do so, reluctant to admit to herself how relieved she felt to have someone so obviously capable taking charge.

Were she not aware of his dark intent, she could have come to rely upon this man.

But that would be dangerous indeed.

"Come on, princess, into the shower, no excuses."

What? Marissa pressed her ear to her door and listened shamelessly. Trust Aurelia to have foiled Marissa's plans! That woman's door opened and closed, but Baird did not come back into the hall.

Marissa heard the water come on in the adjacent room and loathed the mental image that came along with it. She stalked back across the room and snuffed the candles with disgust.

So that was how it was going to be. Marissa surveyed the wilted flowers, the sorry excuse for a romantic dinner that was all she had been able to acquire in town, and grimaced.

She could have accepted defeat, packed her bags, and moved out, but Marissa was not a quitter.

Especially with stakes like this.

But the fact that Baird was already sleeping with Aurelia demanded some hard reconsideration of the facts. Baird might not have time to tire of Aurelia if that woman kept things moving at this pace. They could be at the altar before Baird even noticed that the blonde was not firing on all cylinders.

Marissa eyed her reflection assessingly, her perfect display of decolletage, and reluctantly acknowledged that thirty-five carefully managed years still had a hard time competing with a nubile blonde of twenty. Marissa faced the ugly reality that her charms might not be enough to snare the big fish.

At least not in open competition. She smiled confidently at her reflection, knowing the time for subtlety was past.

It was time to bring out the heavy artillery.

Baird was a bit surprised by how protective he felt of Aurelia. Like a mother hen, he ushered her back into her room and turned the shower on full.

"Come on, princess, you're chilled to the bone."

Baird supposed he should have been encouraged by the fire

that lit Aurelia's eyes. "I will not disrobe in your presence!"

Baird shoved his hands into his pockets and backed away, the steam of the shower encouraging his imagination to run wild. He remembered all too well the flash of her ankles beneath the changing-room door this afternoon.

"Don't I get any thanks for helping you out of that pit?" Baird tried to smile engagingly, but Aurelia wasn't having any of it.

"Thank you," she said frostily. "Now, leave me be."

He was batting a thousand here.

She didn't want him anywhere near her, obviously enough. Not being wanted was a familiar experience for Baird, but this time, the awareness that his presence was unwelcome really stung.

"Fine!"

Baird left the steamy bathroom and returned to his room, unable to completely account for his foul mood. He paced its length and back, telling himself that what he needed was a good night's sleep.

After all, there were more important things on his plate right now than the opinion of one troublesome, deluded princess.

Fifteen

This dream came stealthily and Aurelia welcomed the difference in its tone. This time, she well knew, she would have some answers. The scene was a peaceful one, though Aurelia realized that she occupied the viewpoint of another, yet again.

He was a young man, and he walked down to the sea toward a ship bobbing in the harbor. The ship was familiar to Aurelia, she noted with a start, for it was the Viking ship her sire had kept in good repair. Its high curving prow was carved with a serpent's head and shields hung along the rails. The men were unfurling a great red sail that tugged in the wind as they checked its rigging.

The sky arched blue overhead, the wind ruffled his hair, and though the mood here was festive, the man's heart had only one shadow upon it.

Someone was leaving.

A good friend was going home, a friend whose company he would miss. And they walked together to the harbor. Aurelia glanced at the one who matched his steps to those of the young man and her heart skipped a beat.

The fair-haired and blue-eyed man was none other than her brother, Thord.

She felt the strength of the bond between these two men. They were friends of the heart and this man ached that Thord was setting sail.

Aurelia puzzled over these details. Whose view could she

be sharing? It must be someone of whom she had heard, for this must have happened before Thord's death.

"You must come and meet my sister," Thord said, and Aurelia nearly wept at the familiarity of his voice. How she had missed him! "We could be truly brothers if you two wed, blood brothers, instead of just having fostered together."

Fostering. Thord had fostered with the High King of Inverness. Aurelia remembered that all too well—and he had returned to Dunhelm just shortly before his untimely demise.

His talk had been full of his foster brother, Bridei, the Prince and heir of Inverness. That must be whose view Aurelia shared.

"It is no small thing to have trained in arms together," Bridei replied. The calm assurance of his voice pleased Aurelia and she recalled all too well Thord's certainty that they two would be a good match.

Aurelia wondered what had happened to him in the wake of Bard's capture of Dunhelm.

"We are brothers in deed, Thord, if not in blood."

Thord smiled and gripped his shoulder. "You are the greatest friend that ever I have had. Do not blame my weakness if I would have your friendship closer." He winked and dropped his voice to a mischievous whisper. "Though Aurelia would have a dim view of the havoc we have wreaked among women."

They chuckled together and Aurelia knew fleetingly that this was a reference to some old adventure they had shared. Bridei nudged his friend. "The ale mistress is likely still waiting for you, after last night."

"Oh, after spilling a pitcher on my new tunic?" Thord rolled his eyes. "The Valkyries themselves could not drag me back to that abode. One must wonder whether such people have no idea of the difficulties of acquiring fine cloth."

"Do you go a-viking in Micklegarth before your return?"

Thord laughed. "Ah, the lure of civilization! I am tempted, but my father would have my head if I took such a delay in coming home." His lips thinned. "There is some trouble brewing evidently." He frowned, then clapped his friend on the shoulder. "You must come to Dunhelm, Bridei. And soon."

Aurelia felt a certainty of purpose dawn in Bridei's heart. Here was a man who pledged to do a thing and kept his word. "Do not fear. I will come."

They embraced before the moored ship, then Thord strode across the wharf. "You had best hurry!" he called, his eyes dancing with a mischief that seemed oddly familiar. "Knowing Aurelia, she will have gotten herself into some fix or another."

The affection in Thord's voice brought tears to Aurelia's eyes.

"Did I tell you that she had taken it upon herself to handle a crossbow? A *crossbow*! Leave it to Aurelia! She insisted that men must learn to take her seriously." Thord wagged a finger knowingly. "One of these days, she will get herself into a muddle with no way out. She *needs* someone like you, Bridei, someone of good sense who will pluck her out of trouble!"

"Ha! Where does it say that I want a wife in need only of caretaking?" Bridei called laughingly into the wind.

Thord grinned. "You need a wife who will not bore you and—trust me!—there is never a dull moment with Aurelia around."

Both men laughed and Aurelia's ears burned with the certainty that this Bridei knew a great deal about the trouble she had found in her days. Thord had always been too talkative.

The seamen began throwing off the mooring ropes and the crowd gathered on the beach shouted good wishes. No sooner had the ship been pushed off into the sea than the solidly built ale mistress shoved her way to the front of the crowd. She scowled when she spied Thord, but that man waved merrily to her.

"Farewell!" he cried. "Keep your ale off your patron's garb!"

The woman cursed. Bridei grinned as an unrepentant Thord lent his hand to the work of hoisting the sail.

And Aurelia heard the admiration in his thoughts. *Thord*

*talked a lot, he worried too much about his garb, but his heart
was pure gold.*

It was all painfully true.

Then Thord waved once more, laughed, and he was gone.

And Aurelia felt tears on her cheeks.

The dream blurred and Baird was once again at his first day
of college. Rootless and determined to make his way alone,
he felt once more the fear of being in a new and strange en-
vironment.

Baird should have been used to solitude by then, but the
university was so crowded that it overwhelmed him. Everything was new, everything was different, and everyone else
seemed to know the rules already.

Unlike Baird.

No one had driven him to the dorm, no one had loaded him
up with stereos and books and bedding. No one had waved
good-bye or even wished him well. He would have been confused if they had. Baird had taken the Greyhound bus to the
college town, with one bag holding all his worldly posses-
sions.

It hadn't taken him long to unpack.

Baird had felt more than inadequate when his roommate
arrived with a cheery support team of six and enough stuff to
bury their shared room knee deep. They had embraced him,
this troupe of strangers, offered him snacks, and startled Baird
with their noisy camaraderie.

He remembered now that he had gone early to his Intro.
Psych. class, ostensibly to give his new roommate some privacy.

But there had been no relief at class. At least a hundred
people were already chattering in the hall, all of whom looked
as though they came from secure, happy, middle-class house-
holds.

Baird sat straight in his chair, neither too close to the front
nor the back, sure that he stuck out like a sore thumb.

He didn't need anyone, he reminded himself, he didn't
need to make friends here, he didn't need to count on anybody
because everybody ultimately let him down. No one needed

him, so he wasn't going to need any of them. Baird Beauforte was here for an education and that was all.

But all the old anthems seemed a little thin in that moment. Baird fidgeted in his sleep, remembering the awkwardness of his younger self too easily and resenting that his dreaming mind chose to dwell on old defeats.

Then Julian slid into the seat beside him. Baird looked up and felt a jolt of recognition that now he recalled feeling at the time, although he had quickly dismissed it.

How could he have known Julian?

In those days, Julian had been less flamboyant, though his jeans had been meticulously pressed, his collar buttoned down, his shoes buffed. His sandy ponytail defied anyone to call him a square.

"Hey, I'm Julian Preston," he said with a smile. "Can you *believe* these people? I feel like I fell into a Wonder bread commercial."

And Baird had chuckled despite himself. They had become friends, right then, right there, defying at least one of Baird's axioms about life.

Julian talked a lot, he cared too much about his clothes, but his heart was pure gold.

Aurelia was pacing her room and she was mad enough to spit sparks. The dream was a lie, a crude sham to convince her of something patently untrue.

It *was* Bard who had stolen her dreams. And he was trying to manipulate her in the most appalling way! He would have her believe that he was none other than the High King of Inverness's son, Bridei! He would have her believe that Julian was none other than her murdered brother, Thord!

And that Bard and Thord were *friends*!

It was reprehensible. It was disgusting. It was lower than low. Bard had *killed* Thord. What kind of a man hid from the results of his own foul deeds?

A man who could not be trusted, regardless of his handsome visage, regardless of his charm.

This was an obvious ploy to win her sympathies. Bard and Julian were trying to steal her power for themselves and twisting the truth beyond recognition in the process.

Well, Aurelia was not anyone's pawn! To her mind, this was no less than a declaration of war. Her Dreaming was sacred ground and no one—*no one*—had the right to meddle there.

Even if Julian *did* remind Aurelia of her brother, Thord.

It was a trick! Obviously, the priest had discerned her thinking—Bard seemed to read her thoughts, after all!—and used that against her. Disgusting! Aurelia paced and thought furiously, dismayed at the extent of their success thus far.

How could she defeat Bard? How could she thwart his foul plan when her own flesh was on his side? How could she save her Dreaming from his foul interference?

She could kill him.

Aurelia stopped and stared at the floor, her throat tight with the realization. Julian's magic was powerful indeed, but Aurelia knew that Bard's presence was key. Without an upstart king, there was no need to undermine any support for Hekod.

If they could affect her thinking so severely in merely two days, how much longer would Aurelia be able to keep events straight in her mind? Fear clenched her gut and Aurelia knew she had absolutely no choice.

The deed must be done. Bard must die.

Though how she could kill a trained warrior larger and stronger than she, let alone one who could read her very thoughts, Aurelia had no idea.

There had to be a way.

Well, there was one time when a man was vulnerable beyond all, Aurelia realized, and her heart began to pound at the boldness of her thoughts.

She would kill Bard in his own bed.

And if her chastity was the price she had to pay to ensure Bard slept in her presence, Aurelia would willingly count out the fee. It was a pittance compared to the sanctity of her Dreaming and the potential of being forced to betray her own blood.

Before she could change her mind, Aurelia donned the blue robe and knotted the belt about her waist. Elizabeth had a small but wicked knife in her kitchen. She would fetch that first, then do what she had to do.

It was only fear of discovery that had her heart pounding, Aurelia knew without doubt. It was no small risk she undertook.

She certainly could not be anticipating the heat of Bard's touch.

Baird stared at the canopy over his bed and puzzled over his strange dream. The juxtaposition of the two incidents obviously was supposed to mean something.

Could he and Julian have known each other before? A part of him was sure they had, another part of him insisted that it was all nonsense.

Was he just tossing together bits and pieces from his day to fill in the gaps of his dream? The question about Micklegarth was a direct echo of Aurelia's comments in town. Even though she hadn't been in this dream, her presence had been almost tangible. Thord had talked about her, or at least, talked about his sister, who shared the same name.

The sister he thought Baird should marry. Baird swung out of bed and hauled on his resort robe, certain he wouldn't sleep for a while. He paced, unable to imagine how easily he had taken to the idea of marriage, even in a dream.

What was it about Aurelia that got under his skin?

Was it just the power of desire at work?

Yet Baird knew that it was not something as ignoble as lust that flared through him at just the sight of Aurelia.

She was unlike any woman he had ever met.

Baird liked the way Aurelia's eyes flashed with spirit, he liked how passionately she argued, he liked that she grabbed on to life with both hands and didn't let go.

Baird admired that her thinking proceeded logically from whatever premise she took. She was clever and defiant, opinionated and passionate. He was intrigued that she could be both delicate and resolute, that she refused to back down from any challenge and that she spoke her mind in no uncertain terms.

Aurelia invaded his dreams and stole into his thoughts. And

Baird wanted to know her in every way, he wanted to see her in every light, he wanted to hear her thoughts on every matter and watch her confront every wonder of the world. Baird wanted to solve all the puzzles about her that he had only glimpsed.

But most of all, he wanted to mend the gaping hole her father's loss had left in her life. Not having a father had scarred Baird, but he knew that losing a father would have been far, far worse.

And Aurelia had endured exactly that.

Baird couldn't explain why he felt so protective of a stranger. Unless it was because Aurelia had had the kind of father that Baird had always longed to have himself. He ached now with the dream's unwelcome reminder of his own loneliness.

Baird had never had anyone he could rely on. He rubbed his temples just as a quiet rap sounded at the door.

Aurelia stood on the threshold of his room, wearing a resort robe that matched his own. Her hair was in a braid, she looked young and vulnerable.

And there was a heat in her gaze that echoed Baird's own. His heart thumped and his mouth went dry with the certainty of why she had come.

She wanted him.

Just as he wanted her.

There was no need for words. Aurelia's eyes darkened to indigo as she stepped forward and slipped her hands around the back of his neck. Baird didn't fight the way she urged him closer, his heart hammering with anticipation.

A thousand denials crowded into his mind. He shouldn't. They shouldn't.

But Aurelia did. The sweet seduction of her lips closed over his and swept his rationalizations away.

Again, Baird had that sense of *rightness*.

He couldn't shut out intuition anymore, it took the keys and locked logic securely in the trunk. For the first time that he could recall, Baird Beauforte didn't want to think about anything.

He just wanted to feel.

Aurelia was so welcoming, so familiar yet tantalizingly unknown, and the spell she wove about Baird left no chance of escape. He didn't want to be anywhere else in the world.

There *was* nowhere else in the world.

Baird lifted Aurelia against him, savoring the crush of her breasts against his chest. She was all curves and softness, completely different from him, yet they fit together as though they were each made for the other.

He felt complete in a way he never had before, as though some missing piece had quietly slid into place to complete a jigsaw. It seemed that all his life he had been seeking this elusive feeling. Now he had found it, and in the most unlikely of places.

Aurelia was what Baird had always been searching for. And now that he had found her, there was nothing else that mattered, nothing other than the magic they would make between them.

And that magic would be theirs to remember for all time.

Baird pressed his mouth over hers and their tongues danced together, his blood heating as Aurelia matched him touch for touch. Her cheeks were flushed with passion and when Baird trailed a line of kisses along her jaw, she moaned aloud. Her small fingers clenched in his hair and Baird loved the way she gasped when he rolled his tongue in her ear.

Then Aurelia did the same to him and Baird thought he would explode. He scooped her up in his arms, kicked the door closed, and carried her to the bed. The moonlight slanted through the windows, painting the room in shades of silver and toying with the luster of Aurelia's hair.

She lay back against the rumpled duvet and smiled welcomingly.

Baird slid open the knotted belt of her robe and Aurelia's gaze fixed on him. He stared into the sapphire majesty of her eyes, then lifted the robe away to reveal the perfection of her breasts.

She was so tiny, yet beautiful in every way. Baird slid tentative fingertips over her smooth curves, hip to breast to shoulder, his hand pausing against her jaw in wonder. The moonlight made her look ethereal and unreal. He was half afraid that she was too fragile to touch, that she was an illusion that would disappear if he reached out to her.

Then Aurelia's eyes twinkled with mischief, she turned her head and gave his finger a nibble that was very real. They smiled at each other and Baird, encouraged, couldn't resist that luscious breast any longer.

He bent and licked the nipple leisurely, coaxing it to attention as Aurelia gasped. Baird drew her closer, lifting her from the bed, cupping her breast in one hand, then eased the robe over her shoulders.

It tumbled to the bed with an odd thump, but Baird had only a fleeting chance to notice. Aurelia suddenly locked her arms around his neck and kissed him as though the world were ending.

Her embrace left Baird dizzy and uncaring about anything in any robe anywhere. He scooped her close and rolled across the bed, nuzzling her neck as he went.

When they came to a stop, Aurelia stretched one hand tentatively toward him, but Baird was determined to set that cascade of hair free. He worked the braid loose carefully, then spread the gleaming mass of her hair over her shoulders. It shone in the moonlight like silvered silk and seemed to have a life of its own.

Baird had never seen hair so long, let alone so thick and bouncy. It was nearly straight, heavy in his hand, but silky smooth. He fingered it with wonder. "Have you ever cut it?"

Aurelia shook her head. "It was forbidden."

Baird frowned at the odd confession, then Aurelia's fingers closed over his and the heat fired between them once more. They kissed with fingers entangled, a greedy sampling of each other that left them both gasping for breath.

Aurelia touched his nipple with an exploratory finger. It tightened and Baird caught his breath when she leaned closer to touch her lips to the same spot. Her fingers outspread, she slid her hand down his ribs, across his pelvis, and closed her hand over him.

Baird nearly exploded on the spot.

He caught up Aurelia's hand and rolled her to her back on the bed, leaning over her with purpose.

Aurelia blinked. "You do not like to be touched?"

"I *love* to be touched," Baird assured her, brushing his lips across her brow, the pert curve of her nose, and finally her lips. He lingered there, unable to stop himself, then lifted his head and stared into her eyes for a long moment. Aurelia looked as amazed as he felt at the passion burning between them.

Baird quirked his brow. "I like it so much that we'd be done very quickly if you hadn't stopped."

Aurelia giggled and squirmed beneath him. Baird rolled his hips and let her feel the size of him. She started to smile a very feminine smile of satisfaction, then he captured her breast once more and dragged his thumb slowly across the nipple.

Aurelia gasped as the nipple peaked. She melted as Baird bent and kissed the taut bead with slow deliberation.

Aurelia sighed and arched languorously beneath his caress. Baird suckled first one breast and then the other, loving how she moved beneath him. In this as everything else, Aurelia was honest about her feelings, and she welcomed every nuance of the experience.

Her obvious pleasure brought Baird's own desire to a fever pitch, and he was determined to see that the magic they made surpassed any other Aurelia had ever known.

He wondered if he would ever get enough of her, if she would want more of him. Baird kissed her ears, her jaw, her throat, the underside of her breasts and her navel, and watched a flush slide over her flesh.

There was one way to be sure.

Baird captured the nipple again, then spread his fingers and speared them through the nest of blond curls at the apex of her thighs. He slid his arm beneath Aurelia, holding her fast against his side. Aurelia arched back and gasped when his fingers found the wetness awaiting him there.

Baird caressed and cajoled, loving the way the little pearl hidden there tightened beneath his touch. Aurelia twisted harder beneath him, she arched and clutched at his shoulders.

Baird cupped the back of her head, lifting her lips for a deep and searching kiss. Aurelia clung to him, kissing him as though she couldn't get enough of him. Baird's tongue plundered her sweetness and Aurelia's tongue tangled with his.

His fingers danced and Aurelia gripped his shoulders suddenly. She arched right off the bed with the force of her orgasm and Baird swallowed her cry with satisfaction.

Aurelia fell back gasping against the mattress. Baird cupped her breast and felt the pounding of her heart beneath his hand. His own pulse matched its pace as he bent and brushed his lips across hers.

Aurelia's eyes opened sleepily. Baird had never seen them so darkly blue. "I never imagined," she whispered huskily, and Baird grinned.

"I can imagine a lot more," he teased.

Aurelia's eyes flashed with mischief, giving almost no warning before she had rolled Baird to his back.

"As can I," she murmured throatily. She sat astride him, her feet wriggling against his buttocks. She smiled at him, then closed both hands around him. Baird moaned and closed his eyes. He whispered her name, only to find her soft breasts against his chest.

Baird caught his breath in anticipation as Aurelia perched above him, and then with one breathtaking move, impaled herself on his throbbing erection. The slick heat of her swallowed him, caressed him, and surrounded him with softness and warmth.

"Aurelia!"

Baird gripped her buttocks with both hands just before her lips locked over his. He was beside himself with desire, more enflamed that he had ever been before.

He had been waiting for this woman.

And he had known her from first glance.

Aurelia moved, launching a symphony of pleasure and drawing him deeper into her with every stroke. Baird twisted against the mattress, willing this moment to last, yet unable to imagine surviving her sweet torture for long.

He had to make sure he pleased her again.

They moved together in an ancient rhythm, their breath synchronized, their gazes locked. Baird slid his thumb between the two of them and found Aurelia's secret pearl once more.

She smiled with a delight that warmed him to his toes and rode him even harder.

He felt the shimmer of Aurelia's hair spill over the pair of them, like a net snaring him in her allure. She was all moonlight and magic, her spell of enchantment snaring him in silver cobwebs.

And Baird didn't even want to break free. Aurelia's tiny hands wandered over his skin, caressing and teasing. Her lips drove him to distraction. She touched everywhere at once, it seemed, stoking his passion to an intensity he had never known before.

Her feet slid down the length of his legs and Baird's blood boiled. Baird hung on stubbornly, feeling as though he would burst his own seams if he got any larger. The back of her waist was smooth beneath his hand, her clitoris hardened abruptly beneath his thumb.

Aurelia cried out in ecstasy, stretching for the canopy overhead with both hands. Her breasts bobbed, her hair snared the moonbeams and her delectable toes dug into his thighs.

The vision of her snapped the last cord of Baird's control.

He locked his hands around Aurelia's waist as he thrust into her welcoming heat. Baird heard himself bellow her name, felt his fingers grip her softness, and he finally let Vesuvius erupt.

And the magic had only just begun.

Sixteen

Aurelia watched Bard sleep beside her as she toyed indecisively with the knife.

Bard had heard the blade fall, that much Aurelia knew, but in the moment she had managed to distract him from investigating the sound. Would he recall it later? Would he guess what she intended to do?

How she wished that she could read *his* thoughts as easily as he read hers!

Because now Aurelia was sorely confused. Bard's features were resolute even in sleep, his firm lips only slightly relaxed. Aurelia liked to see his dark hair so tousled, even more now than when he forced his fingers through it.

Bard's strong hand rested on her belly, the curve of his fingers possessive, his skin warm against her own. Aurelia was surrounded by his heat and his scent. After what had been between them, she could not bring herself to plunge the blade into the blackness of Bard's heart.

Could a man of such evil intent have loved her so thoroughly? Aurelia could not believe it. Theirs had been no foul mating, no forced and painful coupling, but an odyssey of pleasure.

She should have been ashamed to find herself hungry for more, but Aurelia was not. Instead, she questioned all her forgone conclusions about the man who slept beside her.

He had shown her only honorable behavior, in this as in all other things.

Was it possible that Bard, son of Erc, was not the villain she believed him to be? Was it possible that he had not been responsible for the death of Thord?

Or was Aurelia merely being skillfully manipulated?

She chewed her lip and watched Bard sleep, her mind riddled with doubts. When he stirred, Aurelia slid the knife beneath the bed, its movement making no sound on the plush carpeting.

She could not strike a blow that might ultimately prove to be an error, however fatal a choice that might prove to be.

Bard's hand slid slowly over Aurelia's belly, then closed over her breast. She caught her breath as his thumb did its magic and watched him smile. He opened his eyes and regarded her drowsily, his green gaze unnaturally dark.

"So you weren't a dream, princess." His voice was low with a satisfaction that made Aurelia flush self-consciously.

"I thought you did not dream."

Bard arched one dark brow. "I never used to." His hand slid over her belly as he smiled. "Maybe I just didn't have anything worth dreaming about."

Aurelia's heart skipped a beat, but before she could say anything more, Bard disappeared beneath the duvet. She felt him nuzzle her pubic hair and caught her breath.

"Breakfast of champions," he murmured inexplicably.

Then Aurelia gasped at the heat of his tongue *there*.

She grasped two fistfuls of his hair, intent on pulling him away, but when he caressed her again, Aurelia forgot all about stopping him.

There was no harm in seeing what he intended, after all.

"I thought you did not like mornings," she said breathlessly.

"I think I may have underestimated them," came the growl from beneath the covers.

Aurelia leaned back against the pillows and clutched the linens as his tongue made its mark. "I may have underestimated them myself," she managed to murmur, certain she had never started a day in such fine style.

Bard did not answer, his tongue resolutely exploring new ground. Aurelia shivered with delight as Bard captured one of her feet in each hand, his thumbs stroking her instep in a seductive caress.

On some level, Aurelia conceded that this deed was not the choice of a selfish man.

Then she forgot everything other than Bard's tongue.

The heat rose beneath Aurelia's flesh, just as it had the night before, but so much more quickly. She writhed and twisted, straining toward release but never wanting this moment to end.

Neither Bard nor his tongue granted her any quarter. He placed one of her feet on his enormous erection and the awareness of his arousal cast Aurelia over the precipice.

She cried out and gripped his shoulders, certain she would drown him with her release. Aurelia was stunned by both the force and the haste of her climax.

She looked down with some embarrassment to find that half smile tugging at Bard's lips as he regarded her from under the bed linens.

Had there ever been a man with such allure? Aurelia smiled back, well aware of the flush that stained her cheeks.

Bard reached up and flicked a finger across the tip of her nose with an affection that melted her heart. "What do you say we blow this Popsicle stand, princess? We could mosey into town after breakfast. . . ."

"You had your breakfast, champion."

Bard chuckled. "Well, *you're* probably hungry." Aurelia's stomach growled in approval of that sentiment. "Then we can have a good look for your father."

"My father?" Aurelia blinked at this sudden return to practicalities.

"Hekod. You remember him." Bard cast himself up on the pillows beside her and rolled to his back. "I tried to phone the police station yesterday, but I couldn't get anything sorted out over the phone. We'll have to go down there to get anything done." He shot her a bright glance. "Any objections, princess?"

How could she protest a day in this man's presence? Although Aurelia told herself she only agreed so that she could study his true character, a part of her denied the justification.

All the same, she would go.

"No."

"Then it's a date." Bard rolled Aurelia beneath him before she could say anything else, bracing himself above her on his elbows. Aurelia's heart began to beat a staccato at the sensual promise in his gaze.

"But first," he whispered, a wicked glint in his eyes, "maybe we should work up an appetite."

Bard bent his head to capture her lips and Aurelia twined her arms around his neck. She was lost in the circle of this man's embrace and, for the moment, did not want to be found.

Baird was whistling under his breath as he poured his coffee. The world was filled with promise. In fact, he didn't know when he'd felt better in the morning.

He hoped Aurelia would hurry.

The sound of a footstep made his head snap up, but it was only Julian. The lawyer's eyes widened at the sight of the *Wall Street Journal* and he pounced greedily on it.

"Ah, the lure of civilization!" he crowed, and cradled the bundle of newsprint like a long-lost lover.

The comment reminded Baird of his dream the night before and he toyed with the idea of asking Julian's thoughts. "It's a week old," he acknowledged absently.

Julian checked the date but didn't look overly disappointed. "But a mere week ago, this paper was in the civilized world." He poured coffee with a flourish. "Not its cradle, mind you, we'd need the *LA Times* for that, but still, closer to the pulse than you or I have been in recent memory."

"You don't have to stake turf," Baird said amiably. "It's all yours."

Julian looked at him thoughtfully. "Are you all right?"

"Never better." Baird grinned and Julian frowned.

"I don't think I've ever seen you so cheerful before ten." Julian waggled his eyebrows. "If that."

"Maybe I just had a good night's sleep."

Julian remained unconvinced, but the lure of the *Journal* was too much for him. "Uh-huh." He unfolded the paper and buried his nose in it with undisguised delight. "God! A sale at Bloomies and I missed it. The things I do for this company. . . ."

Baird cleared his throat. If he didn't ask now, he never would. "Julian, do you know anything about reincarnation?"

Julian lowered the paper so that he could glare pointedly over its top. "Baird, I'm from *California*. Affectionately known as LaLa Land. What do *you* think?" He lifted the paper again and snapped it pertly.

"Well." Baird had a hard time even voicing the question. "Do you think there's anything to it?"

Julian dropped the paper and stared at him. "You might look like Baird Beauforte," he whispered, "but you sure don't sound like him." The lawyer's eyes narrowed and he scanned the hall with mock suspicion. "Where's your pod, Alien? And what have you done with my friend?"

"Come on, Julian, I'm serious."

Julian was not persuaded. "What's in your coffee this morning?"

"Nothing. Really, I'm serious about this. What do you think of that stuff?"

Julian eyed Baird for a long moment, then shrugged. He coughed politely. "I don't see any reason why it couldn't be true. It's not like we have legal affidavits of what happens after we die."

Baird traced a pattern on the tabletop, fighting against the insistence of an intuition he didn't like to acknowledge. "So, places and people could be familiar because we knew them before."

"Yeah, well, why not?"

Why not.

Baird realized his finger was tracing the pattern of whorls that was tattooed on Aurelia's own palm and stopped instantly. "Well, have you ever had the feeling that you knew someone before?"

Julian's eyes appeared above the paper again and his tone was sardonic. "You mean like, my eyes met hers, my heart went thump, and I *knew* right then, right there, that we were destined to be together for all time, despite the odds?"

Baird felt the back of his neck heat. He should never have even brought up the subject. "You're right. It's dumb. Just forget I said anything." He stirred his coffee, wishing he could just drop through the floor.

Or that Julian would stop gaping at him.

Finally Julian cast aside his paper with a noisy rustle, his manner surprisingly aggressive. "Okay, okay, you want to talk about this? I had one time—*one* time!—that I thought I had met someone before. It was weird as hell, but I've never forgotten it, so, you could say that I *do* think there's something to this stuff." He scrambled for the paper again and glared at Baird. "Happy?"

"Who was it?" Baird's question was soft. His skin was tingling with a strange certainty of what Julian would say.

For the first time in living memory, Julian looked uncomfortable with the prospect of speaking his mind. "Remember that first day at college?"

Baird nodded and didn't dare to breathe.

Julian licked his lips and frowned, his voice dropping low with his confession. "I sat beside you because I felt like I knew you already, like we were already good friends, even though I had never met you before in my life. It was nuts, but in that moment, I was sure of it." He frowned at his coffee cup, then turned his gaze to Baird. "And I've never forgotten that."

The men stared at each other.

Baird marveled at what he had just heard. Julian—pragmatic, legal-minded, prove-it-to-me-twice-before-I'll-believe-it-and-put-it-in-writing-besides—Julian had had the same feeling as he had.

And now that man stumbled over his words in his haste to explain himself. "Look, don't be getting any ideas, all right? I mean, you're not my type at all, Baird, I'm as straight as they make 'em and you know it."

Julian rustled his newspaper defiantly. "Don't go thinking that there's some subtext here. I may be a funky, left-tending kind of a guy but I have really, *really* definite ideas about gender." He glared at Baird. "Okay?"

"Okay," Baird agreed easily, more than happy to let Julian return to his newspaper.

Julian's admission encouraged Baird as nothing else could have. Baird respected Julian, he *knew* Julian, had known him for years.

And apparently he had known Julian even before that.

Well, why not? You could only recognize people you had met before, right? And if you hadn't met them in this life, why not in another?

It all made terrific sense, once Baird accepted the premise.

Kind of like Aurelia. And having known her before would explain the sticky problem of how he could recognize her without remembering where they had ever met before.

Perfectly logical.

Which meant that Baird had Dunhelm and its effect on him all figured out. Mystery solved. He'd been here before, maybe as this Bridei guy. Simple. He had known Julian before, he had known Aurelia before. The woman in question sailed into the restaurant and treated him to a breathtaking smile.

Baird's eyes met hers, his heart went thump, and he felt like he had the world by a string.

Now all he had to do was find Aurelia's father.

And in the mood he was in, that looked like a piece of cake.

"Are you not hungry yet?" Aurelia demanded several hours later and Baird looked to her in surprise. She was serious.

Again.

"Let me guess. You are, right?"

Aurelia nodded and watched him expectantly. Baird sighed, admitted that they weren't getting anywhere in a hurry anyhow, and scanned the square.

Hekod was not prepared to be found, despite Baird's earlier optimism. The cops knew nothing of him, no one had seen him in either village on the island, and Baird was really beginning to worry that the old guy *was* dead.

But that was nothing compared to how much he dreaded Aurelia being forced to face that. If anything, his protective instinct toward her had only gotten stronger after the incredible night they had shared.

He didn't want to see her hurt for the world.

But Baird was sure she knew the truth already, at least on some level. But how would confronting it—again—affect her? Not well, Baird guessed, but wasn't sure what to do about it.

Maybe she was right. Maybe he'd think better with something in his stomach.

Baird noticed a tea shop, and turned his steps in that direction. Aurelia sniffed appreciatively as they crossed the threshold, her face lighting up at the sight of an elderly woman sipping tea in the corner.

It was Talorc's mother and she beamed at Aurelia in turn. Relief washed through Baird that *someone* recognized Aurelia. Maybe Ursilla would know what had happened to Hekod. He deliberately took the table next to hers.

"Good morning, Ursilla." Baird nodded at the bags clustered at the older woman's feet. "Out doing your shopping?"

"Gemdelovely Gemdelee! And Mr. Beauforte, as charming as can be." The older lady nodded to Baird, whose heart had leaped at the unexpected mention of That Name again. "You've a sharp eye, as clear as can be, though I wonder if you see all you can see."

As usual, Talorc's mother was a bit confusing to understand. Baird was not surprised that Aurelia settled in beside the dotty older woman with sparkling eyes.

"Like to like," as his twelfth foster father often said.

Baird ordered tea and scones from the bustling matron running the tea shop.

"I do not understand why all insist on calling me Gemdelovely," Aurelia commented with a bit of irritation.

Ursilla smiled mysteriously and stirred her tea.

Baird leaned forward. "Yes, Ursilla, perhaps you could help. Elizabeth said that there's an old story about that name. Would you happen to know it?"

"Oh, yes, indeed!"

"What is it?" Aurelia asked. "Will you tell us?"

Ursilla looked from one to the other as she sipped her tea, her pinkie lifting ever so slightly from the bone china handle. "You do not remember the tale, as old as it might be?"

"I never knew it," Aurelia and Baird said simultaneously.

They glanced to each other as Ursilla laughed aloud. "Is that the truth? Well, we shall see."

She cleared her throat and set her teacup aside, folding her hands primly on the tabletop. "It is said there was once, beyond the sea, a Viking lord who was fine to see. His hair was gold, he could hold his mead, he was strong with sword and brave of deed. When he earned his ship, he put to sea, and with his crew of loyal men, Hekod came to Orkney."

Uh-oh. Baird flashed a glance to Aurelia, who sat stiffly on the edge of her seat. He wasn't quite so sure that this was a good idea anymore, but Aurelia was listening with rapt attention.

The tea came in that moment, cups and saucers settled on the tiny table with a clatter, followed by a teapot in a horrible frilly cozy, a creamer, and sugar. The scones were steaming from the oven and smelled wonderful.

Aurelia, tellingly enough, didn't even notice the arrival of the food. Baird buttered a scone and poured the tea.

Aurelia didn't look away from Ursilla. "Go on!"

Ursilla cleared her voice. "There was a king on the isle, known far and wide in those times. He was named Erc Destroyer and was greatly feared for his crimes. People longed to escape from the heavy hand of their king, but they had not the power before Hekod Viking.

"No sooner had Hekod Viking arrived, his willing men all around, than the people rallied to his side and drove Erc from their ground. The old king was angered his people did not hold him dear, but when he drowned in escaping, the whole of the isle erupted in a cheer.

"Hekod Viking was made king by people glad of his blade, and he, grateful for their praise, took to wife a local maid. Gemma Whitefeather was a witch and a beauty unsurpassed, she gave Hekod a son, shortly thereafter a wee lass. All was happy in their kingdom, they ruled over a prosperous age, and 'twould be long years before tragedy darkened the page."

Aurelia's face, Baird noted with concern, had gone white. He urged a cup of tea toward her and a buttered scone. She smiled thinly and took a bite, but chewed mechanically as she watched Ursilla.

This really didn't look like it had been such a good idea.

But Ursilla wasn't going to stop. "As was told, Gemma was a witch greatly empowered, she gripped many of the world's wonders in her power. There were many of her ilk in those days long forgotten, and the birth of the daughter meant another had been begotten. This child was not only destined to share her mother's gifts, but she was uncommon beautiful, the merest glimpse of her brought a smile to the lips.

"Gemma summoned three of her cohorts to bless the new child, and they all were delighted to share the blessings they had styled. The witches had brought blessings one two three, but evil intruded uninvited, cackling with glee.

"She was Drustic of Sutherland, known as Drustic the Black, and she had come, she declared, to give Hekod his own back. A cousin of Erc, Drustic yearned for vengeance with a thirst, and she had come back to Dunhelm to make Hekod's burden worse. The other witches shrank away while Gemma sheltered her own, and Drustic gave a wicked cackle before pronouncing her doom."

Aurelia leaned forward, her features drawn with tension. Baird opened his mouth to suggest that Ursilla stop this tale, but no sound came out of his throat.

What was going on?

"Oh, you will hear all of this tale," Ursilla told him with a stern glance. "Of that you may be sure, for it is a lesson to us all of what the past can make clear."

Baird figured he should have gotten used to the hair on the back of his neck standing up by now.

Ursilla lifted a finger. "Drustic summoned the forces from the darkness she had roamed, and she bent them on the child, so innocent and alone. Drustic pronounced that the babe would prick her thumb—in the midst of the whorl—and a darkness then would come. She would die from the wound, no one's efforts would avail, and after her demise, Hekod's kingdom would fail. Certain she had wrought all the wickedness she could do on that day, Drustic lifted her bony arms, whistled to the wind and flew away.

"As you might imagine, the witches were distraught. Here was one of their own, cursed with evil she had not wrought.

They thought very busily of what help they could be, then focused their aid on the witch making blessing number three. That witch summoned her powers and focused her will, and she decreed that the child would not die of Drustic's will. The babe would but sleep, if ever she pricked her thumb, and that babe would awaken when her true love did come.

"The witches were quite pleased with all they had done, though Gemma considered matters far from done. Though she thanked her good friends for their gifts made in joint, that night she purged Dunhelm's hall of every item with a point.

"When Hekod protested all that Gemma had seen done, she feared he would think her a fool and make fun. She lied to her spouse and said she feared for her young, that they might stumble in the hall and great damage could be done. Hekod loved his wife clear to the bone, and though he thought her worries whimsy, he ensured her desire in Dunhelm was done.

"And so they passed many years in happiness and peace, until suddenly one winter, Gemma died in her sleep.

"All were dismayed at the passing of their queen, though none more than Hekod, or his children, young and green. It was not much later that tragedy came to pass, and 'twas said it was because the lady's spells could not last. When Gemma passed from this life, 'twas said an age came to an end, and the white-feathered eagles for which she was named were never seen again."

Ursilla sipped her tea and there wasn't a sound in the shop.

"A messenger came boldly, sent by Bard, a warrior true, declaring his lord as a man desiring Hekod's daughter to woo. Now, Hekod remembered well that Erc had had a child, name of Bard, and saw this as a chance to see settled an old scar."

Baird immediately noticed the similarity between his name and Bard's, and wondered if it was just a coincidence that Aurelia had been pronouncing his name as "Bard." Somehow, he doubted it.

"Hekod's son rode out willingly to meet the dead king's spawn, but their trust was poorly served by the very next dawn. On that day, the son's head was returned to Dunhelm— he had been murdered by Bard, though he was son of the realm."

Baird noted with a start that Aurelia was weeping. The tears ran silently down her cheeks as he watched with concern, but when Ursilla paused, it was Aurelia who silently urged her on.

He reached out and took her hand, reassured by her strong grip on his fingers. Baird was determined to help Aurelia face whatever obstacles were before her.

"Hekod was devastated by the murder of his heir, no less by Bard's certain intent of war. The son of Erc was determined to have Dunhelm for his own, and he cared little for any cost paid to win back his father's crown.

"The day Bard's ships were sighted dawned sunny and bright, and Hekod's forces climbed the walls, armed with all of their might. The daughter of Gemma, both lovely and strong, took her crossbow to do her part against this wrong. But no sooner had the Princess of Dunhelm climbed the wall, than her arrow pricked her thumb, in the midst of the whorl. She fell into that slumber, prophesied and foretold, Hekod crying with pain when his daughter he did behold.

"They won the battle that day, and Bard died by his own blade, though the son of Erc had a last word to say. He declared he would be back, that he would make the girl his own, and woe to any man who stood between him and his goal.

"Though the fight had been won, Hekod had paid a heavy toll. It was said he aged a decade and suddenly looked old. Hekod sent word through every kingdom of what had gone amiss, and promised great riches for the man who woke her with a kiss.

"This man would be her true love, Hekod knew that without fail, yet men came one after the other, time passed, and the king grew frail. Hekod stayed beside his daughter, weeping as he died, and clearly 'twas his broken heart that stole Hekod from her side.

"When the great king died, his kingdom crumbled, and the men who had served knew their king and lord would see his daughter's safety preserved. They built her a chamber, a room whose place is lost, and they sealed her inside, sparing no cost. And with every stone they raised and with every hinge they cast, the time of Hekod's happy reign slid into the past.

"When the chamber was done, men of valor wept without

shame, and 'twas after it all Hekod's daughter earned her new name. Spawn of Gemma, yet even more lovely than could be, she became known in Dunhelm as Gemdelovely Gemdelee. A new prophecy was made for Gemdelovely Gemdelee; should her true love kiss her, his bride she will be.''

Baird sat up with a start when he heard the phrase from his dream again. Aurelia inhaled sharply, but Ursilla's words continued, her cadence as rhythmic as a song.

''It is said her true love still searches, as persistent as can be, though no one knows exactly what happened to Gemdelovely Gemdelee. And to this day in Orkney whene'er a pretty lass is seen, folks say she must be the revived Gemdelovely Gemdelee.''

Ursilla smiled at the pair of them and the matron running the tea shop sighed with romantic contentment. ''No one can tell an old tale as well as you, Ursilla,'' she murmured.

But Aurelia was stumbling to her feet.

She stumbled over the chair and Baird reached out to steady her but she evaded his grasp. Her eyes glittered wildly, and she shook her head, her color rising in her cheeks.

''It is not true! It cannot be true!'' Aurelia ran from the tea shop, tripping over the threshold on her way to the street.

Baird lurched to his feet to give chase, but Ursilla latched on to his arm with remarkable tenacity for her age. Her eyes were bright with determination.

''Leave her be, Mr. Beauforte, and you will see, that there is no one stronger than soft Gemdelovely Gemdelee.''

''I can't believe that. She's vulnerable right now!'' He shook his arm but the old woman's grip was strong.

Ursilla chuckled to herself, then wagged a playful finger at Baird. ''Just because you stop believing in things does not mean they cease to be. There's more to you than the world might see—look closely, Mr. Beauforte, and you will see.''

Baird stared at the woman for a long moment, not sure what to make of the knowing smile that danced over her lips.

''She's not Gemdelovely Gemdelee,'' he said finally. ''Aurelia is just a confused woman who needs some help.'' He shook his arm pointedly but to no avail.

Ursilla shook her head. ''The only thing of which Gemdelovely has need is the kiss of her true love, a man loyal in deed.''

''What she needs is to find out the truth about her father,'' Baird said tightly. ''And to shake herself free of a lot of old nonsense.''

With that, Baird freed himself from Ursilla's grip and strode to the door, chafing at his suspicion that the older woman had been ready to let him go anyway. He dropped some money into the hands of the woman who ran the tea shop, ignoring the wonder in her eyes, and dashed out into the square.

And there Baird's fears were proven absolutely right.

There was no sign of Aurelia anywhere.

Baird shoved his hands in his pockets and glared at a kid openly surveying him, the only person on the street. ''Have you seen a blond woman? She just came out of here.''

The boy shook his head and smiled. ''Just you, mister.''

Baird turned away in disgust. He checked the trio of streets that made up the intersection of the town, but didn't see another living soul, let alone Aurelia.

It was as though she had vanished into thin air.

The sign over the Boar and Thistle creaked in the wind when Baird stalked back into the square. Garth's cab was still beside the curb, but maybe Aurelia had gone looking for a ride back to Dunhelm. Baird ran a hand through his hair in frustration. It couldn't hurt to find out.

There was nowhere else to look, after all.

Aurelia ran.

She was out of the town in no time at all, heading for the coast at dizzying speed. All she could think was that she had to get away, away from Ursilla, away from silly stories, away from a tale that sounded far too familiar for comfort.

Gemdelovely Gemdelee indeed!

Aurelia scrambled over loose stones, avoiding the black road, climbing over rocks to the shore instead. The coast was familiar, unlike all that was behind her. She did not want to look at Julian's magic, she did not want to fight to explain great mysteries right now. Aurelia tried to make her breathing come more evenly as she kept her eyes on the sea.

The Vikings would come.

Her father was not dead of grief.

She would not permit Ursilla's story to be true.

Seventeen

~

The Boar and Thistle was busy with afternoon traffic, although some of its clients looked as though they had settled in for days, if not months, before. Some appeared to be as firmly rooted in this place as the furniture.

Although Baird had only come in here once or twice, he was hailed by the regulars as he stood on the threshold, blinking in the dim light. He heard a murmur of conversation slide around the pub, those in the know obviously identifying him to the others.

Baird was very aware that he was the center of attention.

"Left the lady shopping, guv?" Garth demanded, continuing on before Baird could respond. "No place for a man while a woman spends his money," the cabby declared with a wink, and a snort of assent sounded around the bar.

Aurelia was not here.

And she certainly hadn't asked Baird to leave with her. That old sense of being unwanted assailed him and fought with his concern for her welfare. Maybe he should take this opportunity to see whether he could learn anything about Hekod.

"What can I get you, sir?"

A quick survey revealed that everyone drank very dark brew.

"A pint of your best stout."

The barkeeper raised his eyebrows appreciatively, and the men grinned. Baird had been identified as a compatriot.

"Why don't you sit with us, guv, and tell the boys a bit about your work at ol' Dunhelm?"

It was the best opening Baird was likely to get. He slid onto a stool and took a good look around. The place looked positively medieval with its heavy oak beams stained dark and the walls whitewashed in between the trusses. The ceiling was low and made of dark wood. A variety of antique etchings in cheap frames hung on the walls. They had probably been of virtually no value when they were hung—whenever that had been.

The pub smelled of cigar smoke, with a base of spilled beer and a top note of bacon and sausages. There was no clock and the leaded windows emitted so little light that it was impossible to say from inside what time of day it might be.

Baird's beer arrived, frothing over the side and onto the wooden bar. He ignored the foam and lifted the glass to his companions. When he didn't wince at the flavor of the warm, yeasty beer, their amiability increased markedly.

Baird restrained himself from running a tongue over the film the stout left on his teeth. "I don't suppose any of you would know anyone named Hekod?"

"Oh, guv!" Garth exclaimed. "No one uses that name hereabouts!"

"Why not?"

"It's a name of wicked bad luck."

"Powerfully unlucky," contributed another.

"There's not been a Hekod here since the original, they say."

Baird took another sip of his beer and decided it was getting better. "What's unlucky about it?"

"Have you not heard the tale of Hekod?" Garth demanded. Baird nodded and the cabby frowned, gesturing with his glass. "Now, there's a man cursed with foul luck. Everything in the world he had to his name, a beautiful wife, prosperity and two lovely bairns." Garth snapped his fingers beneath Baird's nose. "And every bit of it snatched away from him in his prime."

"Bairns?"

"Babes! A boy and girl, it is said."

Garth drained his beer in one great gulp and set the empty

glass on the bar. He glanced pointedly at Baird, then back to the glass with its residue of foam.

"Another pint for Garth," Baird said to the barkeeper, who shook his head and grinned. He scooped up the glass and pulled another pint, setting it before the cabbie with a flourish.

"Ah!" Garth took a long draught and smacked his lips. "I thank you, guv."

"Now, what about this bad luck?"

"Ah, well, our Hekod lost first his lovely wife, then his son was killed and his daughter cursed. Add to that the destruction of his estate." Garth shook his head. "He must have died an unhappy man."

"It is said he died of grief," added one of the others.

"And rightly so. What man could bear to lose so much?" Garth set his glass on the bar and fixed Baird with a steady gaze. "You're seeing why it would be a horrible burden for any bairn to be granted such a name, aren't you, guv?"

"You're sure there hasn't been even *one*?"

"We've no parents cruel enough to curse their own spawn."

The men nodded sagely at this local wisdom and Baird noticed that the boy who had delivered the pizzas to Dunhelm hovered on the fringe of the group. His eyes were bright and his Adam's apple bobbed with excitement.

No doubt at the prospect of more tales to share with his buddies.

"Why would you be asking, Mr. Beauforte?" he asked.

Baird shrugged as though it didn't really matter. "We were trying to think of a name for the restaurant that we're putting at the top of the tower. One of the marketing people suggested we tie in to Dunhelm's history somehow and wanted to use Hekod's Roost, or something similar."

Baird took another sip, amazed at how readily they accepted his lie. "I just wanted to make sure there wasn't an actual Hekod who might take offense."

Garth gripped his arm with surprising strength, his gaze intense. "You be taking my advice, guv, and don't be using that name on anything at Dunhelm. It will bring only tragedy and unhappiness wherever it is used and you'll not be wanting any of that at the Beauforte Dunhelm Resort.''

A curious silence descended over the group and all drank uneasily.

"Well! I'm glad I asked." Baird forced a smile as he leaned on the counter again. "Do any of you have any suggestions? These marketing people, you know"—he rolled his eyes—"they can drive a man crazy with all their dithering around. I'd love to just walk back in there with the perfect name."

The boy's eyes lit up. "What about The Crow's Nest?"

"Nah," said one of the others. "It should have 'Viking' in it. Viking's Lair."

"And what would a 'lair' be to you and me?" Garth demanded with amiable crankiness. "It's got to be understood by everyone who happens along—you're wanting a name like The Lookout."

"Oh! That's clever!" A chorus of disagreement erupted as the men latched on to the problem.

Baird might even get a name for the restaurant out of this. Even if he hadn't come any closer to finding Hekod. He worried about Aurelia again. Probably she had walked back to Dunhelm. He'd walk back himself after this beer and make sure nothing had happened to her on the way.

As for Hekod, well, that was another problem. If Aurelia's father was alive—and Baird was thinking the chances of that were pretty remote—he must have gone to the main island. Maybe the older man had passed away there. Either way, the next logical step was to go to Kirkwall on the main island, but it was too late to fly there today.

First thing in the morning, then, Baird resolved, and drank more of his stout.

The brew was growing on him, actually.

Aurelia watched the sun sink, its orange rays painting the sea with fire. The wind tousled her hair, the chill of the night rose from the ground.

On this night, she would summon the Dreaming again.

What if she had surrendered her chastity to Bard and had not won back the control of her Dreaming? There was a kernel of cold fear planted where her heart should have been, but Aurelia refused to think any further about Ursilla's story.

Aurelia knew the very moment that Bard came to stand behind her. Her heart began to pound, her skin whispered of his presence, but she did not turn around. For a long time, he did not speak and they stood silently together, watching the sunlight fade.

When the sun finally dipped below the horizon and the sky turned indigo, Aurelia tipped back her head to watch the first stars come out. She took a deep breath, not certain what Bard was thinking and less certain that she wanted to know.

"You don't have to stay out here all night," he said quietly.

Aurelia turned to find Bard's eyes dark with concern. "You have been drinking. I can smell the ale upon you."

"Well, maybe just one beer. All for the good cause of finding your father." Bard heaved a dramatic sigh and Aurelia had the sense he was teasing her. "*Someone* has to do the dirty work."

"Drinking ale?" Aurelia frowned. "This is not labor at all!"

Bard grinned so unexpectedly that Aurelia caught her breath. His stern visage was transformed when he permitted himself to smile.

"You should smile more often," she said, without having any intention of doing so. "It makes you look younger."

Bard's smile faded abruptly. "I'm not *that* old, you know!"

"But you have seen much, I am certain."

And done much, Aurelia knew. Her body seemed to remember some of those deeds quite well. Aurelia's heart pounded as she held his gaze and the air between them heated with rare vigor.

Had there ever been a man whose very glance could make her feel so alive?

"Mmm." Bard shoved his hands into his pockets and watched her closely. "For an uneducated colonial, I've not done too badly." A twinkle lurked in the green depths of his eyes and Aurelia wondered what on earth he meant by that.

What truly filled the secret corners of this man's heart? For a man bent on wedding her, Bard did not seem particularly driven to achieve his goal. It was true that things had moved quickly between them, but at their own speed, not at his insistence.

Or was his manipulation so very skilled that Aurelia could not even discern it?

"You should know that I am not this Gemdelovely Gemdelee," Aurelia said, intending the words to be defiant. Instead her voice broke. "I am *not* a story."

"I know." Bard sobered instantly.

He stepped closer and Aurelia had to tip her head back to hold his gaze. She was encouraged by the sympathy she found in his eyes and liked that he did not believe this tale any more than she did.

It made Aurelia feel less alone in all of this. Bard lifted a hand toward her cheek, hesitating before his palm cradled her jaw.

"You're a woman who has lost someone precious," he said, and his voice was low. "I can understand how hard that must be."

Aurelia's eyes misted with tears and she was confused that the man who had destroyed her family was the one who offered her compassion. Why did *he* have to be the one to witness her weakness?

Why did he have to be the one to make her skin come alive with a single touch?

"It's all right to cry," Bard said quietly.

"I *never* cry!" Aurelia dashed at her tears with her fingertips.

"Of course not," Bard agreed easily, and slid his thumb across her cheek, sweeping away her tears in one smooth gesture. "Vikings never cry." His thumb was warm and Aurelia could smell his skin.

Suddenly she did not want to step away from him. She wanted to go back to his bed, to spend another night locked in his embrace, to spend another night feeling safe, secure, and cosseted.

And it was not because she intended to kill him while he slept.

What was happening to her?

"I asked about your father in town," Bard said gently. Aurelia was surprised at how soothing she found the low rumble of his voice. "And no one knew him. Do you think he might have gone to Kirkwall, on the big island?"

Aurelia had no idea where her sire might have fled. "Why would he go there? He has always stayed at Dunhelm."

Bard shrugged. "Maybe he wanted to go a little further afield again. Find different work, a change of scene." Aurelia examined his toes but he touched her chin with one fingertip, urging her to meet his sympathetic gaze. "Maybe he went a-viking, hmmm?"

Aurelia could not smile at his soft jest.

Bard cleared his throat. "I think we should go there tomorrow and look for him. Will you come?"

Aurelia considered him as the wind danced around them. Maybe he could understand her pain because he too had lost a father. Aurelia remembered only too well that Erc had drowned in his flight from Dunhelm.

Leaving his infant son without a father. Had that been the event that colored Bard's life?

"You know what it is to lose a father," Aurelia said softly.

Bard grimaced and shrugged. "You could say that. It's not important."

Aurelia blinked in surprise. "Losing your father was not important?"

Bard gave her a pointed glance that told her she had asked too much. "Finding *your* father is what's important now. The rest is just history." His lips curved, but the smile did not reach his eyes. "Kirkwall tomorrow? First thing?"

Aurelia was oddly loath to refuse a day in Bard's company. "I should like that," she admitted before she meant to do any such thing, and immediately flushed.

But she did not deny her agreement.

Bard flung an arm over Aurelia's shoulder and turned her back toward his hall, guiding Aurelia in that direction before she knew what she was about. There was something comforting about having the weight of Bard's arm around her and Aurelia liked matching her step to his.

There was an odd sense of security to be found in this man's companionship, one that made Aurelia forget all the dreadful things she knew to be true about him. She felt safe with him.

Was that all part of his scheme? Aurelia was no longer as certain of his dark intent as she would have liked to have been.

In fact, if she could have known for certain that he was honest with her about his character, Aurelia would have had no trouble accepting Bard for her spouse. He felt familiar to her, yet her body tingled with the dawn of something new.

Or was she simply the perfect pawn in his wicked scheme?

"Tell you what, Princess," Bard said with false casualness. "How about you and I make a deal?"

Aurelia was immediately wary. "A deal?"

"Yes." Bard's green eyes were sparkling. Aurelia had to bite back a smile of anticipation. What mischief was he making? "If you aren't going to be Gemdelovely Gemdelee, what do you say about me not being Bard, son of Erc?"

Aurelia was surprised. "You would deny your sire?"

Bard winced. "Erc the Destroyer? He doesn't really sound like my kind of guy and, frankly, neither does his son."

Bard wanted to separate himself from Ursilla's tale. Aurelia's mind flew like quicksilver. Had he seen that she knew part of the tale to be rooted in truth?

Or did he want to change his ways, leaving not only his name but his deeds behind himself? Was it just an undeserved reputation he desired to shake from his shoes?

"Who, then, would you be?" Aurelia managed to ask.

"Baird Beauforte," he said firmly. "I'm Baird Beauforte to everyone in this world except you. I'd like you to call me Baird as well."

Aurelia looked up at her escort and could see no insincerity in his eyes. They stared at each other for a long time, Aurelia seeking some hint in those emerald depths that he lied to her.

But she found none.

Aurelia's words were reluctant when they came and not without wonder. "You are not at all what I expected, Baird Beauforte."

Aurelia's heart skipped a beat when Baird enfolded her chin in his palm. His lips were a finger's breadth from her own, his eyes dark with import. Aurelia could see flecks of gold in his eyes, then his low words fanned her lips.

"And no one could have expected you, princess."

There was an admiration in his words that warmed Aurelia right to her toes and for a dizzying instant, she was certain that she confronted the true man.

And liked him very, very much.

Baird brushed his lips lightly across hers, leaving a tingle in their wake. He hesitated, as though he meant to pull away but could not bear to do so. His gaze darted over Aurelia's face and she could not move, her heart singing when his lips closed decisively over her own.

Aurelia was honest enough to admit that she would have been disappointed with anything less. She stretched and slid her arms around Baird's neck, loving the taste of him, ale and all. Aurelia felt a glow spread around her heart, for there was no doubt that Baird was complimenting her with both his words and his embrace.

And she felt oddly reassured after the tumult of this day.

Baird did not believe she was a mere tale. Baird did not believe that her sire had died of grief. Baird believed they would find Hekod.

And Aurelia found solace in his certainty.

Then Baird lifted his lips from hers and the doubts tumbled back into Aurelia's mind. He gave her shoulders an unexpected squeeze and started to hurry her toward the hall. Baird cleared his throat and cast a smile her way.

"Tell you what, though," he said easily, "don't go telling Elizabeth too soon that you're not this Gemdelovely Gemdelee. She's taken a shine to you and has apparently been cooking up a storm all afternoon. I don't know what she's making but it smells really good."

Aurelia gasped in mock outrage. "And you think that if I tell her the truth, you will not get any of it!"

Baird shrugged, his eyes dancing impishly. "Why take the chance?"

"Why, you shameless cur!" Aurelia pulled away and swatted him on the shoulder. "You would use me to see your own belly filled! You would see to your own comfort first and foremost!''

Baird laughed and stepped out of her range. ''Oh, and you wouldn't do the same?'' He granted her a wicked grin that made her heart jump awkwardly. ''Aren't you *hungry*, princess?''

She was.

Of course.

And Baird *knew* it! That only made his teasing worse. Aurelia's expression must have changed with the realization, for Baird laughed out loud.

''Last one in has to do the dishes,'' he taunted, and ran for the hall.

Aurelia did not know what that meant, but she recognized a threat when she heard one. Oh, and he was so much taller than she! She had to run hard to even catch up with him.

Aurelia bolted after Baird, stretching to tap him on one shoulder. Baird turned to look, and Aurelia darted around him on the other side.

''Cheat!'' Baird bellowed when Aurelia ducked through the door first. They both stumbled laughingly into the hall, and came up short quickly.

Marissa stood with a stranger, a coy smile toying with her reddened lips. ''Playtime over?'' she asked archly. ''We've simply been waiting *forever* for you two to come to dinner. Haven't we, darling?''

And she smiled up at the man beside her.

He was tall and of about the same age as Baird, his sandy hair tousled by the wind. There was a smattering of freckles across his cheeks, giving him a boyish air that was reinforced by his garb.

Actually, it was not his garb that made him look young as much as a general sense that he had slept in them.

Though he was dressed in chausses of ribbed velvet similar to those Baird wore, and his tweed jacket was of clever cut, Aurelia had the sense that this man was permanently disheveled. His leather shoes were scuffed and his creamy shirt was wrinkled.

He pushed his gold-rimmed spectacles farther up his nose

and summoned a grin so engaging that Aurelia could not help but smile in return.

She felt Baird stiffen behind her and was instantly curious. Did they know each other? Was there something amiss between the two? Or maybe Baird did not like his whore lavishing her attention on another.

Whatever the reason, Aurelia knew that Baird was not pleased. That playful side of his nature was banished once again and he looked the grim warrior from head to toe. His lips were tight and she thought she heard a thrum of anger in his voice when he spoke.

Though his words confused her all the more.

"Baird Beauforte," he said frostily, stepping forward to offer his hand as though he would rather be doing anything but. "I don't believe we've met."

Baird had never felt such a strong animosity toward another person, especially one he had never met. The dislike he felt on sight of the other man went against his usual refusal to judge a book by its cover, but he couldn't shake free of it.

The new arrival looked easygoing and innocent. Despite his appearance, Baird sensed malice coming from the other man in waves. Baird fought the urge to toss the man bodily into the street, but was glad he had won the battle just a moment later.

"Darian Mulvaney," the man supplied with a grin that should have been reassuring. "I'm a scholar from the National Heritage Preservation Society. We had word that you had discovered a Pictish site here." He looked as hopeful as a pup. "Would that be true, Mr. Beauforte?"

Baird found himself oddly reluctant to provide details. "I wouldn't know," he said evenly. "It does appear to be quite old." Baird felt his eyes narrow. "How exactly did you hear about this? We only just found the site and haven't had the chance to notify the authorities."

Darian laughed. "Oh, we get phone calls all the time! One of your workmen or someone local might have called it in."

Baird arched a brow skeptically but his tone was scrupulously polite. "You don't keep records of such calls?"

The other man sobered. "Is there an ancient site here or not?" Baird thought he heard the edge of a threat in the man's silken tones. "We had understood, Mr. Beauforte, that you had every intention of cooperating with the authorities in such matters."

"And so I do," Baird said smoothly. "The site has been undisturbed since its discovery—I simply want to ensure that only the *proper* authorities gain access." He smiled with cold charm. "You would, of course, have identification?"

Baird knew he didn't imagine the antagonism that flashed in the other man's eyes. Then Darian bent to rummage for his wallet in pockets apparently stuffed full of miscellanea.

This man would be entrusted to sift through an ancient site?

Three coins leaped to the floor and rolled, followed by a key ring that Darian managed to catch in midair. Aurelia bent to pick up an escaping coin and Baird's gut clenched when Darian winked at her as she returned it.

His fists clenched in his pockets when Aurelia smiled back.

No less than a dozen torn snippets of paper fluttered to the floor like confetti. Four pens, two pencils, a dog collar—that seemed to confuse Darian with its presence as much as anyone else—and a butterscotch candy that looked the worse for wear came to light before the wallet.

Darian triumphantly waved his billfold at Baird, unfolding a picture identification from the society that was obviously his own. Baird examined the photo and felt an unreasonable disappointment that not only the man was who he said he was, but that he could prove it.

Darian meanwhile gallantly offered the butterscotch candy to both women, who politely declined. Darian, untroubled, removed the lint-encrusted cellophane and popped the candy into his mouth, his expression expectant as he watched Baird.

"Well, I suppose you'll want to see the site first thing in the morning, then." Baird handed back the man's wallet, finding it troubling to have the other man's possession in his grip. He fought against the urge to wipe its taint from his fingers.

Darian's eyes gleamed. "Were there any artifacts?"

Baird refused to look at Aurelia, speaking quickly before she could get herself in trouble. This man might misunderstand her confusion, after all. Baird's protective urge was in full armor, especially after the soft confession she had just made to him.

Aurelia might be confused, but no one—no one!—was going to hurt her in his presence.

"No, nothing other than what's still there," he said flatly. "As I said, it's undisturbed. The workmen won't go near it."

"Local superstition, I suppose." Darian rubbed his hands together in gleeful anticipation. "It's been a tremendous boon to us over the years, that's for certain."

Julian made his appearance at that moment and introductions were made. The lawyer glanced fiercely at Baird before turning to Darian. Then he coughed discreetly into his hand.

"You must be looking for a place to stay," Julian began, and Baird's heart sank.

Darian shrugged. "I hadn't actually thought about it, I was so intent on getting here quickly. Is there somewhere you could recommend?"

Baird glared at his friend, who steadfastly ignored him. Julian *wouldn't*.

But he did.

And without hesitation.

"You really must stay with us, we insist. We're still under construction, of course, but the accommodations are as adequate as anything you'll find in town."

Julian coughed again and Baird knew things were going to get worse. "Actually, Beauforte Resorts has made a tremendous commitment on all our sites to preserving the history of the locale. Why don't you join us for dinner, Mr. Mulvaney, and tell us a bit about your work?"

"Oh, yes, darling!" Marissa cooed, linking her arm through Baird's and pointedly ignoring Aurelia. "Just imagine, Baird, darling, an Indiana Jones of our very own! This is *so* exciting! You simply must tell us all about your adventures, Mr. Mulvaney! Baird and I just *love* a good story."

Darian smiled again. "Thank you for your generosity, Mr. Beauforte." For a fleeting instant, his gaze locked with Baird's and Baird caught a quick glimpse of cold calculation.

Then it was gone, leaving Baird wondering whether he had imagined it in the first place.

"You must all call me Darian," the arrival insisted. "After all, I'll probably be underfoot for quite awhile. These investigations take time, at least when they're done properly."

Didn't that just figure?

Julian glared at Baird before he could say anything remotely disparaging, and as much as he hated to admit it, Baird knew that this time the lawyer was absolutely right. This Heritage Society could probably claim Dunhelm in its entirety as some kind of historic site, or encourage the government to do so, and Baird would lose the property he had fought so hard to obtain.

He couldn't let that happen. Darian Mulvaney's presence would have to be tolerated.

But Baird didn't have to like it.

Eighteen

Darian Mulvaney watched the others as they settled at the table, trying to sort out who knew what this time. His memory of the eighth century, of his father, Erc's, demise and his own pledge was crystal clear, but he hadn't been so fortunate each time he and Bridei met.

The fates were capricious when it came to memory. To Darien's good fortune, it seemed that there was still considerable confusion in the others' minds.

Julian, fortunately, had no recollection of the past he and Darian shared. Baird seemed to harbor some animosity—and no wonder after all the times Darian had hacked the life out of him—but apparently his memory was unclear. Darian could use that advantage.

And he would.

Aurelia, the prize herself, was even more lovely awake than asleep. If he had ever seen her like this, he might have taken her on one of his many other visits to Dunhelm. Or let Bridei succeed and steal her from beneath that man's nose.

Which would have been interesting, to say the least. Thus far, his only interest in Aurelia had been thwarting Bridei's goal of saving her from her curse. Obviously Darian's thirst for vengeance had blinded him to the possibilities.

Possibilities that were very interesting indeed.

He'd have to ensure that didn't happen again.

Darian smiled at his reluctant host. "I certainly have to

thank you, Mr. Beauforte, for extending your hospitality to me,'' he said expansively, watching the other man's response with care. "It's such a treat to have a good country meal."

Aurelia leaned toward him with a trusting smile. "Elizabeth is a very good cook," she said with the grace of a queen. "I am certain that whatever she has conjured will be wondrous indeed."

Marissa snorted delicately. "Aurelia, darling, though such home-cooked fare suits a rural appetite like your own, some of us have more sophisticated palates." She slid a hand over Baird's and eyed him through her lashes. "Isn't that right, Baird, darling?"

Ah, yes. Darian swallowed his smile. Dear Aunt Drustic, as malicious a bitch as ever, making trouble as only she could. It was always refreshing to find another being more self-motivated than himself.

Drustic had really outdone herself in the packaging this time, Darian acknowledged with admiration. He might not be adverse to a little family reunion himself.

Not that Drustic's figure seemed to make any difference to her prey—the link between Baird and Aurelia was as hot as a live wire. Once everything was lined up, Darian would take great pleasure in cutting that cord forever.

By the time he was done deflowering the luscious Aurelia and giving Baird Beauforte what he deserved, no one would have any doubt that he was victorious over both Dunhelm and its heiress.

Darian hadn't once been the son of the Destroyer for nothing.

The air at dinner was colored with discomfort, with Julian forcing conversation, Marissa trying to corner Baird, and Baird refusing to do much more than glower at the new arrival. Aurelia was in no mood to manage such a complicated tangle of events.

She did, however, over the course of the meal have the increasing feeling that Darian was trying to goad each of them in turn into revealing something of themselves.

Aurelia told herself that she was only sensitive because of

her concerns about summoning the Dreaming tonight. She escaped from the table early, but had only been in her room for a few moments before there was a soft rap on the door.

Aurelia opened it to find Baird leaning against the frame, his hands shoved into his pockets.

"Like some company?" he asked softly. He was serious, but his eyes glowed with such intensity that her heart skipped erratically.

Aurelia felt herself flush. She was sorely tempted to accept his offer. On the other hand, she had to dream tonight, despite the allure of sharing a bed with Baird once more.

She managed somehow to smile and hoped she looked as tired as she felt. "I am sorry, but I need to sleep tonight."

There was a flash of hurt in Baird's eyes and it pained Aurelia to know that she had caused it.

Then he smiled wryly and the shadow was gone. "And what makes you think I wouldn't let you get any?"

Aurelia arched a brow, feeling no need to say anything more.

Baird almost laughed. Then he touched her chin in the tender way she loved and brushed his lips across her brow. "Pleasant dreams, princess." He flicked a finger across the tip of her nose and turned to stride down the hall.

Aurelia closed the door and leaned her back against it, fighting a ferocious impulse to call him back. Her room looked colder than it had just a moment past, her night of Dreaming less tempting now that she would do it alone.

But this had to be done if she was to know for certain. Let the Dreaming come and show her the shadows of Baird's heart.

By the time Baird got back downstairs, the other two men had retired. He prowled the perimeter of the restaurant restlessly, refusing to admit what was bothering him.

He certainly hadn't been counting on sleeping with Aurelia again. Baird circled the hall, toured the cellars, paced the entire interior of the resort and still wasn't the least bit sleepy. All the same, he climbed to his room, paced its circumference, then poured himself a healthy shot of scotch.

It was Darian's presence that was keeping him awake. It couldn't be anything else. After all, this man could cost him Dunhelm.

And Baird didn't like him.

His sour mood certainly had nothing to do with the way Aurelia smiled and chatted with Darian over dinner, much less that she had suddenly and unexpectedly turned him away.

Baird didn't need Aurelia or anyone else.

The dream took no cautions in its approach this time, it simply exploded in glorious color in Baird's mind, without apology, introduction, or fanfare.

He was in a stone room, the smell of the wind hinting that it stood on high ground. Its furnishings were simple, its occupants garbed in a manner similar to what Aurelia had worn in the well.

An auburn-haired woman slept in the great pillared and curtained bed in the middle of the room. Her features were beautiful, the curve of her lips kindly, the circles under her eyes hinting at her exhaustion. A golden ring glinted on her hand, that hand lying limp on the coverlet. A portly woman changed the linens beneath her, casting those bright with blood into a bucket.

A silver-maned man with a full beard stood impatiently beside the bed, obviously uncomfortable with his role here. He was tall and broad, a man with a muscular back who had labored hard. His hands were calloused, there was a scar on his hardened cheek. A heavy silver chain encircled his neck and he carried himself like a man used to the weight of authority. A golden ring, the mate to the lady's ring, adorned his left hand.

The power of this man's feeling for the woman was a tangible force. He watched her with a vulnerability that surprised Baird.

"She will be fine?" he asked anxiously. This battle-hardened warrior was afraid for his wife's survival, Baird realized, and found himself hoping the woman would be all right.

The glance that the older woman fired across the room revealed that he had asked this before.

Many times. "Oh, yes, my lord. Women have children all the time. All your lady needs is a good sleep."

"But the blood . . ." The warrior shivered with horror and looked at the bucket as though he couldn't stop himself.

"Is not so much as I have seen before." The woman dropped the last length of linen into the bucket, straightened a corner of the fresh ones, then scooped up a red-faced baby from beside the bed. She expertly swathed the child, then handed it to the older man. "You might take the chance to make your son's acquaintance, my lord."

The man looked at the woman again, then accepted the weight of the child with an uncertainty that showed his lack of experience in such matters. He moved carefully to sit in a beam of sunlight, as though he were reluctant to move away from his wife. He cradled the child with the caution and awkwardness of a new parent.

"My son," he whispered to himself, almost as though he could not believe it to be true. The baby clutched at one heavy finger and held on tight, the gesture lighting the father's eyes with joy.

"You be sure you're not disturbing the lady for a while, my lord. She's had a rough go of it, but a good sleep will set her in order." The woman, who Baird realized was a midwife, scooped up her bucket and swept out of the room.

The warrior barely noted her departure. He stared at his son, gradually gaining confidence in handling the boy, and his stern features relaxed into a smile.

"My *son*," he said again, though this time his voice echoed with pride.

The force of the man's feelings assaulted Baird like a wave. He felt the man's rush of paternal pride; he felt the strength of the warrior's commitment to the blood of his blood.

And Baird found himself envying the child who would experience the force of this man's powerful love shaping his life.

"He is the one, you know." An elderly woman separated herself from the shadows, her voice low with import.

The warrior barely looked up. He tickled his son and chuckled when the baby gurgled. "What one?" His tone betrayed his indifference to her comment.

"The one the prophecy spoke of, the one to break the curse laid upon Gemma's daughter, Aurelia."

The warrior scowled. "You are not going to begin that nonsensical talk of prophecies again, are you? I long thought you a woman of good sense, Luan, but this has gone beyond reason."

"It is not nonsense!" Luan argued heatedly. "I was there at the naming! I heard Drustic make her curse! You must betroth this boy to Hekod's daughter with all haste!"

The warrior looked up, skepticism bright in his eyes, reason in his low voice. "Luan, with all respect, you rave like a madwoman in this matter. This child is barely born, the Nairns have yet begun to weave the thread of his fate into their cloth. I cannot commit him to alliances and obligations so soon."

Luan flung her hands into the air. "Do you care nothing for the consequences? Drustic will take him for herself just to keep her curse on Hekod's child from being averted. You know how malicious she can be!"

"Luan, enough!" The man bounced the child lightly, and humor underscored his tone. "My son has yet to even have a name, let alone to know what he wants of this life. Give the child a chance to be whoever he is destined to be."

"He is destined to lift Aurelia's curse."

The warrior's brow arched skeptically. "That would be the curse that has yet to bear fruit?"

"Details!" Luan crossed the room to wave a finger beneath the man's nose. "Can you not see the hand of destiny drawing near?"

"You have little faith in Gemma's abilities, for all the powers you two share."

"I tasted the malice in that curse, brother mine. Trust me, despite the will of all of us, it will come to pass." Luan turned quickly away and her voice grew thick. "I wish, how I wish, that it were not meant to be."

"Perhaps it is not to be."

"Brother! You can stop it! Pledge the boy, pledge him now, and save Gemma's child!"

The man's lips thinned grimly and he pushed to his feet. "Luan, you are my sister, but you push too far in this. This is neither the time nor the place for your argument. I shall keep your advice in mind, but the time is yet too early for the boy to carry the weight of such demands. Let him be a child. Let him become a man, and then we shall talk of his bride."

Luan might have said more, but the warrior left the room, the baby tucked proprietarily against his side. Baird's vision followed him down a dark corridor to the top of heavy wooden stairs. To Baird's astonishment, when the warrior lifted the baby high, it was from the infant's perspective that Baird saw the expectant crowd below.

"Behold, my people," the man bellowed. A sea of faces turned toward him as the hall fell silent. "Behold, the Queen of Inverness has brought forth a son, a son hale and hearty, a son to be the pride of his father's heart!"

"All hail the Prince of Inverness!" a man roared below and the crowd bellowed in delight. Baird felt the king's grip resolute around him, heard the rumble of the man's deep laugh.

For a heady moment, Baird *was* this man's child. He felt the power of the warrior's love for him flow between them and fill the baby with its potency.

It was stronger than Baird had ever guessed such a feeling could be and left him buoyant with the promise of what he, as this baby, might become. He could be a king himself, or a fisherman. He could be a silversmith or a warrior, but whatever he did, Baird knew that this man would be there to catch him if he faltered.

That feeling was the greatest gift he could ever have known. To have a family, to have someone to rely upon, it was everything that Baird had ever wanted and everything that he had been denied.

And this baby had done nothing to earn such a powerful gift, nothing but come into this world, blood of this king's blood. Baird marveled at the power of the human heart as the king held him high.

Then the dream ended with a snap.

Baird tossed in his bed, snatching at the snippets of the vision without success. He sat up in frustration, wide awake, and for the first time, he wished an unwelcome dream had not ended so soon.

But the fire of the king's love glowed in Baird's heart, like an ember left in the cinders of a once great blaze.

What would his life have been like if he had known such a feeling when he was a child?

Aurelia awakened the next morning to an insistent rap on her door. "Come on, princess, rise and shine."

Baird.

She scowled at the window, the sky just barely lightening, then rolled out of bed and shoved her arms into the blue robe. Against all odds, someone still held the key to her Dreaming. She had no understanding of what she had witnessed the night before and that fact had left her irritable.

What good was a Dreaming that revealed nothing?

Aurelia tore open the door and confronted the man she suspected was at the core of her troubles.

Baird smelled delightfully clean, his hair was still wet but already starting to curl in its usual wayward fashion. He wore a plaid shirt and chausses of deep blue, his hooked finger held his jacket over his shoulder.

But there were shadows beneath his twinkling eyes. Aurelia was not the only one who had slept poorly. Sympathy flooded through Aurelia before she caught her wayward response.

Curse Baird and his dangerous charm! The last thing Aurelia was going to do was show him any compassion.

But Baird quickly proved her wrong.

He stepped closer, kissed her with an audacity unexpected, then backed away and winked. Aurelia's unruly heart pounded and she cursed herself for so easily falling prey to his kisses.

"Daylight's wasting, princess, get it in gear."

And with that, Baird turned and strode down the hall, his long legs making short work of the distance. Aurelia pushed back her hair and tried to gather her thoughts, only to have Baird turn back at the hall doorway.

"Chopper's waiting," he whispered loudly, then ducked through the doors.

Chopper must be an impatient chariot driver. Aurelia dove

back into her room, washed and dressed as quickly as was humanly possible, then flung herself down the hall in pursuit.

Baird was waiting at the foot of the stairs. Aurelia barely had a chance to wish him good morning before he had clasped her elbow to steer her outside.

"You make great haste," she dared to say.

He grimaced. "No wind, it may not last."

That made absolutely no sense. Aurelia glanced at her impassive companion and was not surprised that, yet again, she could deduce nothing of his thoughts.

"You would leave Dunhelm to this Darian Mulvaney?"

Baird shot her a very green glance. "You don't like him?" he asked with a smooth disinterest that contradicted the gleam in his eyes.

Aurelia frowned and shrugged. "I am not certain that he should have the ritual well to himself."

"Did you leave anything there?"

Aurelia deliberately avoided his keen glance. "Many have come to their demise there, either by accident or plan."

Baird looked at her hard then, as though she had said something intriguing. Of course, the adventurer with the feathered hat had died in the chamber in Aurelia's dream.

Had Baird witnessed that dream as well? It certainly had been disconcerting.

It was in that moment that Aurelia spotted the silver dragonfly waiting for them. A man sat within it, his eyes covered with shiny black shields not unlike those of the insect in question.

He grinned and waved. " 'Mornin', boss!"

The din of the contraption was deafening.

" 'Morning, Tex!" Baird replied, but Aurelia balked when he would have led her closer. He leaned down and murmured into her ear, "Afraid, princess?"

"I am afraid of nothing!" Aurelia treated him to her most fearsome glare.

The cur's eyes twinkled with mischief. "Into the chopper, then."

"Chopper" was apparently this strange device. It looked dreadfully unstable, but the noise made questions impossible.

There were no horses to pull the thing—like the chariot of the day before—though Aurelia could not have imagined that any sensible beast could have been persuaded to come near this.

Baird had a dangerously daring gleam in his eye. If he expected her to be afraid, then Aurelia would prove him wrong.

She climbed into the chariot and tried not to stare at its whirling wings overhead. Aurelia sat primly as though there were nothing unusual at all in boarding such a conveyance.

Then the chariot rose and wobbled uncertainly just above the ground. Aurelia panicked. Dunhelm dropped away beneath them with dizzying speed and as they moved out over the sea, Aurelia fought against her rising terror.

Never mind Baird's assurances—those were no more than sweet lies to pacify her—he would see her killed! Had he not slaughtered her only brother?

What if Baird had found the knife she had forgotten beneath his bed? He would cast her out of this chariot in the name of vengeance and see her dashed to pieces on the rocks below.

Well, she would not go alone! Aurelia lunged across the tiny chariot and latched on to Baird with all her might.

"You will not be rid of me so easily!" she shouted.

The chariot lurched hard to Baird's side and the ground danced sickeningly before Aurelia's eyes.

"What in the hell?" Baird bellowed.

"Je-*sus! Boss!*" roared the chariot driver. He struggled like a driver settling a wild team, launching a torrent of expletives as he did so.

Baird tried to extricate himself, but to no avail. Aurelia locked onto his shoulders and was not about to let go.

"You will not cast me to a gruesome death so easily!" she shouted at him.

"You're not going to die, unless you keep this up!" he retorted.

"*Ha!* I will not believe your lies, you treacherous cur! My brother learned the price of trusting you to your word!"

The chariot steadied, the driver heaved a sigh of relief and glared over his shoulder. "I *told* you that these small choppers are more unstable than the one we use in the States, boss. What in the hell were you doing back there?"

"Everything's fine now," Baird said evasively.

"Oh, I get it! Lady's afraid of flying, huh?" The chariot driver grinned as though this were a huge joke.

"I am afraid of *nothing*!" Aurelia shouted, her fingers nearly hooked into Baird's flesh. "I am half Viking!"

The driver laughed. "Right! And I'm *all* Texan, but it took some talkin' to git me into one of these babies the first time."

Aurelia glanced down at Baird to find the corner of his mouth quirking in the half smile she found so beguiling. His eyes twinkled and were startlingly green at such close proximity. Aurelia belatedly became aware that she was sitting on his lap, her arms curled around his neck.

He looked straight into her eyes, the very image of sincerity. "You're not going to be flung to your death," he murmured so quietly that Aurelia had to read his lips. Her heart began to pound. "Didn't I give you my word?"

He had.

Aurelia licked her lips, not liking that she had played the fool and provided his amusement. Her face heated with embarrassment.

Baird slid his arms around her waist easily as though she sat thus all the time. "You should have just told me that you wanted to sit in my lap," he teased.

Now Aurelia could not put distance between them fast enough. She darted back to her seat, earning another curse from the driver.

He glanced back with irritation. "Could you-all just decide where it is that you-all want to sit? Go ahead, make my life easier, it won't break my heart."

Aurelia had a hard time understanding his drawling accent, never mind his words, but when she looked at Baird that man winked mischievously. Aurelia turned quickly to the window, her pulse pounding unevenly in her ears.

Oh, he had a dangerous charm!

They were over the sea now and it did not seem that this shiny bird had any intention of falling out of the sky. Fascinated by the fact that they indeed flew like a dragonfly, Aurelia leaned away from Baird and looked out over the landscape.

It was dotted with buildings of marvelous construction that

confused Aurelia once again. Black roads stretched across the land, painted with brilliant yellow lines. Shiny things, much like beetles but in myriad colors, shot along these roads at alarming speeds.

Aurelia chewed her lip. She looked up to the whirling silver overhead and once again felt overwhelmed by the changes Baird had made in her world. It had to be Christian magic at root, for there was no other explanation.

Or was there?

Aurelia found Kirkwall a shock after the small town near Dunhelm. Here there were countless chariots like the one she had ridden in and buildings beyond number. There were more people bustling about than she could have imagined, and many small ships bobbing in the harbor.

She kept silent as Baird inquired after her sire, certain in her heart that Hekod would never have come to this place.

Or would he? Was this not much as she had long imagined Micklegarth? But no one had seen or heard tell of her sire, after all. They trudged from place to place, without success.

When Baird offered a meal called ''brunch,'' Aurelia was glad to accept. The shop they entered smelled so good that her stomach protested its empty state mightily. It was only after she had finished eating her fill that Aurelia noticed the curious glances of those around them.

And Baird's wicked grin.

Baird went a-viking again with the gold card, launching a charming smile at the woman just to smooth the way. Aurelia seethed that he should tease her about her eating, but waited until they were outside to have her say.

''What is the matter?'' she whispered.

His grin widened. ''They must be wondering whether you've got a pair of hungry greyhounds under the table.''

''I have always had a healthy appetite!''

''And an awesome metabolic rate.''

Aurelia did not know what that meant, but it was not flattery, that was for certain. She would have strolled proudly away from Baird, but a window snared her attention.

Aurelia froze and leaned against the glass, her breath fogging it as she strained closer. It was not the window itself that fascinated her—she had already wondered at that marvel—but the item displayed. Aurelia touched the glass in wonder.

It was her mother's own silver bracelet. The same bracelet that had graced Aurelia's own wrist when she climbed to the walls to help defend her father's holding.

"What's the matter? What is it?" Baird asked, his voice low with concern. His hand landed on the back of her waist and in the reflection, Aurelia saw his head bent close to her own.

He looked the very image of a man confused and concerned. Liar! That he should mock her in this was beyond reprehensible!

Oh, he had confused her with his generosity and challenged her assumptions about his character with his pledge to do her no harm. But this—this *travesty* showed his true colors as Aurelia knew them to be.

Aurelia spun to face Baird, her vision blurred with tears. She pushed him away from her, unable to bear such proximity to one who wished her ill.

"How could you do such a thing?" she demanded in a voice that throbbed low with emotion. "How could you steal my only token of my mother? Did they give you so much coin that such a betrayal was worth it?"

Nineteen

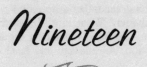

Baird's heart sank as he read the label perched beside the silver bracelet displayed in the museum window.

Pictish bracelet—silver
c. late eighth century
Part of the silver trove discovered in west Rousay, 1934

The bracelet was about three inches wide. A graceful eagle with a long tail was encircled with a Celtic braid to make a medallion. On either side, those same tangled creatures that covered the stone slab in Dunhelm's well filled the width of the bracelet. The bracelet was not hinged, but had a rounded slit that would rest on the inside of the wrist and make it easier to put on.

Baird fought to ignore the way his hair was standing on end.

"Aurelia, this is a museum."

She blinked at him uncomprehendingly, her tears threatening to spill at any moment. Baird gripped her shoulders and stared into her eyes, willing her to believe one less dastardly thing about him. "I didn't sell your bracelet. I've never seen it before."

"Then how did it get here?"

"Apparently it was found somewhere on the island in 1934."

She glared at him. "I do not understand this 1934."

Baird smothered a sigh. She never made a slip in her story, that was for sure. "It's a year, a date, the number of years since the birth of Christ." He frowned. "Well, not exactly, there's a mistake in the calculation somewhere."

Aurelia's face was pale, her tears dispatched and her eyes wide. "Nineteen *hundred* years since the birth of this Christ?"

"Well, now it's almost two thousand, but like I said, the calculation is off—"

Aurelia clutched two fistfuls of his shirt and gave him a shake. Her gaze was fever bright. "How much of a mistake?"

Baird shrugged. "I don't know. Twenty or thirty years. I guess it depends who you listen to."

But Aurelia wasn't listening to him. She turned away and scanned the street, the breath leaving her lungs in a low hiss.

Then she abruptly pivoted back to Baird and her features were drawn tight with fear. What was she afraid of?

"It is spring?"

"Yes. It's March"—Baird checked his watch—"well, it's the twenty-first."

Aurelia waved these details away with a dismissive gesture. "I know nothing of this March. When does the Month of Eostre begin?"

Baird blinked. "Eostre?"

"Eostre!" Aurelia's eyes flashed with impatience. "The festival, in the spring, the beginning of spring." She rolled her eyes, apparently incredulous that anyone could not know such a thing. "Has the day already passed when day and night are of equal length?"

"Oh! The equinox."

"Call it what you will. Has it passed?"

It obviously mattered so much to her that Baird had to find the answer. He'd never paid much attention to all that astronomical junk, but at least he knew where to find it. There was a card shop across the street, and just as Baird suspected, they sold calendars.

He flicked open to March, Aurelia shifting her weight anxiously by his side. "Actually, the equinox is today."

"Today!" Aurelia stepped back and scanned the store, but

Baird knew she wasn't seeing her surroundings.

What was she thinking? She left the shop abruptly and stared up at the clear blue sky, her gaze fixed on the sun.

It was a good thing Baird liked puzzles, because this woman had a million of them. He shrugged his confusion to the clerk, put back the calendar, and followed Aurelia.

She must have heard him because she pivoted and impaled him with an intense glance. "It is not yet midday."

"No." Baird checked his watch. "Just past eleven, actually."

"Do you know the stones of the moon and the sun? They are here, on the big island. Can you take me there?"

Baird frowned. "The stones of the moon and the sun? There's two stone circles here, I know that. The Ring of Brodgar and the Stones of Stemness."

Aurelia jumped at that, her excitement evident. "Two circles, yes! One bigger and one smaller! Toward the sea side of the island. Can we get there by midday? Can we?"

It was obviously so important to Aurelia that Baird could not have refused her.

"I don't see why not," he said, but Aurelia's anxiety did not ease. Determined to see her mind set at rest, Baird stepped out into the road and hailed a cab.

Two thousand years.

As the chariot without horses raced across the countryside, the words echoed through Aurelia's mind.

Along with her father's mocking laughter when told of the faith of the Christians: "Why should I worship a *man* dead eight hundred years? He is no less dead than any of us will be! By Odin, only a fool would worship less than an immortal god!"

What kind of a fool would believe twelve hundred years had slipped away? Aurelia fought against the very idea, pinning her hopes on the moments ahead.

The stones would tell no lies to those who knew their secrets.

The stones had stood for longer than anyone could remember, had been placed by people long dead and forgotten, but still they showed the line of sun and moon with unswerving accuracy.

Aurelia had been there, once a year, every year since she had been ordained priestess. She knew the stones as well as any priestess could, knew them so well that they could not deceive her.

But to her shock and dismay, when the chariot crested a small rise, the stones were not all there. Aurelia was out of the chariot before it had even fully stopped and running across the fields.

"Aurelia! Wait!" Baird muttered something unflattering under his breath, but Aurelia had no time for his concern now.

Where were the stones?

This could not be! If it was the beginning of the Month of Eostre, then only a year had passed since she had stood on this same spot and watched the midday sun.

But that midday sun had risen above a circle of *twelve* stones. Though the four that remained were familiar in shape, of the others there was no sign. They were each taller than her and heavy beyond all. They had stood here since time immemorial.

How could they have been removed without trace in so little time?

The wooden pillar in the middle of the circle was gone as completely as though it had never been. Aurelia crouched and fought back her tears as she ran her hand across the four flat stones arranged in a square in the middle of the circle. The stones were cold with disuse and she guessed no priestess had come this way in many years.

The prophecy could *not* have come true, it could not have.

Baird crouched by her side, his expression concerned. "What's the matter?"

"Where are the other stones?" Aurelia heard the breathlessness in her own voice. Her heart was hammering with a vengeance, a wildly ridiculous premise gaining credibility in her mind with every passing moment.

"What other stones?"

"There should be twelve. Twelve!" Aurelia's vision blurred with tears. "What has happened to them? Where did they go? How could they have been removed?''

Aurelia clutched Baird's shirt and gave him a shake, hoping that she would find him responsible for this desecration instead of more than a millennium stolen away from her. "Why did you have them taken away?"

Baird lifted her hands gently away. He held her hands and Aurelia exhaled slowly, welcoming his quiet strength despite herself. "I had nothing to do with this," he murmured, his green gaze boring into her own.

And Aurelia believed him.

But she could not believe the rest.

Baird must have read her thoughts, for he gave her hands a quick squeeze. "Wait right here. We'll find the answer." He pushed to his feet, and Aurelia was relieved to have his aid in this.

Only now Aurelia noticed that there were others here, oddly dressed people. They stared at her, as though she, a priestess, were the intruder, not all these common people who had no right to be within the circle.

They touched the stones and clicked little black boxes in every direction. What a travesty! This was a sacred place! They had no right to wander here as though it were no more than a patch of earth.

But in her heart, she knew that the common people could not have forgotten the Goddess in a mere year. And Aurelia feared the portent of that.

Baird stepped toward a plump woman in white shoes. "Excuse me, could I borrow your guidebook? For just a second?"

Aurelia refused to watch him work his charm on some hapless female. She watched the sun climb to its zenith and could not swallow the lump in her throat.

Baird hunkered down beside her again and fanned through the book. "Well, let's see. 'The Stones of Stemness. Built circa 2500 B.C.' Yada, yada, yada. Here it is—'originally consisting of twelve stones.' ''

Aurelia looked him in the eye. "I *know* that. Where are they?"

Baird scanned the text. "Doesn't say."

"And the pillar?"

"What pillar?"

"The one in the center, the one that makes the sacred thirteen along with the twelve stones." Aurelia gritted her teeth. "The one that casts the shadow of the midday sun."

"Where should it be?"

Aurelia pointed to the middle of the square defined by the four flat stones.

Baird flicked through the book, his brow furrowed in concentration. "Ah! 'Excavations have revealed traces of a wooden pillar that must have stood in the middle of the circle, though its purpose is unknown.' "

"As it should be by those who have not earned the right to know the sacred mysteries."

Baird looked at her questioningly, but Aurelia shoved to her feet. She backed toward the north side of the circle, her gaze rising again to the sun. She squinted, but could not precisely guess where the shadow would fall if the pillar was still there.

And precision was of import in this.

Baird gave the woman back her book with a smile of thanks and came to Aurelia's side once more. His voice was low. "What is it?"

She sighed, then frowned and fired a frustrated glance at him. "I can tell nothing without the pillar. I need its shadow."

"I can cast a shadow as well as any piece of wood."

Aurelia eyed Baird with suspicion but he did not seem to be mocking her. To have a king lend himself to her service was something she would not have expected, especially *this* king.

"You would do this?"

"If you explain later what this is about."

He wanted her to reveal a hidden mystery in exchange for his assistance. Aurelia hesitated, remembering her vow of secrecy only too well.

But if her fears were right, then the priestess to whom she had sworn that oath was long dead and forgotten.

As forgotten as the Goddess they had sworn it before.

Perhaps the mysteries were not as important as once they had been. Every manner of common person was obviously allowed to wander freely amidst these great holy stones. Aurelia rubbed her forehead, feeling that things were moving too quickly for her.

First, she had to know the truth.

And if that required compromise, so be it.

She pointed to the four flat stones before she could change her mind. "Could you stand in the center there?" she asked quietly, and Baird quickly complied. "I need only see the line of the midday sun."

He did as she bade, and though shorter than the great pillar, his shadow stretched a line across the circle. Aurelia was oblivious to the open stares of the passersby as she traced the direction of Baird's shadow to a stone no longer there.

She did it again and again. She watched the sun reach its zenith and ever so slowly descend toward the earth again. But there was no avoiding the truth.

The sun—and its shadow—were in the wrong place.

When Aurelia last celebrated the rebirth of the sun, a mere year before in her mind, the shadow of the pillar had fallen on the next stone. That stone still stood and was both so large and so well anchored that it could not have moved.

Even in a millennium. Aurelia swallowed carefully.

But the sun would take at least a thousand years to change its shadow so much.

Just as she had known, the stones told no lies. With a pounding heart, Aurelia turned her palm up and examined her left thumb beneath the golden light of Eostre's sun.

Right in the middle of the whorl was a minute scar.

Her breath caught in her throat.

The prophecy had come true! She had fallen into a slumber that had lasted nigh on twelve hundred years. Even with all the evidence before her, Aurelia's reason fought against the conclusion.

It could not be true!

But it was.

Her pulse rose in her ears to the roar of thunder, the sun shone on her brow with a savage heat.

It had all come true.

Aurelia could not tear her gaze away from the scar on her thumb though the world danced around her in a mad swirl. A thousand years had come and gone while she slept. Aurelia felt her knees crumple as a terrible numbness seized her body.

The last thing she heard was Baird calling her name.

Aurelia awakened in her chamber at Dunhelm. Judging by the angle of the light slanting through the window, it was late afternoon, though she had no recollection of leaving the circle of stones.

She propped herself up on her elbows, then froze when she met Baird's steady green gaze. He was sitting in a chair against the far wall, his long legs stretched out in front of him, watching her over the tent of his strong fingertips.

His face was drawn as though he was concerned for her. Aurelia knew that the man who had killed her brother would never have been troubled about her fate.

But then, the man who sat before her had surprised her in many ways already. He was gentle with her, and generous with his purse. He had neither raped nor killed her, nor cast her to his men for their amusement. He had carried her to safety when she was overcome. He had loved her with a passion and tenderness that belied his reputation.

And he had given her his word.

Twice.

Aurelia frowned. But if twelve hundred years had passed, then this man could not be Bard, son of Erc.

Which explained a great deal.

Except for who he actually was.

"What in the hell was that all about?" he demanded in a low voice. "You scared me half to death."

Aurelia thought furiously as she stared back at her benefactor. One thing she had noticed was that he was a man of good sense—and no one of good sense would believe the tale she now knew to be true.

Twelve hundred years! The idea made her own gut clench.

"I do not know," she lied uneasily. "Perhaps it was the sun."

And in a way, it had been.

He rolled his eyes and sat forward to brace his elbows on his knees, apparently reassured by her awakening if not her explanation. The corner of his mouth tugged in that smile that made everything within her melt. "After the brunch you put away, I wouldn't be surprised if your stomach had something to say."

"I was hungry." And no wonder, after over a thousand years with an empty stomach!

"Obviously." Though his tone was light, his gaze still ran over her with concern. "Feeling better now?"

"Much better, thank you."

"I'm sorry we had no luck finding your father in Kirkwall."

Aurelia tried to swallow the lump that rose in her throat and failed. Her father was long dead! There was no point in searching for him now, and a wave of loss swept over her.

Her father was gone. Her Viking relations were gone. The seamstress, the ostler, the cook, and all the others in her father's household were lost to her forever.

Everyone Aurelia had ever known was so long departed from this world that they were completely forgotten. She was alone in a new world, in a new time, rootless as she had never been in all her life.

"We do not have to look for him any longer," she managed to choke out before her eyes blurred with tears. "I understand now that it is futile to seek him."

"What do you mean?"

"He is truly gone," Aurelia said softly. "He is dead and lost to me for all time." She felt one heavy tear slide free.

"Hey!" Baird crossed to her side with one long stride, sat on the edge of the bed, and gathered her into his arms. Aurelia, helpless to do anything else, sagged against him and wept like a babe for all she had lost.

"Go ahead and cry, princess," he whispered into her hair. "It's all right. Everything will be all right. This is good, even though it hurts. It's good that you remember the truth."

Aurelia could not imagine what was good about this truth. She was alone. An ache of loneliness she had never expected to feel cast a shadow over her heart.

Aurelia became aware of the strong arms encircling her, the heady musk of masculinity rising from the chest she leaned against. The weight of a warrior's hand rested gently on her nape and she felt as though she had found safe haven in a storm.

It was tempting to remain in the circle of this man's arms, to rely upon his strength, but Aurelia knew she had already taken too much from him. He was a stranger, he owed her nothing, yet he had taken her in, garbed her, fed her, and shown her kindness.

What if the rest of the prophecy was true? Aurelia blinked in astonishment.

Could Baird be her one true love?

Aurelia pulled back and eyed the sodden mess she had made of Baird's plaid chemise, well aware of his gaze fixed upon her. Her heart skipped a beat. "I have ruined your chemise," she tried to jest.

He pretended to examine the dampness, then flicked a twinkling glance to her. "I'm not made of sugar—I won't melt."

The glow in his eye was nearly her undoing and Aurelia caught her breath. She dropped her gaze and saw that her hand had somehow been captured by his own.

He stroked his thumb across the back of her hand as though he was unaware of the caress he made. "Better?" he asked, his voice a soft rumble in her ear.

Aurelia tingled from head to toe. She blinked the last of her tears back and nodded vigorously, not trusting herself to speak.

It was not enough for her companion. Gentle fingers tipped up her chin until she was forced to meet the compassion in his eyes. "I understand that it must be hard to lose your father."

If he was not Bard, then his father had not been Erc, and his father had not been drowned leaving Dunhelm. When Aurelia stripped away all of her assumptions, she realized that she knew very little about the man before her.

"You said you never had a father."

Baird shook his head, his gaze moving away for only a moment. "But I always imagined what it would be like to have one." His thumb moved across her hand once more and his smile was thin. "Kids have such active imaginations."

And Aurelia caught a glimpse of pain in his eyes.

"You must have been very close to your father to be so affected by losing him," he said quickly.

Aurelia's gaze misted with tears again. "I was." Her voice broke. "Oh, yes, I was." A lone tear fell and splashed against his hand. "We had only each other after my mother and brother died."

Baird touched her cheek. "It's all right if you need to cry."

"No." Aurelia straightened and wiped away an errant tear. She eyed her companion, seizing on the tale of his misfortune to forget her own. "If you had no sire, then you must have known your mother."

Baird's expression turned sad and his voice hardened. "No. Neither of them stayed around any longer than they needed to." He flicked a bright glance to her, then his gaze skittered away. "Apparently she didn't even know his name."

"And you did not ask her?"

Baird shrugged with indifference, though Aurelia knew he cared deeply about this matter. "I never knew her. She delivered me, then left the hospital without a word. They tried to hunt her down to have her sign the forms. I sure as hell wasn't going to go looking for her."

"She abandoned you!"

Baird's green eyes were sober. "That's one way of putting it."

Aurelia was outraged that any woman would treat her child so poorly. "Then who saw you raised?"

His lips twisted. "The good state of New Mexico."

"A state cannot raise a child!"

"A state has no choice when the mother has not released her child for adoption." His expression turned grim. "It's the law."

"Well, it certainly is a poor one. You should demand the king change it."

"Well." Baird shrugged again. "They had lots of foster parents to take me in. I went from one to the next and the next."

Fourteen foster parents he had claimed the other day. This was unheard of! "Did none of them permit you to stay? Were you not entrusted to their care?"

"Oh, they were good to me in their own way." He looked down at their entangled hands. "But most of them wanted to foster a child they could ultimately adopt and that wasn't me." He grimaced. "Courtesy of my mother."

"She served you poorly," Aurelia said tightly. "And your sire no better. You should hunt them down and force a reckoning for their misdeeds."

Baird's gaze blazed into hers for a long moment and Aurelia could not draw a breath into her lungs.

Then he abruptly stood and shoved his hands into his pockets. "Well, I turned out all right, I guess, so it's all water under the bridge." He shrugged. "Being alone isn't so bad. You get used to it after a while."

It was so obviously a lie he made to himself that Aurelia did not know what to say.

Baird cleared his throat and Aurelia guessed that he was not a man who easily talked of matters so close to the heart. "I'm glad you're feeling better." He turned and might have left, but Aurelia bounced to her feet. She felt even more guilty about how poorly she had treated him after hearing this tale. "Wait!"

Baird pivoted slowly and Aurelia suddenly felt very nervous.

"I owe you an apology," she admitted softly, holding up her hand when he might have interrupted her. "I have had harsh words—and even harsher thoughts—for you when you did not deserve them."

Baird said nothing.

Aurelia took a deep breath and forced herself to continue, though it was not easy. "My only excuse is that I believed you to be another man, a man who committed grave wrongs against my family."

Baird arched a dark brow. "The notorious Bard, son of Erc the Destroyer."

Aurelia sighed and rubbed her temple. "Yes. You must understand that he is most evil, and when I thought you were he, I—I . . ."

Her words faltered, but Baird stepped back to her side. "It's all right. It was an honest mistake." The heat of his finger landed against her lips. "You don't have to say any more."

Indeed, what she desired needed no words. And if he was not Bard, son of Erc, then there was no reason to deny this man's powerful effect upon her.

This was the man who had awakened her.

This was the man destined to take her to wife. He had come for her exactly as had been decreed. Aurelia felt as though she was seeing the man before her clearly for the first time.

Baird might not be a warrior in the way Aurelia knew, but he was a man she was proud to take to husband all the same. He was honorable and clever, gallant to a fault, both tender and strong. He made her laugh and held her when she cried. She felt safe in his presence and cherished beneath his caress.

Her father would have liked him well. Confronted with her destiny and finding naught to protest, Aurelia stretched to her toes and kissed Baird Beauforte full on the lips.

Twenty

Baird awakened to the sound of rain drumming against the window. He tucked a dozing Aurelia tighter against his side and watched the dark clouds roll across the horizon as evening fell.

All was right in his world. Not only had he found Aurelia, not only had he proven himself to her, but she had somehow surmounted her fears and faced the reality of her father's demise. Her protective illusions had fallen away like scales from her eyes and she was whole and healthy again.

Everything was going to be fine.

He still couldn't explain the weird dreams that had plagued him since coming to Dunhelm, but it didn't matter anymore. Baird only knew that he felt more complete than he ever had before.

And this was just the beginning.

The old king's love from Baird's last dream resonated in his heart. Baird had never experienced love like that, but now he had a benchmark to measure his own feelings against. So the dream had helped him, really. This was all new ground to him, but for Aurelia's sake, Baird was going to give it his best shot.

He knew somehow that Aurelia was the woman for him—a woman with so many intriguing puzzles he would never figure her out completely—and if nothing else, Baird was learning to listen to those weird gut instincts.

He bent and brushed his lips across Aurelia's forehead, smiling as her eyelids fluttered open. Her small hand landed on his chest in a proprietary way that filled his heart to bursting.

"Sleep well?" he asked, letting his thumb caress the soft sweep of her shoulder.

"Mmm." Aurelia nestled against him. "But I'm hungry."

Baird laughed out loud. "It figures, princess."

. She looked up at him with glowing eyes. "I like how young you look when you laugh."

"Will you give it a rest? I'm *not* that old!"

A wicked glint lit her sapphire eyes. "How old are you?"

"Thirty-four."

Aurelia waved off this confession. "Ah! Ancient, indeed!"

The comment piqued Baird's curiosity. "And how old are *you*?"

"What year is it again?" When Baird told her, Aurelia made a great show of counting it out on her fingers. "By nearest reckoning, eleven hundred and ninety-eight."

Baird blinked, but Aurelia wasn't joking.

His heart sank to his toes. She was supposed to be over all of that! Baird's vision of a glowing future disappeared in a puff of smoke.

She *couldn't* still be nuts.

Baird swallowed his trepidation, rolled to brace himself over Aurelia, and cupped her shoulders in his hands, carefully choosing his words. "Princess, I thought you understood that your father is dead," he said gently.

She nodded. "I do."

Baird was encouraged. "Then you don't have to pretend to be someone out of a history book anymore. Right?"

"There is no need to pretend anything. I now know the truth."

"Great. Do you know who you are?"

Aurelia snorted. "I always knew who I was. I am the Princess Aurelia, daughter of Hekod the Fifth, King of Dunhelm and Lord of Fyordskar over the sea."

Baird blinked. "But—"

Aurelia interrupted him cheerfully. "But what I did not

know was that the prophecy of my birth, one which I always believed to be nonsense, has come true.'' Aurelia offered her thumb as proof. ''I did indeed prick my thumb in the middle of the whorl and I did indeed sleep until my true love—you—awakened me.''

Baird took a deep breath. ''Princess, you can't be twelve hundred years old.'' He borrowed Julian's comment, but left out the sarcasm. ''You would be very dead by now.''

Aurelia arched a skeptical brow. ''Do I look dead to you?'' Baird could only shake his head. Her eyes darkened and she rolled her hips mischievously beneath him. ''And do I *feel* dead, Baird Beauforte?''

Baird bounced out of bed, not trusting his body to remain impartial in this debate, and flung out his hands. ''Aurelia! This is serious!''

''And I am serious, make no mistake.''

She was.

Baird swallowed. ''Are you saying that you really *are* Ursilla's story, after all?''

''Of course not!'' Aurelia propped herself up on her elbows, her golden hair tumbling across the pillows. To his amazement, her gaze was perfectly clear.

She was convinced of her thinking, even if he wasn't.

''My tale must have been the inspiration for Ursilla's story.'' Her lips twisted. ''Trust me, there were none who ever called me Gemdelovely Gemdelee and lived to tell of it. What a woeful excuse for a name!'' She rolled her eyes, but Baird didn't share her amusement.

He frowned at his toes, unsure how to proceed.

''You came to me! You are the one,'' Aurelia insisted in a weird echo of Luan's certainty. ''You are the one who came to awaken me. It's all true. Can you not see? It makes perfect sense!''

''Not to me,'' Baird said stubbornly. ''It doesn't make any damn sense at all.''

''Baird, you must face the truth. We are destined to be together, just as in Ursilla's tale. You have come and awakened me from a long slumber and now our fates are tied together.''

''Aurelia, that doesn't make any sense. That's crazy talk.''

"I am *not* crazy."

"Right." Baird heard the undercurrent of panic in his own voice. A part of him found her argument dangerously seductive, but Baird wasn't going to listen to that.

Oh, he could pick 'em, that was for sure.

He jabbed a finger through the air at her. "If you're twelve hundred years old, then how can you speak and understand plain old English? Nobody spoke that here then."

She couldn't refute that!

But Aurelia did.

"I have the gift of tongues," she asserted without hesitation. She folded her arms across her chest and tossed her hair. "Once I heard you and Julian talk, I could understand and converse in your tongue."

"Well, that's handy if you're going to sleep for ten or twelve centuries! Aurelia, *listen* to what you're saying!"

Her voice hardened with determination. "Do you not remember that I spoke to you in the Pictish tongue first? Then I tried Gaelic and Briton and finally Latin, but to no avail."

She smiled, obviously to reassure him. His gut urged him to believe her, which made Baird just as crazy as Aurelia was.

It was time to get the hell out of here.

Baird snatched up his jeans and fought to get into them as he backed away from the bed. "Look, maybe we can get you some help around here. We'll find someone you can talk to about losing your father. It could straighten things out in your mind."

Baird stuffed his arms into his shirt and made for the door.

Aurelia's words, so low with disappointment, brought him to a halt. "You do not believe me."

Baird sighed. He turned back to face her, saddened that he was responsible for the disappointment in her eyes.

But he couldn't lie to her. "Would you believe me if this was the other way around?"

Aurelia frowned thoughtfully. "No," she admitted softly, then chewed her lip as she studied him. "How could I prove this to you?"

"You can't." Baird heard his own frustration. "No one lives for twelve hundred years. It's that simple." Baird rubbed his temple and had no idea how to make all of this come right. "Look, Aurelia, I've got work to do. Can we talk about this later?"

Though what they would talk about, Baird had no idea. Her disappointment was tangible, but Baird determinedly marched out of the room.

A couple of hours wasn't going to erase the last of Aurelia's delusions. On the other hand, her strange conviction had done nothing to diminish Baird's feelings for her. What could he do?

Believe that she had just had a twelve-hundred-year nap?

Right.

Baird strode impatiently down the hall. Aurelia might turn him inside out, she might be sexy, funny and cute, smart as a whip. She might give him fantasies of a perfect future together unlike anything he'd ever imagined, but she was flat-out crazy.

His eleventh foster mother's doomsaying came to mind: Lucky at cards, unlucky at love.

Maybe he should take up gambling.

Didn't it just figure that Baird would be dealt a winning hand in all the material signs of success? Until he had come to Dunhelm, he would never have complained about the balance, but now Baird felt a yawning hole in the very middle of his life.

And the one woman who could fill it was bonkers.

Baird nudged open his door, freezing in the foyer with the sense that he was not alone.

"Baird, *darling*, I've been waiting just forever for you!" Marissa rolled from the bed and strolled toward him in a black lace negligée and satin mules frothy with ostrich feathers. Her hair was pinned up in artful dishabille, her lips were red, her eyes were knowing. A waft of exotic perfume preceded her arrival and made Baird's nose tickle.

She carried a pair of crystal glasses. "I thought a little aperitif might be in order, darling. We can start with sherry—it's so British, don't you think?" Marissa chuckled throatily and walked her fingers up a stunned Baird's bare chest. "And then, darling, we can see where things go from there."

Baird's nose twitched, then he sneezed violently and completely ruined the ambience of the moment.

Marissa was undeterred. "Have you caught a chill, darling?" She leaned closer and pouted with false concern. "Well, darling, I've just the thing to warm you right down to your toes!"

This was the last thing he needed right now.

"Marissa, this is not appropriate."

She chuckled throatily. "Well, Baird, darling, I have never wanted to be *appropriate* with you." She hooked a finger through his unbuttoned shirt and tried to draw him into the room. "I see you've started without me, darling, but we can certainly progress from here."

"Marissa, I'm serious." Baird glowered. "Please leave."

She pouted. "You don't really mean that, darling. Why, we've had almost no time alone and—"

Baird's tone was nonnegotiable. "I'm asking you to leave."

"And darling," Marissa's gaze hardened. "I will make my staying well worth your while."

"Out," Baird declared flatly. He pointed into the corridor, what might have been a dignified pose ruined by the sock and shoe dangling from his grip.

Marissa looked him up and down, obviously making a point of observing his state of dress. "Well! I see. Is *that* how it's going to be?"

"That's how it *is*."

Her eyes glinted, then her smile turned brittle. "Mark my words, darling, you'll soon be bored with that little package and come begging for more sophisticated fare. Even Darian, sweet boy that he is, was asking when you and I would tie the knot. It seems obvious to everyone but you that we're absolutely perfect for each other."

"Get out *now*!" Baird roared.

Marissa sniffed as she swept past him, both sherries firmly in her grip. "I suppose there's no accounting for taste, is there, darling?"

Baird's only answer was the firm closing of the door. He emphatically shot the dead bolt home and trudged toward the shower, pausing on the way to shove open the window to fumigate the cloud of Marissa's perfume.

Women. Who in the hell needed them?

Aurelia heard Baird's door open, and to her dismay, Marissa's voice carried to her ears. Aurelia could not make out the other woman's words, but she did not have to.

Baird had gone back to Marissa.

It was not fair! How could he deny the truth between them?

Aurelia flung herself across the room and let herself weep. She had lost her mother, her brother, and her father, she had lost her home and everyone she had ever known. And now she had lost the man who was supposed to be hers for all time.

Well, Aurelia was not going to let him go that easily.

Baird was the one, she knew it in her heart. But he was skeptical of the power of his own intuition. He did not trust what he could not hold within his hands. Aurelia sat up and wiped the tears from her eyes.

Would she not have been skeptical in his place?

She would have, she knew it. The prophecy sounded like mere whimsy to the ears of a clear-thinking person. Even she had put no stock in it until the truth had become undeniable.

Somehow Aurelia had to persuade Baird of the truth. If the prophecy intended for them both to spend their days and nights together, it was clear that prophecy needed a little help.

Fortunately, Aurelia knew exactly what to do.

Darian was bouncing like an enthusiastic pup when Aurelia came down to the hall that evening.

"You'll never guess what I found today in the well," he declared as soon as they sat down for dinner.

Darian looked expectantly around the table, but no one responded. Marissa looked sour, Baird dissatisfied, and Aurelia was certainly not in the mood for small talk. She was impatient for night to come so that she could convince Baird of the truth.

And angry with him for going from her to Marissa. She never would have imagined that he could be so shallow and cruel!

Darian's enthusiasm was unruffled by the lack of response.

"Well, I just have a couple of Polaroids of it. Didn't want to disturb it."

"What is it?" Julian asked when no one else did.

With a triumphant flourish, Darian produced a shiny image of something so familiar that Aurelia's breath caught in her throat. "See?"

The image was of Aurelia's crossbow, half buried in the dirt. The gutting was gone, the nut lost somewhere over time, but she would have known the inlaid wood anywhere. Her sire had commissioned the design especially for her when he thought her skill warranted the gift.

She had taken it to the walls that last morning. Aurelia touched the image, but it was flat, though the crossbow was complete in every detail. She swallowed, not daring to ask about this stiff square and its magic, and passed it to Julian.

"What is it?" Julian asked idly.

"I don't know, but it's old, that's for sure." Darian's voice throbbed with excitement.

Baird fired a cold glance down the table. "Don't you follow strict processes for removing and dating artifacts? I had assumed that this was going to be a *systematic* investigation."

Darian fidgeted. "Well, you're right, of course. I was just so excited!" His features brightened. "And isn't it beautifully made? I'm sure that someone can figure out what it's for."

"It's a crossbow," Aurelia said tightly.

Darian looked surprised. "I don't think so, Aurelia. You see, it would have to have a firing mechanism and we know that Picts didn't use crossbows—"

"They most certainly did."

"I thought wood disintegrated in damp places," Baird commented frostily, passing the Polaroid to Marissa.

"Well, well, it does. Usually." Darian toyed with the print now back in his possession. "Maybe it's not as old as all that." He eyed Aurelia speculatively. "How could this be a crossbow?"

He was baiting her and Aurelia knew it, but her temper was such that she responded anyhow. She plucked the print from his hand. "Gutting from here to here, and here to here. A revolving nut here, it's held this way and fires like so." She squinted at the image. "There is the nut, fallen into the dirt directly beside it."

They all stared at her, but Aurelia returned to her meal.

"And Pictish?"

Aurelia glared at him, daring him to challenge her. "Dating from the arrival of the first Vikings."

Darian smiled patronizingly. "Aurelia, the Vikings took possession of the Orkney Islands in the eighth century or so—"

"And Hekod the Fifth claimed Dunhelm, among the first to land in these islands. He married a Pictish woman. The cross-bow is from that time, therefore the Picts used crossbows." Aurelia ate her dinner with resolve but without tasting a single bite of it.

"Uh, well! You certainly seem to know a lot about the period," Darian acknowledged.

Aurelia glanced briefly at him. "You could say that I have lived it."

Marissa laughed nervously. "More silly stories of prophecies for us, darling?"

"Prophecies?" Darian looked to Aurelia with open curiosity.

But it was Marissa who answered, her eyes bright with malice. "Yes, Aurelia has this charming fantasy that she actually is a Pictish princess. Baird found her in the well, didn't you, darling?"

"That's enough," Baird said tightly.

Marissa ignored him. "You know, Darian, darling, it was the cutest little story." She laughed harshly again. "But then, doesn't every little girl dream of starring in her own fairy tale? It's so much easier than actually growing up."

An awkward silence settled around the table.

Darian cleared his throat, apparently uncertain whether to laugh or believe Marissa. Something flickered in his gaze, though, that gave Aurelia an instinctive understanding of Baird's dislike of this man.

"Well, then, perhaps you'd like to help me excavate the site?" Darian leaned closer and smiled charmingly. "I could use all the expertise I can get and if we've got an extra fan of the Picts in the ranks, it would certainly help.''

If Aurelia had not heard Baird go to Marissa, she would never have agreed.

But agree she did.

"I would be delighted to help you," she said proudly.

Baird pushed to his feet, his features grim. "Well, I'm going to bed.''

"Need some company, darling?" Marissa cooed.

Baird's glare was lethal. "Don't push your luck," he muttered, then stalked from the room.

Baird fought the dream tooth and nail, even though it began similarly to the one he'd had of Julian.

But this dream seemed more determined than the others, more purposeful in its invasion of his sleep. Baird had the eerie sense that it was intent on showing him something he had missed.

But that was illogical.

Baird stood in the doorway of the room where the woman had given birth to that child. The furnishings were slightly more worn than they had been before, but the room still had a welcoming feel. A trio of candles burned on a table, filling the shadows with their beeswax scent, and illuminating the proud figure of the warrior standing before the window.

His hands were folded behind him, his back to Baird as he stared out at the stars. It was the same man, with the same heavy silver chain around his neck, though he looked older and slightly smaller.

He turned at some minute sound and Baird saw the passage of the years more clearly in his lined face. His expression was grim.

"Come in, son." He heaved a sigh and frowned, as Baird made sense of his words. "I have some news to share that will not come easily."

Baird must be in the point of view of the son this man had claimed as his own. That would explain the passing of time. He glanced down at himself and saw that he was tall and dressed in a tunic and leggings similar to those of the king.

The old king pursed his lips. "There is no sense in drawing

this out. I have received a missive this day from Dunhelm.''

Baird's heart skipped a beat.

''Bard, son of Erc, perpetuated a cruel ruse with marked success. He sent word to Hekod that he would heal the rift between their families by wedding Hekod's daughter, Aurelia. Hekod, in good faith, sent his son Thord to negotiate the details.''

Baird's mouth went dry, though which part of him was dismayed, he could not have said. The image of his friend at the harbor, the friend he knew to be Julian in the present day, grew clear in his mind.

''Has something gone amiss?''

The king leveled a steady glance at him. ''It was a savage plot. Bard killed Thord and sent his head back to Hekod with the dawn, along with a declaration of war.''

Dismay swept over Baird in a dizzying wave. ''No! Not Thord! He cannot be dead!'' He could not have lost his greatest friend.

The world could not be without Thord's merry laughter.

''But he *is* dead, Bridei, and naught can change that now.'' The king's tone was resolute. He crossed the room and laid a heavy hand on Baird's shoulder, his gaze boring into Baird's own.

''Though I respect that you would mourn, this is not the end of matters. There is little time for such doings now. War has been declared. Hekod has not asked for help, but he will need of it. He has served me loyally all these years and I will send an army to his aid.''

His grip tightened on Baird's shoulder. ''I would have you lead the forces, Bridei. The presence of my only son will show all the strength of my commitment to the defense of Dunhelm.''

Baird straightened and felt an alien thrill of pride course through him. His father trusted him to lead men into battle. He was indeed a man. ''Yes, Father.''

The older man nodded and his tone was grim. ''Perhaps you will be the one to strike the blow of vengeance for Thord. Bard, son of Erc, deserves no less.''

Baird's throat tightened with his own resolve. "Yes, Father."

"Look at you." The older man smiled sadly. "I remember well enough my first battle and can imagine your anticipation. Know that I trust you to do us proud."

"Thank you, Father."

They gazed at each other for a moment, and Baird was sure an echo of the warrior's sadness gleamed in his own eyes. Thord was dead.

"Go, tell your mother the news, but beware she may not take it well. You are her pride and joy, and her only chick, after all."

The king called to him when he would have crossed the threshold, and Baird reluctantly turned back.

"Look well upon the daughter of Hekod," his father said solemnly. "It was said once that much ill could be avoided if I pledged you to her, but I was loath to commit you to anything when you were but a child. Perhaps I erred in this, perhaps this might have ended differently, but what is done is done."

"I do not understand, Father."

His father cleared his throat. "What I say is this—if Aurelia takes your fancy and you hers, know that you have my blessing in making a match."

Aurelia.

There she was again. In every dream, her presence was tangible.

"I shall do so, Father." He bowed slightly. "Thank you for your trust."

The king shook his head solemnly. "You may not thank me, my son, when you witness the foul deeds of which war is wrought."

The dream blurred and Baird had the sense of time passing, of distance flying beneath his feet. He was on the deck of a ship, the sails snapping overhead and the ropes groaning with the tug of the wind. Excitement was high on the ship, every man determined to strike a blow for justice, and Bridei no less than the others.

The ship began to round a jut of land, every eye on the

horizon, and the open sea stretched behind them. Ahead lay their destination, the battle that would prove Bridei's manhood, perhaps the bride he would make his own.

They pulled around the point and the crew gasped as one at the sight. Baird's heart dropped to his toes.

Dunhelm was burning.

He was too late.

Baird sat up and shivered. The acrid tang of smoke lingered in his nose as though the dream had been real. He was chilled to the bone and gooseflesh rose all over his skin.

Failure hung on his heart like a lead weight and Baird felt an urge to weep for what he had lost. He mourned for Thord, even though he knew that Julian slept just a few doors away.

No wonder Julian hated this place so much. He had been Thord, the son of Hekod, who had been ruthlessly slaughtered by Bard.

But that didn't completely explain Baird's sense of loss. He hated the fact that as Bridei he had failed his father's weighty trust. He had not proven himself worthy of that man's powerful love.

And the knowledge tore him up.

Baird took a deep breath, knowing he had never been so twisted around by something he couldn't see or control.

This couldn't go on.

He rolled impatiently to his feet and paced the length of the room. There had to be something he could do to stop these dreams. Intuition came knocking in that moment and, for once, Baird Beauforte was listening.

He would go to Inverness.

Aurelia's eyes flew open, her breath came in spurts, and her fists clenched the linens. Dunhelm was burning! She had seen her father's beloved hall consumed in flames.

But it had only been the Dreaming.

Aurelia sat up and tried to shake off her terror. It had been so real to her, so terrifying a glimpse of the world she remembered with startling clarity.

Dunhelm had burned to the ground.

Twelve hundred years before. It was hard to believe that it had all happened so long ago, or that she had slept through all of it. Aurelia stared at the scar on her thumb.

It was hard to believe that her gift was strong enough to summon such a powerful image.

Even knowing that she was responsible could not slow the pounding of Aurelia's own heart. She slid from the bed and stood at the window, watching the moon. On the eve of the morrow it would be full.

But would her Dreaming, even at the fullness of its power, be enough to convince Baird of the truth? He had been coming for her, coming to aid her sire. He had been Thord's friend, Bridei, and there would have been none more fitting for Aurelia than the high king's own son.

Even in those days, Baird had been hailed as the one for her.

An intense yearning burned in Aurelia's heart. They had been cheated of that time together, so many years ago, and now, Baird's own reservations held them apart. Aurelia bit her lip and hoped fiercely that he had shared the dream again, that he had been persuaded, that she had the ability to convince this man to accept the reality of who she was.

Even though Aurelia knew the truth defied every grain of common sense.

Unfortunately Aurelia knew Baird Beauforte valued common sense above all else. To believe in this, he would have to believe in the urging of his own heart, and Aurelia was suddenly afraid that Baird had learned all too well not to listen to his heart.

His mother in this life had served him poorly indeed.

Suddenly cold, she folded her arms about herself and watched the moon slide across the sky. Aurelia fought the urge to go to Baird, not knowing what his response to that would be, and impatiently waited for the dawn.

She had to convince him.

Somehow.

The sun was barely above the horizon when Tex cleared the peninsula of Sutherland and Baird could see the distant sparkle of Inverness. He climbed into the seat beside his pilot, his gaze intent on the town ahead.

A cliff rose behind the town nestled at the mouth of the Ness River and Baird scanned the details.

There. He picked out a desolate point and knew without doubt that the high king's fortress had stood there.

But how could he know such a thing with such certainty?

Baird couldn't explain it and he didn't care. He had to go and stand right there and he had to do it today.

"Business, boss?" Tex demanded cheerfully.

Baird nodded, not in the least bit interested in conversation. They drew closer at an achingly slow speed, to Baird's mind, the Moray Firth a long vee of sparkling silver below them. Finally they wheeled around the sleepy town at a dizzying angle, the path Tex took giving Baird a bird's-eye view of the harbor with the North Sea stretched out behind.

Baird swallowed. It was the same as his dream.

He knew he had never been here before—he and Julian had flown from Edinburgh on a small jet that had not passed near Inverness. Tex had picked them up at Kirkwall.

At least, he had never before been here in *this* life.

But if Baird knew Julian from the past, it only made sense that he could know Inverness, as well. Inverness was where his dream indicated that he had known Julian, after all.

What if the dreams he had had at Dunhelm were memories?

Twenty-one

Marissa saw the uncertainty in Aurelia's eyes, when that woman came down for breakfast, and smiled to herself. She hadn't been able to seduce Baird while Aurelia was around, which left an obvious solution to the problem.

Aurelia had to be evicted. Then Baird would see what was patently obvious to everyone else.

It had nearly killed Marissa to get up this early, but it was now or never. She smiled in her most friendly manner at the wary blonde and waved a coffee cup in greeting.

"Good morning, darling!" Marissa yawned luxuriously. "Did you have the most wonderful sleep last night? I must say that I"—she giggled—"had a rather exhausting night."

"Did you?" Aurelia's expression was stony, though she summoned a thin smile for Elizabeth when that woman bustled near. "Has Baird come down for breakfast yet?"

"No, my dear, I haven't seen him yet today."

"And you won't." Marissa sipped her coffee, enjoying the way the other women's gazes swiveled to hers. "He's gone off to Inverness, darlings, he was up so dreadfully early, all full of vim and vigor." She chuckled as though recalling morning masculine energy. "Quite unlike him to be so . . . lively in the morning, but I may have had *something* to do with that, darlings."

Aurelia frowned. "Why would he go to Inverness?"

Marissa let her characteristic laughter dance through the air.

"Why, Aurelia, darling, there is nothing like a splendid night of romance to turn a man's mind to a more permanent arrangement, if you know what I mean. And Baird and I have known each other positively forever, after all." She smirked as she drained the coffee cup, then indicated the pot with a regal finger. "Coffee's cold."

Elizabeth snatched up the pot, bright color burning in her cheeks. "Mr. Beauforte must have had business in Inverness this morning," she said stoutly.

"Mmm." Marissa crossed her legs, watching both women eye the expanse of leg revealed by her short kimono. She bounced her feather-trimmed mule on one toe. "Most definitely. I would say he had business with a *jeweler*."

"I do not understand," Aurelia said tightly.

Marissa rolled her eyes at the blonde's persistent stupidity. "He's gone to buy me a great big diamond engagement ring," she declared, then smiled. "And don't worry, darling. I'll accept."

Elizabeth glared at Marissa while all the color drained out of Aurelia's cheeks. "You cannot wed him. We are destined to be together!"

"Haven't you heard, darling?" Marissa said through gritted teeth. "Baird Beauforte doesn't believe in destiny."

Her damage done in a most satisfactory way, Marissa swept to her feet and smiled at the two dumbfounded women. "Don't worry about the coffee, it wasn't very good anyway." She examined her nails. "And besides, I have to decide what would be appropriate to wear to accept a wedding proposal from a terribly eligible man."

Marissa strode from the hall, well pleased with herself.

If she had read Aurelia's expression right, the blonde would be gone within the hour.

And open season on Baird Beauforte could be declared.

By eleven, Baird had climbed up the bluff behind the town of Inverness.

The cab from the airport had dropped him in front of the tourist center. Even though that establishment wasn't open at such an early hour, they had a map mounted on the outside wall to show the local places to stay.

Baird was interested in something less practical. His heart had leaped at the historic site marked at the top of the hill. He memorized the street names that wound their way to the crest and started to climb.

It seemed appropriate to walk to the place Baird was convinced he had known twelve hundred years before.

When Baird reached the summit and could see the view of the bay, his heart clenched at its familiarity. There was where he had said good-bye to Julian, apparently for the last time.

Baird frowned and turned to scan the area. The site was grassy, a few heavy stones scattered about, but devoid of real ruins. A discreet sign was mounted farther along and Baird strolled toward it, liking the clean smell of the air. He didn't expect to learn anything more here, but found himself unwilling to leave just yet.

The picture on the sign made Baird catch his breath.

It showed a heavy silver chain, obviously lying in a modern display cabinet. The links were thick, the catch engraved with a reverse Z entwined with a snake.

It was his father's badge of office.

Images assailed Baird, and he did not fight their advance.

The walls of the increasingly familiar room where he had seen a son born and been himself dispatched to battle rose high around him. A silvery light filtered through rain poured into the single window.

The king braced his hands on the bottom of the window and stared at the gray gloom outside. He had changed, Baird noticed, his demeanor less invincible, his gray brows drawn together with worry, his beard almost white. Where once this king had been a man who laughed boldly in the face of adversity, now he fretted like an old woman. His gaze was anxious and he spun hastily at a rap on the door.

The woman who had slept in the great bed came into the room. She too had aged, the great auburn coil of her hair threaded with silver, though she was still a beauty. Her eyes held a tremendous sadness and she said nothing as she held out a sword on the flat of her two hands.

The old king cried out in pain. "No! Not my son!"

He lunged across the room, falling on his knees before the woman, lifting away his hands before he reclaimed the sword that had once been his own.

"Not Bridei," the king whispered hoarsely. Tears ran freely down his aged cheeks as he looked up at his wife. Baird saw that her eyes were rimmed with red.

"It was supposed to protect him," he whispered, staring at the blade as though he had been betrayed by an old ally. "It was forged with strong runes and blessed with power." He swallowed. "It was supposed to bring Bridei back to us."

Baird's heart lurched with his own failure. Not only had he come too late to Dunhelm, but evidently he had died trying to fulfill his father's command. He had not avenged Julian's death as Thord, he had not upheld his father's honor, and he had hurt these two people who had been good to him.

Now he would lose even the whispered memory of this great king's love for his son.

And deservedly so.

A middle-aged man lingering behind the woman cleared his throat pointedly. Baird recognized him from the deck of the ship, though there was a long gash on his cheek that had not been there before.

The king's lips tightened as he became aware of the man's presence. "Tell me, Angus," he whispered. "Were you there?"

"By his very side, my lord king."

The king closed his eyes and took a deep breath. He seemed to tremble before Baird's eyes, but his voice was grim. "Tell me."

"Dunhelm was burning when we arrived," Angus said, his words falling in a flat monotone. "Bard had already claimed the keep, though the battle was far from won. Bridei"—his voice wavered over the name—"declared time to be of the essence. We dove into battle, assaulting Bard's rear flank and surprising him no end."

Angus swallowed. "He almost single-handedly turned the tide of the battle, my lord."

The king's lips tightened and he stared at the blade. His

wife shook her head, her tears splashing onto the blade. Baird ached that he had caused her such pain.

"How did he die?" the king demanded tightly.

Angus frowned. "Bard was enraged by the threat of victory being snatched from beneath his nose. He challenged Bridei, who willingly matched blades with him. My lord, it was not an easy battle. They fought in the surf, each as determined as the other, their blades flashing in the sun.

"Bridei showed himself well, he fought nobly while Bard used any means he could contrive. After many glancing blows, Bard drove his sword through Bridei's shoulder. We all feared our champion was lost, but he rallied to fight again. That was all we and Hekod's troops needed to regroup and turn back the tide of Bard's victory. The very cliffs echoed with the sounds of swordplay, and still the pair fought in the waves, Bridei bleeding profusely.

"After one arduous parry, Bridei stumbled and Bard lunged in for the kill. We all feared the worst, but Bridei rose at the last instant and impaled the attacker on this very blade."

Angus bowed his head. "He fell, then, his strength gone and too much of his blood mingled in the saltwater. He entrusted me with his blade in those last moments and bade me return it to you, my lord king. He bade me tell you that your will had been done."

A tear slipped from the old king's eye and trickled down his weathered cheek. "But at what price?" he whispered, his gaze scanning the sword.

"Where is he?" the woman asked tightly.

"Hekod had him raised high and sent to his rest with full Viking ceremony, as befits a true hero. His missive and gifts await in the hall, though he bade me confess to you that the price of Dunhelm was far too great."

The woman bit her lip and turned away, her tears falling more quickly.

The king looked up at her and his lips worked for a moment before any sound came. "I am sorry, I am so sorry, my love. I should never have sent Bridei alone on such a mission." He shook his head and his tears scattered like jewels. "I should have gone with him, I should have defended him."

He heaved a ragged sigh and reached up to touch his wife's face. Her tears spilled over his hand. "My son," she whispered brokenly, her voice raw with disbelief. "My only son is lost."

The sight of her pain seemed to renew the king. He rose to his feet and swept her into his arms, casting aside the blade as he held her tightly. She sobbed against his chest and clutched at his shoulders.

The king's whispered words were fierce. "I should never have left unprotected someone we both held so dear. I have failed you, my love, in the one thing that mattered most."

The king took a deep breath and looked deeply into his wife's eyes. "Forgive me."

Though her eyes still shimmered with her tears, the woman's lips set with resolve. She reached up to frame the king's battered face in her hands and pressed her lips eloquently to his.

"You could not have known," she whispered softly, and the king wept anew. Angus discreetly looked away from the pair, a shimmer in his own eyes.

The vision was suddenly gone, leaving Baird cold in the brisk spring wind atop the hill.

He was surprised to find his own cheeks damp with tears and a lump lodged in his throat. He turned to gaze over the awakening town below as he fought to control his emotional response.

Much to his amazement, Baird's father had not blamed Bridei for failing.

In that time, in that place, his father had loved him, without condition or reservation.

And Baird *remembered.*

He remembered not only the events, but he felt again the power of that love lifting in his heart. He had spent this lifetime striving for success, no success good enough because his parents had found him unworthy of their interest even before he let out his first cry.

Baird saw that he had driven himself hard for nothing. His parents in this life had invested nothing in him and deserved no dividend from what he had made of himself. Baird had done it alone, but he realized that it didn't have to be that way. There were those who loved without restraint, without judgment, without condemnation.

As Baird stood above the awakening town, he felt how much difference love could make in his life.

Coming to Dunhelm had brought Baird a tremendous gift. A week ago, he would have insisted that reincarnation was nonsense. Now he knew without doubt that he had lived before. He had known Julian, he had experienced both a father's and a mother's love, he had gone to Dunhelm and died there.

Twice.

Baird shoved his hands into his pockets and wandered back to the cobbled streets of Inverness, thinking furiously the entire way. The musketeer had been him as well, he knew, though that had been at some time between Bridei and now. Baird had come back to Dunhelm again, and he had done so to find Aurelia.

Gemdelovely Gemdelee.

Baird remembered Ursilla's story in every detail and fitted it not only to his own dreams but to Aurelia's story. He had lived not once, not twice, but many times, he was certain. Baird tipped his head back and eyed the windy bluff overhead, acknowledging all the mysteries he could not explain.

A trust dawned within Baird that things could be true even if he couldn't explain them.

In his dreams, he changed. Baird came to Dunhelm in different lives and different skins, each time bent on the same goal that drove his soul. And Julian had been Thord all those years ago. Same man, different vehicle.

But Aurelia was always Aurelia.

Quite simply because she *was* twelve hundred years old. Her wild tale was true, it had to be. There was no other explanation for the fact that she was always the same.

She was always waiting for him. Baird's heart clenched.

At least, he hoped she was still waiting for him. He hadn't been very quick off the mark this time, that was for sure. But whether Luan's prophecy was right or not, Baird was suddenly very determined to prove himself to be the one for Aurelia.

She was everything he had ever hoped to find in a woman,

everything he hadn't even known he had been looking for. He could talk to her, he could laugh with her, he had come looking for her a thousand times before.

Baird couldn't risk losing her now.

As soon as Aurelia heard the distinctive sound of the returning helicopter, she lunged out of the hall and strode across the turf. She might have lost this battle, but she could still make one last entreaty before Baird proposed to Marissa.

She could not let him make this mistake.

She would *not* let him do this.

She understood the power of destiny, even if he did not.

Aurelia marched to the paved pad just as Tex was setting the helicopter down. Baird erupted from the noisy chariot even before it hit the ground. He ran for Aurelia and she was shocked when he swung her up in his arms and kissed her.

Most thoroughly.

Aurelia almost sagged against him in pleasure before she remembered what she was about. She pushed him away and stared sternly at him.

"What manner of man are you to kiss a woman thus when you mean to propose to another?" she demanded, as angry with herself for responding as with Baird for playing her as a fool.

Baird looked stunned. "What?"

"We must have one thing straight between us, Baird Beauforte," Aurelia declared in a stern echo of Baird's earlier denials. "I will not have you toy with me when you mean to marry that Marissa! It will be all or naught between us, no less than that."

Baird frowned, started to say something, then shook head. "But I'm not going to marry Marissa."

So he meant to bed them both and make honorable women of neither of them! Aurelia folded her arms across her chest and glared at Baird. "That is not what she says."

The helicopter quieted to a low roar as they stared at each other. Baird's expression turned grim. "What *exactly* does she say?"

Aurelia was more than pleased to provide details. "That you

went to a jeweler to fetch a token of your esteem—''

"And what if I did?" Baird murmured, and pulled a deep blue box from inside his jacket. A pearly bow perched atop it, looking a little crushed from its transportation.

Aurelia bristled. What kind of man would wave a token intended for another beneath her very nose? Before she could choke out her indignation, Baird offered the box to her.

"It's for you," he said quietly. There was a flicker of uncertainty in his green eyes, as though he feared that Aurelia would scorn a gift from him.

Her anger abandoned her with dizzying speed. Suddenly she could think of naught but reassuring Baird. "For *me*?" She took the box tentatively, all the bluster stolen from her sails with this one gesture.

No one but her father had ever brought Aurelia a gift from afar. "You went a-viking again," she accused softly as she fingered the bow.

Baird laughed, but uncertainty still lingered in his eyes. "I thought it was the least I could do."

Their eyes met for a long moment, Aurelia desperately confused by this gesture. Baird's vulnerability in this touched her heart, just as his decisiveness in other matters of intimacy made her pulse soar.

Aurelia thought of the pleasure they had shared and her mouth went dry.

A smile still played over his lips as he stepped closer and fitted his hands to her waist. She was treated to a heady breath of his scent and desire unfurled deep within her. His thumbs moved in eloquent circles against her belly and Aurelia could not have moved away to save her life.

"Open it," Baird urged, his words a breath against her temple.

Aurelia made short work of the ribbon and opened the box, gasping when she saw its contents. "My mother's bracelet!" She lifted the silver circle with gentle fingers, incredulous that Baird had fetched this for her.

But why?

"Not exactly," he admitted. Aurelia glanced up in time to see him grimace. "It's a reproduction, the best one I could find. They wouldn't sell me the original." His eyes twinkled as he took the bracelet and fitted it to her wrist. His lips twisted ruefully. "But, believe me, I tried."

"I cannot imagine that anyone could resist your charm," Aurelia teased.

Baird sighed with mock resignation. "As much as I hate to admit it, I didn't even come close to convincing them." He traced the central medallion, his warm fingertip brushing against Aurelia's skin with electrifying gentleness. She caught her breath. "Does this signify something?" he asked.

Aurelia forced herself to concentrate on the bracelet. "It is an eagle, the kind that used to frequent the island. My mother always braided one of their long white tail feathers into her hair as a talisman."

"Gemma Whitefeather."

Aurelia nodded. "It was said that her gift for prophecy was like the long vision of the high-flying eagle." She smiled in recollection. "They used to come to her, though normally they were shy of people. They were magnificent birds, and held in great reverence by Pict and Viking alike."

"But there aren't any here now."

"No." Memory tightened Aurelia's throat but she forced herself to share the tale. "On the day that my dame died, a great group of eagles circled the hall, crying aloud. Everyone gathered, for the sound was so mournful that all knew it a sign of ill fortune. I shall never forget the sight of them ascending in a spiral, their white tail feathers trailing behind. They circled once over the hall before they turned as one and flew out over the sea, never to be seen at Dunhelm again."

Aurelia looked up to meet Baird's gaze and found a sympathy there that made her loss seem a little less painful. At least Aurelia had known her parents and their love, while Baird had been alone from his first breath.

"I am sorry," she said in a rush. "You must think me foolish and sentimental."

Baird smiled crookedly. "Those would be the last two words I'd connect with you, princess."

Aurelia did not know whether to take that as a compliment or not. To be certain, Baird had brought her a gift, but it was not this diamond ring that Marissa was certain she would receive. Was this a mere token of friendship, while he brought Marissa a betrothal gift?

After all, this proved Baird had been to a jeweler!

And he had spent the night before in Marissa's bed. What a fool Aurelia was to let his gift distract her!

"I thank you for the bracelet," she said formally, and stepped away to watch Baird's expression. She lifted her chin proudly. "I suppose you have another box with a great diamond ring for Marissa, as she anticipates."

Baird's dark brows drew together in annoyance. Was he angered with her for knowing his intent? "What are you talking about?"

Aurelia straightened proudly. "Marissa declares that you mean to propose marriage to her upon your return."

Baird shoved a hand through his hair and muttered a curse. His bright gaze met hers, gleaming with a sincerity that swayed her conviction. "Princess, I'm not going to propose *anything* to Marissa Witlowe."

Aurelia's heart skipped a beat but she did not ease her stance. "Then why did you go to Inverness?"

Baird's voice softened. "Because I had to see whether something was true." He stepped closer and lifted a hand to Aurelia's cheek, his voice beguilingly low. Her traitorous heart twisted at his touch. "Princess, I'm sorry I didn't believe you sooner, but I believe you now. . . ."

He was making her forget herself again! Aurelia danced away, not trusting herself to listen to him any longer and hold to her will. "Spare me your pretty lies! I would know the truth!"

Baird shoved his hands into his pockets. "Aurelia, I'm not lying to you. I know now that you *are* a twelve-hundred-year-old Pictish princess." A tentative smile tugged at his lips. "I just wish I'd believed you sooner."

Again that fear of rejection filtered through his eyes and Aurelia's heart contracted. She wanted to believe him, but there was one matter that could not be denied.

Aurelia could not keep the hurt from her voice. "Then why did you spend last night in her bed?"

Baird's lips thinned and his voice dropped dangerously low. "She told you that?"

"I heard you go there!"

His eyes flashed with anger. "You heard wrong, princess, and I'm going to prove it to you. I don't know what kind of crap Marissa is talking but we're going to get to the bottom of it right now."

And to Aurelia's amazement, he laced his fingers between hers and headed for the hall at an uncompromising pace. The very purposefulness of his stride made Aurelia wonder if she had misunderstood matters.

Could Marissa have lied?

Did Aurelia dare to hope?

Twenty-two

Marissa was painting her toenails in the west hall when Baird practically dragged Aurelia back into the hotel.

"Hello, darling! Whatever has taken you so long?" The welcoming smile died on Marissa's reddened lips when she saw Aurelia hard behind Baird.

Her gaze dropped to their entwined fingers and she inhaled sharply.

But Baird had no interest in social niceties. And he wasn't going to let go of Aurelia's hand.

"What in the hell have you been saying around here?" he demanded. "Did you tell everyone that we were going to be married?"

"Well . . ." Marissa had the grace to flush.

Elizabeth hovered on the other side of the hall, her eyes bright with interest, and Julian slid through the door to watch.

"I may have *hinted* at such an eventuality, darling. You know, even Darian has said how absolutely perfect we are for each other—"

"Like hell we are!" Baird snapped. "And what's this garbage about our spending last night together?"

Marissa's eyelashes fluttered. "Baird, darling! Don't let's air all our personal details before the staff!" She smiled coyly and returned to painting her nails. "You'll have me blushing, darling!"

Baird bent and snatched away the brush, leaving a ruby trail across Marissa's toe. She looked up at him, alarm lighting her dark eyes for the first time.

The idea that this woman's malicious lies could cost him any chance at persuading Aurelia he was sincere made Baird see red.

"Enough lies," he said sharply. "Time to tell everyone the truth, Marissa. Did we or did we not spend the night together?"

Marissa swallowed. She looked to the group of people avidly listening and her cheeks flamed. "We didn't actually, darling, but we could have." She tried to smile, but Baird wasn't satisfied.

Aurelia's hand was still cold in his.

"Have we *ever* slept together?"

Marissa's lashes fluttered. "Well, no, not actually."

"Actually?"

Her lips tightened with the concession. "Not at all."

Baird straightened and folded Aurelia's hand more securely into his. She was listening, but he couldn't begin to guess what she was thinking.

They might as well have it all as clear as crystal. "Have I ever done anything to make you think that we might?"

Marissa's expression turned mutinous. "No." She plucked the brush from Baird's fingers and jammed it back into the bottle, shoving her feet petulantly back into her slippers. "Have you finished humiliating me?" she demanded in a hostile undertone.

But Baird was fed up with Marissa's interference and troublemaking. It was more than time to do what he had suspected needed doing a long time ago.

"Have you finished the drawings for the Series B guest rooms?"

Marissa sulked. "No, not exactly."

"Series C?"

"No."

"The tower restaurant?"

She fired a glance of loathing at Baird. "No."

"Have you done *anything* since you got here besides complain and upset Aurelia?"

Marissa stood and propped her hands on her hips. Her ruby lips drew to a mean line and she sent her British accent packing. "Now, you listen to me, Baird Beauforte, and you listen good. You're making a fool of yourself with this nobody who doesn't even know how to dress, let alone how to get by in the real world. She's far too stupid for a man like you—"

"That's enough." Baird turned crisply to Julian, whose eyes were snapping. "When does Marissa's contract come up for renewal?"

"April thirtieth," he supplied with a telltale smile.

"You wouldn't!" Marissa breathed.

"I would," Baird asserted. "I don't need people on my staff who don't pull their weight, let alone those who spread rumors and deliberately hurt people close to me."

He gave Aurelia's fingers a squeeze, so she wouldn't miss the reference, and heard her catch her breath.

"Pack your bags, Marissa, and dig out that return ticket that Beauforte Resorts paid for. You're leaving Dunhelm and as far as I'm concerned, you've already left Beauforte Resorts. Your compensation will be paid through the end of your contract. I'll call New York and let them know that you'll clean out your desk by the end of the week."

Marissa's face contorted with a very unflattering rage and her fists clenched. "You can't do this!"

"Actually he can," Julian supplied smoothly, then coughed into his hand as he crossed the room. "That's the true beauty of an employment contract. A per-annum deal has some major advantages on the employers' side of the situation beginning with—"

Marissa spun to face the lawyer. "Shut up!" She pointed a warning finger at Baird, her voice rising hysterically. "I'll fight you! I'll fight you all! I won't let you get away with this! I'll see you in court!"

Marissa stormed from the hall and Julian had the good sense to jump out of her path.

As soon as she had left, Baird heaved a sigh of relief. The air was better in there already.

Julian grinned and rubbed his hands together. "Oh, I can hardly wait. This is the moment I've been dreaming of," he gloated, then winked at Baird. "There is a God, and she loves me very much."

But Baird didn't care about Marissa and Julian anymore. He turned back to Aurelia, his heart leaping when he saw the shadow of suspicion banished from her eyes.

A tentative hope shone in those blue depths.

"You truly were not going to wed her?" she whispered.

Baird smiled and drew her close, his heart swelling with the new feelings he had discovered. "Never crossed my mind," he murmured, tipping Aurelia's face up to his and sliding his thumb across the fullness of her lips. "How could I marry anyone else when I love you, princess?"

Aurelia's lips parted with astonishment, but Baird kissed her into silence. Her arms twined around his neck and she pressed herself against him, as if she too wanted to meld their very flesh together.

Elizabeth hummed cheerfully as she bustled back into her little alcove.

It was some minutes later that Baird lifted his head reluctantly and stared into Aurelia's eyes. He could feel the pulse of her heart against his chest and grinned that it raced as quickly as his own.

"Why did you go to Inverness?"

"I had to find something I'd lost."

"What?" she asked breathlessly.

"My heart," Baird confirmed with a smile. "Just so I could give it to you."

She flushed and suddenly Baird wanted to have her all to himself. He leaned down and whispered into her ear, "Princess, I could really use a shower. Care to join me?"

Aurelia wrinkled her nose playfully. "The road from Inverness is long and dirty indeed." She smiled coyly up at him, a very promising glint in her eyes. "Perhaps I could scrub your back."

"Princess, you can scrub any part of me you want," Baird growled, and when she laughed, he ushered her unceremoniously toward the stairs.

•　　•　　•

From the shadowed entrance of the ritual well, Darian watched an obviously infuriated Marissa march out to the helicopter. She snarled at Tex and practically threw her hand baggage at him, hoisting herself into the chopper. Marissa folded her arms across her chest and waiting regally for the pilot to load her trunks.

If she had been a cartoon character, a black storm cloud would have lingered over her head.

Unless Darian had missed his guess, Auntie Drustic had struck out.

He fiddled in the well until he heard the helicopter lift off, then sauntered back into the hall. The only sound that carried to his ears was Elizabeth's merry humming.

And that woman would be the best source of news.

"Something smells good," Darian declared cheerfully.

The older woman turned with a smile, twin spots of color burning in her cheeks. "Oh, Mr. Mulvaney, you've missed all the excitement!"

"Did I, now? Well, as long as I haven't missed one of your wonderful dinners."

"Oh, Mr. Mulvaney, you've enough charm to even make an old maid blush!" Then she giggled. "But that Mr. Beauforte, well, he'd put any man's charm in the shade. You should have seen what he just did. Like something you'd see on the telly, it was."

Darian hid the slow burn of irritation that he had been compared to Baird and found lacking. "Really?" he managed to ask.

"Oh, yes!" Elizabeth's eyes sparkled and she leaned closer. "Mr. Beauforte went to Inverness this morning and that Ms. Witlowe was telling anyone who would listen that he had gone to fetch her a diamond ring. Well! Aurelia was right upset about it all, and who could blame the wee lamb. Why, even the most daft among us could see that there is something special between her and Mr. Beauforte."

"Anyone." Darian gritted out the word, then forced a smile. "Well, did he bring back an engagement ring?"

Elizabeth's scornful expression said it all. "Not our Mr. Beauforte, he's a gentleman right and proper." She jabbed a finger through the air at Darian for emphasis. "Not only did he set everyone straight on Ms. Witlowe's lies but he *fired* her from the company."

She dropped her voice to a conspiratorial whisper. "I think it was only because she had hurt Aurelia's feelings, though there was some talk of Ms. Witlowe not fulfilling her contract."

"Then what happened?"

Elizabeth drew herself up proudly. "Well, I didn't linger about once Mr. Beauforte and Aurelia started to kiss. It was so romantic, just like one of those wee books my sister Mary likes to read."

She sighed with delight. "I just know they'll be so happy together, Mr. Mulvaney. If ever there was a pair made for each other, it's those two."

She bustled away to check on her dinner and missed the anger that Darian couldn't keep from his features. "Now, you'd best leave me to fixing dinner or there'll be nothing to eat on this night!" Elizabeth chuckled to herself. "Not that I imagine Aurelia or Mr. Beauforte would notice!"

Darian turned and stalked out of the hall, irritated beyond belief that Marissa had failed so completely. But even so, Baird and Aurelia wouldn't live happily ever after if he had anything to say about it.

Fortunately, he had already laid plans for this possibility.

The dream crept into Baird's mind on stealthy feet that night, infiltrating his sleep before he could stop it. He fought against it even as he saw himself descending the steps into the well.

Not again! Everything was sorted out now.

But the dream, characteristically, wasn't very interested in Baird's protests.

It was morning this time, the rosy fingers of the sunrise just cresting the horizon behind him and painting the stone steps with a ruddy glow. The world was framed in black and Baird realized from the distortion of the sound of the sea that he wore a metal helmet.

Baird felt a tremendous weight on his shoulders and in his hand. He glanced down at the chain mail that fell to his knees.

It rattled slightly as he moved, the blue tunic that hung over it flapped in the breeze. He wore leather gauntlets again, though these were rougher than the green ones had been and plain black.

A red cross was stitched on the chest of his tunic. A heavy blade hung in his hand, its hilt graced with a massive red garnet held in place by gold shaped like a hawk's claw. And a single thought echoed in his mind:

He had proven himself worthy.

Baird felt the adrenaline course through him as he descended the stairs and hacked back the thorns with his sword. A horse nickered behind him, but he did not look back, knowing with odd certainty that it was his own steed awaiting him.

As did the lady before him.

The dirt of a dozen cities was on his boots and the dust of a thousand miles embedded in his clothes. He knew with sudden clarity that he had not only seen Micklegarth, but that it was the same city his waking mind called Istanbul. It was strange, as though he were of two separate minds, two minds that were rooted in the same body.

Baird knew that he was this man, that he was witnessing another of his journeys to find Aurelia. Yet the dream Baird who was living this moment was unaware of the presence of his modern counterpart, let alone that man's thoughts.

Dream Baird's thoughts were of crusade and honor, of battles won and lost, of quests to be pursued, and one particular fair maiden to be won.

The slab of stone was locked in place, but Baird bent a shoulder to its weight. He called back and a young boy clattered down the stairs, his eyes wide with mingled wonder and fear.

With a start, Baird recognized the pizza boy. Between knight and squire, they forced the slab aside.

And Baird stepped into the darkness once more. His heart raced with fear at what his last dream had revealed, but the Baird of his dreams was blissfully unaware of any danger here.

The medieval knight was hopeful, expectant. Excited. He breathed deeply of the dank air, his spirit buoyed with the promise of lifting some ancient curse.

The knight stepped forward, his squire lingering in the doorway. The pink dawn light streamed down the stairs behind and illuminated the lady sleeping just ahead.

Both Bairds caught their breath at her fragile beauty.

"Aurelia," breathed the knight. "Lady as lovely as the dawn." He crossed the floor to drop to one knee beside her. He doffed his glove, laid aside his sword, and lifted her pale hand to his lips.

"Lady Aurelia," he murmured. "I have come."

And Baird kissed the back of her hand with exquisite grace.

The lady stirred and her face turned toward the knight, her lips parting beneath the early sunlight's caress.

The knight kissed the inside of Aurelia's palm. She smiled softly in her sleep. Baird tasted the sweet flesh of her wrist, fragrant even in his dream. His heart pounded as the knight he had once been leaned over the sleeping beauty.

He kissed her brow gently. "Lady Aurelia," he whispered. "Awaken to me, destiny mine." The lady stirred ever so slightly and her lashes fluttered.

The squire cried out in sudden terror.

Baird spun to find the boy crumpled to the floor and bleeding copiously. An adversary dressed completely in black leaped into the well, his blade flashing in the ray of early sunlight.

"En garde!" he bellowed, and Baird snatched up his blade.

He was surprised at his own ability, but his opponent was stronger, perhaps driven by madness. The masked adversary feinted and dodged, slashed and stabbed, until finally his sword found its mark.

Baird caught his breath at the explosion of pain in his chest, and he looked down to where the lethal broadsword had cleaved even his mail. He fell to his knees, fearing for the lady in the presence of this blackguard, as mocking laughter filled his ears.

"Do not imagine that I will let you claim what should be mine!"

Baird's eyes flew open in shock, only to find Aurelia's bright blue gaze fixed upon him. The light of the full moon spilled into the room in peaceful denial of the tumult in his veins.

His hands were shaking, his heart was racing. He threw himself out of Aurelia's bed, well aware of her gaze following him, and scanned the shadows. Baird checked every nook and cranny. He checked the closets, looked under the bed, and behind the drapes.

There was no intruder in the room.

Aurelia sat up to watch him, folding her arms around her knees. But Baird didn't have any easy explanation for disturbing her sleep.

His chest ached with the memory of the wound.

Baird dropped into a chair and rubbed a hand over his eyes. He exhaled shakily and remembered his first dream. He had died in that encounter, as well.

Were these dreams memories, too, or were they symbolic?

He swallowed. Maybe he *was* a little worried about Dunhelm's location, despite his assurances to Julian. And if he had chosen the site out of some emotional desire to own it, it might not really be the best place for his resort.

What if he had made a mistake? A shadow of fear crossed over Baird. If Dunhelm failed, the entire company could be in jeopardy because of the cost of this renovation.

Had he stretched too far?

Was that the reason for this nightmare?

"Bard, son of Erc," Aurelia asserted quietly.

Baird blinked. "I beg your pardon?"

"It was Bard who killed you in that dream." Her fair brows pulled together in thought. "It must have been him the other time, as well, though I was not certain before he spoke."

The hair on Baird's neck snapped to attention. Surely Aurelia couldn't know what he had dreamed?

"Spoke?"

" 'Do not imagine that I will let you claim what should be mine!' " She quoted the last line of Baird's dream with eerie accuracy, then shivered. "Truly, the man had a malice that could not be denied."

Baird pushed to his feet and crossed to the bed. He leaned over Aurelia, willing the truth from her. "You can't know that. You can't know what I dreamed."

Aurelia laughed. "Well, of course I do!" She reached out, her eyes shining, and took Baird's hand. With consummate ease, she echoed his own gesture from the dream and pressed a kiss against the back of his hand. " 'Awaken to me, destiny mine,' " she murmured, a smile curving her lips.

Baird snatched his hand away and backed against the wall. "How do you know what I dreamed?"

"Because I made you dream it," she said easily, then patted the mattress beside her. "Come back to bed, Baird. It is too early to be awake. And you, sir, have left me tired indeed."

But Baird didn't move. His gut was tight with the memory of Jessica's coldhearted manipulation.

"How could you make me dream anything?" he asked hoarsely.

Aurelia heaved a patient sigh. "Because that is the second gift from my naming. I have the power to summon the Dreaming. Deep in my mind there is a dreamstone of rare power." She snuggled beneath the covers and yawned. "Could we not talk about this in the morning?"

She had made him dream.

Baird didn't know how she had done it, but the fact remained that Aurelia *had* done it. And all the dreams that unlocked the secret doors inside of him had just been the keys in Aurelia's deception. Somehow she had gotten into his mind and played him like a cheap guitar. Baird didn't know how she had figured out what made him tick, but she had manipulated him brilliantly.

He hadn't lived before.

He hadn't had a father who loved him.

He had never been to Dunhelm or Inverness.

And he certainly wasn't destined to be with Aurelia.

One more time, a woman had played Baird Beauforte for a fool. And one more time, he had seen the truth in the nick of time.

"No, we can't talk about it in the morning," he said tightly, and scooped up his clothes.

Baird knew what he had to do, even though the prospect made him feel physically ill. It was horrifying that even knowing what Aurelia had done didn't loosen her spell over him.

"What do you mean?" Aurelia asked with surprise. She sat up and her glorious hair tumbled over her shoulders, her blue eyes filled with concern.

It was all a brilliant act, Baird reminded himself as his heart clenched. "We won't talk about it, because I won't be here."

Aurelia sat bolt upright. "But where are you going?"

"Doesn't matter," Baird said flatly. "I've had one Jessica in my life and sure as hell don't need another."

With that, he walked out of Aurelia's room.

He should have known better, he told himself grimly as he fought his way into his clothes. No one had ever wanted him just for himself.

And nothing had changed.

By the time Aurelia realized that Baird made no jest, she could hear Tex complaining at being roused from bed. She threw on her clothes and ran down the stairs, but her pursuit came too late.

The dawn was just tinting the horizon when Aurelia burst onto Dunhelm's lawn. She ran for the chopper, but its rotors sped more and more quickly.

It lifted off the ground before she was halfway to the paved pad. Aurelia cried out Baird's name, but he did not look her way. She watched him point to the south. The chopper turned and lifted higher, and in the blink of an eye, he was gone.

Aurelia fought against her tears as she watched the silver dragonfly fade into the pale blue of the morning sky. She could not chase him, she could not force him to listen, she could not take away her hasty words and explain the Dreaming to him in another way.

It was too late. The damage was done.

And Aurelia did not know how she would ever make it right.

She could not go back to the bed they had shared. Perhaps later, she would cherish Baird's scent on the linens, but the blow to her heart was too fresh.

Aurelia lifted her chin and began to walk.

Twenty-three

It was late afternoon by the time she came back to the hotel. Aurelia had no sooner stepped into the foyer than Elizabeth came running to her. The older woman's usually cheerful features were drawn in concern and she twisted her hands together.

"Oh, Aurelia, I do not know what to do!"

And then Elizabeth burst into tears.

Aurelia slid her arm around the older woman's shaking shoulders. "Elizabeth, what is wrong? What has happened?"

"Talorc's mother, Ursilla, she . . . she . . ."

Elizabeth took a gulping breath and Aurelia's heart clenched. "What has happened?"

Elizabeth rubbed ineffectively at her tears. "She passed away in her sleep. The funeral is on the morrow."

Aurelia felt a pang of loss, even though she had not known Ursilla well. There was something about her that drew Aurelia her way. Oddly enough, she had considered seeking out the older woman on this very day.

But she was dead.

"Oh, no, Aurelia, you must not be dismayed. Ursilla was elderly and truly it was the kindest way for her sweet soul to pass from this world. It's Talorc I'm worried about!" She sniffled into her handkerchief and seemed to be fighting to compose herself. "He's not talking to anyone, and worse—"

Elizabeth lifted a pale face to Aurelia. "He will not eat a speck of anything."

She swallowed as Aurelia absorbed this news and within a heartbeat, Elizabeth's words fell in their characteristic torrent again. "It's not good for him, miss, it's not right for a man to lose his appetite. I don't need to tell you that I'm terribly worried about him. He just won't eat a bite!"

She caught her breath. "He looked so drawn and serious when he brought the news, it's not healthy, Aurelia, that it's not. I know they were powerfully close those two, but still, Ursilla led a good long life."

"Surely it is only natural for him to mourn," Aurelia suggested, but Elizabeth shook her head firmly.

"I know mourning, Aurelia, but this is more than that. He's left us, slipped away into some corner of his mind where none can reach him. It's not natural and it cannot be good. Even now, he's a shadow of himself, a man I barely recognize, and that will only get worse if he doesn't eat."

Elizabeth inhaled shakily and her tears gathered as she stared at Aurelia. "I don't know what I would do with myself if something happened to Talorc," she confessed in an uneven whisper.

Aurelia gave the older woman's shoulder an encouraging squeeze. She had noticed the way Talorc's glance followed Elizabeth and despite her own woes, Aurelia could not turn away from the opportunity to lend her help. "Do not worry, Elizabeth. I will talk to him."

"Please, miss. He seems to like you."

Talorc was standing on the cliffs, staring out at sea, his hands shoved deep in the pockets of his baggy trousers. There was something about the way the wind ruffled his hair, perhaps about the way the late sun picked out the silver in the gray that made Aurelia's heart ache with familiarity.

She picked her way toward him, not having the faintest idea what she would say to him or what she could discover to ease Elizabeth's mind.

In the end, she did not have to find the words.

Talorc did.

Aurelia came to a halt slightly behind the older man and he tossed a wry smile over his shoulder. "Don't be telling me you're sorry, Miss Aurelia, my mother had a long and happy life. Indeed, she was blessed with uncommonly good health right to the end." He sighed. "It was easy for her."

"But not for you, I would imagine," Aurelia commented softly as she stepped up beside him. The sea was a silver mirror stretching to the horizon, the lowering sun painting a blaze of orange across its gleaming surface.

Talorc shrugged but did not look to her. "Harder than I expected it to be, that much is for certain." He cleared his throat. "Have you ever had the feeling that you have been through something before? That you have lost someone before and that the ache in your heart is all too familiar?"

He held up his gnarled hand before Aurelia could answer, and she saw a sad smile curve his lips. "No, don't be answering that. It's what she said at the end, preying on my mind and making me fey." Talorc sighed. "I suppose it was a disappointment to see a woman who always clung to her wits losing her grip, even so slightly, at the very end. Sad it was, there's no mistake."

"I thought she passed away in her sleep."

"Aye, that she did, but when my mother went off to her bed last evening, she said the strangest thing. I thought nothing of it at the time but it has troubled me ever since, perhaps only because it makes no sense at all."

"What did she say?"

Talorc exhaled heavily and frowned. "She touched my arm and when I looked at her, she told me not to be afraid, that all that was begun had been set to rights." His frown deepened. "She said that all tasks left unfinished had been done, all debts settled and balances paid."

Aurelia could see nothing confusing about any of this, for she had oft seen that people sensed when they had lived their due. And Ursilla had had time to settle all her affairs to her satisfaction.

But Talorc's silence hinted that this was not all of the tale. "Did she say anything else?"

"She called me Hekod," Talorc admitted, and turned a fierce blue glance on Aurelia.

She caught her breath at the familiarity of that stubborn sapphire stare, but Talorc did not notice her response. He glared out to the sea once more and she could see that his hands had balled into fists in his pockets.

"You must understand that there was a day when my mother often called me Hekod, though it was but a joke between us," he continued tightly. "She meant no ill will by it, to be sure. She often jested that she would have given me the name in truth had it not been such a portent of bad luck. But I, I was blessed with uncommon good luck, despite her nickname for me."

Talorc sighed with the memory. "In my youth, I could not shake the dust of this island from my shoes quickly enough. I joined the merchant marine as soon as they would take me, lied about my age as was easily done then. My mother never protested, though I came home seldom enough in those days." A smile of affectionate recollection curved his lips. "I sent her postcards and she always had them tacked to the walls. Souvenirs from Hekod gone a-viking, she used to say."

Aurelia's throat tightened painfully.

"The war came and, of course, I signed up immediately, anxious in my ignorance to do the right thing." Talorc shuddered. "It was horrible, more horrible than anything I could have imagined, and even after it was all over, it still cast a long shadow in my mind. Perhaps it was the killing, but that taste for travel was my war casualty. The only one and a comparatively low price to pay against that of the many who did not come home again." He took a breath. "I came home, here, to Dunhelm, as there seemed no more right place to be."

"And here you stayed."

"Yes," Talorc admitted thoughtfully. "And have wanted nothing else, all these years." His voice was rough when he finally continued. "But even knowing that, you must understand that her last words gave me a chill. I have to believe that is only because they made no sense at all."

"What did she say?"

Talorc exhaled shakily. " 'Hekod Viking and lover true, my

time is over and yours yet new. Our paths now part, though
memory will be true. Go! Follow your heart now, for its aim
is true.' ''

Aurelia stared at the older man, unable to summon a word
to her lips. Her pulse thundered in her ears.

It was all true. The people she had known and loved all
those centuries before had come back to Dunhelm, drawn here
time and again, to finish the deeds they had left undone.

Drawn here to help her and Baird. Ursilla *had* been her
mother, Gemma, so long ago. A part of her had been compelled to wait at Dunhelm, to try to fix what she saw as her
own failure to protect her daughter.

And she had died only when she believed the matter resolved.

Her words implied that Ursilla would not be back again.

Aurelia wondered how many times Gemma had come, how
many times she had tried to set matters aright. She thought of
Baird's repeated memories of returning here and was humbled
that those she loved cared so much for her welfare.

To her mind, Aurelia had done nothing to deserve such
esteem.

And Ursilla had been right when she declared Aurelia's father to be closer than she believed. Aurelia looked to the
groundskeeper with new eyes, seeing an echo of her sire in
his gruff demeanor and flashing blue eyes.

Talorc carried the soul of Hekod. His traveling, his distaste
of war, the intense blue of his eyes all told Aurelia as much
as Ursilla's teasing nickname.

But Talorc had only the faintest recollection of any of this,
a single ache in the loss of his mother that heated the old
wound of losing Gemma. No more than that.

Perhaps it was a blessing to remember so little.

"And what does your heart bid you do?" Aurelia asked
softly.

Talorc shed a single tear. "It aches so that I cannot hear
anything else it might say." He shook his head, his manner
turning gruff. "Ah, you must be thinking me an old fool, Miss
Aurelia. A grown man weeping for his mother as though there
was something unnatural between them."

His glance quelled any protest Aurelia might have made. "She was a fine woman, a woman of rare intellect and insight. I respected her as I have never respected another and there was nothing more than that between us. In truth, it seemed that no other woman could measure up to her standard. We had an uncommonly close bond, more like powerful friends than mother and son. We were good company each for the other and I shall miss her sorely."

"Miss Aurelia?" Elizabeth's call carried from the terrace and both she and Talorc turned to look. The woman's wave was more tentative than usual and Aurelia thought there was an uncertainty in her voice. "Would you have some dinner?"

"That woman is always cooking," Talorc muttered, and shook his head. "Every time I turn around, she is trying to stuff some food or another upon me. By the heavens above, she will make me fat yet!"

"She is worried about you."

Talorc looked at Aurelia, his somber glance speaking volumes. "She is a good-hearted woman, Elizabeth is."

"Is that what your heart says?"

Talorc snorted. "You have a measure of my mother's insight, that much is for certain." He squared his shoulders and looked toward an obviously anxious Elizabeth. "What do you think she has been cooking all this day?"

Aurelia smiled. "Whatever is your favorite dish."

He stared at her for a long moment, then shrugged again. "You have caught me in a rare mood this day, that much is for certain. And there is no need to hurt a good woman's feelings over foolishness." He cleared his throat. "But, before we go and eat whatever it is Elizabeth has been busying herself with making, there's one thing I would say to you, Miss Aurelia."

Talorc fidgeted, awkward with such confessions, and Aurelia simply waited.

"I have never had a child, and at this point, I sorely doubt that I ever will. But there is a spark in you, Miss Aurelia, that warms an old man's heart. If ever I were to have a daughter, I would be proud beyond all if she had the good fortune to be like you."

They stared at each other for a long moment as the sea crashed far below their feet.

Aurelia finally managed to coax the words past the lump in her throat. "You remind me most vividly of my own sire," she admitted softly.

"Is that the truth of it? Well, then I was not such a fool to say such a thing." Talorc jammed his old felt hat on his head and waved to Elizabeth. "Are you coming along to eat?"

"No. Not just now."

Aurelia watched as Talorc strode back toward the hall, a definite bounce in his step. "Elizabeth, you've not been cooking all the day long just for the two of us, have you? By the saints above, woman, how many people are you thinking you'll be feeding in this place?"

Elizabeth laughed, then her scolding tones carried to Aurelia's ears though her words were not clear. Aurelia knew that she did not imagine the other woman's relief.

And what of her own? Aurelia turned to pace the length of the cliff face. Baird's dreams had been right, though it was no consolation to think of that now. The tangle of their fates compelled them all to return to Dunhelm, to try and fix a muddle gone sorely amiss.

This time, things had changed. Aurelia had been awakened but Baird was gone, no longer her lover true. He was lost to her, as surely as he had been each time he died within the walls of the ritual well.

Men seldom wed their whores. Gemma's voice rang in her ears, prompting Aurelia to wonder whether she had made such an old mistake.

Had she truly been no more than that to Baird?

Julian slipped into the tiny church wearing a suit with too much of a hint of burgundy to be truly called black. His white shirt was crisp and his golden tie remarkably sedate in what was obviously a concession to the occasion.

When the funeral service was over and Ursilla had been walked to the cemetery, Julian fell into step beside Aurelia. "Nothing more fun than a funeral," he muttered.

Aurelia glanced pointedly at him but kept up her brisk pace.

"I was surprised to see you here. Did you know Ursilla?"

Julian shook his head. "Corporate presence. Boss's request." He met Aurelia's gaze with a glance so knowing that she had to look away. "Got to wonder why the man isn't here to do such things himself."

Aurelia stared at the ground.

Julian's tone was idle. "You wouldn't happen to know anything about his sudden departure, would you?"

Aurelia's cheeks flamed and Julian pounced.

"Aha! I should have known. You two had a tiff, and I was left holding the bag in this godforsaken place!" He positively bounced alongside Aurelia, showing an annoying contentment at solving the puzzle. "So, what did you fight about? Anything meaty?"

Thord had done that all the time. As endearing as her brother had been, he showed an irritating tendency to ignore any hurt that was not his own. Of all the things she had tried to change . . .

Aurelia turned and stared at Julian in sudden understanding. Julian *was* Thord. She had been so busy dismissing her earlier conclusion that Baird had been trying to affect her dreaming that she had forgotten all about Baird's dream comparing the two.

And now it seemed so painfully obvious. Julian was Thord, drawn to the site of his own murder to see this matter set to rest. Aurelia's heart swelled in sudden understanding of why Julian found Scotland so offensive.

It had nothing to do with the weather or the food.

She could trust Julian with the very secrets of her heart. The fact that he had come back again was yet another testament of the old link between the two of them.

And he was friends with Baird, which meant he might be able to answer something that had been bothering Aurelia.

"What does it mean to be a Jessica?" she asked.

Julian winced. "He called you that?"

"Yes, but I do not understand."

"Oh, but I do. That explains *everything*. No wonder he took off like a bat out of hell." Julian clucked his teeth and walked ahead, pausing to glance back at Aurelia. "So, what? You want his money?"

Aurelia stiffened. "I care nothing for hard coin."

"What is it, then? The fancy lifestyle? Lavish accommodations? You want him to introduce you to fatter fish?"

Aurelia treated Julian to her most scathing glower. "Baird and I are destined to be together."

"Uh-huh." Julian's skepticism was tangible.

"It is true!"

"Whatever." Julian made a face. "So, what did you *do* to him? Why did he compare you to Jessica?"

Aurelia shrugged. "I do not know."

Julian studied her for a long moment, then nodded to himself. "You know, maybe I should tell you about this Jessica bitch. She kind of spoiled Baird for anyone else, if you know what I mean."

"No, I do not understand."

"Well, Jessica was a piece of work, probably still is." Julian shoved his hands into his pockets and started to walk, Aurelia fast on his heels. "Gorgeous woman, all curves and auburn hair and come-hither glances. She laid one of those on Baird once she decided he was a man with a future." Julian shook his head. "You know, anyone else might have seen right through her, but Baird . . . well, Baird had been alone so long that he fell for her like a ton of bricks."

Aurelia's mouth went dry. "He loves this woman?"

"He thought he did." Julian fired a bright glance Aurelia's way. "It wasn't as though he'd had a lot of experience in all that."

She nodded, aching for the loneliness Baird had known. "He told me of his fostering."

Julian ran a hand over his bald pate. "Well, yeah, he hasn't had it easy, that's for sure. And Jessica was good, you know. The Manipulation Queen. She knew when to push and when to leave it alone. It wasn't long before Baird was completely in her pocket." Julian stuck out his tongue. "It was really a drag, because everyone else could see that she was playing him for a fool, but our noble Baird wouldn't listen to a word against his lady."

Aurelia's chest tightened. Did Baird still love this woman? Had Aurelia inadvertently reminded him of this lost love?

Julian scuffed his toe. "Problem was, Jessica was no lady."

"What happened?"

To Aurelia's surprise, Julian looked sheepish. "Well, he wouldn't listen. I didn't want him to get hurt—you know, that's what friends are for."

Had they been discussing anything else, the lawyer's defensive manner would have made Aurelia smile. As a child, she had always been amused by the way Thord would squirm when caught in an awkward situation.

"What did you do?" she demanded with no small trace of sisterly affection.

Julian colored. "Well, I set her up. She deserved it!"

"How?"

"I, uh, happened to come by some information about a little liaison Jessica was planning. Purely by coincidence, Baird was heading home early from some overseas meeting—"

"Coincidence?"

"Well, maybe I helped speed things up a bit. He's my *friend*!" Julian hurried on as though he did not want another interruption. "And so I suggested that instead of calling ahead he should just surprise Jessica. After all, didn't he have a key to her place?"

Aurelia gasped. "He walked in on them?"

"Flagrante delicto," Julian confirmed with gusto. "Worst thing was, she had hopped into the sack with some business associate of Baird's, a highflying type that Baird had introduced Jessica to. What a slap in the face! It must have been some kind of show." He whistled through his teeth. "I wish I could have been there."

Aurelia knew her eyes were wide. "Did he spurn this woman for her faithlessness?"

Julian grimaced. "You know, I'm not sure he would have. Baird was really smitten. Maybe he would have been able to forgive and forget or take it as a one-off, but Jessica made a big mistake that night."

"What did she do?"

"She laughed at him." Julian's gaze was sober. "She told

him flat out that she had used him to meet wealthier men, that Baird was taking too long to make his millions. This guy she was with was busy setting her up in style as his mistress—''

Aurelia was incredulous. "He was not going to wed her?"

Julian's tone was dry. "He already was married."

"Such a man is no better than vermin!"

"I tell you, they were two of a kind." He cleared his throat. "Then she invited Baird to visit her penthouse, just to play."

Aurelia could well understand how hurt Baird would be by this betrayal. He would have put everything into the first loving relationship of his days, and to find himself used and deceived would burn deeply.

She was astonished that he had come to trust her the way he had. It could not have been easy for him to grant his heart to Aurelia. If only she had known more of Jessica before! Never would she have admitted to summoning the Dreaming— or at least, she would have made her role in the generation of those dreams more clear.

But now, Aurelia did not know whether she would ever have the chance to explain.

Julian walked more quickly. "Well, she showed her true colors and Baird was out of there. And funny thing, Beauforte Resorts doesn't buy linens from Carson Quality Supply anymore."

They walked in silence for a long moment, but Aurelia had to ask. "Baird still loves this woman, despite her faithlessness?"

"No! He's not an idiot, you know." Julian shrugged. "He just thinks women in general are manipulative and self-serving. He's steered a pretty wide path from romance since Jessica."

"But to deny your own happiness because of one foul person is not idiocy?" Aurelia asked impatiently.

Julian stopped, then jingled the change in his pockets and surveyed Aurelia. "Not learning from your mistakes is. I've got to wonder why he turned and ran all of a sudden. It's not like Baird to leave something half done." He leaned closer. "Were you manipulating him, Aurelia?"

Trust Thord to make her face an awkward truth.

She swallowed carefully. "I fear he saw it as such," Aurelia admitted softly. "I only used the power of my dreams to show him the truth of our shared destiny." She felt her tears rise but fought against them valiantly. "And now I have sent him away forever. I wish—I wish that I could have the opportunity to explain the truth to him."

Julian's stern expression eased as he stared at her, obviously seeing her discomfort. He reached out and patted Aurelia on the shoulder, urging her to continue walking toward the resort.

"I never thought you were cut from the same cloth as Jessica," he admitted with an encouraging smile. "I'm going back to the States this afternoon—let me see what I can do."

"I would greatly appreciate the chance to talk to Baird again."

"Well, I'll try, but he can be pretty stubborn." Julian forced a smile and pointedly changed the subject. "You know, Aurelia, I've had a good feeling about you for a while. I know you're really stuck on this eighth-century thing, but is there any chance we met somewhere before? Maybe you were friends with my sister or something?"

Aurelia turned a smile on the lawyer. "Maybe I knew you in the eighth century."

Julian looked momentarily startled, then met her glance and grinned back. "Yeah, could be. I mean, why not?"

Twenty-four

~

Aurelia prowled the perimeter of Dunhelm restlessly, fed up with her own company. Two months of missing Baird was enough to make her dread a lifetime alone.

As she had been alone for countless centuries. On this day, it was threatening rain and the air was damp. The shadowed steps of the ritual well beckoned to her, the weather reminding Aurelia all too clearly of the day she had first met Baird.

Aurelia heard Darian murmuring cheerfully to himself as she descended, and thought his company might be good tonic.

For twelve hundred years Aurelia had slumbered in this ritual well, she marveled as she descended the stairs, and ran her fingers along the fitted stone walls. And yet she had not returned here since the day that Baird awakened her. She paused in front of a carved stone slab, remembering when many such stones dotted the landscape.

This one evidently had served to seal the well.

"It's a beauty, isn't it?" Darian asked pertly, ducking his head out of the well's shadows. They exchanged greetings, then looked at the stone in unison. Darian demonstrated the mechanism that opened and closed it.

"Remarkably well preserved, probably because it's been out of the elements. We'll never figure it out, of course, no hint these days as to what these things meant." He pursed his lips. "These stones must have been important once, seeing all the work people put into them."

"Oh, yes," Aurelia breathed. "They were."

She stepped closer, ignoring the considering light in Darian's eyes. This was the stone raised in memory of her. The crescent moon signified her status as priestess, the arrow arched against the curve of the moon showed her mastery of the crossbow. The fact that the arrow was broken signified her passing away.

And the world serpent encircled it all just as he surrounded the world and held it intact, consuming his own tail in an endless cycle of death and birth.

Aurelia ran her fingertips across the relief sculpture of herself, thought of all the men who had put their labor into seeing her safe beyond the days of their own lives, and she felt newly humbled by their esteem.

Their efforts had been for nothing in the end. Aurelia had been protected, she had survived, but she had awakened to a barren new life.

Too late Aurelia realized not only that she could love Baird but that she *did* love him. Wildly, madly, and passionately.

But she had figured out the truth too late to make a difference. If Aurelia had been able to confess love when Baird feared she was manipulating him, would it have made a difference? Her heart ached with the weight of that possibility.

But Baird was gone as surely as he had been over the centuries. New York was as remote as the shadowy otherworld of the Dreaming that Aurelia glimpsed. How could she pursue him across the seas, without ship or sail, without Tex's helicopter, without this coin they all held in such esteem?

Without Baird, Aurelia was alone as she never had been before. Only now she understood the full weight of the solitude he had endured as a child.

Falling in love, if indeed Baird had, would have been a tremendous shock to him. New ground, as it were, instead of the appearance of the trusted and familiar, as it was to Aurelia. That coupled with the dreams, for a man who did not dream, would have challenged all he knew to be true.

In five days.

Aurelia sighed, hindsight showing all too clearly that things had moved overly quickly between them. If only she had known then what she knew now, all might have gone differently.

But it was too late. Her pride nudged her with the unwelcome reminder that Baird did not want her, that whatever interest he had had in her had been exhausted in her bed.

"Look at this inscription," Darian urged, and Aurelia shook her head at this reminder of the other man's presence. "Too bad modern scholarship doesn't have the key to read these letters anymore."

Aurelia studied the familiar runes and easily read them. "Here lies Aurelia, daughter of Gemma and Hekod, priestess high—"

"Cursed to sleep until her lover is proven true."

Aurelia's gaze flew to Darian in surprise. His eyes shone with an odd brightness and she suddenly did not feel safe in his presence. "I thought you could not read that," she said cautiously.

Darian smiled and there was something in his expression that made Aurelia aware of the damp chill of the old well.

"No, I said modern scholars couldn't read it. But I remember many, many things that others have carelessly forgotten." He winked with confidence. "Must be a sign of superiority."

A lump rose in Aurelia's throat and she took a step away. "I do not understand."

Darian grinned. "Of course you do, Gemdelovely Gemdelee. We both understand and remember a great deal more than everyone else." He moved quickly to block Aurelia's path to the stairs. "Maybe that's why we're meant to be together."

"We are *not* meant to be together!"

Darian's voice turned hard. "If you're hoping for Bridei to come back, you'll have a long, long wait, Aurelia. This time, I've really scared him to the core, thanks to that dream. He won't be back."

Aurelia's mouth went dry. "What do you know about Bridei and his dreams?"

"More than you, obviously," Darian said with assurance. "He and I have met here many, many times, but you slept right through it all."

The breath left Aurelia's lungs in a rush. "You are *Bard*!"

A malicious smirk twisted on Darian's lips. "None other than the son of Erc himself," he said cockily.

This was the man at the root of her woes! Fury rolled through Aurelia and she lunged at the other man.

"You murdered my brother!" she bellowed, an ancient part of her bent on taking vengeance out of this man's hide.

Darian was flattened against the wall by Aurelia's assault. He swore as she raked her fingernails down the side of his face, then snatched at her wrists.

Aurelia struggled against his grip, furious that he was so much stronger than she. If only she had her crossbow!

"Temper, temper!" Darian slammed Aurelia's back against the wall, looming over her as he held her wrists above her head. She fought to free herself, loathing the way he leaned his chest against her breasts.

"You know, you should have married me when you had the chance, and all of this could have been avoided."

"I had no chance! That was all a lie to draw Thord into your web of deceit!"

Darian laughed and Aurelia despised him doubly for what he had done. "You *do* remember everything! Good, then there won't be any pretending between us."

"There will be *nothing* between us!"

"Oh, really?" Darian sobered. "I swore a pledge a long time ago, Aurelia, a pledge that both you and Dunhelm would be mine." He pressed against her and Aurelia was revolted by the press of his erection against her belly. "Although I never expected you to show such promise."

He closed in for a kiss and Aurelia spat in his confident face.

"Bitch!" Darian grimaced and held her wrists with one hand while he wiped away the spittle. He glared at Aurelia. "I could take you now," he assured her darkly. "But I'd rather wait for you to come willingly to me."

"Never! I will *never* surrender to you!"

Darian chuckled and the cold sound sent a shiver over Aurelia's flesh. "That's where you're wrong, Princess Aurelia."

He slid his free hand down the length of Aurelia, pausing

to pinch her breast. "You know, I like a woman with some fight in her."

If he wanted fight, he would get it from Aurelia. She slammed her knee up into his groin.

Darian howled and loosed his grip. Aurelia squirmed free and dove after the pickax he had been using in the excavation. She pivoted as she swung the weapon high, only to find Darian leaning in the doorway. His arms were folded across his chest and a smile played over his lips.

"Go ahead," he invited.

He thought she would not be able to kill him!

Aurelia stepped forward, not fooled by Darian's bluff. "You should not be so confident that I will not strike a blow," she assured him. "It was I who made the first kill for my father's forces on the day you invaded." She heard her voice turn cold. "Would that it had been you who took that arrow."

Darian's smile broadened and he did not step away from Aurelia's advance. "Well, it wasn't then and it won't be today."

"You are overly confident!"

"Just imagine what the murder of a society archaeologist at Dunhelm would do to Baird's reputation," Darian mused. "Especially when it's already well known that the owner of Beauforte Resorts is fighting this historic investigation tooth and nail."

Aurelia paused. "But Baird has supported your work all along. Indeed, he seems more concerned about details than you!"

"Ah, not according to the reports I've been making to the society." Darian's smile flashed. "Apparently he's been most obstructive, coming within a hair of tossing me off the property."

"But that's a lie!"

"And just between you and me, the chairman of the society is this close"—Darian measured an increment between finger and thumb—"to demanding the government seize Dunhelm as an historic site. You know, this place is so historic, a real cultural gem, that it would be irresponsible to let it pass into private hands, especially private hands that have no respect for the past.''

''You cannot do that to Baird! He has invested heavily in restoring Dunhelm! Dunhelm means everything to him!''

''Exactly!'' Darian confirmed with relish. He flicked a glance to the pickax that Aurelia had half lowered to the ground. ''So, go ahead, kill me and bring this all to a quick conclusion.'' He snapped his fingers. '' 'Hotelier's Lover Murders National Heritage Preservation Society Archaeologist.' The government would seize Dunhelm in a flash.''

''It's all lies!''

Darian smiled coldly. ''Well, it's not my favorite solution, since I'd be deprived of having Dunhelm myself, but it would certainly destroy Baird. Again.'' His gaze hardened. ''Trust me, Princess Aurelia, I can make it so.''

Aurelia felt sickened by this confession. Too late, Aurelia saw the hatred that motivated Darian, a hatred that echoed too clearly of the Bard whose deeds she knew too well.

How could she have missed the obvious?

But she would not give Darian the tools to steal Dunhelm away from Baird. Even if Baird had spurned her, she knew how important this place was to him. And she would do what she could to keep Darian from destroying all Baird had built.

The power of her love was far, far greater than her need for vengeance. Aurelia cast aside the pickax and Darian chuckled.

''You cannot make Dunhelm your own if the government seizes it,'' she declared, but her bravado was weak.

''Close enough.'' Darian shrugged. ''I'll be in charge of the site, and eventually, if all goes according to plan, the society itself will be mine, as well.''

''You cannot do this to Baird,'' Aurelia whispered. ''It would break his heart to lose Dunhelm.''

''That's precisely the point.'' Darian moved suddenly and braced his hand above Aurelia's shoulder, leaning so close to her that she recoiled in distaste. ''Although there is still one pesky detail to be resolved.''

Aurelia could barely form the word. ''What?''

Darian's eyes gleamed. ''I also vowed to lay claim to Hekod's lovely daughter.''

"No!" Aurelia pushed past him and ran for the stairs.

Darian's mocking laughter followed her and Aurelia remembered his assertion that she would come willingly to him. "No! Never!" Aurelia scrambled up the stairs in her desperation to escape.

She had to help Baird!

There was one thing Aurelia could do, one thing she had to do, one thing she had never dared to do before. It was a once-in-a-lifetime solution and she would never be the same afterward.

But the stakes were high enough to merit the deed. Aurelia had to summon Baird, and this time, she had to make him fully understand the threat against him and Dunhelm.

The moon, mercifully, would be full on this night.

Perhaps that was a portent of success.

Aurelia rushed into the hotel and Elizabeth turned in surprise. "Where can I find someone to cut my hair?" she demanded breathlessly.

It was six o'clock on a Thursday night in May and Baird was staring out the window of his office at the city far below. New York was the same as it always had been, but Baird knew he was different.

The business ran as well as ever, better in fact since Baird had acknowledged the power of his own intuition. He made decisions more quickly now, trusted his gut instead of wasting time chasing supportive statistics. If anything, Beauforte Resorts was a stronger company than it had ever been.

But success had become hollow.

Maybe it always had been, but Baird had needed Aurelia to open his eyes to the facts. He jingled the change in his pockets, not quite ready to admit he needed her more than that.

Baird's apartment in the Manhattan Beauforte was the same, but its plain functionality no longer pleased him. He found himself rattling restlessly around in it at night.

The apartment was empty, just like his life.

Baird had always been alone, that wasn't new. What had changed was that he didn't want to be alone anymore. The yawning emptiness that he'd actively chosen now bothered him as it never had before.

He often caught himself staring into space when he should have been working, lost in a vision of blue, blue eyes with a faint rim of silver-gray.

Just as he was now.

The dreams had stopped as soon as Baird left Dunhelm, although that moment in Inverness had proven to be the beginning of something far worse. What had been his dreams now came at any hour of the day, bursting into his mind with a vividness that competed with his own photographic memories.

The slightest thing brought them on—a snippet of William Morris wallpaper reminded him of a Victorian parlor he had abandoned to seek Aurelia, a waft of incense brought memories of a Byzantine church where he had turned back to the Orkney Islands. Each and every one of them was a testament to a time he had proven himself worthy, then gone to seek Aurelia's hand.

Baird had a hard time believing that they *weren't* his memories.

If they were, he had spent twelve hundred years going back to the same place, over and over again, undeterred by his own repeated failure to achieve his goal.

A goal named Aurelia.

A woman whom he loved against all reason.

If the visions told the truth, if he had *actually* gone back to Dunhelm all those times, then this would have been his greatest failure of all. Baird had awakened Aurelia, he had fallen in love with her, but he still found himself unable to trust her.

And he had left her in Dunhelm.

Baird frowned and called up the bookings for Dunhelm one more time on the in-house computer system. He had to acknowledge that they were looking good.

The place wasn't even open yet and the reservations were more than decent all the way through to the fall. And Christmas looked very promising. Baird leaned back in his chair and tapped his pen on the desk. It was small consolation that his gut had been right about Dunhelm.

Baird missed Aurelia enough to have been right about her, too.

"Hey." Julian lounged in the doorway, looking uncharacteristically haggard.

"Looks like Marissa's giving you a run for your money," Baird commented, grateful for the distraction from his thoughts.

Julian flashed a wry look at him and dropped into one of the leather chairs opposite. "That would be *your* money."

"I'm surprised you haven't settled things yet. You two aren't enjoying yourselves, are you?"

Julian's glance was lethal. "Hardly! The woman fights like a demon over every comma in the settlement contract."

"Careful, Julian." Baird scanned a memo Darlene had dropped on his desk. "That's starting to sound like admiration."

Julian grinned suddenly. "Well, there's nothing like a worthy adversary to make the victory sweet."

Baird glanced up. "So you're close to settling?"

"Oh, yeah. There's no court case here and she knows it." He ran a hand over his head and yawned. He feigned casualness so well that Baird almost missed the signs. "So, how's Aurelia?"

Baird's heart leaped, but he tried to school his expression. "I wouldn't know," he admitted coolly.

"Maybe you should find out," Julian dared to say.

Baird glowered across his desk. "Look, you're way out of line here. . . ."

Julian, undeterred, leaned forward to brace his elbows on the desk. "I don't think so." His eyes shone with sincerity. "She's not like Jessica, Baird. You know it and I know it."

"I only know that she tricked me!" Baird retorted.

"No. You got your wires crossed somehow." Julian looked out the window for a long moment, but when Baird said nothing, Julian met his glance again. "Look, you trusted my instinct on women before. Think about it—I think there could

be something good between you two, if you have the balls to
go back and talk to her.''

Baird bit back a curse. ''I'm not afraid of Aurelia, even if
she does think she's a half-Viking Valkyrie.''

''Yeah?'' Julian pushed to his feet. ''Then tell me why you
aren't booked to go to Dunhelm Resort's grand opening. This
was your baby, as no other site has been.'' Julian pointed a
finger at his friend as he retreated. ''The Baird Beauforte I
know wouldn't let the way a little blonde turned him inside
out stop him from being there.''

With a grin that showed he knew he was right, Julian
ducked out the door and was gone.

And he *was* right, damn him.

But Baird still wasn't going. He combed a hand impatiently
through his hair and turned back to his laptop.

The moon rose round and orange, then climbed slowly in the
sky. Aurelia was on the farthest point of Dunhelm from the
resort, on the spot where she believed she and her dame had
done their rituals long ago. It had been a strong place, but the
rhythm of the land was faint now and harder to discern, even
by those who listened closely.

This place would have to do.

The sea surrounded the tiny point on three sides and the
land dropped from the plateau to a ledge out of view. The
drop was only the height of a man but it was enough to keep
prying eyes ignorant of what Aurelia meant to do.

The night wind felt strange against her skin. Aurelia felt
lost without the protective curtain of her hair. As the moon
rode high, she lifted the weight of her shorn tresses out of the
bag she carried them in.

The braid was long and thick. A decade of growth, the hair
carried the full import of her magic from the onset of her
courses. It was filled with blessings and rituals, strong with
the power she had learned. A priestess was to use her hair
sparingly, for it was uncommonly powerful, but Aurelia had
known that this moment would take no less than all she had
to give.

She sacrificed the full power of her magic to ensure Baird

did not lose the only thing she knew for certain that he held dear.

Dunhelm. Aurelia could not stand by and let him lose what he had built, knowing how important success was to him.

How she wished she could have summoned him for herself instead.

When the moment was right, Aurelia raised her hands to the moon. She called to the four directions to witness her spell, she summoned the winds, she saluted the elements. She raised her voice in the ancient chant she had never expected to use.

The reflection of the moon obediently slid down into the waiting chalice of water. Aurelia lifted the chalice, gazing into the glow of the moon's light, recounted a chant and raised it to her lips.

The moon slid into her, its silver strength rolled through her and when the water was gone, Aurelia was the Goddess.

The power of infinity coursed through her veins, the dreamstone throbbed with a secret light. The elements and the winds cavorted to her bidding and Aurelia felt Gemma's presence behind her left shoulder. When she raised her voice to chant, she did not speak alone, Gemma and countless others were whispering in unison.

In her mind's eye, Aurelia suddenly saw a child with Baird's dark hair. She felt the faint pulse of a new life within her belly and wondered how she could have not known sooner.

Then the Goddess struck the flint and the flames leaped high at her dictate.

And she cast Aurelia's hair into the fire.

The flames licked greedily at the hair and sparks flew in all directions as its power was consumed. It burned with a blue flame that the Goddess drew higher and higher. When the last of the hair was consumed, the Goddess bent the flame to her will, drawing it high, gathering it to direct its power. . . .

And a shower of cold water doused it all.

No!

The magic disappeared with an audible snap. Aurelia cried out as the Goddess abandoned her and the blue flame vanished. She spun to face her attacker and her heart sank when she met the smug grin of Darian Mulvaney.

"I won't let you call him," he said.

The moment of magic was lost. Aurelia could have wept. A black spot on the earth was the only remnant of her glorious hair. The Goddess had come, the magic had been gathered, but its power had been dissipated before it could be directed.

She had given her all for naught! Already the moon was sliding away, the Goddess' eye turned to other matters. Aurelia ached that her hair, the crowning jewel of her powers, had been shorn for naught.

She would not accept failure.

She rounded on Darian and let him feel the brunt of her anger. "I will not permit you to destroy him! I will fight you every step of the way, with every power I can rouse."

"Well, then, maybe we can make a deal." Darian closed the distance between them and Aurelia was furious that she had to make any kind of bargain with the likes of him. "Marry me, Aurelia, and maybe I'll leave Baird a crumb."

She did not hide her animosity. "You concede little."

He laughed. "I don't have to concede *anything*. What you were doing here could be called witchcraft, and I've got to tell you that witchcraft isn't very popular in these times."

Aurelia eyed her attacker, uncertain whether to believe him. Had the role of the Goddess sunk to such depths?

Darian shook a finger at Aurelia. "Rumors of a satanic cult active here could completely destroy this resort's credibility even before it opens." His smile turned cruel. "That might be kind of fun, wouldn't it, for *you* to be the reason Baird's investment fails?"

"No! You cannot spread these lies! You cannot ruin him!"

Darian spread his hands. "Then marry me." He shrugged. "What have you got to lose?"

There was the issue in a nutshell. Aurelia certainly had nothing to gain. She loved Baird, though, and if nothing else, she would see his dream of success secure.

Her heart ached with the certainty that Baird would probably never know what she had done. Elizabeth had said that he was not even coming to the grand opening of the resort.

And Baird certainly would not come to Dunhelm because

of her miserable excuse for a summoning. Aurelia already
knew that Baird no longer wanted her.

She had made the oldest error known to womankind. Men,
after all, seldom marry their whores. And being pregnant out
of wedlock made her tainted goods by any account. No decent
man would want her now.

Although a most indecent one did. Aurelia surveyed the
blackened scorch, which was all that remained of her hair, and
knew that she did not have the power to fight Darian's foul
intent.

She had bet everything she had and lost. All she could do
now was try to save some shard of Baird's dream of Dunhelm
from the vengeful Bard. She would figure out later how to
save herself, and Baird's child, from this loathsome man.

With a heavy heart, Aurelia took Darian's outstretched hand
and nodded her agreement. Perhaps she and Baird were not
destined to be together, after all.

Baird was working late—again—still trying to erase Julian's
certainty from his mind when the vision hit him right between
the eyes.

Dunhelm was burning.

And Baird was there. Orange flames rose high to consume
it, a black billow of smoke rose high in the air. The heat
pressed against his skin, his eyes narrowed against the soot
tossed through the air. He could smell the smoke.

But there was one critical difference. This was *his* Dunhelm
going up in flames, not some old Viking hall.

*Do not imagine that I will let you claim what should be
mine!*

Baird heard the threat again from the last dream he had had
at Dunhelm.

And suddenly the words made perfect sense.

Bard, son of Erc, had pledged to make both Dunhelm and
Aurelia his own.

Aurelia!

She had said she could make him dream. But what if she
didn't make the dreams themselves? What if her Dreaming
had only been a way of forcing Baird to confront his own
memories of Dunhelm?

Just as she had shown him the power of his own intuition.

It would be just like Aurelia to take matters into her own capable hands. She wasn't one to sit back and let matters take their own course.

Baird sat up as understanding flashed through his mind. This vision wasn't about losing Dunhelm. It was about losing something—or someone—much more important. And his intuition was screaming to get his attention.

Well, Baird was finally listening. He couldn't change the fact that he had run from Aurelia like a coward, but he could go back and fight for what he wanted.

Just as Aurelia did.

Just as he had in so many other lives.

But he had never come so close to success before. He would be an idiot to let Aurelia and her love slip through his hands.

Baird was on his feet, closing his laptop and heading for the door before he could think twice about it. He snatched up his raincoat, sailed across the reception area of the executive offices, and pivoted as he punched the elevator button.

"Darlene, could you get me a flight, please?"

Darlene looked sternly over her glasses. A matronly paragon of efficiency, she kept everyone at Beauforte on a tight leash.

Including Baird.

She was as stern as a schoolmistress. "And where are you off to at this time of day?"

"Dunhelm."

Her eyebrows rose. "Tonight?"

"It's important."

"Uh-huh." Darlene looked pointedly at her watch. "You're going to have to move if you're making any trans-Atlantic flight tonight."

"Right." Baird shrugged into his raincoat, delighted to find his passport in the breast pocket. He wouldn't even have to duck upstairs to his apartment. "So why don't you find me a flight while I flag a cab to JFK?" He gave Darlene his best smile and she shook her head.

She pulled off her glasses and tossed them on the desk as she surveyed her boss sternly. "You sure have been acting strange lately, Mr. Beauforte." Her eyes narrowed. "If I didn't know better, I'd say you were a man in love."

Baird felt the back of his neck heat tellingly and a reluctant smile curved his lips. "Well, maybe you do know better."

Darlene shook her head and picked up the phone. "You'd better have your cell phone with you, Mr. Beauforte," she said testily. "Otherwise you're never going to know how you're getting from here to there."

"Thanks, Darlene." The doors slid open and Baird paused in the act of stepping into the elevator. "You *were* taking tomorrow off, weren't you?"

She wasn't and they both knew it.

Darlene flashed Baird a rare smile as she punched in the number. "Am I?" she asked archly.

"Oh, I think you should," Baird said with a solemn nod. "Weren't your grandchildren coming down for the weekend? And besides, what else are you going to do around this place?"

Darlene threw a wad of paper at him with deadly accuracy. "Get out of here, you devil, before you go giving everyone a day off!" She sobered as her call was answered. "Yes, do you have any seats available to Heathrow tonight? Only business class?"

She looked inquiringly to Baird and he nodded just as the elevator doors slid closed. "Fine. I'd like to make a booking for Mr. Baird Beauforte, please. And can you book connecting flights through to Kirkwall? Yes, I'll hold. . . ."

A man in love.

Baird hoped like hell he wasn't too late.

Twenty-five

~~~~~

Baird shared a helicopter from Kirkwall with Colin Russell, the head of the National Heritage Preservation Society. To Baird's surprise, Mr. Russell was en route to Dunhelm to decide whether his society should recommend Dunhelm become public property.

The burly man was a gruff bundle of tweed with a hearty handshake. Mr. Russell seemed oddly nervous, which was odd since Baird was the one with the most to lose.

It figured that Darian had not let Baird get a whiff of this.

Baird's mood was grim as the helicopter lowered to Dunhelm's helipad. He forced a smile for Mr. Russell. Baird chafed with impatience to find Aurelia, but the other man's words brought him up short.

"I must say that I didn't expect you to be here, Mr. Beauforte."

"It's purely a coincidence, Mr. Russell, but a happy one. I'm glad to have the opportunity to express Beauforte's interest in maintaining the historic value of Dunhelm." Baird looked to the hotel but there was no sign of Aurelia.

Mr. Russell glanced at Baird. "I had thought that you objected to any investigation here." At Baird's obvious surprise, he continued. "At least, I was given to understand that you presented numerous obstacles to Mr. Mulvaney's work here."

"On the contrary," Baird said through gritted teeth, "my concerns were purely that the investigation be done systematically. Mr. Mulvaney initially showed an 'enthusiasm' that raised some questions in my mind about his experience.''

Mr. Russell cleared his throat a number of times. "I see, I see. Well, I must apologize on behalf of the society. . . .''

"That's not necessary," Baird said smoothly. "I simply want to see this site explored in a professional and academic manner." He smiled again, trying to guess where to look for Aurelia first. "I suppose it's natural for anyone to be excited about a new find."

Mr. Russell frowned. "No serious professional would permit that to interfere with his work," he said with a severity that didn't bode well for Darian.

Good.

Mr. Russell cleared his throat once more. "Am I to understand, then, Mr. Beauforte, that you have no objection to our excavation of the site?"

"None whatsoever." Baird met the man's gaze. "As long as it's done properly."

"Of course, of course. Eventually, we would like to see such a site opened for public interest." He looked inquiringly to Baird.

"There is no problem with public access," Baird confirmed.

"Well." Mr. Russell frowned. "You must understand, Mr. Beauforte, that this is completely opposite to the understanding I have been given of the situation here." He pulled a handkerchief out of his pocket and wiped the perspiration from his brow. "It seems that the situation may have been misrepresented to me. Might I assume that we could put this arrangement in writing?"

"Of course." Baird watched relief wash over the older man's features, though he still looked troubled.

"I believe Mr. Mulvaney is expecting me at the well. Perhaps you could join me, Mr. Beauforte, and we could get to the bottom of this matter."

Baird tried not to show his frustration. There was no good way to refuse Mr. Russell, but then, he might find Aurelia in the well.

She had agreed to help Darian, after all.

Baird agreed and the men matched steps as they crossed the lawn.

Aurelia's heart stopped cold when she heard the low murmur of Baird's voice.

Then it raced madly.

She rose to her feet, not daring to believe she heard right as footsteps echoed on the stairs to the well. A portly man descended first, his bright gaze scanning both Aurelia and the room before he looked at Darian. He scowled and the antagonism between those two men was tangible.

This must be Mr. Russell, to whom Darian would recommend Dunhelm be stolen from Baird. Darian had not been able to keep Aurelia away from this presentation, for all that she felt powerless to change the results. A part of her had hoped desperately that she might be able to persuade Mr. Russell otherwise.

But that man looked like one who made up his own mind. There was a determination in the set of his jaw when he glared at Darian that gave Aurelia a tentative hope.

Perhaps this would not be so easy as Darian believed.

Then Aurelia saw Baird and she cared nothing for Darian and his games. Baird was as tall and broad as she recalled, and the sight of him had precisely the same effect upon her as before.

If anything, two months without him had made her more susceptible to his allure.

Baird's charcoal suit was like the one Julian had worn the first day they had met, but more conservative in cut. He looked austere despite the burgundy silk knotted around his throat, and the subtle gleam of gold at his wrists. His dark hair had been compelled to some kind of order, his gaze was as vividly green as ever, but there were shadows beneath his eyes.

He looked to have lost some weight.

Did Aurelia dare to hope that Baird had missed her?

She could not summon a word to her lips when his intense gaze met hers. Baird scanned her as hungrily as she had studied him and Aurelia's heart began to sing.

Perhaps all was not lost. Her cheeks heated with self-consciousness as Baird stared at her shorn hair. Aurelia saw the question flash through his eyes before he frowned and looked at the other men.

If only she could have the chance to explain.

"Welcome, Mr. Russell," Darian said expansively. His charming smile grated on Aurelia for all its dishonesty. "And Mr. Beauforte"—his voice hardened—"your presence was hardly expected."

Baird's lips thinned. "So I gather."

Darian chuckled softly. "Well, if you've come to defend your ownership of Dunhelm, I'm sorry to tell you that you've come too late to make a difference. Mr. Russell and I have already had numerous discussions and it's quite clear that our recommendation to the government will be that Dunhelm be made an historic site." He smirked. "With no resort development."

"Our recommendation is far from decided," Mr. Russell interjected tightly.

"Is that so?" Darian asked silkily.

But Baird only stared at Aurelia. "I didn't come for Dunhelm," he said quietly. Aurelia's heart rose to her throat as he crossed the room with purpose. "I came for something much more important than any piece of property could be."

Baird offered Aurelia his hand, uncertainty lurking in his eyes. "Can we talk, princess?" he asked, the words for her ears alone.

Aurelia reached out but before she could put her hand in his, Darian interrupted.

"I'm not sure it's terribly appropriate for you to be exchanging secrets with my fiancée," he said coldly.

Baird's gaze flashed at him, then back to Aurelia. Disbelief shone in his eyes. "Is this true?" he demanded incredulously. "Are you going to marry *him*?"

Aurelia fidgeted. "I did agree to his proposal, but you must understand—"

Baird dropped his hand and stepped away. "There's nothing to understand," he retorted, and spun away from her.

"No! Baird, you must listen!" Aurelia cried, but Baird kept

on walking. The stiff set of his shoulders told her that this time he would not be back.

But Aurelia was not going to let Baird Beauforte walk out of her life again, at least not without knowing exactly what was in his heart.

And she knew exactly how she was going to get his attention.

"How unfortunate that the course of love does not run true," Darian murmured mockingly.

Aurelia stormed over to the display he had carefully prepared of the found artifacts and snatched up the replica he had made of her crossbow.

"Hey! You can't take that!"

"I can and I will." Aurelia snatched up a trio of arrows and glared at the man who had ruined her chances for happiness so many times. "You owe me no less."

Baird couldn't believe that Aurelia would marry Darian Mulvaney. He *wouldn't* have believed it if she hadn't admitted it herself. He stormed across the perfect lawn, furious with her and with himself. How could he have been so dumb as to hope she cared for him?

Something whizzed past Baird, within a finger's breadth of his ear, and made him jump.

The arrow buried itself in the turf ahead, the fleche quivering with the force of its landing.

Baird glanced over his shoulder, only to see Aurelia loading her crossbow for another shot. She looked like a vengeful pixie with her hair cropped so short.

She lifted the crossbow and aimed straight for him.

That was enough! Baird stood his ground and flung out his hands. "Why in the hell are you trying to kill *me*?" he roared in frustration. "You're the one who wants to marry someone else!"

Aurelia lowered the crossbow for a heartbeat and her tone was grim. "If I wanted to kill you, Baird Beauforte, that arrow would never have missed."

Before Baird could make sense of that, Aurelia cocked the

crossbow and fired. Her next shot landed quivering an inch in front of his well-polished wingtips.

Baird jumped backward.

And the way Aurelia proudly lifted her chin told Baird that that was precisely where she had intended for the arrow to be.

He cleared his throat and propped his hands on his hips. "Then what do you want?"

To his relief, she lowered the weapon and strode across the turf, challenge bright in her magnificent eyes. "To get your attention."

Baird pushed a hand through his hair. If nothing else, the woman could keep him guessing!

"Consider it yours." He studied her as she closed the distance between them. Aurelia looked more fragile than she had before, despite her defiant manner. Perhaps it was her cropped hair, or the faint shadows beneath her eyes.

"I do not want to wed Darian Mulvaney," she said flatly. "He is Bard, son of Erc, and true to his foul character, he cornered me so that I had no choice but to agree."

She took a ragged breath as Baird came to terms with that. "He declared he would not destroy all you had built if I took his hand, and I know full well that Dunhelm is of all import to you."

Aurelia impaled Baird with a bright glance. "I would not see you lose all you hold dear, so I made this concession though it went against my own heart and mind."

They stared at each other.

Aurelia didn't want to marry Darian!

But she had been going to do it for *him*.

Baird was humbled by her confession and wondered suddenly what Aurelia's heart desired, if it wasn't Darian.

She gestured resignedly to the well behind them, apparently misinterpreting his silence. "I have had my say, for whatever it is worth, and you should go back if you mean to influence their decision. It is why you are here, after all."

Baird's heart began to pound. "Princess, I didn't know anything about this meeting. It's not why I came back."

She lifted her gaze to his and Baird's gut wrenched at her uncertainty. "Then why?"

"I came back for *you*," he said simply, and her eyes widened in surprise.

Well, even if she didn't like the idea, Baird had to know the truth.

"I love you, princess. I should never have left in the first place." Baird swallowed before he could continue, Aurelia's silence eroding his nerve. His voice was hoarse. "I had to know whether you could love me."

"Oh. *Oh!*"

Baird was not expecting Aurelia to throw herself into his arms with such enthusiasm. When she rained kisses all over his face, his heart swelled enough to burst and Baird wondered how he could have ever doubted her.

He would never do it again.

Ever.

Aurelia caught his face in her tiny hands and stared deeply into his eyes. "I love you with all my heart and soul, Baird Beauforte." Her words were fierce and she glared up at him. "Do not even dream of leaving me like that again."

Baird laughed in his relief. He raised his eyebrows at her. "Mmm, I wouldn't want to have to answer for that," he teased, and swung her high into the air.

Aurelia wrapped her arms around his neck and smiled just before Baird kissed her soundly. Aurelia's embrace was welcoming, familiar, and tantalizing, her tongue reminding him all too well of the pleasures they could give each other.

For all time.

"What do you say to a wedding, princess?" he growled against her throat, and Aurelia pulled back.

A twinkle lurked in the depths of her eyes. "Are you certain you would wed a woman whose womb is already full?"

Baird blinked. "You're pregnant?"

Aurelia tapped him in the middle of his chest, a coy smile curving her lips. "With your seed, sir. I shall expect you to make an honest woman of me."

He was going to be a father! The prospect was both exciting and terrifying. But thanks to the dreams he and Aurelia had shared, Baird had a better model for parenthood than he had had before.

Baird pulled Aurelia close, barely able to believe that his life could be so filled with promise for the future. "How soon can you be ready for that wedding, princess?"

Aurelia answered him with an enthusiastic kiss.

When he finally lifted his lips from hers, Baird ran his fingers through the short remainder of Aurelia's hair. "Why did you cut it?" he asked, unable to keep the disappointment from his voice.

Aurelia grimaced. "It is a long tale that I will tell you sometime." She smiled up at him. "Suffice to say that it was a price well worth paying."

"Really?" Baird knew his skepticism showed.

She tilted her head pertly. "Do you not like it short?"

Baird rubbed a thumb across Aurelia's lips and fought not to grin. "You know, I wouldn't have said anything, princess, but you *did* ask. It, um, it makes you look awfully cute."

Aurelia straightened proudly. "I am not cute! I am a warrior princess!"

Baird bent and plucked one of the arrows from the grass, waving it playfully beneath her nose. "Cupid's own weapon of choice," he told her with a smile. "But he never had such good aim."

"I do not understand."

"It's an old story of a god who makes people fall in love." Baird twirled the arrow. "By piercing their hearts with a magic arrow." He sobered as he held her gaze. "Just as you pierced mine."

Aurelia snuggled against him, her eyes shining. "I had no such magic, but I like the tale well enough." She fingered her hair. "And fear not, my hair will not only grow again but be all the thicker for the change."

"Good." Baird bent and kissed her soundly, loving the way her curves fit perfectly against him.

As though they were made for each other.

"Our recommendation is far from established, despite your apparent certainty," Colin informed the confident young man before him.

"My intention is clear," Darian retorted.

"But you are not the deciding force within the society," Colin said tightly. He scanned the display mockingly, angry that the site had not been cordoned off properly. "Your work here is amateurish and threatens serious scholarship in what might be a critical site for our understanding of the Picts."

"Careful, Mr. Russell," Darian said softly.

"I will not be careful! You have lied to me and manipulated me long enough!" Colin puffed out his chest. "And I do not appreciate that you have misrepresented Mr. Beauforte's interests in all of this. In our brief discussion, he has shown a marked willingness to work with us in exploring this site."

Darian grimaced. "He just wants to protect his investment."

"And I see no reason why he should not."

The two men stared at each other, then Darian smiled slowly. "But it doesn't really matter what you think, does it, Mr. Russell?"

"Of course it matters!" Colin blustered. "Whether you like it or not, young man, I am the founder and president of the National Heritage Preservation Society and my will matters considerably more than yours!" He jabbed a finger through the air. "You are removed from our staff, Mr. Mulvaney!"

"No, Mr. Russell, that's not how it's going to be." Darian unfolded himself and crossed the room. He paused directly before Colin, menace in every line of his body. "Not agreeing with me is a mistake you'll regret. You're going to make me the president and deciding voice of the society and you're going to do it today."

"I will do no such thing! The society is mine!"

"Not without Mrs. Russell's support," Darian threatened.

"Why, you cocky young pup!" Before he considered what he was doing, Colin shoved the man so intent on destroying everything of merit in his life.

Darian cried out, obviously not expecting the older man's rage. Colin meant only to push him hard, but Darian slipped on the damp floor.

And fell, his head cracking against the lip of the ritual well.

Colin gasped as the younger man's limp body slid into the murky water. He couldn't bring himself to go any closer. His first response was a rush of pure freedom, his second outright terror.

What had he done?

And what would this cost his beloved society?

A bellow from the well was the only thing that could have made Baird stop kissing Aurelia. They stepped apart, exchanged a glance of confusion, then Baird snatched up her hand and they ran across the lawn together.

They darted down the stairs and paused at the bottom. It was only now that Baird noticed the open square on the opposite side of the chamber from the slab that had served as Aurelia's bed. A stone rim about two feet in height surrounded it and Darian was sprawled across that rim. His feet dangled above the floor, but his head and shoulders weren't visible. Mr. Russell was backed against the far wall, his expression horrified.

Baird crossed the floor with three long strides and reached into the well to lift Darian's head from the dark water. There was an ugly gash on his temple where he had evidently hit the stone and the water below was tinted red.

There was no pulse at Darian's throat.

"He's dead," Baird said numbly.

Bard, son of Erc, was dead. Baird felt suddenly that an ominous shadow that he had barely acknowledged no longer dogged his footsteps.

"He slipped and fell," Mr. Russell declared quickly. "It was an accident." His expression showed that he did not regret the fact, although his explanation didn't exactly ring true.

Aurelia lingered on the stairs, her own lips tightening at the news. "Like father, like son," she whispered, and crossed her arms over her chest.

Baird glanced up, knowing she wouldn't regret this death any more than he did.

But her words made him remember that Erc had died in Hekod's victory over Dunhelm. Baird scanned the chamber, then looked back at Mr. Russell. "What exactly is this place?"

Mr. Russell brightened at the chance to explain. "It's a ritual well, markedly like the one at Burghead, but in fine

condition. The details here, the door and so forth, are astonishing in their complexity, and frankly, I can't wait for the
opportunity to explore them at leisure.''

"But what's it for?"

"The Picts used ritual wells for the drowning of undesirables in their society. A sort of capital punishment, if you
will.'' Mr. Russell peered over the stone lip of the well. ''The
water is probably only four or five feet deep—usually rainwater accumulated by some clever means—but the typical victim had no chance to escape. The beauty of it is that their
death would not taint the water supply of the settlement.''

Baird's scalp prickled. "What kind of undesirables?''

"Traitors," Aurelia said flatly. "And much-loathed kings."

Baird met her gaze and understood.

This was where Erc had drowned.

And not of his own choice.

Mr. Russell smiled, quite unruffled by the loss of one of his
employees. "Quite. I'm certain we'll find some very interesting relics once we pump out the water here. Could we sign
that agreement shortly, Mr. Beauforte? I'd like to get a team
working here.''

"First," Baird said grimly, "we'd better call the police."

In one of the smaller conference rooms on the sixty-fifth floor
of Beauforte Resorts' Manhattan Retreat, Julian dropped the
firm's best and final offer onto the cherry table with a disdainful flick of his wrist.

"That's as good as it gets," he informed Marissa. "You
won't get another dime.''

He braced himself for her response, a part of him admiring
the way Marissa fought for what she thought she deserved. He
was kind of looking forward to going another round.

Little did Julian know that the document hit the table at the
exact same moment that Darian's skull cracked on the stone
lip of the ritual well.

To Julian's complete amazement, Marissa took one look at
the contract and burst into tears.

"Aw, now, come on, that's not fair!" He shifted his weight
awkwardly from foot to foot, but Marissa just wailed. Julian

waved his finger at her with bravado. "If you think you're going to make a better deal by using those feminine tricks on me, you've got another think coming!"

Marissa wept.

Julian fidgeted. He had only one weakness that he acknowledged. He just couldn't bear to see a woman cry.

"You know, I don't appreciate this," Julian said, trying to sound unaffected by her tears. "I expect better of you, Marissa. I thought you'd fight the good fight here."

"I can't believe how badly I messed up!" Marissa wailed, mascara streaming down her cheeks. Julian squirmed before this unexpected display of emotion.

Marissa wiped at her tears and smeared makeup across her cheeks. "I don't know what I was thinking," she confessed, then buried her face in her hands. "I never wanted to marry Baird, really. I knew he wasn't interested in me. I just had this idea that I *should* get to marry him. It just got into my mind and I couldn't get rid of it."

She looked up at Julian through her tears. "Have you ever really, really wanted something, more than anything in the world, then been relieved when you couldn't actually have it?"

"Well." Julian frowned. "There once was this Calvin Klein suit that I really coveted, but then I saw it on some guy and it made him look so *old*." Julian shuddered in recollection and Marissa smiled.

"Well, something like that," she acknowledged softly.

Julian looked up at the odd sound of her voice and found himself snared by a very alluring dark gaze. Julian realized in that moment that Marissa was actually quite an attractive woman. When she smiled at him like this, well, it tingled some part of him that hadn't tingled in quite a while.

He pulled his new Gucci handkerchief from his pocket and offered its perfect whiteness to her without a second thought.

She blew her nose enthusiastically and wiped away tears and makeup. "It's all right, I don't expect you to understand," she informed him. "It's crazy and I halfway don't believe it myself."

To Julian's surprise, Marissa's Midwest twang wasn't as

offensive as he recalled. And the usual hard edge to her lips
was gone, leaving her rather enticingly feminine.

He slid into the chair beside her. "There's a lot of craziness
going around. Try me."

Marissa wrung his handkerchief in her hands and it didn't
even upset him. "You'll think I'm nuts, but I always had this
horrible feeling bearing down on me that everybody owed me
something, that I had to really fight to get what I deserved and
to keep people from snatching away what should be mine."
She glanced to Julian and flushed in a most intriguing way.
"Well, it's just gone."

Julian again had the sense that the aliens were substituting
pod people for everyone around him.

But this was an alien who really intrigued him. "What do
you mean, gone?"

"All that bitterness, it just went away when you gave me
that contract." Marissa frowned. "I feel empty, like someone
waved a magic wand or something. I feel *free*."

She shrugged as though she were suddenly self-conscious.
"Like I said, it's nuts. I guess that's why I cried, it's so weird
to be without all that anger driving me on." She smiled up at
him. "Feels kind of good, actually."

Julian pursed his lips as his heart lurched. "Nothing crazy
about feeling good."

Marissa laughed in a self-deprecating way that he wouldn't
have ever expected to hear. "Well, I shouldn't have said anything." She fingered the contract, flipping through it quickly
but not reading the terms. "I guess I fought too hard for Baird.
It's kind of embarrassing to think about how I threw myself
at him."

"You were persistent, I'll give you that."

Marissa shrugged and wiped away the last remnants of her
tears. "I behaved really badly over this, but Baird is a decent
guy. The way I see it, any settlement is more than I deserve."

"The cash is pretty good," Julian admitted, still trying to
make sense of the woman before him. He told her the page
number, Marissa turned to it, and her eyes sparkled with
delight.

"Oh, you know, I could set up the most darling little shop

with that!" She leaned across and pressed his hand, and Julian, oddly enough, had no desire to pull away. "I probably shouldn't say this, but hotel rooms are so *boring* to design. Baird did me a favor here—I'm ready for something with a little more meat on the bone."

And before Julian's amazed eyes, Marissa signed a settlement agreement that she hadn't even read. He coughed into his hand. "I really think you should read the terms. . . ."

Marissa laughed. "Why? The money's good, there's probably a noncompete, but I don't want to compete with Beauforte Resorts anyhow. I'm going to try something different, make a new start."

She looked down and seemed to notice the condition of Julian's handkerchief for the first time. "Oh, I can't believe I did this. Look, Julian, I'll get you another one. I've seen them at that new shop, Abernathy's."

"Yeah, I bought it there."

Marissa's eyes shone. "Don't they have the most wonderful things? There's this fuchsia cocktail dress that has absolutely stolen my heart away"—she wrinkled her nose—"but it might be a little too flashy."

"The one in the window?" When Marissa nodded, Julian waved off her concerns. "You could carry it easily with your coloring, as long as you had an appropriate event to wear it to."

"Mmm." Marissa jammed the handkerchief and contract into her purse. "Well, I guess shopkeepers don't go to that kind of party very often," she commented with a smile devoid of malice. "I'll keep it in mind, though. See you around, Julian."

Marissa got to her feet and made for the door, but Julian wasn't quite ready to see the last of her.

"Tell you what, Mort." Marissa glanced back in surprise and Julian shoved his hands nervously into his pockets. "You buy that dress and we'll go to Sebastien's farewell dinner together."

"I don't have an invitation."

"I have two."

Marissa chewed her lip. "I don't know if I should. I mean,

I'm not with the company anymore and wouldn't want to embarrass Baird.''

"He's not even going to be here. Think about it, Mort. Sebastien's farewell feast. Portobello mushrooms . . ." Julian teased and Marissa caught her breath before she laughed.

"Oh, Julian, you're making my mouth water!"

"Well, then?"

They eyed each other warily, and Julian thought he saw an answering glimmer of excitement in Marissa's eyes.

"You don't have to do this, Julian," she said softly.

"I want to."

And he did. "Besides, it's my obligation as Beauforte's legal counsel to make sure you understand the ramifications of the agreement you just signed."

Marissa laughed out loud. "Bull! You didn't cough before you said that!"

Julian felt his color rise.

"You just want an excuse to buy that black Hugo Boss tux they have at Abernathy's!"

Julian caught at his heart as though he had been lethally wounded. "Caught! The lady's too smart for me." Marissa laughed again and Julian felt oddly lighthearted.

Better the devil you know, after all. He had seen Marissa at her worst and still loved matching wits with her.

And her best was looking very, very promising.

"So, what do you say?"

Marissa smiled, revealing a pair of enchanting dimples. "How could I possibly refuse?"

Julian crossed the room and took Marissa's elbow, savoring the waft of perfume that tickled his nose. "Could I see you out, Ms. Witlowe?"

Her dark eyes twinkled. "Via Abernathy's?"

Julian coughed deliberately. "I could offer counsel on that dress."

"Oh, and we wouldn't go near the men's department!"

Julian frowned with sudden concern. "Marissa, you don't think the tux is too staid, do you? I don't want to look old."

"Well, maybe the way they have it displayed it looks conservative, but I tell you, Julian, I saw this jacquard vest and bow tie at Bloomingdale's that just screamed your name. . . ."

"Ooh! What color?"

"Framboise. It was absolutely luscious—elegant yet audacious, you know? It was perfect!" She practically dragged him to the elevator. "Come on, I'll show you!"

And Julian was only too happy to go.

Epilogue

~

It was a glorious day for a wedding. The sun sparkled on the sea and Aurelia awakened with anticipation filling her heart.

Baird's single comment that he preferred traditional weddings had opened the issue of whose traditions to follow. Aurelia had vetoed the very idea of having a priest officiate, while Baird had not taken well to the idea of entertaining everyone within a day's sail of Dunhelm for three days and nights.

In the end, they had decided on a morning handfasting in the gardens. A quiet ceremony with their friends alone, at Dunhelm to close the circle of what had been begun here so many years before.

And on the morrow, the Beauforte Dunhelm Resort would open with a fanfare. Aurelia had laughed aloud when Baird unveiled the resort's logo, his wink telling her exactly why a single arrow had been worked into the design.

Cupid's arrow indeed.

Aurelia smiled to herself as she dressed. Her dress was simply cut and wrought of ivory silk. It fit her figure smoothly, flaring to swirl around her ankles and leaving her shoulders bare. There was a band of embroidery in the same creamy shades across the neckline and around the hem. She had decided to make her vows barefoot and had told Baird as much.

Just to keep his interest.

Aurelia eyed her reflection critically once she was dressed and hoped her hair would grow back quickly. The power of the Dreaming was vastly diminished without her hair and even when the locks grew back, Aurelia knew they would never have their former strength.

She could not blame Baird for preferring it long, for she did as well, but given her choice and the same circumstance, she gladly would cut it again. It had been a small price to pay for Baird's happiness.

And what need did Aurelia have of the Dreaming when everything she had ever desired awaited her in Dunhelm's garden?

There came a knock on the door and Aurelia knew it was Talorc. When she learned of the custom of fathers escorting their daughters down the aisle, she had immediately asked Talorc for his aid. The old man had unabashedly blinked back a tear before he agreed.

And today he looked as splendid in his tux as an older Julian might. He winked at Aurelia. "Are you sure about this young man of yours, Miss Aurelia?" he demanded gruffly, the merry twinkle in his eye belying his protective tone.

"Oh, yes." Aurelia felt herself flush, but Talorc merely smiled and offered her his elbow with a paternal air.

And as they left her room, Aurelia could feel Gemma's presence keeping step.

A harp was playing as they stepped out onto the lawn and Aurelia's smile widened when she saw Baird.

This time he waited for her, his hands folded, his morning suit impeccably cut. The suit emphasized the broad width of his shoulders, showing his height and lean strength to advantage.

Baird's eyes glowed as Aurelia stepped into the circle of roses and stephanotis laid on the grass. She thought her heart might burst when the heat of his hand closed over hers. They clasped hands left in left, right in right, and faced each other before the crashing sea. The wind lifted her skirts ever so slightly as she smiled up at the man who held her heart.

"Ready, princess?" he murmured.

Just past Baird's shoulder, Aurelia saw the faint shadow of the King of Inverness and his wife, their faces wreathed in

proud smiles. And Julian was there beside Baird, Thord's mischievous smile dancing on his lips. She looked back to Talorc
and caught a glimpse of her father in his blue eyes, then
Gemma/Ursilla's merry twinkle right beside a glowing Elizabeth.

Beyond them all lingered three figures in white, the Nairns
themselves who wove the fate of all men into their cloth, the
features of three great priestesses cast like shadows upon their
faces. Even the priestesses who had graced Aurelia with their
gifts now came to wish her well.

She and Baird were not alone, they never had been. On this
long-fated day, they were surrounded by all the ones who had
loved them so dearly, in this life and all others.

The pulse of Baird's child murmured in her belly of the
future and Aurelia turned back to Baird with tears shimmering
in her eyes. "I love you so very much," she whispered.

Baird's lips tugged in the half smile that heated Aurelia's
blood. "I'll take that as a yes," he murmured. When Aurelia
smiled in turn, he squeezed her fingers, then began to recite
the vows they had written themselves.

Aurelia watched as Baird pledged himself to her, his voice
ringing with quiet conviction. She did not falter in her own
oath, then Baird slid a simple gold band onto her finger. The
heat of his hand lingered over her own.

"And so it was," Aurelia said softly.

"And so it is," Baird concurred.

They stared into each other's eyes and simultaneously declared, "And so it always shall be."

And when Aurelia turned laughingly into the hail of rose
petals, she saw that the shadows of those gone before had
faded like the morning mist. The power of their love lingered
in her heart, and Aurelia knew it always would be there.

Just as she knew even when this life was far behind them,
the wheel of life would circle once more. She and Baird would
return, they would find each other and share again the power
of a love that never died. The threads of their destinies were
woven tightly together and would remain entangled for all
time.

So it was, so it is.

And so it always would be.

Author's Note

~

Dunhelm, of course, does not truly exist, although it is an amalgamation of many Scottish castles that I have had the good fortune to visit. In my mind's eye, it occupies the northwest tip of the island of Rousay in the Orkney Islands, though—of course!—you won't find it there.

Nor will you find a description of the Picts in any book as they appear here. As Talorc's fictitious book indicates, there is very little actually known of the Picts, other than their apparent preference for tattoos and for carving monumental stones. Aurelia's stone is consistent with the symbolism of Pictish stones, with the exception of the image of Aurelia herself, though the interpretation is entirely my own. When in doubt, I've given the Picts characteristics and/or habits known of the Celts, since one prevalent theory is that the Picts are descendants of the Celts.

Since the Picts left no records other than their List of Kings, their religious beliefs are also unknown. I've taken the liberty of making them pagans, like the Celts, and their religion Goddess based, as was common throughout Europe before the wave of conversions to Christianity. Neopagans and students of European paganism will recognize the triple aspect of the Goddess, as well as Her association with the moon.

The Stones of Stemness on the Orkney Islands are as described, though no interpretation of their positioning exists as explained in the text. These stones form the oldest "henge" in Europe, though, and studies of others like them—for example, Stonehenge—have revealed their ancient use as observatories. Aurelia's name for the Stones of Stemness and the nearby Ring of Brodgar are my own invention—both circles were named in the nineteenth century, so needs demanded that she call them something else.

The fertility festival of Eostre was celebrated by European pagans, most particularly the Saxons (who passed the event to the Norse). The Moon of Eostre began on the first full moon after the equinox, and was the time when the Goddess was "pregnant" with the promise of the growing season. The festival also marked the Goddess' victory over the underworld and her triumphant return to the land of the living, bringing spring and rebirth in her wake, an aspect echoed in the Christian celebration of Easter.

In addition, Christianity adopted the timing of Easter (which is still calculated on Roman calendars as the first Sunday after the first full moon after the equinox) from this festival, as well as the fertility symbols of the egg and the hare.

The egg as a symbol of birth and renewal is pretty self-explanatory, but the hare's symbolism has nothing to do with that creature's reproductive abilities! Many ancient cultures saw a Moon-hare in the full moon instead of what we commonly call the Man in the Moon. Since the full moon symbolized the Goddess at the height of her power, the hare became sacred to Her.

So next time the moon is full, take a good look at those dark marks and decide what you see!